"You do like to argue, don't you, Countess?" He brought her hard against him. "It's been my experience that women fight what they want the most."

Lana felt the taut musculature of his body, felt his thighs against hers. Touching a man in such a way, even with layers of cloth between them, startled her, and she fought for breath. "I can imagine the women who have provided that experience," she managed. "Someone like Isa—"

She got no further. Tony's lips came down warm and firm on hers and his hands moved to her back, pinning her to him. Her hat cocked at an angle on her head, and she felt the loosened wisps of hair trail against her neck.

Every sensation of passion was new to her, and a source of wonder. She wanted so many things, things she didn't understand. Most of all she wanted this moment never to stop . . .

BOOK YOUR PLACE ON OUR WEBSITE AND MAKE THE READING CONNECTION!

We've created a customized website just for our very special readers, where you can get the inside scoop on everything that's going on with Zebra, Pinnacle and Kensington books.

When you come online, you'll have the exciting opportunity to:

- View covers of upcoming books
- Read sample chapters
- Learn about our future publishing schedule (listed by publication month *and author*)
- Find out when your favorite authors will be visiting a city near you
- Search for and order backlist books from our online catalog
- Check out author bios and background information
- Send e-mail to your favorite authors
- Meet the Kensington staff online
- Join us in weekly chats with authors, readers and other guests
- Get writing guidelines
- AND MUCH MORE!

**Visit our website at
http://www.zebrabooks.com**

MIDNIGHT SINS

Evelyn Rogers

ZEBRA BOOKS are published by

Kensington Publishing Corp.
475 Fifth Avenue
New York, NY 10016

Copyright © 1999 by Evelyn Rogers

Kensington and the K logo Reg. U.S. Pat. & TM Off.

First Printing: June, 1999
10 9 8 7 6 5 4 3 2 1

Printed in the United States of America

Zebra Books
Kensington Publishing Corp.

http://www.zebrabooks.com

ZEBRA BOOKS are published by

Kensington Publishing Corp.
850 Third Avenue
New York, NY 10022

Zebra and the Z logo Reg. U.S. Pat. & TM Off.

First Printing: June, 1989
10 9 8 7 6 5 4 3 2

Printed in the United States of America

*To Frankie, Edna, Nelda, Joy, and Billie
who swear they would be fans even if
I had not married into the family*

Prologue

Countess Svetlana Alexandrovna Dubretsky leaned back in her shabby carriage and stared with pleasure at the crowded streets of St. Petersburg. An unexpected sense of well-being washed over her. It had been a long while since she had been to the city of her birth, but she still remembered the untroubled years spent there when her parents had been alive.

There was much evidence of changes wrought by Czar Nicholas. New government buildings, the Hermitage Museum which held the Imperial art collection, the National Library—all held her in thrall.

It was the spring of 1851, but the trees along the cobblestone streets had not yet begun to bloom. Across the Neva River, still marked with ice floes, was the Winter Palace, and nearby was Senate Square, where riots against the crown had taken place on the night she was born.

Could that Decembrist uprising have been only twenty-five years ago? At times Lana felt at least a thousand years old. Marriage had done that. She had been widowed a busy six months, but memories of the late count were not removed in so short a time. In the dark of night she could still hear his imperious voice echoing down the hall outside her door; in the gray winter afternoons she sometimes felt his unyielding stare still on her, as though he weren't buried deep within the family crypt, as though he still had the power to inflict on her his curious kind

7

of pain.

And now had come the death of her father. After a simple funeral at his country estate, she was traveling into town for the reading of the will.

She let the street noises fill her mind. "How wonderful everything seems," she said to the servant Boris, who sat opposite her, his long-fingered hands neatly folded in his lap, his angular body held erect. As long as she'd known him, and that had been most of her life, Boris never seemed to relax.

"Look at the street musicians," Lana prompted. "And all the people." She thought of the worn black gown of mourning beneath her cloak. "How fine they look."

Scantly turning his narrow, gray head in the direction of his mistress's gesturing hand, Boris sniffed. "They are just ordinary townsfolk, Countess. You have been too long associating with serfs."

Lana threw back her head and laughed. "What a snob you are. You know I only teach them to read."

"You raise expectations among them which can never be realized."

"I plant hope amidst despair."

She looked in defiance at her old confidant, all thoughts of her unstylish clothing gone. How good it felt to argue with him once again. Even though he had been with her during the four years, three months, and two days of her marriage, there had been few times for such talk. And certainly no laughter.

"Hmmph!" was his brief rejoinder, and Lana smiled triumphantly. She knew he was secretly pleased at her efforts to bring reform to the workers on her inherited and sadly impoverished estate.

The smile died. How could she be so lighthearted? Here she was on the way to the lawyer Balenkov's office to hear the words that would sound the final death knell over her father. The occasion should not hint of joy.

Not that Papa had seen her much in recent years. Since the death of her mother . . . since the sudden departure of Nicholas following an especially bitter argument with

8

their father . . . since her seclusion on the count's land which bordered the far more prosperous family estate . . . There were so many events that had forced a separation from Papa.

But always Boris had been there. "He's like a Russian nanny," her English-born mother had said, "the way he looks over you and little Nicholas."

If only her mother could see him now. Like a martinet more than a nanny, Lana thought. He could correct her as he saw fit in both English and Russian—and didn't hesitate to do so. But, she also realized, he would lay down his life without pause to save her from harm.

Lana turned her black eyes out the window and spied a flower stand. Where the flowers came from she couldn't imagine, but they aroused in her a feeling of hope, of rebirth, that she had not felt in a long while. How frivolous, she thought, to think of buying a bouquet, to spend a ruble or two on something that wasn't food or medicine or a scrap of cloth to keep out the winter chill for one of the children on the farm.

And yet she couldn't help thinking how welcome a little frivolity would be. Maybe, after her morning meeting, she just might indulge herself with a pansy or two.

When she arrived at the gloomy office buried deep in the bowels of a cold and dank stone edifice, she drew close to the Kasatsky family lawyer and her heart sank. From her childhood she had remembered him as a handsome, kindly man who had dandled her on his knee. Today there was the smell of brandy on his breath, and signs of the depravity rumored to have overtaken St. Petersburg were carved into his bloated face. During the past years, Lana had become an expert on depravity.

She shuddered. Stories of the rebellion against Czar Nicholas's restrictive regime had made their way even to the country. The Iron Czar, he was now called. The festive crowds and the beautiful buildings led her to believe that the city still held an innocent charm, but there was no more innocence in the world. Of that she was sure.

Maybe she would just forget those flowers. After getting

official word that Papa had left her the Kasatsky family land—and after receiving the small trust fund from her mother that was due at the same time—she would go back to the country to continue the rejuvenation of her property and the education of its serfs.

"Dearest Lana," a voice behind her said. "More beautiful than ever."

She whirled to face her distant cousin Rudolph. Her first thought was that as a child she had been right. He really did have the face of a ferret. And the soul of a thief.

How obvious his letters had been since her widowhood. She knew he wanted to marry her and claim ownership of both the Kasatsky and the late count's estates. Rumor had it that the Czar had threatened him with exile to Siberia if he didn't clear his debts, which were formidable enough to require the income from both properties. It was hardly a romantic reason for seeking a union with her, but then Lana had long ago given up her girlish dreams of romance.

He surprised her by grabbing her hand and raising it to his lips. His kiss was wet and cold.

"Rudolph," she said with a curt nod and pulled her hand free to thrust it in the folds of her cloak. She did not like to be touched by a man.

"Perhaps I am too familiar," he said, "now that you are a countess." He let her title roll on his tongue. Oh, how he liked that sound of it, she knew. To wed and bed a member of the aristocracy—even one such as she who had come to the class through marriage—would give him status and, what was more important, save him from Siberia.

"Countess," he repeated, "you are quiet today. I share with you the sorrow of your losses. A husband and a father, and so close together. So sad."

What a fraud! So convenient was more likely his thought. She quietened him with an icy stare, a look of haughtiness she had perfected as protection against some of the more forward men her husband had brought home.

She turned to Balenkov. "Shall we proceed?"

A dark look—was it sorrow? distress?—passed across the

10

lawyer's face. "Of course," he said.

She sat in one of the chairs facing Balenkov's desk. Rudolph took the other one, and behind her Boris stood like a guard at the door. Of the three men, only the servant knew of her desperate need for the Kasatsky land.

Balenkov took a long drink from a brandy snifter on his desk. "Perhaps," he said, clearing his throat, "we should begin by saying a few words of remembrance. As a member of the Imperial Guard, your father served the Czar well."

"And was rewarded," said Rudolph, "with title to a very fine estate."

Lana gave in to a brief moment of indulgent memories. How dashing a man Papa had been, with hair as black as her own. She had inherited her long-limbed figure from him, too. Often he had taken her to the Winter Palace, where, in those first years of Nicholas's reign, she had been a favorite.

She glanced up at the small likeness of the Czar which hung on the paneled wall, and her thoughts turned from Papa. It was hard to reconcile the grim-faced ruler in the painting with the man she remembered, the once beloved ruler for whom Papa and Mama had named their only son. Like Balenkov, Czar Nicholas had changed—and not for the better.

"Please," she said, pulling herself from her thoughts, "I want to return home this afternoon. May we proceed?"

Balenkov shrugged. "Of course." The trust fund from her mother was the modest sum Lana had expected, the lawyer reported. Then it was on to Papa's legacy. Balenkov lifted a folded parchment and broke the seal. First he read the expected stipulations of modest sums bequeathed to the faithful who had served him through the years. She was pleased to hear Boris had inherited a generous amount.

Now would come the part that would put her mind at rest.

"The rest of my properties and all income resulting therefrom I leave to my son Nicholas Alexandrovich Kasatsky . . ."

11

Lana gasped.

". . . providing he lay claim to them in St. Petersburg no later than two years from the reading of the will."

"I am ruined," Rudolph muttered.

Lana sat in stunned silence. Nicholas had inherited everything! How could such a thing be?

"For my beloved daughter Svetlana . . ."

Lana stifled a cry of hurt.

". . . knowing she has been well taken care of in marriage . . ."

What an absurdity! And she'd thought herself strong and wise to keep her impoverished state a secret.

". . . I leave the jewels of my late, beloved wife."

Lana struggled to accept Papa's reasoning. He would have no idea his daughter could have any use for the land. But the jewels, ah, that was the proper inheritance for a woman. He had locked them away after his wife's death, and Lana had understood. The sight of them would have brought back too many memories of the beautiful woman they had adorned and of the brief illness that had taken her life.

She tried to remember exactly what the pieces were. Certainly there were pearls and a ring or two, a cameo brooch, a diamond pin. But all faded beside the memory of the collection's most valuable item: a fifty-carat ruby called the Blood of Burma for the country in which it had been found and for its deep red color labeled pigeon's blood by connoisseurs. The sale of such a jewel would provide many rubles for the improvement of her estate.

"What happens," said Rudolph, "if my cousin does not return to claim the estate within the stipulated time?"

"As the sole remaining male heir, you would receive title to the lands."

Lana was positive Rudolph was smirking, but she refused to look his way. "Do you have the jewels here?" she asked the lawyer.

Balenkov downed another glass of brandy. "I have the strongbox entrusted to me by your father when he knew the end was near."

Lana found his nervousness catching. "I trust you have inspected the contents. Can I see them now?"

Balenkov shrugged. "There is nothing to be gained by postponement."

Lana wrung her hands and watched him lift a small wooden box onto his cluttered desk. He extended the key.

"Countess, perhaps you should be the one to . . ." His voice trailed off into the stale office air.

She didn't hesitate to accept. The key turned smoothly in the lock. With Rudolph breathing hotly down her neck and the lawyer taking a step backwards, she lifted the lid. The velvet-lined interior held the remembered pearls, the rings, the pin and cameo, and an unexpected necklace of finely carved jade. One by one she set the pieces on the desk. Frantic fingers searched for more. She turned the strongbox upside down. Nothing remained. The Blood of Burma was gone!

"Where is it?" she demanded, her dark eyes pinning Balenkov against the shelves of lawbooks behind his desk.

"Nicholas . . ."

"My brother?" she said.

"Hardly the Czar," muttered Rudolph.

Balenkov cast a covetous glance toward the decanter of brandy. "Nicholas came to St. Petersburg before he left and gave me a message for your father. Alexander Kasatsky, stubborn man that he was, refused to read it. Perhaps it should go to you."

Lana quickly ripped open the proffered envelope. Her eyes raced down the single page, and she said in a strangled voice, "He took what he thought was rightfully his. The land he left for me."

"It is too bad, Svetlana, that your father did not agree with his son's apportionment."

She thought of the fair young brother so like the carefree woman who had given them birth. Lana loved him with all her heart, but right at the moment she was having difficulty holding back her newly born resentment toward him.

"Nicholas and my father seldom agreed," she said.

"Nicholas was violently opposed to the marriage Papa arranged for me." She clutched at the letter. "He says here that one day I would be needing income from the family estate."

"Surely there he was wrong," said Balenkov. "The count was a wealthy man, although a much older one."

Lana declined any refutation. "Did you know Nicholas had taken the ruby?"

Balenkov shook his head. "Not for a long while. Your father wanted the jewels close by his side, unseen though they were. I had warned him about keeping such valuables in his desk. But Kasatsky was a stubborn man. Only after his death did I open the strongbox. When I saw the ruby was gone, I assumed what must have happened."

Bitter thoughts tumbled through Lana's mind. Nicholas was in a far land with her inheritance; she was in Russia with his. At least such was the case if her dear, free-spirited brother had not managed to separate himself from the jewel. It was another unpleasant thought that she brushed from her mind.

She allowed herself a quick glance at Rudolph. He *was* smirking. Would he follow her father as owner of the Kasatsky estate? And what was far worse to contemplate, would he succeed the count as her husband? Had she any choice, if she were to keep the serfs from further suffering and the land from being lost to taxes?

She most certainly had!

She turned to Boris, who had moved close behind her. "We must leave immediately for the country. There is much that must be done."

He looked at her in bemusement. "You have a plan, Countess?"

"I have a plan." She turned to the lawyer. The time for dissembling was gone. "Please see that these jewels are sold for as great a price as possible." Silently she prayed for her mother's forgiveness; somehow she knew Mama would understand.

Balenkov cleared his throat and asked, "For what purpose?"

"For immediate funds to run the estate. I will use the trust fund to pay for the journey."

"Journey?" he asked.

"Yes. The letter also says where my brother has gone. He is seeking his fortune in a new land where a great discovery of gold has been made. A place called California."

"California?" Rudolph croaked.

"Yes, in America. There is only one thing for me to do. I must go there and bring him and the Blood of Burma home."

Chapter One

Lana looked long and hard at the litter-strewn expanse of mud that was San Francisco's Pacific Street. Across the way sat a row of dingy clapboard buildings, among which was her destination—the Gut Bucket Saloon. After months of sea and overland travel, she simply could *not* let a little muck stay her from reaching it.

From the shadows of St. Petersburg's Winter Palace to the Gut Bucket . . . what a journey, she thought. If she ever got her hands around brother Nicholas's fair young throat, she would make him beg forgiveness for causing such trouble.

On this gray Monday afternoon in October, the narrow dirt walkways that ran close to the saloons and gaming halls of Pacific seemed uncommonly crowded with the most unlikely host of revelers she had ever seen, all scurrying as though they shared an emergency. Some were in flannel shirts and woolen trousers, others in the deerskin breeches and fringed shirts she had read about, and one or two in top hat and tailcoat. Many had the rolling gait of sailors long at sea.

No matter their dress, they all had one thing in common: a wild light in their eyes.

The only women she saw—and they were few in number—were gaudily clad and, if she were any judge of their purpose, saucily plying their trade. In the short time she had been observing, none of the *filles de joie* had been

17

particular about patrons, nor waited long before getting to work.

If it had not been for such transactions, however, Lana would have thought a riot was about to erupt. She was certain the watching Boris, who hovered close behind, shared the same concern. At least in Russia one knew when an attempted revolution was imminent. In America, she must learn to look for clues other than this apparent panic in the streets.

Just as she was about to venture onto the quagmire, a burly, bearded man jostled her, muttered something that sounded lascivious in a language she didn't understand, and then shrugged when she let lose a diatribe of Russian invective. She straightened her cloak and looked past him. *Revelers,* she thought as he shuffled away, was too complimentary a description for the motley horde. Drunks and rowdies came closer to the truth.

"Countess."

Lana ignored the imperious tone of her servant.

"Countess," repeated the indefatigable Boris, "I would not advise the course you have chosen. I will prevail upon another carriage for hire to get us to our destination."

"Nonsense," she said, brushing at the tendrils of dark hair that curled in the damp air from beneath her astrakhan hat. "The saloon is only twenty feet away and there's not a carriage in sight. Besides, someone has thoughtfully filled some of the larger holes . . ."

"With the morning's garbage," Boris said with a sniff.

"With enough discarded crates to allow me safe passage."

"I do not like the look of these men," Boris said with persistence, his eyes casting critically along both sides of the street.

Lana agreed with him. Even the worst of the carousers brought home by the count had never been as openly interested in her as the strangers eyeing her now.

But she would never put her thoughts to words. Boris would be too quick to state once again she had been foolish to venture onto the uncivilized San Francisco streets.

She had been guided to this heart of the Barbary Coast by her only acquaintance in America, a Russian emigré named Peter Androv—Andrews he called himself in his new land—who came from the village near the Kasatsky estate. He had seen Nicholas a few times in San Francisco, although not in the past month. The only specific place her brother had mentioned visiting was the Gut Bucket. It seemed he had located a poker table there where he could earn his daily keep without venturing into the mountains to labor for gold. How like Nicholas that sounded.

The thought occurred to her—as it had in several unguarded moments since she left lawyer Balenkov's office months ago—that Nicholas might have separated himself from her jewel. That he might even be without resources of any kind. But Peter had said Nicholas always appeared prosperous and in good spirits, and she decided her worries were without merit.

It was necessary, however, Peter had pointed out with a nervous shrug, for Nicholas to be constantly alert in the vicinity of the Gut Bucket, lest he find himself shanghaied by one of the area businessmen. If not watchful, a patron of such a place could easily end up working on a boat bound for Melbourne or Peking.

Lana had stifled a cry. Could her brother—her only family—be even now headed for a faraway port, slaving for some inhumanly cruel sea captain? Nicholas, with his soft hands and ready smile, wasn't at all used to hard work. For stealing her ruby he might deserve such a fate—almost. She simply had to find out where he had gone.

Lana had left her luggage with Peter and his wife Sophia, planning to search out a hotel room later in the day, and hired a carriage for the saloon. Throughout the slow journey along seemingly impassable streets, she had been treated to an unsavory view of the city.

The driver, a small man with a nervous tic, had sounded proud as he pointed out the cheap clothing stores and pawnshops, the gambling dens and saloons—places with names like Boar's Head and Fierce Grizzly, Fat Daugherty's and the Crutch. Occasionally he singled out a disreputable place he referred to as a "slop shop," and Lana had decided the Gut Bucket sounded right at home.

He'd been particularly proud of the bawdy houses, which seemed to occupy every other building. During the ride, St. Petersburg seemed farther and farther away.

With a gap-toothed grin and a twitch of his head, he had grabbed his exorbitant fee and, after depositing her and Boris unfortunately on the far side of the street, whipped his sluggish nag through the mire and out of sight.

Lana tugged her dark cloak close, fearful that one of the hell-bent men swarming along the sidewalk would approach her the way they did the whores. She had no doubt she could put such a boor in his place, but she would be successful only if Boris gave her the chance. He did insist on attending to his self-appointed role as her protector, even, she feared, resorting to fisticuffs if he decided the situation required.

As it was, she didn't like the determined look in his eyes. If she didn't move quickly, her gallant old friend would no doubt heft her into his arms and set course across the way. She imagined Boris's legs much too spindly to handle both her weight and the suction of the mud.

"Can I be of service?" a baritone voice offered.

Lana's head whipped around, and she found herself staring at the open throat of a midnight-blue work shirt. For a moment she was mesmerized by the exposure of wiry curls of black hair and by a strong, sinewy neck. Bristles shadowed a lean face, accenting prominent cheekbones and giving her accoster a feral air. When she glanced up into a pair of amused eyes that matched the color of the shirt, she looked no further. Here was only another man seeking a brief and, for him, pleasurable time. For that, he would need a woman far more willing than she.

She turned hurriedly back to the street. "Come, Boris." The tip of her tightly laced shoe edged toward the mud.

Again came the deep voice. "I wouldn't do that if I were you."

She found herself looking at him once more. This time the amusement had spread to the man's lips, and she couldn't help thinking that when he smiled, his teeth looked extraordinarily white against the contrast of his bronzed, bristled skin.

Her gaze rested on his smile. She had grown used to weak mouths that showed cruelty and petulance and, occasionally, soft carnality—mouths not at all like this man's. In the curved set of his lips she saw masculine humor and an invitation that was far more compelling than any spoken demands she had ever heard.

As if an onlooker, she heard herself respond. "I must get to the . . . Gut Bucket." The name sounded silly on her lips.

The stranger's grin broadened, breaking the sharply hewn planes of his face. "You must have a powerful thirst. I'd avoid drinking from anything other than a newly opened bottle, however. Never can tell when you'll be served a Mickey Finn."

Brash American! She put weight onto her extended foot and immediately sank ankle-deep into the mud. With a plop! she pulled free and stared in dismay at her shoe. America was certainly proving to be inconvenient.

Without warning she felt herself being lifted from the sidewalk and cradled against the stranger's body. One of the man's powerful arms slipped under the crook of her legs; the other wrapped around her back and held her against his broad chest. She looked in astonishment at his maddeningly cheerful countenance. A narrow-brimmed hat was tilted rakishly on his forehead, exposing a shock of black hair, and his blue eyes were lit with the same appreciation she had seen in the burly oaf who collided with her minutes before.

Men! This one might be considerably better-looking than the other, taller and for all his leanness more powerfully built, but just as she had figured when she first

21

stared up at him, he had the same thing on his mind. And his touch was no more welcome.

"It just so happens I'm headed toward the Gut Bucket myself," he said. "No reason we can't make our way across together."

Lana arched a brow. The time for icy reserve was overdue. "I can think of several," she said. Absolutely refusing to struggle like a cat in a trap, she held herself stiff in his arms.

Then she remembered Boris and worried that he would throw himself against the virile stranger. At fifty, her old friend was probably fifteen years older and certainly no match for the muscled strength she could feel beneath the stranger's close-fitting work clothes. But when she looked past the American's shoulder, she was amazed to see Boris studying the pockmarked surface of the street as if determining the safest route across.

"Hold on," the stranger advised, gripping her tighter, and his long legs carried them away from the hard-packed dirt of the walkway and into the mire. Startled, Lana did as she was told, forcing her arms around his neck. He had a pleasant, manly scent about him—if she was interested in such things—and his stride was surprisingly steady, considering the circuitous path he took toward the Gut Bucket.

The only truly disturbing movement was the shift of his hand as it rested against her breast, an unnecessary placement she thought. It was surprising how she could feel his fingers through the double layers of cloak and dress. And even more surprising, she had no inclination to stiffen and pull away.

When they reached the opposite sidewalk, Boris close in their wake, the American stood for a moment with his lips close to hers. Lana's heart quickened inexplicably.

"Put me down," she said, not quite so firmly as she had intended.

"You didn't order me to do that over there," he said, nodding to where they had stood only moments before.

"I—"

"A practical woman, I see," he said, "as well as a thirsty one."

She fought against scratching his smug face. "Put me down," she ordered again, this time with the haughtiness she wanted. He complied, depositing her unceremoniously on her feet beside him.

Snapping open her small purse, she pulled out a coin and thrust it at him. "For your trouble, sir."

His eyes drifted slowly down her body. "I've already received my reward. Such as it was. You don't exactly warm a man, do you?" He shrugged. "And that's a waste."

Lana's cheeks burned. "From what I've observed in America, you can find the sort of woman you obviously prefer on every public street."

"Where a woman puts herself certainly doesn't mean much, does it? After all, that's where I saw you." His eyes glittered a dark warning. "And if you're not after the gold these miners bring into town, I suggest you not hang around where they are. A man is likely to misunderstand."

She watched, openmouthed, as he turned and disappeared through the swinging doors of the Gut Bucket. She could think of several things to call him in Russian, but the English she had learned from her mother didn't include such a rich vocabulary.

She glanced at Boris, who stood nearby, stone-faced and silent. "We'll have to ignore such insults if we're to stay long in America," she said. "I want to thank you for your restraint."

"I saw," he replied, "that you were in no danger. The man only did what I was about to do. Indeed, Countess, he sacrificed himself most graciously in your behalf."

Lana's dark eyes widened. *"Sacrificed?"*

"His boots, Countess. The street is quite impossible. As you found out when you attempted to cross."

Lana glanced down at her mud-encased slipper and attempted in vain to wipe some of the muck against the dirt walk. She gave up with a shrug. "I'd hardly call ruined

23

footwear equal to . . ." She stopped. Equal to the way she had allowed an intimate brush of his fingers against her breast, she was about to say. But where the stranger touched her was nobody's business but her own.

"Enough," she said with a wave of her hand. Such an imperious dismissal was the only way to deal with Boris when he was determined to debate her every word. Sometimes the dismissal even worked. Without a thought for the wisdom of her actions, she hurried into the smoke-filled interior of the Gut Bucket Saloon.

Chapter Two

"Hoo boy!"

The shout, which filled the Gut Bucket's smoky air just as Lana moved through the swinging doors, startled her into forgetting both Boris and the would-be gentleman from the street.

"Ain't seen nothin' like this since Alabam!" the voice added.

Moving deeper inside, Lana cast a quick look around the saloon's lone room. Furnishings included scattered tables and chairs and a bar, such as it was—one long plank of rough-hewn wood propped onto stacks of bricks. Apparently the Gut Bucket hadn't gone in for extensive redecorating after San Francisco's latest fire, a summer conflagration that her Russian friend Peter Andrews said destroyed most of the town.

The Bucket's customers were no different from the assorted throngs outside, including a few women who sat amongst the men. One table was crowded with a group of cardplayers. Light from a half-dozen kerosene lamps attached high on the plank walls reflected eerily onto the smoke-filled room. The stranger from the street was nowhere in sight.

And neither was Nicholas. Lana shuddered. She seemed to have the attention of every person in the room. Too late, she agreed with Boris that she might have been precipitate in hurrying to the Barbary Coast her first day in

San Francisco.

"Come on, girlie," drawled the same loud voice that had greeted her, and she turned to see standing between her and the swinging doors a short, stocky man dressed in the same dark coat worn by the deckhands on the ship that had brought her into the bay. His face was covered with a scraggly red beard, and long, greasy hair the same color was knotted at the back of his neck. "Ain't a woman around here says no to Big Jake. Especially after months at sea."

Stale whiskey breath enveloped her, and she coughed delicately, at the same time waving a slim hand through the smoky air. "Mister Jake, I really must ask you to cease and desist."

"Whatever that means, girlie. Maybe I will and maybe I won't. Got a few things for you to do, too."

Around them rose coarse laughter, and Lana cast a longing thought to the late count's dueling pistols packed away with her other belongings. Right now she could be stroking one of them the way she had stroked the tattered blanket of her childhood—and receiving far more practical comfort. But it had been early afternoon when she left Peter Andrews and his wife, and she hadn't really gotten a good look yet at San Francisco. In her ignorance, she had felt perfectly safe.

She tried a bluff. "I must warn you," she said, eyeing the overly amorous if somewhat soiled Jake, "I am not without resources."

Jake wiped his fat, pink lips on the sleeve of his sailor's coat. "Resources, eh? Is that what you call 'em? I figure you got all the necessaries I'm looking for. And you're gonna find out why they call me Big."

The man was hopeless. Lana watched him bow to the laughter of the crowd.

"Countess," Boris said from behind her, "step aside."

She swallowed. The last thing she wanted was a brawl with Boris in the midst. Surely such a wrangle could be avoided. Standing firm, she leveled a cold stare at Jake, leaned close, and said in a low voice that only he could hear, "Mister Jake, if you so much as put one begrimed finger on my person, I will personally see that certain portions of your anatomy are amputated, rendering you useless for any such assaults again. And," she emphasized, "costing you the name you're so proud of. As a countess, I have many men ready to do my will."

What a prevaricator she was. She'd never had *one* do much of anything she asked. But Big Jake didn't know that, and just possibly he was stupid enough to believe her.

Big Jake hesitated, pondering her words, his low-slung brow wrinkled in thought, and with no further comment settled his barrel-like frame in one of the nearby chairs.

Lana decided that as long as she had the attention of the Bucket's customers, she would turn it to her own cause. "Perhaps you can help me," she said loudly. "You or one of the other men here."

"I'll gol-durned try!" someone yelled.

"I'm looking for a man," she explained.

"Ain't we all, sugar?" one of the women shouted over the whistles of the men.

"Nicholas Kasatsky," Lana said, then remembered the name Peter Andrews, formerly Androv, said her brother was using. "Nick Case."

Her dark eyes cut around the room, searching for someone to respond with the information she sought. Leaning against the bar was the stranger from outside. He must have come through the back door behind the bar because he certainly hadn't been there before. Obviously he was no stranger to the Gut Bucket. Its crudeness probably appealed to the same quality in his own nature.

The smile was gone from his face, and from beneath the angled brim of his hat he studied her thoughtfully. She raised her eyebrows, as if asking whether he could help with information, but he merely shrugged.

Suddenly she was seized by a pair of rough arms which wrapped around her middle and pulled her off her feet. She found herself sitting on Big Jake's shallow lap, her hat tilted to one side and a long curl of black hair hanging across one eye.

"Decided you was lying to me. Countess, is it? I seen you riding on the ship. Shared a room as I recall with some other women. No men to take care of you then, and there ain't none now."

The man's touch was repulsive, and she struggled to get free.

Boris stepped forward and, without a word, swung a long, thin arm at Big Jake. His fist whisked past Lana's cheek and sank into Jake's beard and flesh. Jake's only reaction was to frown.

Boris shook his head in disgust and, ignoring Lana's plea to retreat, planted his feet more firmly onto the floor, his fists raised as if he were prepared to meet a boxing foe. "Leverage, Countess. I did not properly prepare."

Jake held his grip on her, obviously unfrightened by Boris's stance.

A broad hand gripped Boris's arm. "Allow me." Once more, the stranger was interfering.

As Lana stared up in amazement, Boris paused for only a brief moment before stepping aside, but she could have sworn he looked disappointed that he would not have another chance at striking Big Jake. In disgust, she blew at the irritating curl of hair.

"Mister," Big Jake said, tightening his hold on her middle, "I ain't got no quarrel with you. Nor with that old feller. But I saw 'er first. She may be a-squirmin' now, but once I get atop, she'll stop that soon enough."

"*Nyet*," Lana hissed.

"I think the lady's declining your offer," the stranger said.

"It ain't exactly an offer," Jake said, his button eyes narrowing.

"Better watch it," one of the Bucket's customers yelled. "That's Tony Diamond you're fooling with now."

"*He* better watch—" Jake stopped in midsentence as Diamond stared down at him.

The tension in the room was as thick as the air. At last the seaman looked away, and Lana could feel the hold on her lessen. Jake felt the same power from this man that she

28

had experienced out on the street.

Lana took advantage of the moment and jerked free, moving quickly toward the bar where not even the hem of her cloak was within Big Jake's grasp. She watched as he grinned nervously up at Diamond.

"Guess maybe I'm more thirsty than anything else right now. Kinda' got my appetites confused."

Tony Diamond nodded in agreement. "Let me treat. A long time at sea, a man builds up a big thirst."

Of all the nerve, Lana thought as she straightened her hat and tucked the errant curl once more out of sight. The men were going to share a drink. But she saw she was wrong as Diamond signaled to the bartender and turned his attention to her. The crowd around them returned to their earlier pursuits, and Boris, with a nod of appreciation for Diamond's help, positioned himself at watch close to the swinging doors.

"Again I am in your debt," she said stiffly, leaning against the bar's rough edge and giving a quick glance at her rescuer's muddy boots. "I had thought a fight with Big Jake was a certainty."

"I never use more violence than is necessary."

"You seem very confident of yourself, Mister Diamond."

He answered her with a maddening smile. "You have the advantage of me. You know my name."

"Only because you are known by others here." She fought against his compelling midnight blue eyes. "I am the Countess Svetlana Alexandrovna." Purposefully she omitted her married name, even while she used the identifying rank of aristocracy that had come with it. She had been no more proud of the title than she was of the man who had given it to her, but sometimes it came as a handy weapon of defense.

"Countess," he said, bowing. Despite the rough cut of his clothes, he seemed smoothly sure of himself as he addressed her, and not particularly impressed. "Your name is quite a mouthful for most Americans. If you plan to remain in San Francisco, I'd advise something shorter. Lana Alexander, for instance."

Lana started. Until Mister Diamond, only her mother had called her by the more familiar form of her name. "I do not plan to stay longer than is necessary," she assured him. "Since you are obviously a habitué here—"

"Don't use such a word to anyone else. They'll think you're calling me something obscene."

"Which I was. As I was saying, since you obviously frequent the Gut Bucket, perhaps you can help me. I'm looking for a young man who calls himself Nick Case."

Tony's face grew solemn. "Isn't that his name?"

"In Russia he is known as Nicholas Kasatsky."

"Which is where you and he knew each other."

Diamond seemed to put an unpleasant and sexual meaning to his words. Lana decided perversely not to tell him the truth about her relationship to Nicholas. Let him think what he would.

"I am told he comes here often," she replied.

"As a matter of fact, he does."

"You know him?" Lana asked excitedly.

"I've gambled with him once or twice." He turned to the bartender, who was standing close by. "Nick Case been around here lately?"

"Ain't seen him in a long time, Tony."

Tony shrugged. "You are out of luck, Lana. Is the matter urgent?"

Lana started to respond with the truth, but something about the intense look on the man's face held her back— that and his easy familiarity with her. In Russia no one would have been presumptuous enough to address a countess by her given name unless he had known her a long while.

"Nicholas needs to return to Russia," she said.

"Are you his wife? Nicholas is a lucky man with such a beauty waiting for him, as well as a title."

Diamond was goading her for information, why she couldn't imagine, but even knowing what he wanted, she couldn't help but respond. "I am not his wife. And my title comes from my husband."

Tony's face hardened. "Then the count is a lucky man."

"The count is dead."

"Not so lucky then. He has left a lovely widow."

Lana certainly didn't care to discuss what kind of widow the count had left behind. If she had, Tony Diamond would have been more than just surprised. As would a large portion of St. Petersburg, including the Czar.

"I need to leave word in case Nicholas . . . Nick comes around."

Tony gestured toward the bartender. "I'm sure such a thing is possible. Where are you staying?"

"I've yet to secure a room. Boris"—she glanced at the tall, erect servant standing at attention by the door—"and I have only just arrived. Friends told me about the Gut Bucket, and since I was eager to begin my search, I decided to find a hotel later in the day."

"Boris, I take it, is a servant."

"And friend. For many years."

"You may be out of luck. Rooms are very difficult to find in San Francisco, what with so many gold-seekers pouring in."

"I am prepared to pay." Lana thought of the funds tucked away with her belongings. "Up to five rubles . . . that is dollars a day."

Tony's lips twitched. "That much, eh? Perhaps you would allow me to help you one more time. Without," he hastened to add, "any unwelcome conditions."

Pulling a notebook from his shirt pocket, he scribbled a message, then handed the folded paper to her. "There's a hotel on Telegraph Hill called the Ace. Give this to the clerk. Perhaps he can find accommodations for you and Boris."

Lana hesitated, then took the proffered note. Diamond, she figured, must be friends with the clerk, perhaps, she speculated, acquaintances from the gaming tables. A man like Tony would be good at cards. There was a controlled sureness about him that would intimidate his opponents and enable him to succeed with the most outrageous bluffs.

"Now," Tony said with a smile that lightened his dark

31

face, "how about that drink? Surely we can get the barkeep to break the seal on a new bottle for such a distinguished guest."

Lana declined with a haughty shake of her head. "Perhaps you can get that Mister Finn to join you in my stead," she said. "If hotel rooms are really as scarce as you say, I must make sure that accommodations are found before night."

Minutes later, as she settled back in the carriage he had insisted on summoning, she rested her mind on one point. This brash American with his surprisingly smooth ways had manipulated her all he was going to. If she didn't like the look of the hotel, she could certainly decline to stay there. A niggling curiosity ate at her mind. What kind of place would Tony Diamond recommend? It would probably be like the hastily built structures she had seen on her ride to the Gut Bucket and one no more architecturally appealing than the saloon.

Back in the Bucket, Tony took a long drink of whiskey and thought about the mysterious countess. How out of place she had looked standing on the dirt walkway in the middle of the roughest part of San Francisco—and in this town that was saying a great deal. Tall and long-limbed and elegant, she had been, with eyes as dark as ripe plums.

According to Big Jake, she had traveled to California with only her servant and without a great deal of funds. At least she had been quartered with other women and not in a private stateroom. There was much to speculate about this countess, who seemed innocent and worldly at the same time.

Tony's mouth twisted into a grin. Mickey Finn as a drinking partner! Five dollars a day for a room! The Countess Svetlana Alexandrovna had much to learn about this untamed town.

No matter her situation, her title suited her. She definitely looked aristocratic, with her high cheekbones and ivory skin and the long, slender curve of her neck. She had a curious way of holding her head at an angle, as though listening for something . . . like a wild animal in the forest, although she wouldn't care for the comparison. She would not like to be considered wild in any respect. Probably not even in bed.

So why was she looking for Nick? He was much too young and callow to attract a woman like her. Tony stopped himself. Maybe Nick satisfied her. After all, women had a way of being perversely unpredictable. It was why Tony had stayed single his thirty-five years. He didn't like surprises. Life presented enough unpleasant twists and turns without seeking out more. Besides, there were enough willing and amusing—and warmly predictable—female companions in San Francisco to satisfy a man all he wanted without tangling with a haughty beauty like Lana Alexander.

The thought brought him back to Nick. What would the countess think if she knew Tony wanted to find him as much as she seemed to? And all because of that ruby Nick was so proud of.

Nick was headed for trouble. Tony had realized it the moment he saw the fiesty young man across a poker table months ago. Gambling too much, drinking too much, and definitely going after the women with a store of energy that indicated he was away from home unsupervised for the first time in his young life.

Tony actually knew little about Nick, only that most of his family was dead and that he had come like thousands of others from around the world seeking his fortune. But that hadn't been what interested Tony. Right away Nick had reminded him of someone he knew a long time ago. The memory had brought pain, but it had also brought an interest Tony didn't ordinarily feel toward the wild young bucks flooding California in search of gold.

That special interest was why he had left his import house early today, still in his work clothes, to take a quick trip to the Bucket, one of Nick's less reputable haunts. He had even checked the alley to make sure Nick hadn't skedaddled outside. After all, he was running from Tony as well as from the irate father of his latest conquest.

The thought brought him full circle back to the

countess. Her curious English-Russian accent was much like Nick's. What a tempting armful she had been. She must have given the late count a difficult time.

He waved to the bartender. "Send word if Nick shows up. I'll see that the lady gets the message, too."

"Sure thing, Tony. How about another whiskey?"

"No, thanks. I've got one or two more places to check. Then I'd better get back to the Ace and see how the countess is getting along. There are a few things about her accommodations that I don't imagine she'll care for." His dark face broke into a grin. "No, I'm quite confident she won't care for them at all."

Chapter Three

Lana's room on the top floor of the five-story, brick Ace Hotel wasn't nearly as bad as she had expected. With its oaken furniture, tapestry draperies, soft feather bed, and the spectacular view of the city from its wide window, it was almost worth the five dollars a day she had agreed to pay. Boris was staying in another room somewhere below hers at a greatly reduced rate.

The clerk, waving the note she had handed him and smirking, asssured her that both prices were very fair indeed. Tony Diamond must have suggested that for her the normal rate be doubled. She should have ignored her scruples and read the folded missive.

What had surprised her more than the charm of the porticoed building and the comfort of her room were the guards placed in the hallways.

"It would seem," Boris had observed, "that rowdies and thieves are known to pounce on unwary guests at some establishments in town. The owner has made certain such will not happen here."

Somehow she had not found the sentries comforting but rather a reminder of why they were needed in the first place. More than ever she wanted to find Nicholas and get back home.

But where to look for him? Only now was she beginning to appreciate the enormity of her problem. Both Peter and Sophia Andrews had tried to warn her, but she had been so sure of meeting with success. What she had actually been was ignorant. All she really knew about her brother's habits was that he liked to gamble and disliked work. In San Francisco, there were establishments he could frequent on every street.

But she hadn't come thousands of miles to give in so quickly to adversity. She had tried what surely must be the roughest part of town. Tonight she would see another, hopefully tamer, side. When Boris had returned from the Andrews' home with their luggage, he delivered an invitation for her to join Peter and Sophia at a gathering of some of San Francisco's leading citizens. The local *boyare*, Boris had called them. The Andrews would stop by the hotel within the hour to pick her up.

How ambitious Peter was, how eager to be a part of the upper class. Back in Russia he had been associated with the dissidents who were unhappy with the Czar. In America, he had proudly told her, anyone could be treated like a king.

If that was what he wanted, she could only wish him the best, although she had yet to see any signs of regal living in California. Even the Ace Hotel, comfortable and charming as it was, could not compare with the hostelries of St. Petersburg.

Not that Lana was looking for anything finer. She had had enough aristocratic living to last a lifetime.

Despite the unpleasant memories of recent years, a wave of homesickness overcame her. She missed the orderliness, the sense of timelessness of St. Petersburg and the surrounding land. Besides, there were responsibilities calling her to Russia, people who depended upon her, and she must return as soon as Nicholas could be found. Her foray tonight simply presented another chance to continue her search.

For such a purpose, she looked presentable enough, considering the closeness of her finances. Her dress of purple silk still fit her slender frame the way it had when she bought it as part of her trousseau five years ago. Low necked and nipped in at the waist, it accented the rise of her breasts and the curve of her hips. She had stupidly thought the count would appreciate such a gown, but in that as in many other things she had been woefully wrong.

She gave only a brief thought to the pearls that had been sold to help finance the running of her estate. No jewelry would adorn her tonight; she would have to make do with a black velvet ribbon around her neck and a matching feather tucked into the mass of curls atop her head.

The cloak she had worn during the day was mud-stained around the hem, and the October night was not cold enough for her sable cloak. As she headed for the door, she grabbed up a shawl, brightly woven by one of the women workers on her estate and presented just as she was about to leave for America. She wrapped it lovingly around her shoulders and took courage. In its way the shawl was more valuable to her than the sable.

Downstairs, she looked carefully around the crowded lobby and realized with a start just what she was doing—searching for Tony Diamond. As if he would be at such a hotel, even if he had recommended it. On this cool October evening the men were dressed in formal wear, and the women bedecked in fine jewels.

Tony Diamond's clothes had labeled him a laborer of some kind, even though his manners had been smooth. She told herself she was glad he was not there. She would not see him again, not unless she found it necessary for a return trip to that netherworld called the Barbary Coast.

"Papa," she heard a young girl say from behind a potted palm, "there's no need for you to go tonight. I'll be all right."

The accent was decidedly British, as was the answering bark.

"Nonsense! I don't intend to let you out of my sight again."

The girl gave a squeal of dismay. "You yourself said this party is likely to be very dull. If one could even call it a party! I couldn't possibly get into trouble, not at any place called the Benevolent Society."

"Elizabeth," her father's voice thundered, "you could

37

find mischief in a nunnery. Which is where I'll try putting you next, if you give me any more argument."

Lana cleared her throat, announcing her presence.

A pair of wide gray eyes peered around an arched frond, and Lana found herself smiling at the heart-shaped face of the distressed Elizabeth. With her upturned nose and froth of yellow curls, the girl looked more pixie than human.

Lana's first impression was strengthened when Elizabeth stepped from beind the palm. She couldn't have been more than five feet tall, at least six inches shorter than Lana, and at least five years her junior.

The charming face broke into a grin. "I ask you," she said, "could you think of a safer place for a young lady than the Benevolent Society?"

"I certainly hope it's safe," Lana said, "since that is also my destination."

A round-bellied man in tailcoat and top hat stepped beside the girl. A pair of wary eyes looked out at Lana from beneath bushy gray brows. Lana met his stare straight on and waited for him to speak.

He cleared his throat and said, "I don't believe we've had the pleasure. I'm Lord Dundreary of Sussex. In England, you know. And this is my daughter Elizabeth."

Another proud man with a title, Lana thought, and deliberately she dropped her own. She only needed it as a defense against such boors as Tony Diamond and Big Jake.

"Lana Alexander," she said. "And I know where Sussex is. My mother was English and while I never visited there, she talked often about the country."

Whether she meant to or not, she now had made a friend.

"Thought I heard something in your voice that sounded of London. What a relief it is," Dundreary said, "to run into a lady at last. Not many here in America."

"Have you been here long?" Lana asked.

"Almost two months," he said in disgust. "A member of the British diplomatic corps, retired. With my wife dead, decided to take Elizabeth on a world tour. Heard much about San Francisco, but when we landed here for what was to be a short stay, the entire crew of our vessel deserted for the gold fields. We've been waiting for passage on another ship."

Elizabeth Dundreary's face dimpled into a smile. "Don't let Papa's complaints fool you. He's been kept occupied at the gaming tables. And very successfully, too."

Dundreary cast a look of longing across the lobby toward the double doors through which most of the men and women entering the hotel had passed. "Imagine the faro tables are already busy."

"I'm sure they are, Papa," Elizabeth said. "And you're welcome to visit them. I'll be all right."

Lana could see indecision on the man's face, but the duties of fatherhood won out. "The tables will wait until we're back and you're safely in your room."

"Lord Dundreary," Lana suggested, "I'm waiting for a friend and his wife to stop by for me. Your daughter is perfectly welcome to attend the party with us."

Dundreary hesitated a moment, then cast another brief look at the double doors. "Thank you kindly for the offer," he said at last, "but I'd best not shirk my responsibilities. Most certainly I can give one evening to Elizabeth. Want her to meet the right people, you know."

Lana could see the girl stiffen and the light in her eyes dim. She obviously had plans for herself far different from those of her titled father. Remembering the way her own father had arranged her disastrous marriage, Lana felt her heart go out to the girl. After all, the count had been considered a right sort of person by most.

Before she could say more, Peter Andrews and his young wife Sophia arrived. After brief introductions, she was whisked in the Andrews' carriage to a one-story brick structure atop another of San Francisco's steep hills, Lord Dundreary's conveyance close behind.

The crowd inside the large room was not nearly as motley as the one she had seen on Pacific Street. The men were dark-suited and, she noticed with dismay, the women clad primarily in shades of gray. In her purple silk and brilliant shawl, she felt uncomfortably like a tropical bird caught in a flock of sparrows.

A silly comparison, she decided. She was from the north of Russia, and there was nothing tropical—or warm—about her.

Lord Dundreary arrived and, depositing his daughter beside Lana close to the front door, joined Peter in a trip across the empty dance floor to the punch bowl where most of the men had gathered. Elizabeth glanced around the room, her features wrinkled in a frown. Lana was tempted to question the girl about whatever was troubling her but, knowing the value of privacy, instead asked, "Are most gatherings like this one? The women to one side and the men to the other?"

Elizabeth shrugged. "I've not been out lately. Papa thought it best . . . well, he wanted me close to the hotel."

Sophia, Peter's quiet-spoken young wife, offered, "The men will be talking politics. Someone will make a speech about something or other, and then the music will begin." She smiled at Elizabeth. "There'll be dancing. I'm sure the young men will crowd around you."

Elizabeth's face took on a stubborn set. "And I'm sure I won't be interested."

A man, thought Lana. Only a man could make a young innocent like Elizabeth Dundreary—who must still be filled with the beguiling fantasies of romance—scoff at a host of swains begging her to waltz.

Lana had no intention or desire to step foot on the highly polished dance floor and let a man take her in his arms. She much preferred to remain here near the door where the air was fresh.

"And here," came a masculine voice, "are three young and charming ladies I've not had the pleasure to meet."

Lana turned toward the voice. Stopping beside her was a smiling man she guessed to be about forty. His dark hair was tinged with gray and slicked back from a broad face. Pale, close-set eyes assessed her, flicked momentarily toward the younger women, then settled once again on Lana.

40

"Allow me to introduce myself. Maxwell Shader, a simple, hard-working businessman who hopes only to make this city a better place to live. Which is why I've gathered together some of her leading citizens."

A full-throated laugh interrupted him. "Maxwell is far from simple, I assure you. Before the night is out he'll have everyone here supporting him in his latest cause."

Even in a high-necked dress the color of iron and with her auburn hair curled over each ear in tight chignons, the woman with Shader made a spectacular appearance. Full-bosomed and full-lipped, she stood as tall as Lana and seemed far more self-assured.

"I'm Isabel Wright," she continued, "your hostess for tonight. Maxwell allows me to perform such small favors for him to show my gratitude. When my husband met an untimely end in a mining accident two years ago, Mister Shader was very kind and supportive."

"Come, come," Shader said. "I merely helped you with a few investments. You were not left a poor widow, Isabel."

Americans were quick to reveal their private business, Lana observed. Already she knew more about the relationship between Shader and Isabel Wright than they would ever know about her—so much, in fact, that she wondered if there weren't more between them than had been indicated.

Lana brushed away the thought. Too many years with the count had made her skeptical about the entire human race.

She smiled a greeting at Isabel. The woman had not been left poor, according to Mister Shader. In that respect, Lana thought, she and the widow Wright were not alike. And she suspected, giving the woman a close look, there were probably other, very important differences as well. Something about the hard look around the woman's mouth, perhaps, or the watchful look in her eyes, indicated as much. But there she went again . . .

The introductions were completed, Lana's title and marital status omitted, and she said, "You have a cause,

41

Mister Shader?"

"Indeed I do. If you've been in San Francisco long, and that can mean only a few hours, you'll no doubt have noticed signs of the lawlessness which abounds. If we are ever to be a real city and offer safety for our citizens, we must see that justice is sure and swift."

"I warned you," Isabel said, smiling at Lana.

"You tease me, Isabel," Shader said, casting her a quick look, "but you know I am right."

"Surely," Lana said, "there are authorities hired for the purpose of law enforcement."

"Which does not mean they are adequate." Shader's voice rose in volume as his enthusiasm grew. "Women and children are not safe on the streets, what with the strange characters who lurk about. Hundreds of foreigners pour in every day. From points as far away as China and Chile. They come for gold, and are not too worried whether they find it in the ground or in another man's pocket."

Around them talk had ceased, and a man said, "You're right about the police. But what about the Vigilante Committee? They've already hanged a man for stealing. Seems to me they've taken up where the authorities have failed."

"They're of good purpose," Shader agreed. "But in the midst of all this iniquity, there has been only the one hanging, and the culprit was one of the notorious Sydney Ducks that even the police might have caught."

He saw Lana's questioning look. "An unusual name for thugs, I agree, Miss Alexander. They're from Australia, ex-convicts mostly. And there's not much they won't do in the way of wickedness."

"So what are you proposing?" another man asked.

"Only what seems obviously essential. Another body of citizens determined to do whatever is necessary to achieve our worthy purpose. We need organization. Men recruited for patrols, citizen's arrests made, and once and for all our streets cleared of those who would be a threat."

A chorus of agreement rose around them. Remembering the streets through which she had passed and the crowd

42

she had observed at the Gut Bucket, Lana felt herself in sympathy. Maxwell Shader presented an eloquent case.

As the noise subsided, a lone voice of dissent sounded out.

"And who would decide which men would be eliminated? You, Max?"

The deep baritone was startlingly familiar to Lana, and she whipped her head around to see the tall, lean figure of Tony Diamond standing in the doorway that led to the street.

Chapter Four

Tony's appearance was far different from the one he had presented to Lana on Pacific Street. Gone were the work clothes of the afternoon, replaced by a double-breasted tailcoat and trousers that appeared tailored for his muscular frame. He was hatless, and hair as black as his clothes brushed against the velvet collar of his suit.

Different, yes, but she would have recognized him anywhere. He still had that dark, devilish look on his face and an all-seeing gleam in his eyes.

"Diamond!" Shader growled. "What the hell are you doing here?"

The room was still as Tony said, "I heard you were holding open house for those interested in reform. This is my town, too. Thought I might make sure you didn't do anything to harm her. Or any of her citizens who might not meet with your approval."

"See here, Diamond, if you're referring to what happened to Jess Tucker—"

"Leave Jess out of this," Tony ordered. "He's long dead and buried. I'm talking about what you're planning tonight. Not the past."

Lana's eyes stayed pinned on her rescuer of the afternoon. She couldn't look away. For her he had become the focal point of the room. His clothes, his bearing were similar to the other men's, and yet he had outdone them. He seemed more elegant, and at the same time more intense, the one man present to be reckoned with.

Everything she'd thought about him before—his power, his strength of will—seemed magnified tonight. And she wasn't the only one who felt it. Otherwise there might have been others coming to Maxwell Shader's defense. They had agreed with him vocally enough before Diamond appeared.

Coming quietly out of the night as he had done, Diamond looked somehow . . . dangerous. It was the only word she could think of. She was reminded of the wolves which prowled the countryside near her estate. Only Tony Diamond's domain was the wilderness called San Francisco. Whether in a Barbary Coast saloon or soiree, he made himself at home as much as did the wolves in the Russian woods.

The sudden sound of violins sawing away in the far corner cut through the tension-filled air.

"Come, gentlemen," Isabel said brightly from her position beside Shader, "enough talk. The ladies grow bored."

Speak for yourself, Lana thought. She had been waiting to hear what Tony Diamond would say next, and how the righteous Maxwell Shader would respond. How nice it was to listen to other people's problems for a change, problems that didn't in the least concern her.

Tony moved deeper into the room, and Isabel stepped between him and Shader. "Mr. Diamond, welcome. Maxwell needs to hear dissenting opinions once in a while. It keeps him from taking himself too seriously." Her full lips widened into a smile. "Do you dance?"

Tony's eyes rested on Lana. "I was about to ask the countess the same question."

"Countess?" Shader exclaimed in surprise.

Tony nodded toward Lana. "I see I have revealed your secret. Allow me to apologize while we dance."

Before Lana could protest, he swept her into his arms and whirled onto the still empty floor in the center of the room. She'd had no intention of accepting such an invitation from anyone, but Tony Diamond wasn't a man to await permission.

As the music swelled around them, other couples joined in the dance. Lana was barely aware they were close by, caught up as she was by the same feeling she had experienced when he carried her across the muddy street. One of his gloved hands rested warmly against the small of her back, and the other held her hand. She didn't welcome his touch any more than she did any other man's—and yet she couldn't pull away.

And what a superb dancer he was. How long it had been since . . .

She pulled away from her memories, wondering what on earth there was about Tony Diamond that made her think and act so uncharacteristically. It had been years since she had thought about such frivolous indulgences as a waltz.

As they danced around the edges of the floor, Lana caught him glancing speculatively at Isabel Wright, who was talking to a small group of men by the punch bowl. A slight, unexpected sting of displeasure disturbed her.

"Are you sure you wouldn't prefer another partner?" she asked.

"It's only that—" Tony paused and looked down at her. "There's something about that woman—"

"That keeps you from finishing a sentence." Lana cast a quick look at Isabel, whose full-bodied figure showed to good advantage as she stood in profile close to the wall.

Tony laughed. "It seems I have two things for which to apologize. Mentioning your title and giving far too much attention to a gray dove when I hold such a beautifully feathered creature in my arms." The pressure of his hand at her back increased. "And one who dances so well."

Lana started. His comparison of birds echoed too closely her own thoughts when she had first come into the room.

"If you're referring to my dress—"

"Which is lovely." His eyes lingered for a moment on the swell of her breasts. "I must admit it's a big improvement on that drab cloak of this afternoon."

47

"As are your clothes," Lana snapped. "You surprise me."

Tony's lips twisted into a smile. "Good. I don't imagine that happens too often. And I'm sure you don't like it."

"Tell me, Mister Diamond, do you Americans always call attention to yourselves in public places? The people of my acquaintance in Russia are more private."

He leaned close, his breath stirring the feather in her hair. "If you're hinting we find a place where we can be alone—"

Lana refused to be intimidated. "Like most men, you think along singularly narrow lines."

"Perhaps," Tony said, pulling back and looking carefully down at her, "you would prefer a man like Maxwell Shader. When I came in, he had your undivided attention."

"He spoke on the side of law and order."

"As he sees it. A dangerous position, you must admit."

"But one more understandable than yours. Would you really let criminals run unshackled in the streets?"

"Of course not. But neither would I round up everyone who didn't meet with my approval and hang them from the nearest tree."

Lana caught a sharpness in his voice she had heard once before—when Shader had mentioned someone named Jess Tucker. She suspected Tony was thinking of Tucker now.

"I don't see," she said reasonably, "why there shouldn't be some compromise between the two positions. I saw much in my short ride today that could be improved."

She could feel the tension leave Tony's body.

"I'm sure you did," he said. "What particularly impressed you?"

Lana gave his question serious thought. "Curiously, it was not anything critical. It was the excitement, I suppose, the activity. No one seemed at leisure or even to have much purpose in scurrying about. But they all seemed to be having a good time." A thought struck her. "Tell me, Mister Diamond—"

"Tony."

"I forget how informal you Americans are. Tell me, Tony, just what *is* a slop shop?"

"Why?" he asked, grinning. "Are you planning to visit one tomorrow?"

Lana found herself grinning back. "That depends on your answer."

Tony's grin died. "For your own safety, you'd better not venture onto the streets with only a servant in tow. Although the shops are innocent enough. They're nothing more than cheap clothing stores." He glanced down at her gown. "Not anything a countess ought to be concerned about visiting."

Lana bit back a retort. He had no idea the kind of worn clothing she had brought with her from her near-destitute country estate.

"You say I should avoid them for my own safety. It seems we've come full circle to Mr. Shader's arguments about criminals on the streets."

"We Americans might talk about ourselves too much, but you Russians don't give up an argument easily, do you?"

"Not when we're in the right."

"Then consider all the facts. You come from an autocratic country. California has been a state for just over a year; she must do the best she can with democracy. Which doesn't mean Americans don't care for titles. If you wanted to impress Maxwell Shader, you should have revealed yours. I thought this afternoon you were filled with pride. Is there some reason in particular you did not want to mention the late count?"

Lana stiffened. "Not that it is any of your business, Mr. Diamond, but I *never* want to mention the count."

"Tony, remember? And why not talk about your late husband? Is the memory too painful?"

How inadequate a word, she thought. "The count was an older man," she said, as if that could dismiss him from their conversation. "His death was . . . not unexpected."

"Was it unwelcome?"

She looked up in surprise. "Even coming from an

49

American, I fear such a question is far too informal for me to answer. You dare a great deal."

Tony didn't miss a beat of the music as he whirled her around, giving her no chance to pull free without causing a scene.

"I dare more than that. What about this Nick Case you are seeking? As I recall, he is not a much older man."

Lana drew on her reserves of patrician hauteur. They had worked with cousin Rudolph back in the lawyer Balenkov's office and they would work with the man holding her now.

Casting a cool eye up at him, she said, "My interest in Nick Case has nothing to do with you, Mr. Diamond."

She found out right away she was wrong.

"Perhaps, but you have aroused my interest," he said, not the least subdued. "It is not, I must admit, what women with your beauty usually arouse."

She muttered an expletive in Russian, then settled for the less expressive English. "A crude remark from a crude American. Such is what I would have expected."

"You'll have to insult me far more than that to kill my interest. Why do you seek Nick? Could it have anything to do with his being hard-bodied and handsome?"

Lana stifled a cry of outrage. Not even the count in his most obnoxious moments had penetrated her self-control. Even in that last dreadful moment of his death. She was not about to let Tony Diamond accomplish what no one else had managed.

"I have a headache," she said icily. "Please allow me to leave."

Tony came to a halt at the edge of the floor. "Could I see you to the hotel?"

"I'll see you in perdition first before I'll allow you to escort me anywhere."

With those words she pulled free of his hold on her and, grabbing up the shawl and reticule she had left on a table by the door, whispered to an openmouthed Sophia she would be waiting outside.

Tony was much more insistent than she had figured.

50

"That might not be wise," he said as he kept close to her side. "Remember all those criminals on the streets."

"How can I help but remember?" she asked, pausing in the doorway. "That is where I first met you, is it not?"

"Lana." Tony hesitated. "About Nick Case—"

For a moment she thought he was going to apologize, this time with more sincerity than he had evinced on the dance floor. She gave him no chance. "Nick is no concern of yours. And neither is my business with him. You made the mistake of judging me by your own standards. I sincerely hope you do not have that opportunity again."

She hurried through the open door and into the cool dampness of outside. There was no danger waiting for her in the dark that would upset her more than the man lurking inside in the light.

The sound of footsteps sent her anger on the rise once more. "What must I do to discourage you?" she hissed, turning to face her tormentor. In the dark she could make out the figure of Elizabeth Dundreary. The girl let out a faint sob.

"I'm so sorry to bother you. Countess, isn't it?"

"Elizabeth," Lana said apologetically. "I thought you were someone else."

Again came the pitiful sound of a muted cry. Elizabeth sounded like a frightened kitten lost in the dark.

"I couldn't help overhearing you as you left," she said at last. "When I heard Nicky's name, I had to come outside."

"Nicky?"

The girl's voice strengthened. "I haven't even whispered his name in weeks. Well, maybe late at night. You're looking for him, too, aren't you? I put up a brave front. Anything else upsets Papa and makes him hate Nicky all the more."

"Nicky?" Lana repeated, unable to say more. She was beginning to think she had been struck simple by the girl's words.

Elizabeth brushed a nervous hand through her blond curls. "I wanted so much to get out tonight. Maybe I might see him and know he was all right. But as soon as I arrived,

51

I saw how silly I had been. Oh, Countess, you must tell me the truth. You're so beautiful and sophisticated. All the things I'm not. Yet I'll bet you've given in the same way I did. Nicky,'' she said in the tone of a pronouncement, ''has ruined you, too.''

Lana shook her head weakly, for the moment robbed of speech. Fog diffused the light spilling from the open doorway to the Benevolent Society, yet she could still make out the tall, lean figure standing behind a very young and vulnerable Elizabeth Dundreary. As he seemed always to be doing, Tony Diamond was watching her, waiting for whatever she had to say.

Chapter Five

Tony leaned against the frame of the doorway and waited for Lana to handle Elizabeth Dundreary's tremulous question. The countess—the beautiful, aristocratic Russian with her usually cool ripe-plum eyes and unreadable face—hadn't looked this shaken when she'd been grabbed by Big Jake in the seamy Gut Bucket Saloon.

Nick Case was important to her all right, more important than Tony had figured when she asked about him at the Bucket. The knowledge disturbed Tony more than he liked.

Lana's gaze was trained on Elizabeth. "There is unsettled business between my . . . between Nicholas and me." She seemed to be choosing her words carefully. "A legal matter. Nothing more."

Her dark eyes blinked rapidly, then opened wide, and Tony wondered if maybe she were lying. He didn't know her well enough to tell, but give her a few more chances to play with the truth, and he would find out for sure.

"Is Nicky in some kind of trouble?" asked Elizabeth.

Lana reached out and took her hand. "Not that I know of. But you said . . . Are you all right?"

From Tony's position behind Elizabeth, he could see the young woman's shoulders straighten. "I will be once he returns. I know the trouble. Papa has scared him off."

Alfred Dundreary wasn't the only one who had set Nick to flight, but that was knowledge Tony preferred to keep

53

to himself for a while.

As if summoned by his daughter, Dundreary bulled his way past Tony into the thickening fog outside the Benevolent Society. "Scared who off, Elizabeth?" He waved a stubby-fingered hand. "No need to answer. That rascal Nick Case again, no doubt. He wouldn't be running off if he hadn't done us both an injustice."

Elizabeth whirled and frowned stubbornly up at her father. "Nicky's not a rascal, Papa. Why don't you believe me?"

"Too much evidence to the contrary. Been around too long not to know when a man is up to no good. Anyone avoids a gambling debt is no gentleman, that's for certain."

"You and your gambling, Papa! Is that all you can think about?"

"Unfair, child. Don't forget I caught him kissing you. Not at all the thing, an innocent girl. Even in this godforsaken land. That's why I keep you close beside me. So no one will try it again."

So her indignant Papa didn't know everything Nick had done. Tony glanced at the ruddy-faced English lord. The man would probably explode when he did learn the truth. A gentleman from the Old World, Dundreary judged a kiss without a betrothal a disgrace. In San Francisco, a kiss was a way of saying hello.

If this was Dundreary's reaction to a supposedly chaste kiss, it was no wonder Nick had run. Elizabeth was fully capable of blurting out a few more details, just as she had done to Lana. *Ruined,* she had said. Once Papa found out, Nick would find himself shackled in marriage before he knew it.

And of course the reckless young man had Tony on his trail, too. Dundreary didn't have the primary claim on any gambling debt of Nick's. Tony did. On that last night he had been seen in town, Tony had gambled with him first.

Maybe what rankled the most was that in disappearing with the ruby he was so proud of, Nick seemed to have outsmarted them all. If the young fool hadn't got himself shanghaied . . . or worse . . . he was better off keeping out of sight.

"It's time we were getting back to our rooms," Dundreary continued. "Madame," he said, nodding to Lana, "sorry to inflict our problems on you. Not at all the thing."

"I understand," she said, a catch in her voice.

"You're a lady. Knew it the first time I saw you. Can't imagine why you didn't use your title before. Nothing shameful about it, even if these Americans think we're all related to royalty. Comes in handy, sometimes." He glanced toward his carriage, which was hitched near the street lamp. "You can ride back to the Ace with Elizabeth and me. Already informed your friends I would see you home."

For a moment Lana's eyes locked with Tony's. She was the first to break away. "Thank you, Lord Dundreary, for the kind offer. I'm sure we've provided quite enough entertainment for anyone insistent upon listening."

She whirled around to face the mist-laced street, her bright shawl close to her shoulders, but even with her back to Tony, her ridiculous feather waving in the night breeze off the bay, she couldn't hide the slender, curving lines of her body beneath her dress and the provocative tilt of her head. A damned fine-looking woman she was, even if she did put out the warmth of a block of ice. How soon would she melt, Tony wondered, in the heat of a man's desire? How often had she already done so, and with how many men other than the count?

For all his traveling around the world on clippers and traders and wherever else he could find work, he had learned damned little about the Russian aristocracy. They rarely visited the holds or masts where he had plied his sailor's trade in those poorer days before he had made his fortune.

Even after she had ridden off into the night with Dundreary and his daughter, and Isabel Wright had drifted outside to loop her arm in his, he kept his thoughts on the enigmatic countess. He had gotten one smile out of

55

her, when they had talked about the slop shop. She ought to smile more often. It had lightened the entire room.

Suddenly he realized Isabel was talking.

"I hope Maxwell didn't upset you too much with his vigilante talk," she said, her full breast pressed against his arm. "It's just that he cares so much about San Francisco and the safety of its citizens. And with all of your investments around town, you certainly qualify as one of those."

When Tony failed to respond, she moved slightly, her breast rubbing against the sleeve of his coat. "Either he really has upset you, or you're thinking about a woman. Men do let us creep into their thoughts when the mood strikes them."

The bitterness in her voice caught Tony's ear. He turned his head to look at her and found her lips close to his. He didn't need instructions as to what he was supposed to do next. She was waiting for him to kiss her, but Tony was too filled with thoughts of an elusive dark-haired beauty to comply.

The most he could do was wonder once again where he had seen Isabel Wright before. On Maxwell Shader's arm, certainly, on the few occasions when their paths had crossed. A grateful widow is how she described herself, one who served as Max's hostess. Tony had no doubt she served in other capacities, as well.

But she was Maxwell Shader's goods, and that made her unappealing to him. Max had landed in San Francisco about the same time as he and Jess Tucker, when gold fever was just hitting the state, but their paths had separated. Unlike Tony, Max was always flaunting his wealth and power, always trying to get the Sierra Nevada dirt from under his fingernails.

And then there was Jess. Damn Max for mentioning him again!

Tony stared at the fog into which Lana had disappeared. Jess and he had shared the same taste in women. His late partner would have appreciated the countess's cool beauty, would have wanted to thaw her out almost as

56

much as Tony did.

Ignoring the sensual pout on Isabel's face, he quickly made his excuses and took his leave. The Widow Wright might be a ripe fruit, ready to burst its skins, but he was fast developing a taste for caviar.

For her first night in months off shipboard, Lana had expected to indulge in a deep, relaxing sleep, but too many thoughts kept her mind disturbed. By the time a shaft of morning sunlight drifted through the hotel window, she seemed more tired than when she had gone to bed.

During her long periods of wakefulness, the sounds of shouts and laughter drifting through her open window from the street five stories below, she had thought mostly about home and Nicholas and how much she had missed him since he had left. Where could he be? What had happened to him?

For all she knew, he could be accumulating more gambling debts somewhere in the city, risking *her* ruby or—a horrible thought struck her—trying to win it back.

Then her conscience struck her. He could also be injured or held captive in some faraway ship. As horrible as the thought was, in some ways it seemed more likely. The daredevil Nicholas she remembered wouldn't have run away from his troubles.

Poor, darling Nicholas! He might be needing her as much as she needed to find him. And not only for the ruby. He was the last family that she had in the world.

And then, when dawn began to lighten the room, she remembered Elizabeth Dundreary's worried pixie face. Nicky, indeed! She had no doubt whatsoever about what had happened between that rascal brother of hers and Elizabeth.

The young Englishwoman might have been eager for everything Nicholas had done—some women enjoyed such things—but she was still young and innocent, far different from that charming rascal Lana remembered from his days in the village near the family estate. Papa

57

had tried to keep a close rein on his son, but that hadn't stopped the girls in the village from pursuing him. To Lana's knowledge—which she admitted was limited—Nicholas had never turned down one of their offers.

Whatever punishment Dundreary decided to inflict—from a public flogging to a trip to the altar—Nicholas would deserve it. If only Elizabeth were not hurt by events more than she already was. As much as Lana loved her brother, she knew from personal experience it was the woman who always paid.

Once Lana knew for certain Nicholas was all right, she could wish all sorts of troubles on his head.

As well as on the head of Tony Diamond. She lay still in the bed and thought about the two times they had met. What an insinuatingly rude man he was, with his talk of the count and Nick. What must he think of her to speak so boldly? Could he possibly suppose that women would welcome anything he said?

Just because he looked the way he did . . . and had the aura of power about him . . . and a sense of self that would intimidate most other people . . .

Nyet! She would think of him no longer. If only she hadn't given one last glance out the carriage window and seen his head bent to the voluptuous and very close Isabel Wright. It had been impossible to tell where one body ended and the other began. Maybe he had a preference for widows, thinking them lonely and experienced. As far as Lana was concerned, he could not be more wrong.

With a tingle of anticipation, she threw back the covers of the bed and rose to begin her first full day in San Francisco. The sooner she completed her task, the sooner she could return to her estate . . . no, farm was really a better name for the run-down land she had inherited from the count.

One glance at the well-worn dresses in her wardrobe brought Tony briefly back to mind. So he thought she had no business in a slop shop, did he? Little he knew!

Where she would go this morning, she had no idea. She would think about it over coffee. For her as-yet-unplanned

58

excursion she chose a plain gray dress. Pinning up her hair beneath the astrakhan hat, she grabbed up the cloak that Boris had somehow managed to clean and made her way down the hall. The guard on duty near the stairs greeted her with a smiling "Good morning!" She fervently hoped it was.

Boris, as usual impeccably dressed in black suit and high-collared white shirt, was waiting for her downstairs in the lobby. "I've ordered breakfast for you, Countess," he said with a bow.

Lana breathed a sigh of relief. Having Boris with her made her longing for Russia seem not quite so acute. And his formal manner that was so endearingly familiar, coupled with that critical look in his eye that was supposed to put her in her place, told her that no matter where they were, she was not really alone.

She ate simply—toast and coffee—with an uncomfortable Boris across from her swearing he had already eaten. She doubted he would ever get used to sitting at the table with her, but in America the old rules seemed foolish and unnecessary.

"I suppose we'll need to visit some more gaming halls," she said as she set her napkin aside.

Boris's eyebrows rose. "Another Gut Bucket?"

Lana grinned. "Surely Nicholas visited more reputable establishments, too. I have a feeling all of them are open for business night and day."

"Which could be of benefit, if I am allowed to bring up so distasteful a subject as finances, Countess. It may become necessary for you to raise additional funds. Breakfast was, I regret to report, almost as expensive as the room."

Lana looked at him in dismay. "It couldn't have been!"

"I took the liberty of adding it to the charges for our rooms."

As they strolled into the busy lobby, Lana glanced toward the double doors leading to the hotel's gaming hall. She knew Boris was intimating that she might have to try her luck at one of the tables inside. The idea wasn't farfetched. For all his evil ways, the count had taught her several useful skills, among them how to fire a pistol and how to win at cards. She had taken to them with equal ease.

Holding tightly to her reticule, she smiled up at him. "Let's hope such drastic action isn't necessary. I would hate to risk the few rubles I have set aside for our return journey.

"Of course," she added, "I could use one of the dueling pistols to rob a bank." She ignored the disapproving look on Boris's face. "From the talk last night at the Benevolent Society, I gather it's a popular local custom."

With a blink he dismissed her suggestion. "Allow me to inquire about some of the nearby establishments where we might look for Master Nicholas. Some of the patrons here will surely know." As usual, Boris didn't wait for her compliance, instead moving quickly through the double doors.

She was about to slip into her cloak when she spied by the check-in desk a familiar figure, this time clad in a dress shirt and brown trousers, the matching suit coat thrown over his arm. His back was to her, but of course she identified him right away. She should have known he would be there. He was everywhere she went! The situation was intolerable, and she knew from bitter experience that her troubles did not take care of themselves; they had to be confronted directly. She strode quickly to the desk.

"Mister Diamond," she said to his back.

Tony turned, recognition for a moment easing the hard lines of his face. "Formal again this morning, I see," he said with a nod. "Good morning, Lana."

She eyed him haughtily. "A little formality would certainly improve your manners."

"I've been told that before." He eyed her high-collared gown. "I see you're wearing your saloon-visiting clothes again. I rather prefer the plumage of last night."

Lana's cheeks warmed. "What utter nonsense you speak. As usual. Are you by some chance following me?"

"Tony—" the clerk began.

He waved the man to silence. "You seem irritable this morning, Countess. I hope your bed was comfortable enough."

"Neither my bed nor my clothing should be of concern to you."

"Could that possibly be a complaint?" He gave her no chance to respond. "As for being followed, I was about to ask you the same thing."

Lana's fingers itched for that dueling pistol. No man had ever so unnerved her.

"What an absurd idea," she said in a raised voice, ignoring the crowd around them. "I have absolutely no interest in you."

Tony's eyes glittered. "Oh, no? I've been wondering about that. Let's see whether you're lying or not."

He tossed his coat onto the desk and without further warning grabbed her by the wrist, pulling her through a nearby door which he slammed firmly behind them. Lana found herself in a darkly furnished parlor lit only by a single dim lamp. Her cloak and reticule fell to the floor as she tried to free herself from Tony's grasp, but he only tightened his hold.

"You do like to argue, don't you, Countess?" He brought her hard against him. "It's been my experience that women fight what they want the most."

Lana felt the taut musculature of his body, felt his thighs against hers. Touching a man in such a way, even with layers of cloth between them, startled her, and she fought for breath. "I can imagine the women who have provided that experience," she managed. "Someone like Isa—"

She got no further. Tony's lips came down warm and firm on hers and his hands moved to her back, pinning her to him. Her hat cocked at an angle on her head, and she felt the loosened wisps of hair trail against her neck. Her own hands curled into fists and she tried to pound against his chest. He paid her no mind.

At least he paid no mind to her protests. He was giving

61

great attention to their kiss and embrace. He moved his lips against hers while his hands tightened their hold, stroking her back, forcing her breasts to shift against his chest. Through his slippery silk shirt she could feel the firm contours of his body—and knew he could feel the soft contours of hers.

At that moment Lana's body decided for her what she would do. Her hands flattened against his chest, stroked him as he was stroking her. Her fingers moved slowly to the dark hair that brushed against his collar and on up to the thick curls against the back of his head. His breath was hot on her cheek, his lips hard, then soft, and hard again, each change in pressure sending tentacles of pleasure throughout her.

She felt her breasts swell, a sensation she had never experienced before. But then every sensation of passion was new to her, and a source of wonder. How could she want to bare her body to him, she who had never before known such desire? And yet she did. Uncontrollably. She wanted so many things, things she didn't understand. Most of all she wanted this moment never to stop.

It was Tony who broke their kiss. He rested his forehead against hers, his chest heaving as he strove for breath. Lana trembled against him and fought for control. She needed to free herself from his embrace, to slap him, to scream imprecations against his audacity.

But not just yet. Her fingers curled around the folds of his shirt until her breathing could become more regular, until her heart could stop pounding, until the warmth that had spread so quickly throughout her had cooled.

Tony Diamond was an impudent bastard, but he had shown her one thing. She could respond to a man's kiss as any other woman could. She who had never intended to let a man so close. The discovery left her embarrassed, as though she was the one who had done something wrong, something dirty for which she should apologize.

With that embarrassment came the anger she should have been feeling all along, and she was able to free herself from his touch, her patrician mask back in place.

"Lana—"

She forced her eyes to lock with his. "Surely you don't intend to apologize."

"It's just that you . . . surprised me," he said huskily.

"Which, as you said about me last night, doesn't happen very often. And you, too, probably don't like it."

"There's not a man in the world who wouldn't have liked your kiss."

So Tony had enjoyed their kiss, had he? She regretted the tingle of pleasure that resulted from the realization.

"I do not want such a thing to happen again," she said.

"Are you sure?"

Lana blinked, then her eyes widened. "I'm sure."

Tony stared down at her for what seemed an endless moment. "I wonder, Countess. I know as little about you"—his eyes glittered—"or almost as little as I did before."

He reached up and straightened her hat. She jerked away.

"I can do that." She took a deep breath. "Please give me a moment to compose myself. You may be used to . . . to furtive kisses in a darkened room, but I assure you I am not."

"It doesn't make much sense to me," he said softly, "considering the way you cooperated, but for once, Lana, I suspect you are telling the truth."

This time he closed the door gently behind him, and Lana collapsed on a nearby settee. She brushed her fingers against her lips, which felt swollen and bruised. She had never been kissed like that before . . . never really been kissed, since she could hardly consider the chaste touch of the count's mouth against hers that sealed their wedding vows.

What had she done? What was happening to her? On her first journey from her homeland, had she so easily abandoned all that she believed about herself?

In the close air of the parlor, her mind went back to memories she thought had been thrust away forever . . . to that wedding night almost five years before when the drunken and perspiring Count Dubretsky had stumbled into the bridal bedchamber of his youthful countess and, lifting her gown, attempted to do what he called the "necessary thing."

She had known so little about a man's body. She had long been without a mother to instruct her as to what to expect. But even then, in her innocence, she had realized that Dubretsky failed to accomplish his task. And that somehow she shared that failure.

It wasn't until two weeks later, when she came upon him unexpectedly in a guest bedroom undressing another man, that she realized she would have to suffer no such failures again. The burly count, noted far and wide for his hunting and drinking parties—a manly man, it was said of him—did not like women at all.

He had not acted ashamed, as she had been, merely ordered her from the room. She had kept his secret well, throughout the almost five years of their marriage, through similar assignations with men he brought to the estate. Some cast equally lustful looks at both the count and his countess. Always she kept her head high, but she was careful always to lock her room.

Until that night when Dubretsky, fifty-five and determined it was time he had a male heir, broke down that door and attempted to correct his previous failure.

The doctor said his heart gave out.

"Too much excitement," had been his words, and there had been a knowing leer in his eyes. As though she had worn out the count's heart with her demands. She had almost laughed in the doctor's face. She had learned by then something of what was supposed to happen between a man and a woman. Let him examine her, if he would. He would find her still a virgin. There would be no heir other than she.

Until today she had never wanted another man to touch her, never thought she could respond. Each time she caught someone's eye and read a questioning look on his face, she had remembered Dubretsky's corpulent body collapsing on top of hers, heard that last gasp for the precious breath of life, and had been repulsed.

Tony Diamond had changed all that. In his arms, she was aware only of the strength of him, the masculine power, and the overwhelming desires that he had aroused. No, she had not been repulsed. Weak as other women, she had been out of control. For that knowledge she could only curse him. And pray that she never kissed him again.

Chapter Six

When Lana emerged from the dimly lit parlor a few minutes later, her black cloak resting on her shoulders and hat and hair in place, she blinked at the brightness of the lobby. Whoever owned the Ace Hotel didn't spare expenses when it came to lamps and chandeliers.

She focused her concentration on the large room's lighting fixtures, then on its oak paneling and the richly colored Aubusson rug that covered the expanse of floor. She studied anything that might help her forget what had just occurred.

At last sure that she had regained her composure, she surveyed the lobby for the familiar, long-legged figure of her servant. She was relieved to detect no sign of Tony Diamond and bothered that Boris was also not in view.

"Countess."

Lana jumped. "Boris, I didn't hear you walk up behind me."

"The countess was thinking of other things."

How did he know? Lana declined to inquire. Boris always seemed to know things that were none of his concern, and he always let her know that he knew.

She felt Boris's critical eyes study her.

"Is the countess all right?"

"Considering the circumstances under which we were forced to journey to this god-forsaken land, I am in splendid condition."

Ignoring her acerbity, Boris said, "I witnessed Mr. Diamond's leaving the parlor and entering the gaming hall. And then you, of course, soon appeared. I was relieved to see you had been in safe company."

Lana bit her tongue. For some reason she couldn't readily understand, Boris liked Tony Diamond. She could describe an incident or two that might change his mind, but then the telling of those incidents would be like reliving them. And she might find herself telling the complete truth. Let him continue with his misconceptions.

Diamond's scurrying toward the double doors told her at least one thing. He gambled at the Ace; that must be how he knew the clerk through whom he had procured her a room.

He was trying his luck right at this moment, was he? After having succeeded with her in the parlor, he must have figured the signs were right to test himself at cards.

"Enough dallying," she said with a wave of her hand. "Were you able to learn of some places we might visit?"

"The croupier assures me a place called Portsmouth Square is surrounded by the most elegant of the city's gaming halls."

"Which probably means the clientele use spittoons instead of the floor."

"The countess is testy today."

"The countess simply wants to accomplish her task and go home."

With a sweep of her cloak, she turned and marched out the main door of the Ace Hotel, impatiently waited for Boris to indicate the way, and strode down the brick walkway along Kearney Street toward Portsmouth Square, where, Boris assured her, they would find a half-dozen halls in which news of Nicholas might be learned.

The first establishment they entered proved his information had been correct. Cut crystal chandeliers, antique mirrors, a quartet of violins thrumming in the background beneath the low talk at the tables—all added to the air of elegance she had not expected. There were no Big

Jakes here.

Lana was grateful to see she was not the only woman in the room. A few of the feminine participants at the tables even looked respectable, not like the heavily painted *filles de joie* who seemed to comprise most of the distaff portion of town.

Still, standing in the doorway, she attracted unwanted attention from the men in the room. At first came a glance and then a questioning look in their eyes, but it was more attention than she desired. Instinctively she assumed her aristocratic role, waving her hand to summon the host. She put her question to him. Did he know Nicholas Kasatsky? No? Then what about Nick Case? This time a light in the man's eyes gave her hope.

"But," he said with a heavy French accent, "I fear the *mademoiselle* must be disappointed. *Monsieur* Nick has not been here in some time."

Worse, he could give her no indication as to where Nicholas might have gone.

With Boris by her side, Lana met with the same disappointment as she made her way around the square. Elegant halls but only shakes of the head. Everyone she asked seemed to know her brother; no one knew where he had gone. She felt the edge of desperation grow sharper as the day progressed.

She heaped curses on the head of Tony Diamond! The discomposure he had caused this morning seemed to be growing worse. And on her first full day in town.

Several times she had the feeling she was being followed, but when she looked around, she could see no one who looked suspicious. Or rather, she could see no one who did *not*. The tall, dark, and leering San Franciscan she might have most easily recognized was nowhere in sight. For that, if for nothing else, she was grateful.

It was well past noon by the time she and Boris made their weary way around to the gaming hall where they had begun. Toast and coffee seemed a long time ago. Through her mind drifted visions of *borscht* and of *shashlik*, the skewered lamb that tasted so good cooked over a wood fire.

Of course there would be the dark, crusty Russian bread that she had learned from the peasants how to bake. All washed down with a glass of icy vodka and then a cup of real coffee made in a samovar. And for dessert *blini*, those wonderful thin pancakes that went so well with caviar or jam.

"Countess, I think we need to eat."

Lana pulled herself upright. "Someday, dearest Boris, you are going to regret reading my mind. But not today. Let's go down this street and see if we can find something that won't cost us a czar's ransom."

Like so many other streets in town, the way was narrow, muddy, and rutted, but it featured what surely must be the strangest-looking gentleman in this wild country. Standing halfway down the block and given wide berth from the passersby, he stood six feet tall with tufts of gray hair encircling the bald dome of his head. His face was round and lined, a kindly face with a beatific light in its pale eyes. She guessed his age near sixty.

His portly body was clad in frayed formal wear and there was a fingerless glove on each of his broad hands. In the lapel of his tailcoat he sported a red carnation. Other than the bouquets in the Ace Hotel lobby, it was the only flower she had seen in town.

Lana looked more closely and saw that, except for a few scurrying individuals, the people weren't just walking in a circle around him; they were giving him a slight bow or curtsy, as though paying him deference.

"Your highness," she heard more than one man or woman say, and the gentleman would respond with a wave of his half-gloved hand.

San Francisco was filled with lunatics!

Light-headed from hunger or lack of sleep—or the ever nearing desperation that threatened her—she felt a little lunatic herself. That playful side of her nature, the one buried for so long, surfaced for a brief moment. Approaching the strange but benign figure, she genuflected deeply as she always did when she visited the Czar. With head bowed, she waited for the summons to rise.

"Child," a voice boomed out, as big as the man who spoke.

She lifted her head and saw that the beatific gleam had been replaced by a more personal look of appreciation. He gestured for her to rise.

"We see," he said in stentorian tones, using the royal we, "that you know how to address a king."

"King? I had wondered what the title was, your highness."

"Surely you have heard of us. The King of California." He smiled. "You may call us King. And which of our subjects are you? We have not observed you in our kingdom before today."

Boris stepped forward and bowed. "Allow me to present the Countess Svetlana Alexandrovna Dubretsky of St. Petersburg."

"In America simply called Lana," she added.

"And what brings a Russian countess to our humble shores?"

A bearded man in a fringed leather coat brushed past her, almost knocking her to the ground.

"Churl!" the King growled.

That he might be, but Lana took care to stand against the wooden edifice where the King was holding court.

"Come," said the King, lifting a basket that rested at his feet. "It is time for a repast. Join us and relate your tale."

Never one to deny a royal command, Lana followed him, with Boris close behind.

Somehow the King managed to find a small grassy area off a nearby alley and, miracle of miracles, a small oak shade tree that was struggling to survive. It wasn't exactly like one of the Imperial parks where the Czar hunted and rode, but to her it was beautiful.

Spreading her cloak, Lana sank gratefully to the soft ground, the men on either side. Even more gratefully, she accepted the loaf of bread and basket of oranges that the King set before her. Boris, never one to stay in the background long, insisted upon breaking the bread and

71

peeling the fruit. They dined in silence for a while.

Lana was transported back to those times when she sat in a shady area on her estate and ate along with the peasants. Then, too, the juice would run down her chin, only the fruit was more likely melons or grapes. She thought that nothing in her life could ever taste better than those sweet, ripe oranges did in that dusty alley on that autumn afternoon.

"Now tell us, Lana," the King said when they were done, "why have you come to America?"

And she did, thinking as she spoke that she was becoming like so many of the Americans she had met, telling her personal truths to a stranger. But there was something about the King that invited confidences, something that had nothing to do with his commands. Maybe it was the kind look to him or the way he had shared his food—or just that he seemed interested in her plight without any shadowy purpose for personal gain.

And so she told him about Nicholas needing to claim his estate and about the Blood of Burma ruby that he had taken. Even Cousin Rudolph, with his eye on both her and the Kasatsky land, came into her report—everything but her marriage and a few details concerning her experiences since her boat had docked yesterday.

"I've visited the gambling halls where Nicholas frequented, although certainly not all of them. His chances for an inheritance will be long gone by the time I visit them all."

The King's eyes twinkled. "Perhaps we can be of help."

Another delusion on the gentleman's part, she figured, but again she went along with his innocent pretense.

"You know Nicholas?" she asked politely.

"We know all our subjects. A handsome, fair-haired young man with an eye for the gambling tables as well as the ladies, is that not right?"

Lana's eyes widened. "You *do* know him."

"Alas, we do not know where he is."

She sighed. "I am not surprised."

"Ah, but a king has sources of information that lesser mortals do not."

72

Lana tried not to show her discouragement. Even the Czar would have difficulty discovering all of the potentially disruptive activities taking place in Russia under his regime, much less the location of every man. And Czar Nicholas was a real ruler; as charming as he was, the King of California was only a sham.

Boris tended to label her a cynic. She knew she saw the way things were.

Still, she didn't want to hurt the King's feelings. "It would be kind of you to help," she said, smiling.

"Noblesse oblige, child. We are obliged to try. Ah, but it might take some time. Do not rise just yet. We must send out queries. In so uncivilized a land as ours, sources of information are not always available."

The King stroked one of his gray, healthy eyebrows. "Perhaps you could return later today."

"Such a visit, your highness," Boris said to the King, "should be mine. I can tell the countess what you have learned."

"Splendid. We concur."

Lana couldn't figure out whether Boris was humoring the King or truly believed he might help, but it made no difference. She was grateful to let the two of them assume responsibilities for a while, even if their activities would come to naught. She would like to reimburse this wonderful, eccentric old man for the food she and Boris had consumed, but she knew to do so would insult him. Members of royalty demanded tribute more readily than they accepted payment for goods. The King would prefer conforming to propriety, and she vowed to replace his basket of fruit and bread by tomorrow.

She took her leave, making sure she kept her head low as she backed from the alley. Boris did the same. Once again in her hotel room, she dropped onto the bed. The day had contained more ups and downs than a ride through the Ural Mountains. She was much too tense to sleep, of course, but perhaps she could rest a brief while . . . until Boris returned and gave another discouraging report. Being a cynic, she thought as she closed her eyes, was not a great deal of fun.

A knock sounded at the door, and she thought surely the King hadn't reported his failure so soon. Opening her eyes to a darkened room, she bolted upright. What time was it? Could she really have fallen asleep?

The knock sounded again, and she hurried to open the door.

"Countess, forgive me for being so long, but I have news."

Shaking off the effects of her deep sleep, she grabbed Boris by the sleeve of his coat and jerked him into the room.

"Do not play games with me, Boris. Tell me everything."

Boris tried to speak slowly, to impart each detail of the King's inquiries, but Lana would have none of it.

"I don't mean *everything*. If you know where Nicholas can be found, then say so."

"That I do not know. But the King did learn where Master Nicholas might possibly have gone to hide. A most unlikely place, and one that is dangerous for a white woman to visit."

"Boris," Lana said threateningly.

"You have noticed the Chinese on the street?"

She nodded. "They all wear that single pigtail down their backs."

"Which are, I believe, called queues. Like the rest of the San Franciscans," Boris said, "they have established gambling halls."

"I could have guessed as much."

"Master Nicholas has become practiced at their game of fan-tan. One place in particular he was wont to frequent, on Stouts Alley in the sector some call Chinatown. Or the Celestial Empire, as the residents prefer. The owner of this particular establishment, a Celestial named Sam Chin, has a white wife and speaks English. Sometimes he allows players other than Chinese. Master Nicholas has often been one of those players."

"And Nicholas might have gone there to hide?"

"It is an area not frequented by white men, except those few who care to try their luck. And he was seen there within the past two weeks."

Lana allowed her hopes to rise. Could that dear, deluded King of California have discovered what she so desperately needed to know?

There was only one way to find out, but she knew without saying a word that Boris, her friend and protector and—when he deemed the occasion warranted—her jailer, would never let her pursue the most obvious course, which was for her to journey to this fan-tan parlor with all deliberate speed. He would want to call on help, or go himself, but he didn't have the faintest idea how to protect himself, a fact he had displayed when he tried fisticuffs against Big Jake.

Whereas she had those wonderful dueling pistols the count had so providentially taught her to use, as well as her incredible luck at all the games of chance she had tried. For once she felt almost kindly toward her late husband.

She glanced toward the dark outside her window. "Shall we inspect this Celestial Empire in the morning?"

"It would seem a wiser course if I went alone. The Celestial name, I understand, is more glorious than is called for."

Lana had learned a thing or two about handling her stubborn companion. She had to be stubborn, too, and in so being, obscure her real plans.

"I insist on going with you. This is my search more than it is yours."

"The King did not think that would be wise."

"The King isn't looking for a brother. I promise to leave immediately if I find this Chinatown looks unsafe."

Boris looked at her suspiciously.

"But I don't expect to," she added firmly. "Besides, I'll have you with me as you were yesterday at that saloon."

"If you recall, Countess, it was necessary to obtain help from Mr. Diamond."

"Only because we didn't know what to expect. We certainly won't need him in Chinatown. Tomorrow we will be looking for trouble. If there is evidence that we are not completely safe, I promise to leave immediately."

She saw the hesitation on his face.

"Go to your room and get some rest," she said. "I will meet you in the lobby early tomorrow. And say a prayer that we meet with success."

At last Boris agreed. As Lana closed the door behind him, a determined smile settled on her face. He was so sure she would give him a difficult time in the morning, he hadn't considered what she might do tonight.

But if Nicholas were going to make an appearance, it wouldn't be during the light of day. He obviously was running because of some gambling debt and a threat from an irate father. She truly wished he were not, for his sake more than for hers. Accepting the discouraging fact that he must be hidden somewhere, she knew he was smart enough to show himself only in a location and at a time that Lord Dundreary would never discover.

If only she found him in good health—and in possession of the Blood!

She didn't bother to change clothes. The gray dress would suffice for a night-time visit to Stouts Alley. The black, hooded cloak covered her head and much of her face; in its deep pocket, close to her right hand, rested a pistol.

She waited an hour before leaving. The guard on duty in the hall eyed her curiously, but she ignored him, slipping down the flights of stairs and fairly skulking from palm to palm across the hotel lobby. From habit, she glanced around for Tony Diamond, but he was not to be seen. If he was anywhere around, it was behind those double doors.

It took longer than she had thought possible for the doorman to summon a carriage. All might be quiet upstairs, but the streets were almost as crowded as they had been during the day and most of the vehicles for hire were already claimed.

The driver, a twin of the weasel-like little man who had taken her yesterday to Pacific Street, almost balked when he heard her destination.

"Chinatown ain't no place for the likes of you," he proclaimed.

She had heard similar words only that evening. The world was full of men like Boris.

"I'll pay double," she said, shoving a disgraceful number of coins over the edge of the seat. He nodded once. She had found a language he understood, and the carriage took off.

The town really wasn't very large, she realized, when he stopped a few blocks later.

"This here's Grant Street," he said. "That alley down the way is Stouts."

"I don't suppose I could convince you to wait here for me."

"Not unless you find a gold mine down there."

"I just might do that," she said as she climbed out of the conveyance and gingerly stepped from the mud onto the dirt-packed walk. "At least a ruby mine," she added to herself.

As the carriage pulled away, flinging mud onto her cloak as a parting good-bye, Lana took in her surroundings. A cold fog was rolling in off the bay, and she pulled her wrap tight against her, making sure her face was obscured by the hood and that the pistol was in her hand.

The gun was French, a forty-bore gold overlaid percussion pistol with trailing vines in relief. The one she had selected from the matched pair shot slightly to the right, a flaw for which she knew to compensate, but she had no intention of firing the weapon, only to wave it about if necessary. Looking down Grant Street, she thought such an event unlikely.

The Celestials, men in blue coats and wide pantaloons, moved down the crowded street as quickly as everyone else in San Francisco, only their slippered feet stayed close to the ground as they shuffled along. Many carried bundles suspended from bamboo poles slung across their shoulders; others kept their hands inside their sleeves. They walked or rather ran, in single file, the long braided queue of glossy black hair stark against the blue of their coats.

The buildings were brightly colored and ornamented with fluttering ribbons and paper, and everywhere she saw the curious calligraphy of the Chinese written language. It was a land of wonder, full of bustle and noise. The sounds of the strange, high-pitched speech filled the night air.

She made her way slowly, occasionally extracting an excited, unintelligible comment from one of the Celestials, but nothing that put her in fear of her life.

Until she turned into Stouts Alley, which was dark and lined not with bright lanterns and paper but foreboding edifices that spoke of evil deeds behind their closed doors.

She shook off her fright. She was the woman who had withstood years of degradation, the countess who had supervised work in the fields of her destitute estate, who had learned to bake and stitch when others of her class refused to dress themselves without help from a maid. She was not about to cringe before a darkened door.

She moved deeper into the alley and saw a door open to admit a pair of Celestials. In the few seconds it took for the men to enter, light and noise spilled into the night and she caught a glimpse of tables surrounded by blue-coated men. She caught a whiff of the air from inside. It was sultry and oppressive. Grimly she walked toward the door and knocked.

A Celestial answered. His forehead was shaved and his hair pulled back so tightly into the queue that he was left without expression.

She asked admittance in both English and Russian but received only the same blank stare.

"I am Sam Chin," said a second man, who took his place. Unlike the other Celestials she had observed, Chin wore an elaborately embroidered coat. "How may I be of service?" he asked. His English was formal and clipped, and he slurred the *r* in the last word.

Realizing any attempt at meekness and disguise would do her no good, she tossed back her hood and gave him her haughtiest countess stare. "I understand there is a game offered here called fan-tan. It is something I have not tried before, and I would very much like to play."

Again she was met with an inscrutable look, but unlike the first man, Chin stepped aside and gestured for her to enter. She stepped into the smoke-filled room, listened to the excited chatter of the men fade as they turned to stare, and, with a firm grip on the pistol hidden beneath her cloak, said, "Show me where I may sit."

Chapter Seven

Lana's eyes roamed slowly around the room, as if she were challenging anyone to deny her entrance to the gambling den, but her purpose was far different. She fought back disappointment when she returned her gaze to Sam Chin. Nicholas was nowhere in sight.

Maybe he had seen her before she could see him, but, no, that was impossible. There was only one exit other than the one leading to the alley; from its overhead frame were suspended strings of beads in place of a solid door. The beads hung silent and still. No one had scurried through them in the past several minutes.

"It is a most unusual request that you make," Chin said without expression, his head nodding once. "You honor our humble establishment."

His greeting, Lana decided, was not completely truthful. Not if she was interpreting correctly the stares of the other Chinese, who didn't appear in the least honored. She kept her own countenance as inscrutable as theirs, a difficult feat since her eyes were already watering from the acrid air. Each breath she inhaled burned her throat.

At least, she thought grimly, Chin was right about one thing. The establishment was humble. Six tables were crowded into the single room; with a croupier standing and gamblers seated around each one, there was little floor space on which to move about.

The walls were bare and the lighting simple. Each table

79

held a small candlestick supporting a bowl of oil. Burning wicks rested close to the rim and emitted a thin stream of smoke.

The residue of another smell hung in the air. Identifying it, she was scarcely able to conceal a shudder. Opium. She had been introduced to the odor at one of the count's more dissipated parties. She could see no one smoking it now. Motionless, as if in a painting, the blue-coated men with their inevitable queues appeared to wait for nothing more than for her to leave so that the games might resume.

"You are most kind, Mr. Chin," she managed, determined not to be frightened away. "I request only a brief description of your intriguing game and an opportunity to try my luck. I was told that fan-tan is simple. And also that a white woman could not win. Such a challenge I could not ignore."

"An understandable reaction, madame, but you ask much. Even in this new land of America, the old traditions must be observed. Fan-tan is a game for a man."

"Nonsense."

A rustle of beads drew Lana's attention to the rear door. A slender, fair-haired woman in a high-necked white dress stepped into the haze and made her way around the tables toward her. The American wife that the King had mentioned, Lana was certain.

Lana smiled. "In choosing a wife, Mr. Chin, you have broken with tradition. I congratulate you on your good sense."

She turned to the approaching woman. "Madame Chin," she said without preamble, "surely your husband can be persuaded to take my money. Or perhaps he is afraid I will be too successful tonight."

A look passed between husband and wife. Lana didn't have the vaguest idea what it meant.

The smoky light reflected off Chin's embroidered satin coat. At last came the obsequious dip of his head. "My wife has convinced me of my mistake, madame."

While Lana was wondering how the silent woman had managed to do that, Chin barked something in Chinese, then directed her to a table near the beaded doorway, a placement she found pleasing. She could easily see anyone who entered either portal before he was able to see her.

The four Celestials seated there immediately abandoned their chairs and edged away from the table, as though Lana had brought with her a cloud of ill luck. The croupier did not move.

With a bow, hands pressed flat against one another as if he were in prayer, Chin directed her to one of the chairs. He probably was uttering a silent hope that she would lose her money quickly and leave, allowing the real gamblers to get back to their game. Madame Chin assumed a standing position behind her.

Lana sat as though she were taking her rightful place on a throne, but despite the closeness of the room she did not remove her cloak. Even though she had no intentions of using the gun, she wanted it close at hand.

"Mr. Chin," she said, "the instructions, please."

Only a few objects were needed to play: the foot-square pewter slab covering the center of the table; bronze buttons, which Chin called cash; and a small bowl. On each side of the slab were marked the numbers one, two, three, and four.

With gestures and occasional help from the English-speaking Chin, the croupier gave a quick demonstration. From the pile of cash in front of him, he separated a part of the heap without counting them and placed them under the bowl. Lana was then to place her bet beside the number she selected to win. He lifted the bowl and, using a chopstick, proceeded to count the cash off four at a time; the number left at the last count decided the winning number of the fan-tan slab.

If Lana had placed her money on number three and there were three pieces remaining, she would triple her wager—minus, Chin was hasty to point out, a percentage for the croupier.

Lana listened carefully. It was a game of pure luck and no skill, the kind of gambling at which she had proven most successful in the past. She anticipated that her luck would not change.

She was right. In a brief period of time the coins she had thrust into her pocket beside the gun increased tenfold. She was joined by first one, and then another, and at last the remaining two Celestials who had been at the table before her arrival. She knew they were betting against her in hopes that she would lose. Her luck couldn't continue indefinitely.

They were wrong. Occasionally another Celestial replaced a disgruntled gambler as the stacks of coins in front of Lana increased in size. Always she kept her attention divided between the game and the two doors, but her only success came on the pewter slab.

"I don't suppose," she said at one point to the ever-present Chin, "that you have seen a friend of mine. I'm told he sometimes gambles here. Nicholas . . . Nick Case."

"The white men who gamble here do not identify themselves," Chin said.

Directing her attention once again to the slab, Lana was positive another look passed between Chin and his wife. She swore to stay around and try to interpret those looks.

As the game progressed, the noise around her increased. She became the focal point of the room. Excited, loud voices shouted unintelligible comments; from the agitated, alien sound, she knew the men were not at all pleased. Each one seemed to think she was stealing money from *him*.

What poor losers they were, she decided as she raked the money in. Her eyes and throat grew accustomed to the unpleasant air. Always she kept part of her attention divided between the game and the doors, but the experience of winning was heady. Before tonight, she had been limited to gambling with the count and his companions, occasions she had tried to avoid. Dubretsky had insisted, as though he were proud of her unusual talents.

Tonight for the first time she, too, was proud of them, and she began to understand the lure of risk and the excitement of victory. And she also learned to count to four in Chinese Mandarin. If she listened closely enough, she was certain she could pick up an obscene phrase or two.

A sharp knock at the alley door sounded above the noise, and Lana caught her breath. None of the other players diverted their attention from the play. Without thought, she shoved a stack of coins beside the number three and kept her eyes riveted to the door. As usual, side bets were placed that she would lose.

The door opened, and through the haze she could see a black shirt sleeve, not blue as the Celestials wore. Could it be Nicholas? Her heart quickened.

But the man stepping into the room was far too tall to be Nicholas, and his hair was dark instead of fair. Her eyes widened as recognition struck her. Tony Diamond had decided to call.

A low cry escaped her throat. *Of course* it was Tony Diamond. She felt giddy. How could she have been stupid enough to expect anyone else?

If she were marooned on a desolate island and a dinghy fought its way through the swells to the sandy beach, Tony Diamond would step ashore. If she climbed the tallest of the Urals, she would find Tony Diamond waiting for her at the snow-capped crest. If she . . .

"Three," the croupier said in Chinese as he shoved a stack of coins in her direction and raked in the Celestial wagers.

A frenzy of chatter went up around her. It had taken on an ugly edge, but Lana paid it no mind as Tony made his way across the room. She turned her head sharply to the sound of the beads and saw Madame Chin disappear from the room.

"Madame," said Chin, bowing and speaking close to her right ear, "I am unable to insure your safety. I must ask you to leave."

Tony came to a halt at her left. "A thousand pardons," he said to Chin, then glared down at her. "What the hell do you think you're doing?"

It was Tony, eyes glaring and lips tight, who held her

83

attention. She had never seen a man so angry. Her own temper flared. She knew it was a mistake to lose control, but she couldn't help it.

"You *are* following me."

"Tonight I am."

"Madame," Chin said.

Lana gestured toward the money in front of her. "You've wasted your time, Mr. Diamond. As you can see, I'm doing quite well."

Tony muttered an expression Lana hadn't learned from her mother.

"What I see is a very stupid woman," he shouted over the tumult.

"Madame," repeated Chin.

"Stupid!" Lana shrilled. "I'm not the one who disrupted a perfectly peaceful fan-tan game."

To the Celestial protests were added broad gestures and raised fists. The formerly imperturbable Sam Chin was wringing his hands.

Lana made her second mistake. Pulling the pistol from her pocket, she waved it under Tony's nose. "I wasn't stupid enough to come here without protection."

The exclamations from the Chinese increased to a roar as they dived under the tables.

"Damn!" yelled Tony, reaching for the pistol.

"Watch out," Lana yelled back. "It has a—"

Hair trigger, she was going to say. She never got the chance. The explosion of the gun resounded throughout the room, deafening her. A particle of ceiling fell onto the pewter slab. Tony was shouting something at her—everyone was shouting something at her—but she could hear only the echoes of the gunshot.

Tony grabbed the gun from her hand, and she covered her ears to stop the pain. His fingers closed around her arm and he jerked her to her feet.

"Time to leave, Countess," he said, shoving the gun beneath his belt.

This time she heard him. All was confusion around her, but only Tony's words got through.

And this time she agreed with him—but she was not

going without her winnings. Scooping up the coins, she shoved them by the handfuls into her pocket. A hand snaked out and grabbed for one of the stacks; determined, she slapped it away.

With imprecations of she knew not what filling the air, she felt herself borne away toward the door, her feet barely touching the floor. With his hand firmly gripping hers, Tony pulled her down the alley toward the lights of Grant Street. Coming up fast behind them were a crowd of angry Celestials. They were the poorest losers Lana had ever seen.

She felt like a salmon swimming upriver as they turned onto the street and moved fast against the single file of Chinese going the other way. With her free arm she suported the cache of coins in her pocket. They grew heavier the farther she ran.

She had to duck in order to avoid the occasional bamboo poles resting on the shoulders of the men they hurried past. Once she got caught in a stream of colored ribbons, but Tony didn't stop and the ribbons became a tangled decoration for her hair, which had become unpinned.

Her side hurt, her feet hurt, she couldn't catch her breath, and with the little thought she could manage she wasn't at all sure this insane dash was necessary. She had done nothing wrong.

When they came to the edge of the Chinese section, Lana was sure Tony would behave rationally and slow down. As he flung the two of them into the crowd moving along Clay Street—did San Francisco never go to bed?—he quickened the pace. Lana thought he had lost his mind.

Suddenly Tony took a sharp left, and she found herself in an alley off the busy thoroughfare. Dark and quiet. And deserted. He pulled her deeper into the inky blackness.

"Now really!" she exclaimed as he shoved her against the wall and pressed his body against hers, his hands tight on her shoulders.

"Quiet," he ordered.

Her fingers pulled at his shirt sleeves, and the handle of the dueling pistol pressed against her abdomen. She lowered her voice to a hiss. "I do not—"

She swallowed her words as his lips came down hard on hers. All was quiet save their breathing. Seconds passed, and from the street came the familiar chatter of agitated Celestials, a sound she knew well.

She held still, opened her eyes, and tried to look sideways toward the lighted street, but Tony had her pinned securely to the wall and his lips remained covering hers.

The threatening noise from the Chinese gradually faded. Instead of drawing back, Tony simply softened the pressure of his mouth on hers, and the gesture that had at first seemed an angry restraint became a kiss. Lana forgot the Celestial Empire.

Her hands uncurled and caressed his upper arms. Through the cotton shirt she could feel his sinewed strength. If he chose, he could crush the life's breath from her body; instead, he held her sweetly, his hands stroking her shoulders, his fingers playing in the locks of her hair which had fallen free during the chase.

Giving in to an urge, she let her own hands trail up to his neck and she entwined her fingers in his hair. Coarse and thick hair that fell against the collar of his shirt, not fine and wispy like a woman's. A man's hair. Everything about him was manly.

In a rush of desire she felt soft and vulnerable. Her breasts tingled, her fingers tingled where she touched him, every nerve ending seemed on fire. She crushed her softness against him, ignoring the uncomfortably hard handle of the gun and the press of the coins between her thigh and his. He shifted both weapon and coins to the side and thrust his hips against hers.

She was immediately aware of another kind of hardness pressing against her, not the irregular, unnatural feel of the gun handle but something different, firm and insistent. It took her a moment to figure out just what it was. His body was responding to hers. This hardness was not the least uncomfortable. Stronger, hotter sensations shot through her, and she made a soft mewing sound. When his tongue demanded entrance, she could do nothing less than part her lips and give in to that demand.

The intimacy of his invasion startled her. She held her breath and gave all thought to the rough texture of his tongue against hers and to the faint whiskey taste mixed with another taste, that elusive quality of manhood that had aroused all of her senses.

She clung tightly to him, letting his kiss deepen, crushing her breasts his chest. Her embrace was born of sweet desperation, an unsprung need that coiled around her and would not let her go.

His hand moved to the tie which held her cloak secure at her throat. Deftly he worked at the strings, pushed them aside, and moved to the top buttons of her dress. His fingers stroked their way beneath the coarse cloth to the swell of her breasts and burned against her skin. She was at once thrilled and appalled that he could take such liberties.

Tony's head bent to the widening throat of her gown, and the passions coursing through her were stilled. She had never been bared in such a way by a man; no man had ever seen her breasts unclothed. Only the count had pulled at her gown, but in those two disastrous occurrences that began and ended their marriage, he had not wanted to look, not really wanted to touch.

She had been a necessary evil. He had told her as much.

She heard only the count's last breath, felt the weight of his body against hers. Not Tony's body. Not anymore.

She jerked her head aside. "Please, no," she managed, humiliated that she should be pleading, unable to do anything less.

Tony's fingers stilled. She remained wrapped in his embrace, but the spell of desire was broken as quickly as it had been cast and the tight, heated space in which they stood became oppressive and unbearable.

He backed away, and Lana retied the cloak string tight at her throat. "They've gone," she said. She was proud of the strength in her voice.

Tony didn't move.

"Don't you think we can leave now?" she asked. When he didn't respond, she forced herself to look at him. With her eyes accustomed to the darkened alley, she could make out his face, the harsh set of his mouth, the glitter in his eyes.

"You send out misleading signals, Countess." His voice was low yet cutting. "It's wearing on a man's body. But I imagine you know that."

She almost blessed him for insulting her; with that insult came anger. "Imagine what you will," she said with a wave of her hand, then pulled it back against her body, praying he hadn't seen her tremble.

"I'm not one to go in for fanciful thinking. It's evidence I go by," he said.

"And so do I. My observations indicate you have an inordinate interest in my activities. What possessed you to behave as you did tonight?"

"If you're talking about what just happened, I would say you possessed me, although it's damned difficult to figure out, just now, exactly why."

With anger burning out her shame, Lana was feeling better all the time. "What romantics you Americans are. I meant why did you insist upon interrupting the game. I can see, however, I'll get no sensible answer. Please see if you can summon me a carriage."

"Of course, your highness." But he didn't move.

Something about the way he stood there sent a chill down her spine. Maybe she had gone too far in ordering him about. Tony Diamond wasn't a man to do anything he didn't want to. She had known that the minute she set eyes on him.

But Lana had her pride, too. She didn't need the help of a man.

"I'll summon it myself," she said, twirling around toward the street. Her coins shifted with a clunk.

Tony gave an exclamation of disgust. "You probably would, too. Stay back here until I call for you."

He didn't wait for a reply. As he strode down the alley, his long legs taking him swiftly back to the busy street, she began to count to ten in English. And then in Russian. At last she tried her meager knowledge of Chinese. None of the languages seemed to satisfy.

When Tony waved to her from the lighted street, she

supported her winnings once more with one arm and walked as regally as she could manage to the awaiting carriage.

"I believe the Celestials have returned to their empire," Tony said, settling in beside her as the conveyance joined the flow of traffic.

"They weren't angry until you arrived."

"Wrong, Countess. You just didn't understand what they said." Pulling a piece of ribbon from her hair, he placed it in her hand. She jerked away.

"A remembrance of the occasion," Tony said.

Lana crushed the ribbon and patted the coins. "I have all I need right here. If they really were angry, I can't imagine why."

"They distrust the white man, and the white woman is beyond their understanding. It's a condition I fully share."

"How did you know I was there?"

"The King of California is an acquaintance of mine. He suspected you might do something foolish tonight and summoned me."

Lana ignored the insult, which was becoming commonplace. With a stab of remembrance, she thought of all she had told the King while they ate—about home and Nicholas and a little about her plight.

"Did he tell you why I might go to Stouts Alley?"

"He was quite taken with you. Wouldn't divulge any confidences. I assume you're still looking for Nick."

"Which was no reason for the Celestials to get so upset."

"Look at things from their way. To them China is the Flowery Kingdom to which they all plan to return. They're here for the same reason as everyone else—for the gold. But like everyone else, they have weaknesses. Gambling is one of them."

"And opium."

"Unfortunately true. You were taking their money, and somehow they became convinced you were cheating."

"Impossible!"

"Or had perhaps cast a spell over the cash. You do have a way about you, Countess, that stirs a man to strong feelings."

Tony had a far different view of her than she had of herself, but she didn't try to argue.

"I didn't see any women Celestials," she said.

"Thus far only a few have sailed to California, but they'll be here. Like death and pestilence, they're inevitable."

"Bitter, Mr. Diamond? I got the impression you like women."

"So I impressed you, did I?"

In the small space Tony's thigh was warm against hers. "You *assaulted* me," she said in defense.

"Now, now, Countess. Be honest. I didn't do anything you didn't want me to do."

Lana was grateful that the carriage jerked to a halt in front of the Ace Hotel and she was saved from a dishonest protest.

"Shall I walk you to your room?" Tony asked as he escorted her into the lobby.

"Nyet."

She turned with all her Russian dignity to stride up the stairs, regretful only that the weight of the coins pulled her cloak at an unsightly angle on one side.

"Countess," came a call from the desk.

She turned.

"There is someone waiting for you." The clerk gestured toward the private parlor, then exchanged a glance with Tony.

Lana went over the short list of people she knew in America. She could imagine none of them coming to call so late.

Unless . . .

She ran to the parlor, Tony close behind, and threw open the door.

The figure of a man stood in the dark. He stepped closer, and Lana's heart sank.

"Rudolph!"

"Dearest Svetlana," her ferret-faced cousin said, smirking as he brought her hand to his lips. "I have been waiting for hours. At last you are here."

Chapter Eight

Lana jerked her hand from Rudolph's grasp. "What are you doing in California?"

Rudolph looked crestfallen. "After such a long and tedious journey, I had expected a much warmer greeting, Svetlana."

"Don't work on my sympathies, Rudolph. Right now I don't have any. Please answer my question."

"How can you ask?" Rudolph responded, the hurt expression remaining on his narrow face. "We are so close."

Lana considered an ocean and the continent of Asia separating them close enough. She heard Tony stir behind her. Whatever she had to say to her cousin—and she could think of a great deal—there was no reason to have him as a witness.

"We would like to be alone," she said, turning to face him.

"My dear," Rudolph murmured behind her.

When Tony's eyes held hers, Lana knew just what he was thinking.

She also knew the two things he needed most: a dose of self-restraint when the two of them were alone and, when his thoughts went down their usual lascivious way, some of that inscrutability of the Celestials.

"Of course," Tony said and walked from the room.

Even though she had asked him to leave, she felt an

91

unreasonable pang of disappointment that he had chosen so quickly to comply. He thought she wanted to be alone with Rudolph. That much was true, but not for any reason he believed. Or Rudolph, either, for that matter.

She turned back in time to catch her cousin staring speculatively at the closing door. His eyes shifted to her loosened hair. In his evil little mind Rudolph had worked out what she and the American had been doing while they were gone from the hotel. In some ways all men were alike.

She stood tall, once more the countess, and said firmly, "It is after midnight and I grow weary. Please tell me exactly what you hoped to accomplish by traveling all this way."

Rudolph shrugged, his benign expression back in place. "I grew worried about your foolish journey. The lawyer Balenkov, too, was concerned. I have traveled far, my dear, simply to offer my help."

"The only thing worrying you was that I might find Nicholas. You must have left right after I did."

"Tut, tut, Svetlana," he said, shaking his head and attempting to take her hands in his. She pulled away, and he gave a curious look to her cloak when the coins shifted in place. "How could you be so cynical? Remember our family ties. Surely you realize that we share mutual needs."

"Your primary need is for land and money."

Rudolph looked truly surprised. "You have changed since last I saw you, dear cousin. Your tongue has been sharpened in this uncivilized land, and after such a short while."

"I've learned how to express what I feel. It's an American custom, one that you might adopt instead of always trying to obscure your purposes." She ignored the startled look on his face. "Tell me, is your presence here connected to a possible threat from the Czar?"

"There was," Rudolph said with a wave of his hand, "talk of Siberia. I chose California instead. It was, as you have said, a hasty decision." He grimaced. "Until I arrived today, I felt sure I had made the right choice."

"You didn't," Lana said bluntly, then sidestepped from the strict truth. "I have definite information as to Nicholas's whereabouts. I expect to talk to him in the next day or two so that we can return to St. Petersburg in time to claim his inheritance. You made a long, hard, and expensive journey for nothing."

The benign expression dropped from Rudolph's face. His pointed chin jutted stubbornly. "No, my cousin. I expect some reward."

Lana's eyes widened in surprise. She was not the only one to have changed. Before her was a new Rudolph, a more forceful man, and one she liked even less than the obsequious ferret.

He moved close, backing her up to the settee. "You have changed in more than just your outspokenness." His long fingers stroked her unbound hair. "There is an untamed spirit about you that drives me wild. We were meant for each other, Svetlana. Admit it."

Before she could react, he jerked her against him and pressed his cold, soft mouth against hers. At first Lana was more shocked than she was repulsed. Kissing Rudolph was like kissing a worm.

He had a wiry strength about him that kept her from pushing him away. She decided to hold still and wait for him to be done. Her mind worked. As repulsive as Rudolph was, he didn't share the count's perverted interests. Rudolph liked women, even if he didn't seem to know how to handle them. She could have a lifetime of such encounters if he managed to claim the Kasatsky inheritance and force her to marry him.

Never!

He lifted his head.

"Are you finished?" she asked flatly.

"I see the cold Russian blood still runs in your veins. You must be taught warmth."

He seemed ready to move in again.

"And you must be taught your place," Lana declared.

Remembering Boris's stance in the Gut Bucket, she planted her feet firmly against the carpet, pulled back her fist and brought it hard against Rudolph's pointed nose. It was a direct hit; blood spurted onto her hand and trailed down to Rudolph's lips.

He let loose with a loud squeal, followed by a decidedly unaristocratic spate of Russian invective.

"Don't ever try to kiss me again, Rudolph," Lana said as the door opened behind them. She turned and saw a bemused Tony Diamond staring into the parlor.

"I heard a cry and wondered if you might need assistance," Tony said, "since you were without this." He waved the dueling pistol in the air. "I was wrong."

"You often are," she said, wiping her hand on her cloak. Then to Rudolph, "For heaven's sake, go somewhere and clean yourself. You're dripping blood on the carpet."

Rudolph exuded righteous indignation. "We will talk tomorrow, Svetlana." He dabbed at his nose with his sleeve. "You have not heard the last from me."

He stalked past her and Tony, leaving them alone.

"Don't say it," Lana ordered.

"I don't intend to utter a word. I might end up as bloodied as Rudolph."

"Rudolph's advances were mild compared to yours. The Imperial Guard couldn't deliver what you deserve."

"Similar sentiments have been expressed before." A gleam lit the depths of Tony's eyes. "This Rudolph seems an unlikely swain for the countess."

"Since coming to California, Mr. Diamond, I don't often get to choose whom I would kiss."

"*Touché.*"

Lana gave up. There was no way she could get in the last word, and she clamped her lips tightly closed. Sweeping grandly past him, she took care to grasp the dueling pistol he was dangling in the air. She thrust it into her cloak beside her winnings and hurried for the stairs.

On the long climb to the fifth floor, she had time to think. Too much time. Rudolph had offered his assistance; Tony intimated the same thing when he came to her rescue in the parlor. Liars, both of them. Outside of Boris, no one was here to help her. Even the King of California had betrayed her and set Tony on her trail.

She had already learned in life that there was no better help than that which she gave herself. Finding Nicholas was her chore. The best clue she had unearthed had to do with the Celestial Kingdom. Nicholas was in there somewhere, or there were Celestials who knew where he was.

The only thing she knew to do was return to Stouts Alley when this long night was done and confront Sam Chin and his silent wife with her suspicions. Without the gun. Without Tony Diamond.

Chin had treated her with respect; the other gamblers were the ones who had become so upset. She would simply explain to him that she was seeking her brother for his own good and that she wished nobody harm.

The sun was already creeping over the eastern horizon by the time Tony collapsed wearily onto his Ace Hotel bed. Down the hall, no doubt sleeping peacefully, was the Countess Svetlana Alexandrovna, the cause of his exhaustion. She had no idea their rooms were so close.

Maybe he ought to go down there, wish her good morning, and tell her what he had learned in the early morning hours while she slept.

For all he knew, she wasn't in there alone. Maybe she had changed her mind about Rudolph. The sharp-faced Russian might very well be enjoying the charms she offered to Tony and then so abruptly withdrew. He was getting a permanent ache in his loins. A man could take only so much.

He was tired of playing games with her. Finding Nick and sending her on her way had become his top priority. That was the reason he had returned to Sam Chin's fan-tan parlor after checking with the fifth-floor guard that she was safe in her room.

He shifted restlessly in the bed and felt every one of his thirty-five years. He was getting too old for such middle-of-the-night antics.

Accosted in the quietened fan-tan parlor, Sam had been willing to talk, all right. Tony had never seen the man so excitable. Lana had won far more than could reasonably be expected. The other Celestials wanted their money back and, worse, were also seeking revenge.

"Many of the Celestials were born in the slums of Shanghai," Chin warned. "They are dangerous and will not rest until their honor has been avenged." A raised fist punctuated his words. "You must command your woman not to return."

"I'll do that," Tony replied.

The longer Sam talked, the more philosophical he became and the excitement died. At last he shrugged. Women, he seemed to be saying. What more could a man expect? With that indisputable fact settled between them, a camaraderie was established and they proceeded to talk about Nick.

Chin had seen the young Russian, all right, and even had an idea where he might have gone. As a result of that conversation with the Celestial gambler, Tony found himself caught in a dilemma. He had some thinking to do, some hard decisions to make. Since the beautiful Lana had landed in town, his life had become unexpectedly complicated.

Giving up on sleep, Tony wrapped his naked body in a robe from the foot of his bed and stumbled over to the chair by the window. Damn Nick for running away!

A glass of whiskey went down smooth. The warmth spread, doing what he had hoped it would do, and he poured himself another drink.

Better not overindulge. He would become maudlin and start thinking of things that should remain forgotten. But already he knew it was too late. Already the image he carried of Nick began to fade, replaced by one of Jess Tucker.

Jess with that laconic Texas way of talking and a fair-haired look of innocence that attracted the women. He had always been up to deviltry of some kind and usually got away with it.

Jess, you bastard, why did you have to get yourself killed?

Tony poured another drink and gave in to the memories. He had met Jess in a New Orleans saloon two years before anyone had ever heard of Sutter's Mill, California. The Texan had been in a brawl, the first but not the last Tony was to save him from.

"The wrong woman," Jess had explained later when they were sharing a drink in another part of the city. "How was I to know her husband was the barkeep? She came on strong, sitting down and rubbing her hand on my leg. Hell's fire, Tony, I'm not made of stone."

No, Jess, you proved that for all time.

Jess returned the favor the next night, when Tony found himself looking at the wrong end of a Philadelphia derringer. One of the New Orleans gamblers objected to his filling an inside straight. A sharp blow on the head from Jess convinced the gambler it could be done.

"Ain't got no family. Comanches got 'em a while back," Jess told him that night.

Tony's family was long gone, too, wiped out in an influenza epidemic that had swept the East. It was natural for the two men to start traveling together. In time, they were like brothers. Tony, the elder by five years, took the lead.

Jess's only problem was he drank too much, and he got mean sometimes when he did. It was the main way he and Nick Case were different.

The sea called Jess and Tony for a while, and the drinking didn't seem a problem. Then came the lure of gold. California! The name had a romantic sound, and there had been romance in their souls. And a healthy dose of greed. Gold would set them up for life. Tony had passed his thirtieth birthday a couple of years back, and Jess would be facing it soon enough.

They would quit roaming. Maybe find themselves a couple of women and settle down.

"Some pretty little gal to keep the home fires burning," Jess said. "Chili on the stove. And something just as hot in bed. I tell you, Tony, it'll keep a man home at night."

It sounded like a fine idea. Tony was already weary of roaming. He had spent the first half of his life without a peaceful place to rest his head. The idea of a woman and children settled nicely in his mind. It was a dream to work for.

Along with half the fools in the world, they landed in San Francisco in '49. Maxwell Shader was one of those joining them. Their savings had gone for placer-mining equipment and grub. With hundreds of others swarming in the same direction, they struck out for Sacramento and on to Hangtown. At first Max was alongside.

Jess and Tony decided they wanted no part of him. Even in those days, he liked to preach too much. Tony always had the feeling that despite his lofty sentiments about right and justice and keeping things orderly, he was really looking out for himself.

Tony and Jess settled in deep in the Sierra Nevadas in a valley where no one ever wandered. The story went that there was no gold in those particular hills. When the spring thaw came and a mountain stream brought the sparkle of gold right outside the door of their cabin, they didn't say anything to change anyone's mind.

Staking a claim, they panned from dawn to dusk each day, usually turning up gold dust, but there were occasional flakes and nuggets, enough to make a man keep working harder than he ever had, enough to make him want more. The weeks, the months hurried by, and after a hard winter came another spring.

"I'm getting the itch," Jess announced one day.

Tony knew what he meant. Jess wanted a woman and a drink. There was nothing big brother Tony could do to hold him back. Jess returned from Hangtown a week later, red-eyed and with a smile on his face.

"Found me a redheaded whore at the Fat Lady Saloon," he announced. "She scratched me just where I wanted her to. Didn't have to draw her a picture."

Tony felt a surge of jealousy. Jess wasn't the only one who felt nature's urges. But soon . . . soon they would be set for life. The gold was playing out in their second year, and they both knew it was just about time to leave.

The choice was made for them the next morning when a gunman ambushed them and took their gold, all of it save for a cache Tony had hidden at the top of one of the hills.

"I'm going back for that whore," Jess announced before Tony could tell him about the gold he saved. "I musta talked too much during the night. Otherwise no one could have found us here."

Tony never saw him alive again. And he swore never to return to those hills. The hidden gold got him started in San Francisco. He was in the right place at the right time. Now he was a very wealthy man.

But no one ever got close to him again—until Nick. And then the countess had shown up. He didn't seem to have a lot of sense when she was around.

Like that stupid stunt in the alley. He had meant to do no more than stop her talking, but when he had touched her he forgot why they were there.

And so did she. That was the hell of it. She didn't fight him, not when her hands were roaming and her hips were tight against his. She had opened her mouth readily enough, as if to say *come on in*.

She didn't fight him until she had him out of his mind. And then she played the innocent, so well that there were times he almost believed her. Could the fire with which she responded to him really be igniting for the first time? Impossible! She was a widow looking for one man, and tonight she had another one hot on her trail.

He felt almost sorry for Rudolph, whoever he was. At least Lana hadn't struck Tony in the nose.

Tony held tight to his empty glass, thoughts of Lana bringing him full circle to his dilemma. She wouldn't leave until she found Nick. She would go back to Stouts Alley and confront Sam Chin. The less than honorable crowd of Celestials she had angered would see her, the countess being a difficult woman to miss. She was as likely as not to end up with a knife in her back.

No, she wouldn't leave without Nick. And Tony knew

where he was, or at least had a strong suspicion, thanks to Chin.

Nick knew about the cabin, the result of a late-night conversation with Tony after too many drinks.

"Tony is bound to find me here in Chinatown," Nick had said to Chin a week ago, "and I'm not ready to pay him back. Or Lord Dundreary." He had proceeded to talk about a place he could hide in the mountains where no one could find him. He needed to let things cool down, then find a gaming table where he could win enough money to pay off his debts.

Good for Nick. He had all his problems worked out. For Tony, they had only increased.

His choices were clear: he could forget all about Nick's debt to him—and his own determination to teach the young rake a long overdue lesson—and let the countess solve her own problems, or he could go against his vows about returning to the cabin. The sun was high in the sky before he made up his mind.

Chapter Nine

Boris was at his imperial best as he sat across from Lana for their late morning breakfast. He had consented to her request that he share a meal with her, but he was making up for the concession with an unending series of questions and probing looks.

Questions like, "Is there some reason the countess looks exhausted this morning?"

And, in a more indirect way, "The countess has ordered us a full meal at a great cost. She seems to have improved her financial situation since yesterday."

When Boris talked about her as though she weren't present, she knew he was incensed. Somehow he suspected that after he left her last night, she had been up to something without his protective presence. He was much too well mannered to declare his displeasure with her, and much too intrusive to keep it entirely to himself.

Wait until he found out Rudolph was in town and had talked to her in the middle of the night. Surely her venal cousin had the good sense to keep secret the punch in the nose. Boris would never let her forget that particular lapse from good breeding. She might toil alongside the workers in the fields and the kitchen, receiving his silent blessing and occasional praise, but pugilistic encounters with a fellow member of her exalted class, untitled and boorish though he might be, was another matter entirely.

Besides, she suspected that Boris would never forgive

101

her for being more successful with Rudolph than he had been with Big Jake. She was the one who had drawn blood.

So many secrets! She was overwhelmed by them this morning, and she knew to keep quiet. Ignoring Boris, she tried to enjoy her steak and eggs.

For a while he gave up his inquisition.

"I assume we are fortifying ourselves for the excursion into the Celestial Kingdom," he said when they had both had their fill.

This time she answered. "Yes, we are." He would find out soon enough that for her this was a return trip.

"The countess remembers her promise that she will leave at the least sign of danger."

"The countess remembers."

Silently she renewed that promise. She didn't worry so much about herself as about Boris. There was no way she could get away from him this morning and return to Stouts Alley alone.

What if she met with an unfriendly reception? The thought was more than just a possibility, considering the way she had taken her exit last night. For all that Tony threw her thoughts into a tumble, she had to admit he was right about the anger she incurred. If the Chinese were anything like the Russians, they would maintain that emotion far longer than just overnight.

In defense of his countess, Boris was fully capable of doing something foolhardy and brave, but he wasn't a predator from the San Francisco jungle the way Tony Diamond was. He couldn't survive on his instincts and prowess the way Tony could.

Unfortunately, rather than admitting his shortcomings, Boris viewed himself as her protector. He would lay down his life if necessary in the performance of his duty. That wasn't at all the way Lana viewed their relationship. It was up to her to protect him from unnecessary risk.

How had the King put it? *Noblesse oblige.* It was the same concept underlying her labors on her Russian estate, the strong sense of responsibility she felt toward the peasants, the worry she felt in being away from them so long.

She reached for her awkwardly heavy reticule, which was stuffed with her winnings from last night—in case she was forced to return the money in exchange for news of Nicholas.

"The countess is carrying an unusual amount of money this morning," Boris commented.

Lana ignored his questioning look. Boris knew full well she hadn't possessed so much money last night.

"I would rather pay for our meal now and not run up too large a bill at the hotel," she explained, pulling out a few of the coins. With them was the piece of colored ribbon that Tony had given her in the carriage. She thrust it back in her purse before Boris could add it to the evidence he was gathering against her.

She shouldn't even be carrying it. All it did was remind her of the way Tony had touched her hair to retrieve it . . . and the warmth of his fingers when he pressed it in her hand.

She pushed all thoughts of the darkened alley from her mind and, fortified by her breakfast, allowed herself to think kind thoughts of him. She couldn't be a cynic all the time.

Tony really had saved her last night, even though she doubted she had been in any physical danger. The frustrated Celestials probably just wanted their money back. The important thing was that *he* thought she was; furious for what he called her stupidity—that particular thought still rankled—he had come to her rescue. And he had carried her across an impossible street the first time they met, moments later subduing Big Jake.

All when he had no reason whatsoever to involve himself with her and her problems. Nicholas had been an acquaintance of his, true, but then Nicholas had apparently known half the people in town.

Admittedly, Tony had been bold, far bolder than any gentleman had a right to be, but then he wasn't a gentleman. He was a Californian. She had to make exceptions. And, her conscience insisted, maybe she had

103

led him on just a bit.

But not because she had wanted to encourage him. She had been ignorant; he had simply taken her by surprise.

She could feel almost kindly toward him now that she sensed her search for Nicholas was nearing an end.

"Woolgathering, Countess?"

It was an expression her mother had used, one that Boris had soon adopted, and she smiled at him. He had taken care of her and Nicholas since they were toddlers; she would feel lost without his concern.

"There is much to think about in America," she said, and for the first time realized she would miss the constant excitement when she was gone. Duty lay back in Russia, along with a sense of accomplishment and pride. But the days there were routine, and the nights long and lonely. No King of California. No Celestial Empire. No fan-tan games at midnight.

And no Tony Diamond. She was startled that the notion should strike her with such force.

"We must leave," she said, standing abruptly and heading for the door.

For once she took Boris by surprise, and he had to scurry after her, her cloak draped over his arm.

Elizabeth Dundreary met her in the lobby. "Countess . . ." Her voice was close to a sob. "Lana . . ." Her lips trembled. "Nicky is in terrible trouble."

The pixie-faced young woman had Lana's full attention.

"Have you seen him?"

Elizabeth shook her head, sending her blond curls flying.

"Heard from him?"

Again, no.

"It's Papa! He's going to have Nicky killed."

Lana's heart was in her throat. "Does he know where Nicholas can be found?"

"No," Elizabeth wailed, "but that doesn't mean he won't find him. I've never seen him so upset."

Lana forced herself to take several deep breaths. Here

was simply another crisis confronting her. She must learn to take them in stride. Nodding at Boris that everything was all right, she grabbed Elizabeth by the wrist, then strode across the lobby and into the small parlor she now regarded as hers.

An elderly gentleman with full gray beard was sitting by the upturned lamp, a newspaper in his hands. He looked up in irritation.

"Please, sir," she said, "do forgive our intrusion, but the young lady and I have business to discuss. I pray we don't disturb you. There may be tears involved." The last was said in ominous tones.

His irritation turned to horror. A woman's tears! With paper rattling, he exited fast.

"I will stand guard," Boris said from the doorway, "to see that you are not disturbed."

Boris didn't like tears any more than did the gentleman.

Lana brushed aside a sting of conscience that she had routed the elderly gentleman with such ease.

"Now, Elizabeth," she said, handing the girl a handkerchief from her reticule and drawing her down beside her on the settee, "dry your eyes and tell me exactly what you mean."

Sniffling, Elizabeth caught her breath, then honked indelicately into the white linen cloth.

"I am sorry to have caused such a scene." She squared her slender shoulders. Clad in a blue dress, ruffled and lace-trimmed, she was a delicate, pitiful sight.

"Nonsense. We must think of Nicholas, not of ourselves. Is he really in trouble?"

"I'm afraid so. Papa . . . Papa *knows!*"

Lana didn't have to ask what Papa knew. Nicholas had ruined his daughter.

"I assume you told him."

Her blond curls bobbed. "He forced it from me."

Lana doubted that. Elizabeth had confessed all to her the first night they had met, after hearing no more than Nicholas's name.

"That is," Elizabeth added hesitantly, "he did in a way.

But all Papa could talk about was that stupid old ruby! As though that were the only thing that mattered. I had to let him know there were other things important."

Lana could concentrate on only one thing. "The Blood of Burma?"

"Nicky lost it to Papa in a poker game, and no one has seen him or the ruby since! If it hadn't been for that stupid game, he would have offered for me. I'm sure of it. And now it's too late."

Tears welled in her eyes, but she managed to keep all save one from trickling down her cheek.

Lana's heart went out to the girl. "And why is that?" she asked gently.

"Papa would never agree to let me wed a man that he says gambles so recklessly."

Lana paused before responding. Here was a situation that called for delicate handling. As loyal as she was to her brother, she suspected Elizabeth was wrong about his honorable intentions. Unreasonably, she also felt a surge of impatience with Lord Dundreary. What he really didn't like was a man who gambled and lost. She would bet her fan-tan winnings she was right.

But never the ruby! She would never have gambled with that. Right now, if she let herself, she could easily join Elizabeth in a bout of tears.

"I assume your Papa has taken some kind of action against Nicholas."

"He's hiring those dreadful Sydney Ducks to find him. And when they do . . . Everyone knows they're killers. You heard that Mister Shader talk about them the other night."

Lana remembered a mention of the Australian convicts. They had sounded like unpleasant sorts.

"We'll just have to find Nicholas before these Ducks do."

"Oh, you do care for Nicky, don't you?" Suddenly Elizabeth's cheeks reddened.

"Of course I do, dear. He's my brother."

Elizabeth's eyes widened. "Your brother?" She held her breath for a minute, then said in a gush, "Then that makes you practically my sister!" She grabbed Lana in a tight hug and proved herself surprisingly strong for so slight a girl.

Lana found her arms stealing around her. An unexpected affection for the girl warmed her heart. "I suppose in a way I am."

They sat in silence for a moment.

Elizabeth sighed. "So how do we go about finding him?" she asked.

Her answer was interrupted by a knock at the door. She straightened and looked down at Elizabeth. "Through with your tears? Good. Now put that curl back in place and smooth your dress. This is a public room, after all. You must never let anyone see you upset."

It was advice a mother might have given, advice that had served Lana well.

"For Nicholas," she added, "as well as for your own pride."

Elizabeth nodded, and the door opened to admit Rudolph.

"He insisted upon seeing you, Countess," Boris said, his censuring eyes on her. "Again."

So Rudolph had blabbed about seeing her last night.

"Bid him enter." Her permission came a little late as Rudolph was already in the room. She introduced him to Elizabeth as a cousin, praying the girl wouldn't claim him as her cousin, too. Elizabeth showed good sense and kept quiet.

"Could we speak in private?" Rudolph asked.

"Whatever you have to say can be said in front of Elizabeth. She is my good friend."

Elizabeth reached over and squeezed her hand.

"Very well." Rudolph bowed stiffly from the waist. "I wish to apologize for last night. It was unforgivable on my part to greet you so enthusiastically. But, as I said, the journey was long and I was so relieved to find you in good health."

As apologies went, it wasn't a very good one, but Lana accepted it graciously. Especially when she could see that

Rudolph's nose was swollen and red.

Again came a knock at the door. Boris peered in, this time with a smile on his face. He was enjoying all this!

"Another visitor, Countess."

Maxwell Shader entered the room. He was dressed in a finely tailored suit, his graying hair slicked smoothly back from his broad face. He looked prominent and proud . . . and disappointed that he didn't find her alone.

"Since the other night, I was worried about you," he explained. "What with San Francisco being the way it is, and you a stranger in town, I wanted to make sure you were all right."

He sounded reasonable enough, and Lana could think of no reason to doubt what he said. Except that she had a well-cultivated distrust of all men.

"As you can see, Mr. Shader, I do not find myself in solitude. You remember Elizabeth Dundreary, of course. And this is Rudolph Levin from St. Petersburg. Rudolph, Maxwell Shader is one of San Francisco's most prominent leaders."

Rudolph clicked his heels together and bowed from the waist. Shader nodded uncomfortably, as though he wanted to respond properly but didn't know quite how.

He returned his gaze to Lana. "You flatter me, Countess. As I said, I am here solely in your behalf. I noticed Tony Diamond paying attention to you at the Benevolent Society. For a woman as lovely as you, that can mean trouble."

Rudolph cleared his throat.

Maxwell Shader's forwardness irritated her, and she came to Tony's defense. "He has caused no trouble," she said, blinking and widening her eyes. "On the contrary, he has proven to be a friend."

"Glad to hear it," Shader said, but he didn't look at all glad. "I worried things might be different, especially since you were staying here at the Ace."

She had no chance to query him about that peculiar statement. After a sharp knock at the door, Tony entered the room. Boris must have given up and retreated from the scene.

"Do you think there's room for me in here?" Tony asked. "Considering the site you've chosen, I assume the public is invited to your court."

"Of course," Lana said, no longer surprised by his appearance. Or the handsome figure of a man he was, in his brown suit and with those dark eyes concentrating on her. But he needed to train his hair to stay in place and not fall casually across his forehead. That lock of black hair accented the hard lines of his face in a most disconcerting way.

Rudolph and Maxwell Shader shifted away from the door, and Lana rubbed at her neck. She was getting a crick from looking up at so many men.

Or maybe the problem was that she grew impatient to leave. If Nicholas really were hiding in the Celestial Kingdom, she needed to hurry there as soon as possible. She had made light of Elizabeth's news about the Sydney Ducks for the girl's peace of mind, but Nicholas could be in real danger from them.

The difficulty lay in getting away from Tony, who would of course object to her plans. She glanced up at him and felt a sudden chill. A quiet had descended upon the room. For Tony, only one other person seemed to be present, and that person most certainly was not she.

Tony was watching Maxwell Shader with unmitigated scorn, and for the second time since she had met him, Lana was suddenly reminded of the Russian wolves.

Chapter Ten

"What are you doing here, Max?"

Tony's voice cut through the stillness of the small parlor.

Lana stirred nervously. She didn't like such scenes of tension. They took her back to those unpleasant times on her estate, those endless days when the count was alive and she carried a constant burden in her heart.

"I'm making sure the countess hasn't come to any harm," Shader said. "As I said the other night, San Francisco is a dangerous place."

"I made that observation yesterday," interjected Rudolph, who seemed oblivious to the change in the room. He shook his head. "Ruffians everywhere."

His comments ignored, he fell into silence, and Lana thought that now even Rudolph must feel the tension. Beside her, Elizabeth remained still.

Lana looked from Tony to Shader and back again, trying to determine just what animosities lay between them. What had ignited that scornful light in Tony's dark eyes? Deciding she had nothing to lose, she asked, "Have you two known each other long?"

Tony was silent; it was Shader who answered.

"Since the early days of the gold strike. We both hit it lucky up in those mountains. At least I did. Tony made his fortune in town."

Tony spoke at last. "I hear you are having troubles,

111

Max. Some of your investments not turning out the way you had hoped?"

For a brief moment Shader's eyes darkened with hate. Lana had been far too mild in thinking their differences mere animosity, or even scorn.

"I'm doing all right. What I need," Shader said, "is a five-story hotel like the Ace. At twenty-five dollars a day per person, and with rooms as scarce as they are, I figure you're pulling in quite a haul. Close to highway robbery."

"Max," Tony said, "anyone ever tell you that you talk too much?"

Lana sat stunned, Shader's revelations coming at her like gusts of wintry wind. Tony owned the hotel he had recommended. And she was paying only a fraction of the standard rate.

She turned rounded eyes on Tony. "Is what Mr. Shader claims the truth?"

"In this case, yes." His gaze remained on Shader.

Elizabeth spoke up for the first time since Tony had entered. "Papa says the rooms are worth it," she said, as if in Tony's defense. "Other hotels charge as much, and they're not nearly so nice."

"But are there any other cheaper accommodations one might find?" Rudolph asked.

No one replied.

"I think it best I leave," Shader said, straightening his lapels. "A meeting of the newly formed Citizens Committee is scheduled at noon. Ladies."

He nodded at Lana and Elizabeth, then made a circle around Tony and let himself out the door.

The tension of the room did not lessen after he was gone, only this time Lana felt it was between her and Tony. She had a desperate need to throw a few pointed questions at him. Whatever his problems were with Shader, he would have to worry about them some other time. Right now, he had to worry about her.

She stood, and Elizabeth followed suit. "Remember our discussion?" she asked the girl. "It's time I got to work on it. Please go to your room, dear, and wait for word from me. And don't worry. Everything will be all right."

Elizabeth started to protest, then summoned her dignity and nodded with a smile. "Of course it will."

Lana was proud of her as she slipped from the room.

She turned to Rudolph. "I have accepted your apology. I assume you have nothing else to discuss. Since you're staying here, I'm sure our paths will cross."

"My dear." Rudolph couldn't go without lifting Lana's hand and pressing it against his lips. Again she thought of a worm.

"By the way," she asked when he was at the door, "how did you find me? Was the Ace Hotel by any chance recommended in some saloon?"

"I made inquiries. Dear Svetlana, others beside Mr. Shader have noticed your presence in town."

Rudolph's departure left her alone with Tony, and she got right to the matter at hand. "I demand an explanation. Why did you not tell me that you owned this hotel?"

Tony shrugged. "I also own an import business, as well as several other interests. Would you like to hear about them, too?"

"If you sold me their goods at reduced rates, yes, I would. Or do you simply offer rooms to women you meet in places like the Gut Bucket?" Her cheeks burned with shame.

"You seem determined to think the worst of me. Or of yourself. If I hadn't offered this place, where would you have gone? You seemed short of funds."

"And one of your other interests is charity? Please, Tony, you called me stupid but I'm not."

"I think you're operating on cold logic half the time and emotion the rest. But you're more used to the logic, and the emotion has got you upset. You fight the power it could have over you. You'll be one hell of a woman, Lana, once you give in."

What an absurd idea! Tony had no idea what kind of woman Lana was, and she waved her hand as if fending off his ridiculous words. She had no intention of letting him know how they had weakened her knees.

113

"Is that why you arranged for my room?" she asked. "So that you could be witness to my giving in? Or better yet, perhaps be its cause?"

She gave him no chance to respond. "I have never asked for charity, and I never will." She picked up her reticule filled with last night's coins. "You will be paid in full."

"You're a proud woman, Countess, and a stubborn one."

He stood uncomfortably close. If only he wouldn't look at her that way, she might have better control and not think about reaching out . . .

Calling down a silent curse on his head, she started for the door.

"Nick's not in San Francisco."

She came to a halt and slowly turned. "You know where he is?"

"I'm pretty sure I do."

She moved closer and looked into his eyes, her anger recast into fear. "You're not lying to me, are you? Has he been"—she swallowed—"shanghaied?"

"He's in a cabin in the mountains."

Lana let out a sigh of relief and gripped her hands to keep them from trembling. Only then did she realize the depth of her worry about Nicholas. Laughing, handsome, fair-haired Nicholas, who from the beginning of her marriage had been the only one away from her estate to see the edges of her despair. Right now the Blood of Burma seemed of little import.

"I must go there immediately."

"Not possible, Lana. You would never find it. And that's no reflection on you. Not many people could."

She felt bounced back and forth between good tidings and bad. "How do you know about this place?" she asked. "And what makes you think Nicholas is there?"

"The King was right about Nick's spending time in Chinatown. He told Chin that's where he was going."

In answer to her query, Tony admitted he had returned to the Celestial Kingdom during the early hours of the morning. "I figured I had to move fast to get there before you. One rescue a night is enough."

Lana ignored his sarcasm and settled on the heart of his report. "If this cabin is so hard to find, how do you and Nicholas know about it?"

"Because it's mine. I described it to Nick one night when we'd both had a few drinks."

Lana wasn't at all surprised Tony owned this hideaway; after today's revelations, she wouldn't be surprised to learn he owned half the state.

"Do you think the Sydney Ducks could find it? Lord Dundreary has decided to set them on his trail, too."

"The Sydney Ducks?" Tony shook his head. "That's hard to say. I don't think so, but I wouldn't want to risk leaving him up there until he decides to come back to town."

Without thinking, she touched his arm. "We can't leave him up there, Tony." His strength communicated itself through no more than the slight pressure of her fingertips.

Tony studied her hand and slowly brought his gaze to her face. "You really care about him, don't you? I noticed the women usually do."

Lana pulled away, hurt and anger vying for control. "You see everything in one way, don't you? What difference does it make why I want to find him?"

Tony's eyes locked with hers. "I don't suppose it makes any difference at all, Countess. I've already decided to go up there and bring him back."

Lana's cynicism returned in a rush. "Why? What do you hope to gain?"

"Just say I've got a few ghosts to bury. I haven't gone back in a couple of years. It's time I did. Bear in mind that I'm not sure the place is still there."

"I'm going with you."

"Impossible!"

Lana's head lifted defiantly. "Then I'll follow you. Surely I can find some kind of guide in town."

"They're expensive."

"Everything is."

"Winter is coming on," he threw back at her. "There

115

will be snow already in parts of the mountain.''

Lana was reminded of how her overseer had objected to her plans for salvaging the estate. She was right then, and she was right now. Waving her hand in dismissal, she said, ''You're talking to a Russian. I understand snow and ice. Besides, I've got a wonderful sable coat.''

She held her ground, waiting for his next excuse. She didn't wait long.

''We can only go so far by boat,'' Tony said. ''Then we must change to horses.''

''I ride. You can think of a hundred more excuses, but not one that will convince me. You think I'm soft. I'm not. I'm as tough as the situation calls for.''

''A woman on the trail is impossible.''

Lana met his determined gaze with equally determined eyes. She might harbor some doubts about herself as a woman, but the past few years had taught her that she could survive.

''You've already made that point. Other women, but not me. I am not like other women.''

Tony nodded his head. ''Now there I will agree. You're the most pig-headed, infuriating female I've ever met.''

''As well as proud and stubborn and logical—and wasn't there something else? Oh yes, cold. If you've finished assessing my character, then I suggest we start making plans. Of course I will pay you for your efforts. Since you will get nothing personal out of this.''

Except—his words suddenly came back to her—the burial of a few ghosts.

He started to say something, but held back.

''I assume the journey will take some time?'' she asked.

''Depends upon the weather. A couple of weeks maybe.''

She grabbed her reticule. ''Then I have a few preparations to make, too.'' With Tony close at her heels, she walked out to the lobby desk. ''I would like to settle up my account,'' she said to the clerk. ''And please, none of this nonsense about five dollars a day. I wish to pay you the full amount.'' When she had finished her business, the reticule was still half-filled with coins.

She turned to Tony. "And now for the expenses of our undertaking. Your personal fee, of course, should come first."

Tony's eyes drifted slowly down to her slippered feet peeking out from her gray gown. "My price is very high. I'm not sure you want to pay it."

"You're quite mistaken, Tony. You think I don't have the funds and will have to rely on other . . . ways to settle my debts. That may be the way with other women in this town, but not with me."

She glanced toward the double doors.

"I assume that since you own the hotel, the gaming room is included. Last night was not an accident. There are certain areas of accomplishment I enjoy that might take you by surprise. Gambling happens to be one of them."

If she thought she could unnerve him, she was wrong.

"Care to tell me what the other areas might be?"

"Let's stay with one accomplishment at a time. I'm going to take great pleasure in winning enough at your own gaming tables to pay you in full."

For a change she got the last word.

Four hours later she finally made her way to the fifth floor of the hotel, triumphant, smiling, and with an armed and heavily laden guard in her wake.

She stopped before a partially opened door down the hall from her room.

"Does Mr. Diamond live here, Andy?" she asked the guard.

"Sure does. Don't know why it's open."

From the hallway Lana could hear a woman humming. It was not even three o'clock in the afternoon. Could Tony possibly be . . .

Of course Tony could.

"Better let me check that out, Miss Alexander," Andy said. He shifted a money bag to his left hand, freeing his right to rest against his holstered gun.

"That's not necessary," said Lana, her foot nudging the door open wider. One look told her the maid, a young Mexican girl, was inside putting fresh covers on the bed. Tony was not with her. Annoyed by a feeling of relief, Lana took a step forward.

"Miss Alexander, you can't go in there. Nobody goes into the boss's room unless he says so."

Lana glanced over her shoulder at Andy. A pair of worried eyes peered from under a broad-brimmed hat, and his weathered face was set in a frown of disapproval.

"I assure you it's all right. Mr. Diamond is expecting me to leave the package."

"I don't know. My orders were to get you safely upstairs with all this cash. Nothing more."

Lana turned to face him. "Surely you don't believe I've come to rob the man." She gestured toward the money bag. "I could buy everything in that room and not be impoverished. Mr. Diamond and I have a business arrangement."

She ignored the knowing look that momentarily replaced the frown.

"I've come to leave money, Andy, not take it."

He shook his head. "Highly unusual."

Lana sensed his weakening. "Mr. Diamond is an unusual man. But then, I am an unusual woman. Have you ever known a winner at the tables to return her winnings so directly?"

By this time, the attention of the maid had been attracted. "Andrew," she said, opening the door wider, "let the senorita enter, *por favor*." She shifted a bundle of linen against her hip. "I wish to lock up and go home. It will soon be the dinner hour and my work here is done."

Andy shifted his hand away from the gun and scratched his jaw. "Can't argue with two women. Guess there's no way *leaving* something can do any harm. You go on, Maria. I'll see everything's squared away here."

Maria gave Andy a smile of gratitude and left. Lana took the money bag from Andy's hand.

"Oh," she said as it dropped almost to the floor. "It's

118

heavier than I thought."

Andy grinned. "They'll be talking about you for days down there. You're likely to become a legend. The Countess Who Broke the Bank, or some such."

Lana returned his smile. "Not quite, but I must admit the roulette wheel was kind."

"You did all right at faro, too."

"That was my first time to play."

"And it sure irritated some of those men down there. They'll be looking for another go at the money you took from 'em."

"My gambling days are over, Andy. I won what I need. It was exciting at first, but then it became routine."

Andy shook his head. "I wouldn't mention that downstairs if I were you."

Lana thought of the fan-tan players and the look in the gamblers' eyes today. "Men do take their gambling seriously, don't they? Wait right here while I find a place to put this." She would have waved the bag nonchalantly if she had been able to lift it higher. "You will be staying up here to watch the hallway, won't you?"

"All night."

"Good. I want to make sure Mr. Diamond receives what I promised him."

Which wasn't at all what he had intimated that she should pay him. Imagine trading her "accomplishments" as he called them in exchange for his services as a guide! It was something that only someone like Tony Diamond could suggest.

As though she had any accomplishments in bed.

She slipped into his room. This closer view was about what she had expected: dark paneled walls, a bed and wardrobe, fireplace with a large chair angled in front of it, and by the draperied window another chair and table. Everything neat and oversized and manly. Not a frill in sight.

She stood still inside the doorway, her impression of manliness strengthening. The skin on her arms tingled. She could feel Tony's presence in the room. The scent that had enveloped her each time he embraced her—the odor of indefinable masculinity that was so foreign to her—hung subtly in the air. It was almost as if he held her in his arms again.

She closed her eyes and her body swayed. She felt his breath stirring her hair, the press of his lips against hers, even the sound of his deep, insinuating voice . . .

"Care to tell me what you're doing here?"

Lana's eyes opened wide, and she whirled around to stare into Tony's mocking face. Behind him the door to the hall was firmly closed. Andy was nowhere to be seen.

Chapter Eleven

Lana's heart pounded in her throat. She had not heard Tony enter, not heard him shut the door, all because of her ridiculous flight of fancy. Her cheeks reddened. What a romantic fool she had become!

And he wanted to know what she was doing in his room. Remembering . . . imagining . . . dreaming . . . She pulled herself up short and dropped the moneybag to the floor. It landed with a heavy *thunk*. The sound cleared her mind.

"What am I doing here? Paying your salary, that's what," she shot back at him.

Tony nodded knowingly. Once again he was in the laborer's shirt he had worn at the Gut Bucket; following the muscled contours of his arms and chest, it gave him a virile look.

His lips twisted into a smile. "You are a cool one, aren't you, Countess? And determined, too. I didn't think you could manage it, but they told me downstairs what you had done. Too bad that I'll be paid in something so ordinary as money."

Summoning her inner strength, Lana stared scornfully at him. "It's certainly not too bad for me. I can't imagine what gave you the idea I was that sort of woman."

"Let's see," he said, lifting his hand and touching his fingers one at a time. "There was the count, of course, but then you two were wed. All honorable, I'm sure. Then

Nick and your other Russian friend, Rudolph. After two days in town, you have Maxwell Shader paying you court. Quite an accomplishment. He's usually directing his attention to much loftier causes."

Tony stepped closer. "You've even had me going a couple of times, although there I've met with disappointment."

Lana's pride flared, and she ignored his ramblings about the other men. "If I was a disappointment, you certainly didn't show it."

"Countess, it was the brevity of those occasions, not your skill that I question."

"Skill! As though lovemaking is some kind of practiced attainment. I doubt that you know how to make true love to a woman." She forgot that she didn't know what she was talking about. She could fling out insults, too.

Tony's eyes glittered dangerously. "Shall we find out? I've wondered if I could thaw you out. And I still don't want that cash."

Lana stared at him defiantly. Curse the man for his insolence. Let him demand his way with her! She would maintain her anger and deny him what he wanted. It had happened that way before.

She held her ground, waiting for his assault.

But Tony was a surprising man. He took her hand in his and brought it to his lips, pressing featherlike kisses against her fingertips and then against her palm. She stared at his bent head, and her hand trembled. She knew she must pull away, and yet the denials that formed in her mind refused to be translated into action. She also wanted him to continue.

The wanting won. Closing her eyes, she let the light kisses tantalize her wrist.

He lifted his head, his fingers stroking the sleeve of her gown. "You wear a lot of clothes, Countess."

Her eyes opened. "Tony—"

The feeble protest died in her throat as his hand moved slowly up her arm. She stood with weakened knees and watched his inexorable progress. Through the woolen cloth she could feel his touch and marveled at the tingling in so ordinary a part of the body as the arm.

She looked in wonderment at him. This was a new Tony Diamond, this gently insistent suitor. He was a man against whom she had no defense.

His eyes held hers, trapping her with the fires of desire that she saw in their depths. He seemed so calm, so deliberate, yet he was caught in the power of the moment as much as she.

She tried again. "You don't understand." She spoke in a breathy voice she had never heard before. An unconvincing voice.

"Not yet, I don't. You tempt me as no woman ever has."

It was madness, she told herself, one moment to hold such anger toward him, and the next . . . She admitted the truth. All she really wanted right now was to be held.

"Tony."

This time his whispered name was an invitation, and the embrace that she had imagined became a reality as he wrapped her in his arms, his hands firm against her back, his hips tight against hers. Her fanciful images when she thought herself alone paled in contrast to the actuality of him—the broad, hard chest pressed against her breasts, the warm, insistent lips covering hers, the length of his unyielding body so easily sensed through the layers of clothes that separated them.

Her head reeled. The safe, chaste world in which she had hidden was about to shatter. It was as certain as the rise of the moon, and yet she wasn't ready to unleash the stirrings she felt inside. Not yet. *Coward*, she called herself even as she tried to summon the memory of those disastrous moments with her husband, memories which before this moment had killed all desire.

She could think only of Tony and the way he set tentacles of pleasure radiating through her body. She longed for more, for the revelation of secrets long hidden from her. The repulsion she sought as the last armor against his subtle assault eluded her; instead, she was thrilled.

She curled her fingers in his hair. No longer could she offer pretense as the haughty countess demanding obedience. She was a woman wanting a man.

With the lightest of pressure, he caught her lower lip between his teeth. She melted against his strength. The tip of his tongue traced the edges of her mouth as if sampling the goodness she offered. His hands cupped her face, and he brushed his lips against her eyes, her cheeks, and the throbbing pulse point at her throat. His touch was gentle, an overture to the harmonious blending of their desires.

The last resistance within her died. She had waited all her life for this moment. This time when he began to work at the opening of her gown, she did not recoil. His fingers burned against her skin as he deftly unfastened the hooks and buttons that had been part of her armament. No man had touched her breasts, no man had seen her naked body, but she felt no shame, only a wondrous pleasure, and a wish that she would not disappoint him.

He pulled her gown aside and lowered her chemise, freeing her full, high breasts. His sharp intake of breath was as inflaming as his touch.

"Beautiful," he whispered. His hands stroked the fullness, his thumbs teased the taut peaks, and he looked in her eyes to whisper once again, "Beautiful."

He bent his head to place his lips where his hands had been. She gripped his shoulders for support, her lips pressed against the midnight black hair at his temple. The gritty texture of his tongue against her softness weakened her even more to his will, and at the same time gave her a will of her own.

A man's muscled chest must surely respond in the same way. Her palms rubbed against his shirt, and she fumbled at the buttons. She was not so dexterous as he, but at last her goal was achieved and she was rewarded with the sensation of wiry curls of hair, of taut sinews moving under her fingers, and of nipples hardening under her touch.

With a low cry, he pulled her hard against him, trapping her hand between their bodies. She freed herself

124

and felt the glorious sensation of her breasts against the solidity of a man. Everything she was experiencing was wondrously new, a discovery both frightening and exhilarating. Her body throbbed with an urgency unlike anything she had ever known as he gripped her buttocks and held her tight against his own need.

"Lana," he whispered into her hair, "you are everything I have imagined."

With swift, sure movements he lifted her in his arms and carried her across the room. As they stood beside the bed, he loosened the pins from her hair and began slowly to undress her. One by one her clothes fell to the floor. Her shyness returned when at last he came to her petticoat, the garment he had left for last, but she was powerless to turn away.

He unfastened the closure and moved the ruffled cotton slowly down her hips, his head bent, his thumbs trailing against her heated skin. The petticoat pooled at her feet, and she stood naked before him.

He gave her no time to give in to her shyness. Gathering her in his arms, he laid her on the bed. She gripped at the covers and waited for the asssault that was sure to come. She could only imagine what would happen next: the demanding roughness, the quick taking of what he wanted. Surely the gentleness would end now.

But Tony was still the surprising man. He stripped the clothes from his body. She watched in wonderment. Liquid pleasure poured through her as she watched for the first time the unveiling of a man. The strong column of his neck, the broad chest darkened with wiry curls, the thickening darkness of his abdomen.

And at last the power of his masculinity in full arousal. She was at once fascinated and frightened. She knew what was to happen: somehow her body was to enfold him. Impossible! She had to tell him so.

He stretched beside her and covered her mouth with his. The subtleties of what had gone before were burned out in the heat of his ardor. Hands and lips stroked her, and she found her hips undulating in supplication for their inevitable joining. Instinct replaced fears. Nothing that seemed this right could be wrong. He couldn't hurt her. Not when he thrilled her so much.

When his fingers moved to her inner thigh, she parted her legs; when he found within the secret folds of her skin the pulsating bud of her desire, she became his. Slowly, expertly, he took her to ecstasy.

Trembling against him, she became a wild thing, her kisses burning against his face and throat, her hands exploring the firm length of him. She took him in her hands; he had to slow her down and show her what he wanted.

And then he stopped her. "I want to be inside you when it happens," he said huskily. And then more urgently, "Now!"

Roughly he parted her thighs, and it was too late to tell him that he was the first. He plunged deep. She cried out. She had not meant to, but the shock of pain was too harshly contrasted to everything that had gone before.

He embraced her tightly, his words unintelligible. His breath stirred her hair and warmed her neck. At last she understood his urgent message—"it will be all right"— whispered over and over and his thrusts began slowly, and then quickened.

This time she felt no thrill, no wondrous rapture, but at least the pain had lessened as he said it would. His own passions drove him on and on, his body boundless with energy until with a shudder he held still, then embraced her before collapsing at her side.

She lay quiet and alone beside him, the thrill of passion dissolving into a sense of loss that she could not explain. He had . . . what was the word the count had used when describing his encounter with a young man who visited the estate one night?

She translated it into English. Tony had *satisfied* her. And she had satisfied him.

Surely that incredible peak of intensity when his hand had rested on her was what satisfied meant. So what was this feeling of desolation? How could she ever put into words that this sexual act about which so much was intimated somehow wasn't enough for her? As glorious as that brief moment had been, she wanted more . . . to have this joining with Tony more than just physical.

She had tried to tell Tony that he didn't understand about her, but now she was the one who didn't understand. Listening to the sound of breathing, his deep and uneven, hers shallow and smooth, she waited for what would happen next.

He reached out and placed his hand gently on her abdomen. She pushed it away, pulling the covers to hide her nakedness. He didn't fight her. She stared up at the swirled ceiling; tears—unwanted signs of an unexpected weakness—filled her eyes. She blinked them away.

Tony propped his head against one hand and looked down at her. "Want to tell me what's going on?" His voice was low and deep and filled the room.

She closed her eyes. When she had made the decision not to deny him, she hadn't thought about the time after. She hadn't really been thinking at all.

All right, she told herself, *you got into this situation of your own free will. Now escape it without losing your pride.*

"I think the word is deflowered, isn't it?" she said without a quaver. "Sometimes my English is weak."

"Lana—"

"*Nyet!* If I hear one word of regret in your voice, I'll go back downstairs and really break the bank."

She was relieved to hear him chuckle. "Now that sounds like the countess I know. Break the bank, will you? You know how to hurt a man."

And you know how to hurt a woman.

But really, how had he? Nothing had been done by force. He had been, as far as she could judge from her inexperienced past, a considerate lover. No, the cause of her dissatisfaction must rest with her.

A hell of a woman, was she? Silently, she disagreed.

From the way she had behaved around him, he had every right to be surprised by her virginity. Somehow she had to

127

explain a little about her past.

Her fingers tightened around the protective covers. "The count and I were not compatible."

"I don't know how it is in Russia, but over here even when a man and wife don't get along, I think they manage to make love at least once."

"It is probably the same in Russia, but the count thought otherwise."

"Then the count was insane."

Incredibly, she found herself smiling. "It was a condition I more than once considered possible."

"How long were you married?"

If only Tony wouldn't look at her, all this might be easier.

"Four years, three months, and two days," she said, counting the time off by rote. "He died last year."

"And in all that time you never . . ."

"We never." Lana's pride came to the fore. "Don't misunderstand me or, God forbid, feel sorry for me. I never encouraged the count. It was only to be expected that he left me alone, although I wasn't sure how easily you could tell."

Lana kept her own gaze firmly pinned to the ceiling. If she were to look into the dark depths of his eyes, she would rest her head against his chest and confess the truth. Somehow, she didn't think he really cared to hear the ugly details.

He wasn't her confidant. He was her one-time lover.

"I could tell, Lana. I always suspected an innocence about you that puzzled me. But you're so damned beautiful and self-assured. And you seemed surrounded by men."

"People usually attribute motives they don't know for sure to two sources, greed or passion. You simply picked the latter. It was the wrong one."

"I didn't know you were a cynic."

"Admit it, Tony. You didn't know me. Please," she said, gripping the covers, "this is difficult for me. Couldn't you get dressed or something?"

128

He leaned down and kissed her once, gently, on the lips. She risked looking at him. The lines of his face were somehow softer than they had been before, the glint in his eyes replaced by something else.

"I'm afraid I disappointed you, Countess."

She looked away before she completely lost control. "Not at all," was all she could manage.

She listened to his breathing. At last the bed shifted as he lifted his weight to stand. He stood with his back to her and reached for his clothes; her eyes were drawn to him. Unable to do otherwise, she watched his every move as he slowly pulled black trousers over his long, powerful legs and lean buttocks. She was surprised to realize that a man's body could be so beautiful.

A longing stirred deep inside her, the same way it had when he kissed the palm of her hand. It took all of her strength not to call him back.

Again she studied the ceiling. "Nicholas Kasatsky is my brother. It is imperative that I find him. He's taken something that belongs to me, but more than that, he needs to return home to claim his inheritance. Otherwise, the family estate goes to our cousin."

Tony tugged on his shirt. "Rudolph Levin, I assume."

"You are an intelligent man."

"The truth is, I feel pretty stupid right now." He turned to look down at her. "I hope I didn't—"

"No," she said, interrupting him, "you didn't hurt me."

He made a gentlemanly turn, his back to her, his gaze directed away from the bed. Deciding that staying where she was involved more danger than getting up, she threw off the covers and grabbed for her gown.

She tried not to look at her body where Tony's hands and lips had been. Surely the skin would carry his imprint. Surely she would look different in some way.

She concentrated far more than necessary on the buttons of her dress. "Now then," she said at last, trying to smooth her tangled hair, "I'm sure there is much I have to do in preparation for our journey. When do we leave?"

Casually asked. As though she were asking him to pass

the tea. As though she had not a care in the world.

Tony turned and slowly shook his head. "You really are an amazing woman. Most of the females I know are either too much at home at the Gut Bucket or are too timid to set foot in the place."

He walked past the bed to stand in front of her. Lana managed to hold her ground.

"You carry yourself like an ice queen," he continued, "as though no ordinary mortal could ever warm you. And yet—"

He glanced at the bed, then back at her. "I believe that for a short while there I managed to arouse a little heat. Not enough, of course, but I tried."

Tony was as far from an ordinary mortal as Lana could imagine. She kept the thought to herself.

"Then there are your clothes," he said, fingering the frayed collar of her gown. "You wear something like this and speak of a sable coat for the winter. Even in Russia, such things don't come cheap."

The coat had been a wedding gift from the count. No, Lana thought, such things don't come cheap.

"You haven't answered me," she said, stepping away from him. "When do we leave?"

"No more confessions?" He continued to stare at her in that unnerving way of his. At last he shrugged. "Maybe there will be time for them later. We leave tomorrow morning on a steamer for Sacramento. I'll do a little confessing myself," he said, raking his fingers through his uncombed hair, "I had decided to leave without you. Or at least try. I've a feeling I wouldn't have gotten very far."

"You most certainly would not." Lana reached for her reticule. "Be sure you have a ticket for Boris, too. He's out purchasing a few supplies right now. Don't worry," she said at Tony's look of alarm, "he rides even better than I, and he will be impossible to live with if I leave him behind."

Lana took a quick look into the hall and was relieved that Andy was not in sight. She paused in the doorway, knowing one thing had to be made clear. "Please don't misunderstand this afternoon. You are a tempting man, and it was time that I lost my innocence, but if you've decided I'll be a diverting companion after today, you are wrong." She held her head high. "For us there will not be a second time. I know all about men that I want to know."

"Do you?" Tony's eyes glittered. "I doubt that. I have no way of predicting what will happen out on the trail, but to my way of thinking, Countess, we've both got a great deal to learn."

Chapter Twelve

The following afternoon Lana, draped in her sable coat, stood on the teeming Market Street wharf and watched as Tony made his way through the crowd to her side. "I have the tickets," he said. "Three staterooms on the upper starboard deck. They will be cramped, but I don't think you'll be too uncomfortable. The ride to Sacramento is less than twelve hours."

"I'm sure they will be more than adequate," Lana responded, matching his politeness and irritated even as she did so.

Since yesterday, Tony had set the tone for their relationship—all courtesy and concern. Afternoon-with-the-Czar manners, her mother had called them. Maybe Lana should have welcomed such treatment; it was certainly nothing she could complain about, not like his previous arrogance.

But complain she did, if only to herself. In subduing his attitude to her, he seemed to be saying that she was someone to be handled carefully, a pitiful creature who had been through a difficult time.

He had no idea how tough she was. And she wasn't pitiful, no matter how strange her married life had been! Different from most women, maybe, but not pitiful!

After hours of solicitude, her nerves were frayed. Tony might think he should do nothing to upset the despoiled virgin, but what she would have preferred was a roaring fight.

Around them, everyone seemingly hurrying to some different spot on the wharf, were sailors, dock workers, passengers—in short the town's usual motley assortment of humanity.

Clad in a dark blue woolen coat that matched his eyes, Tony stood close enough to touch if she were to take only one small step. His black hair was tousled by the breeze coming off the bay. An image flashed across her mind of what he was like without all that covering—brown skin stretched over taut muscles, slender hips, and long, powerful legs.

She cursed him and then herself for being so weak. He wasn't inviting such thoughts.

Suddenly Tony's eye was caught by the half-dozen portmanteaux and boxes resting near her feet. His lips twitched.

"Where did these come from?"

"These are supplies," she answered. "Boris delivered them while you were at the ticket office."

She waited for his response, hoping it would be curt.

Tony's lips flattened. "You know, of course, that most of this will have to stay behind."

Good, a chink in his armor of unemotion. "I know nothing of the sort," she answered in challenge.

Straightening her hat, she removed the sable coat from her shoulders and draped it across one arm. The late October day was far too warm for such a wrap, but she had been unable to fit it inside any of the tightly packed bags to which Tony objected.

Silently she urged him to start issuing orders, condemning her good sense, scoring her with his sarcasm—anything to show that her brief descent into licentiousness was past and forgotten. Yesterday should not make any difference to him; there had been many women before her, and she certainly could not have been anything special.

"Were you planning to take several pack mules up into the mountains?" he asked.

That was more what she had come to expect.

A burly, bearded man in a fringed leather shirt stumbled over one of the boxes and, as he righted himself, colored the air with his displeasure before disappearing into the milling crowd. Lana, hardened to the ways of America, didn't bat an eye.

"Boris was not instructed to purchase all of this," she said matter-of-factly, "but since he did, I'm not going to suggest we leave any of it behind. As we find something cumbersome, we'll simply set it aside and retrieve it on the way back. Remember, by then we'll have Nicholas to help us."

Tony nudged one of the boxes with his foot. "I find this one cumbersome right now. What's in it?"

"A samovar."

His eyes barely flickered. "What every traveler needs."

"When you're served a cup of tea on the first snowy morning, I don't imagine you will complain."

His answer was lost in the long, low whistle of the *New World*, the five-hundred-and-thirty-ton side-wheeler on which they were to ride. Around them their fellow passengers converged on the gangplank. Most were men in work clothes with no more than a blanket under their arms, but Lana saw a few bonneted women and a vermilion plume on the fancier headgear of one berouged blonde. Part of her work clothes, Lana thought.

The bay was crowded with every kind of vessel—from three-masted clippers to houseboats—but she concentrated on the long, graceful ship that was to take them to Sacramento, wondering if the throngs scurrying aboard would be able to crowd onto the lower and upper decks.

The *New World* had been around Cape Horn from New York, Tony had said on their long, uncomfortable ride from the hotel, and was now one of the many steamboats crowding the river. Ribbons of white smoke rose from her twin stacks and disappeared into the gray autumn sky.

A fog rolling across the bay obscured the forest of masts and spars surrounding the *New World* and gave the ship a spectral look as she sat still in the water. Lana shivered as if overcome by a sudden premonition of trouble ahead. She brushed the thought aside, unused to such fanciful thinking. Nicholas was somewhere ahead of them. They would find him and bring him back.

"Countess," said Boris, who had walked up as the whistle's summons died in the thickening air, "it is time."

Lana welcomed his arrival. With the stern-faced, dependable servant beside her, she could give no foolish thoughts to omens or ghosts.

"We'll need help in boarding," she said as she reached for the nearest portmanteau.

"I have matters in hand," he responded as he gestured to a pair of overall-clad boys beside him. "Gentlemen," he said, waving his long-fingered hand, "these must be taken to the second deck."

One of the youths spit a stream of tobacco juice through a gap in his teeth. It landed with a splat on the deck.

"Sure thing, Mr. Boris."

Tony simply shook his head and joined the procession up the gangplank behind Lana. Leading the way were Boris and the heavily laden youths. Without warning, the bent figure of a man scurried past, almost jostling her into the murky bay water between the wharf and the ship.

"Tony!" she cried out, retaining enough presence of mind to hold tight to her coat. Tony grabbed her by the waist.

The overeager passenger, the tail of his shirt flapping, elbowed his way by so quickly no one had a chance to protest his rudeness; he disappeared into the crowd on deck.

Suddenly from the dock came the shrill whistles that indicated authority, followed by shouts of "Stop him!" and "Don't let him get away!"

Still pinned in Tony's arms, she looked back to see a half-dozen men snake their way through the throng on the still crowded landing. Screams and shouts marked their progress as they made no attempt to slow down for whoever was in their path.

"He's up here," one of them yelled as he headed for the gangplank.

From her perch, Lana got a good look at his moustached face. She could have sworn she had seen the man before.

As had the lone man before them, his pursuers thundered up the narrow plank leading to the ship. No more than a minute, two at the most, had passed since the hunched figure first startled Lana. Still held in Tony's arms, she looked at him for explanation. Somehow he always seemed to know what was going on in this crazy land.

Whatever it was, the scowl on his face indicated he didn't like it.

"Were those the police?"

"They'd like to think they are, but they're as bad as the outlaws they claim to be after."

"Shader's committee?" she asked, glancing toward the deck. "Of course." She answered her own question. "That man in the lead. He was at the Benevolent Society a few nights ago."

"Here are the tickets," Tony said, freeing her. "I'll see you in the stateroom. Are you all right, Boris?"

"The young gentlemen and I will join you as soon as we gather our packages again. We can be grateful none went overboard."

Tony hurried after the vigilantes and disappeared into the excited crowd onboard, leaving Lana nothing to do but make her way after him with Boris and the two boys. Occasional shouts and heavy footsteps signaled the route the vigilantes had taken. She could almost feel sorry for the culprit and wondered what he had done to send such an angry group of men after him.

Boris cleared the way up the stairs to the upper deck where their staterooms awaited on the starboard side away from the dock. The people they passed were craning their necks to find out what was going on, but no one seemed to know more than she did.

"Some said the bastard killed a woman," she heard.

"I heard it was two little girls. And he did more'n shoot 'em," came the reply.

"Hope they catch the son-of-a-bitch!"

Lana agreed as she opened the stateroom.

"Countess," Boris said, handing her a portmanteau. "You will, of course, stay inside with the door locked until the culprit has been apprehended."

She didn't need any urging to do just that. Closing the door behind her, she tossed her coat onto the bunk that ran the length of one wall. Her hat followed.

Slowly her gaze drifted around the small room—from the built-in bed, to the clothes hooks on the wall, to the washstand at her right. It was a Spartan room, but far more spacious than the room she had shared with two other women on her odyssey to America. It was hard to believe that longer journey had ended less than a week ago.

A movement . . . a sound . . . some barely perceived stimulus penetrated her senses and told her she was not alone. Slowly her eyes lifted to the mirror hanging above the stand. She froze. Staring back at her was the reflection of a man.

"Don't you yell out, lady. I've got a knife."

Lana would have had a difficult time summoning so much as a whimper. She kept her eyes locked onto the reflection, certain that she looked at the man who had almost knocked her down. The killer of women, maybe of children.

She forced herself to breathe deeply. No good would be served if she submitted to panic. Her mind raced. He must have been behind the door when she entered. She had not checked to be sure, had not even glanced backwards when she closed the door. Suddenly the cabin seemed not so spacious anymore.

She thought of the dueling pistols carefully packed away in the portmanteau at her feet. Could she possibly get at them? It was a foolish thought. She could never be fast enough to avoid a slashing blade.

Once more panic bubbled within her. She mustn't think of the knife. Something peaceful, something calming. Miles of undisturbed Russian snow . . . minarets rising into the St. Petersburg sky.

The words came, but for the life of her she couldn't

summon the images to her mind. All she could do was stare at those eyes in the mirror. Wide, brown eyes reflecting the same panic that she was feeling.

The thought was sobering. As she looked closer at the culprit, she realized he was no more than a boy, not too many years older than the pair Boris had hired. Eighteen maybe, twenty at the most. He looked as frightened as she felt.

She could almost feel relief—except for the knife he had claimed. He was old enough to know its use. Outside the stateroom people were passing and talking excitedly. What if someone knocked on the door? What if Tony entered? He said he would see her in the stateroom.

She couldn't stand here doing nothing, waiting for him to come in and maybe be injured . . . or worse. Summoning her courage, she said the first thing that popped into her mind. "I heard you killed someone. Is that true?"

He wiped his brow with a sleeve; in his hand was a wide-bladed knife. It was the biggest knife Lana had ever seen.

He hesitated. The moment was crucial. His eyes squinted at her, and at last he said, "You believe me if I say no?"

"I . . . I don't know," she answered, relieved that he seemed willing to talk.

"Well, I didn't. Not that it matters what you think. You ain't out to string me up like those bastards outside."

She thought his guard relaxed for just a minute and she turned to face him. "If you're innocent, why are they chasing you?"

"'Cause they're crazy, that's why." He suddenly realized she had turned. He brandished the knife. "Don't do nothing stupid. I know how to use this."

"I promise I won't." She paused, then tried again. "If you haven't done anything, why don't you just give up? Surely some judge would listen—"

"I'd never get to no judge, not with those hanging bastards on my tail. Besides, I never said I didn't do *nothing*. Just nothing agin any law that I ever heard tell of. Tried a little gamblin' at the El Dorado and got in over my head." Despair burned in his eyes. "I'm a dad-burned fool. Never did have no luck."

Lana felt an urge to step closer and put a consoling hand on his arm, but there was still the knife and that desperate edge to his voice.

She settled for talk. "They couldn't hang you for having a gambling debt. Not even in San Francisco."

Voices grew loud outside the door, and he motioned her quiet with his knife. Gradually the sound receded, and once more Lana's heart stilled.

"They claimed I was cheating. Ain't no man gonna say that about Lucas McBride. I upped and challenged the liar to a fight. Didn't have no idea he had one of those little sugar titty pistols up his sleeve."

"Was someone hurt?"

"Woman passing on the street caught it right in the heart. Everybody was swearin' I did the shooting. I hightailed it out of there, and before I knowed it, there was these men after me. Musta been meeting somewhere close." He shook his head in disgust. "I never did have no luck."

Lana gave a moment's thought to the poor woman whose only mistake had been walking along the street. Her luck was worse than his.

Lana became the voice of reason. "If that's what happened, then you must say so. Someone will believe you. I do. We'll get you a good lawyer."

"Lady, you've gone plumb loco. Where do you expect to find a good lawyer in this town? And if'n one showed up, who would pay him? Besides, those vigilantes got their own judge and jury. Everybody knows that. Far as I can see, I as much as said I done it when I skedaddled."

From the distance came the sound of a stateroom door slamming closed. Men's voices sounded from the walkway outside, moving closer, and they could hear the door of the stateroom next door open . . . more voices . . . then the second door slammed shut.

"Seems like they're searching," Lucas said, by now blinking back tears. He shook his head slowly. "Never shoulda left Tennessee."

"Now stop that kind of talk. All we have to do—"

A hard knock at the door stopped her.

"Lana? It's me, Tony." His voice was muffled through the door. "Are you all right?"

"Of course." Her eyes told Lucas to be quiet.

"These fools out here are searching the staterooms. Citizens Committee for a Safe San Francisco, they call themselves. You might as well let them look around."

"I'm not dressed," she called out.

"Throw on your coat. They're liable to do something stupid like shoot the lock."

"Ain't no use," Lucas cried, his eyes wild with panic. "I'm a dead duck if I stay in here and let 'em take me without a fight."

"No—"

But he had already flung open the door. The suddenness of his action caught Tony by surprise, and Lucas knocked him back against the group of searchers behind him. Pulling himself upright, Tony grabbed for the boy, but Lucas was already shoving his way down the deck.

Behind Tony the moustached leader of the vigilantes raised a gun and pointed it at the fleeing boy. The few passengers who hadn't disappeared into open staterooms hit the walkway.

"No!" Lana screamed, trying to throw herself between the vigilantes and Lucas, but there were too many people crowded in too small a space.

A warning shot exploded; the sight of the gun lowered. Lana spied another armed man round the far end of the deck beyond Lucas. The boy was trapped.

The gun clicked, and Tony whirled, the edge of his hand coming down hard with a numbing blow against the man's wrist. Caught by surprise, the vigilante dropped the weapon. It clattered against the deck.

But Lucas was unaware of Tony's help, and Lana tried to cry out to him. Too late, she watched in horror as he pulled himself onto the railing and flung himself outward, arms raised, legs flailing, as if he could run in the air and make good his escape.

He seemed to hang against the gray sky forever before starting his downward journey to the crowded waters of the bay. The prow of a passing schooner caught him just as he hit the choppy surface. When the ship had sailed past, there were only roiling waves in its wake.

Stunned, Lana stared in horror into the foaming swells. Tony's arms wrapped around her. Burying her face against his shoulder, she fought against the images that would not go away.

The captain of the *New World* agreed to delay departure while the area was searched for Lucas's body. The search was brief and the corpse taken ashore.

Later, when they were getting under way, Lana stood with Tony at the rear of the *New World* and related to him all that Lucas had said. He assured her the boy had probably not been aware of his fate.

"His last feelings must have been of flying through the air. Of freedom. And he was right about what awaited him. If he had survived today, he wouldn't have lived to see the end of the week. Our esteemed committee to protect us all has been itching to prove itself."

Lana stared into the distance as the boat slipped smoothly across the bay, headed for the Sacramento River which fed in from the east. Beneath them they could feel the powerful steam engines at work; from both starboard and port came the *thunk thunk* of the paddle wheels as they hit the water.

The fog had lifted, and she watched the sun dip below the edges of the watery horizon, purple light diffusing the juncture of ocean and sky. Pink-tinged clouds hung above the sunset, decorating the peaceful scene.

The beauty was lost on Lana. Heavy in her heart was the feeling that she had been right in her premonition of trouble. Lucas's death could be only the beginning. Her worry had not lifted with the fog.

She wanted to lean against Tony's strength, but she

could not. He had comforted her in that horrible moment when Lucas plunged into the river and when she lost control. But not now. Too long she had relied on her own will. To do otherwise would be a weakness she could not accept, and she held herself apart.

Still, she needed to understand. "What kind of a country is this that you live in?" she asked. "There seem to be no rules."

Tony shrugged. "You ask an impossible question. It's not really a country yet. We're not even a hundred years old. Not like Russia with its centuries of tradition."

She turned to him. "Will it ever be?"

"I guess that's up to whoever settles here, and what we do with the gifts that have been given us. The gold won't last forever, not like the land."

His eyes locked with hers, and her heart missed a beat. "Still, it's interesting to contemplate the possibilities of bringing together men—and women," he added hastily, "from all over the world to settle a new land. It's too bad, Countess, you won't be around to see how it all turns out."

Chapter Thirteen

Maxwell Shader sat before the parlor fireplace of his Russian Hill home overlooking San Francisco Bay, brandy snifter in hand, and watched Isabel Wright rise from her nearby chair. Tight, neat coils of auburn hair were twisted above each ear; her high-necked black gown rested lightly against her full-breasted figure.

Max looked away, not interested. A restlessness ate at him, a stirring he couldn't understand. For a change he had things going his way . . . the committee, some interesting prospects for improving business, a growing reputation in town. So why the worry?

Isabel drew close, her skirt brushing against his boots. "You're too tense, Max. Too much on your mind," she said. "You need something to help you relax."

Kneeling in front of him, she began to work at the buckle of his belt.

A discreet knock at the closed door interrupted her progress, and she rose to stand by the mantel, her painted fingernails stroking the silken folds of her black gown.

A white-gloved butler peered inside. Max almost smiled. He liked the touch a butler gave to his home. White gloves. Now that was real class.

"You have a caller, Mr. Shader."

Max nodded and set the snifter on the table between the two chairs, not bothering to ask for a card; no one in this town seemed to know what they were for. Most of the hundreds he had ordered engraved a year ago still rested in his desk.

"Captain Otto Baylor," the butler announced.

Baylor entered. He seemed short of breath and his face was flushed; even his normally well-groomed moustache looked unkempt.

"I rushed right over here as soon as I could, Maxwell. Thought you would want to hear the news."

Max was immediately alert. Otto was the closest thing he had to a confidant among the respectable leaders in town.

"What's wrong?" he asked. "Something happen at the committee meeting?"

Baylor caught his breath. "It went about the way we planned, down to the details for holding trials, but a whole hell of a lot has happened since." He shook his head. "Seems a week ago instead of only a few hours," he added, glancing at Isabel.

"It's all right," Max assured him. "You can talk in front of Mrs. Wright. We were sharing a glass of brandy before dinner. Help yourself and then tell me everything."

Max's relationship with Isabel was a confidence he didn't share with anyone. Not because of her reputation, but because of his.

Baylor quickly did as he was instructed, taking the chair that Isabel had vacated. "Thought for a while today we were going to have us another example of justice at work. And we did, in a way. A young drifter tried to shoot up the El Dorado just as the meeting was ending across the square. He killed a woman out on the street."

Baylor took a long swallow of brandy while Max watched impatiently.

"And the committee members couldn't catch him, I assume."

"Maxwell, I never moved so fast in my life." He brushed at his moustache. "Too old for these shenanigans. We need to hire us some younger men."

He finished his glass, then hurried on at Max's gesture of impatience. "A half dozen of us chased him all the way

146

down to the dock. We even got him cornered on one of the boats." He coughed nervously.

"So what went wrong?"

Baylor poured another drink, this time sipping while he talked. "Tony Diamond was on board, along with that Russian countess who was at the meeting the other night."

Max tensed. "What was Diamond doing there? Seeing her off?"

"Far as I could tell, the two of them were traveling together. Ship was the *New World*, bound for Sacramento. Didn't bother to ask around about why they were going there. I assumed you would want to know right away about the boy."

Max didn't really give a damn about some young killer, not when Tony was in the picture, but he didn't tell Baylor that. He settled back in the chair, one hand working into a fist on the upholstered arm.

"Let me describe for you what happened, Otto. I know the man well. Diamond interfered in committee business and allowed the killer to get away."

Baylor nodded in disgust. "He interfered all right, managed to disarm me, even though I put up quite a struggle. But I scared the boy. He jumped overboard. Stupid move on his part, with all the traffic on the bay. Big ship caught him soon as he hit the water."

"How terrible," Isabel murmured, then grew silent at a glance from Max.

"You have to look at it this way, ma'am," Baylor added, "I don't imagine he would have lasted long under our care. Not if justice were served."

"I would hope that is true," said Max.

"His body is down at the mortuary," Baylor continued. "I don't imagine anyone will claim it. At least, we can put it on public display as a warning to others like him. And it doesn't hurt to let the people know we're protecting them."

"You'll take care of the details, of course," Max said in dismissal.

"Of course." Baylor reached for the bottle of brandy,

147

caught Max's eye, and set down his glass.

"And keep your ears open for word about Diamond," said Max. "He's against us, you know, and all the good work we're trying to do. There's not much he can do to stop us, not with the public on our side, but we still need to know what he's up to."

"Sure thing, Maxwell. I'll let myself out. No need to call that man of yours."

Max barely heard him. Alone with Isabel, he stared into the fire and tried to figure out what was going on. Tony had sworn two years ago never to go back to those mountains. If he wanted to spend a little time with the countess, he would be looking for another place besides that cabin.

Had he discovered anything more about what happened up there? He had certainly never forgotten Jess Tucker. Without knowing all the facts, he blamed Max for his partner's death. Tucker had been an impulsive fool, but Tony sure as hell wasn't. Max had spent two years watching him, letting the hate grow. Unlike Max, who had made a few unwise investments, everything the bastard did turned into success.

And now Tony even had the countess in bed. Max was sure of it. His loins tightened at the thought. He would like to get a part of that action himself.

"It really is too bad about the kid, isn't it?" Isabel said. "And the poor woman."

"What? Oh . . . sure," Max said, coming out of his thoughts. He smiled. He might not have the countess to do his bidding, but Maxwell Shader was not without compensations. There was always Isabel. She pulled off the role of widow lady just fine, but she had the heart and soul of a whore.

As well she should. She had been working the mining camps when he first met her—face painted, hair dyed redder than nature intended—and her manners had been straight out of the backwoods. Under his guidance, she had come a long way.

And, he had to admit, she had taught him a thing or

two. He glanced up to see her staring down at him, her eyes on the rise in his trousers.

"I see you're getting ready for me," she said.

"Then do what I pay you for." He liked humiliating her, liked the feeling of power it gave him.

Once again she kneeled in front of him; he reached out and squeezed her breast. She cried out softly but didn't pull away. Women liked pain, liked the shame a man handed them.

Her hands reached for his belt, fingers stroking between his legs and catching his growing fullness before moving to the fastenings of his trousers.

When she had freed him, exposing his full arousal, he caught her head and pulled her down against him. Ah . . . for a time he could forget his worries. With eyes closed, he imagined the lips of the haughty countess rubbing against him. Her hot breath . . . her tongue . . .

Does she do this for you, Tony?

In that moment of climax he swore that someday the Countess Svetlana Alexandrovna would kneel before him and do exactly as he wished.

Chapter Fourteen

Early morning found the *New World* running behind schedule. What should have been a dawn arrival at Sacramento was now predicted for eight o'clock, Tony explained when he joined Lana on the starboard deck outside their connecting staterooms.

Lana greeted him with a smile, glad she was able to look at him without the uneasiness of yesterday. She attributed the change to the way they had both responded to the tragedy on board. By the time she returned to Russia, she would no doubt have forgotten what they had done in his Ace Hotel room.

Together they watched the sun rise over the snow-capped Sierra Nevadas. On both sides of the wide, brown river stretched the Sacramento Valley, still verdant in autumn with oaks and evergreens. The banks were dotted with camps, and the river itself was as crowded as the San Francisco streets.

"We passed an accident during the night that held us up," Tony explained. "As far as I could tell, a couple of barges rammed a big steamer and had it crosswise across our path."

Lana thought of the Neva River near her home and the orderly flow of ships and barges during the few summer months when it was navigable. "Are American rivers all like this one?"

"No river is like the Sacramento. It's the main route to

151

the northern gold fields. Somebody will have to do something pretty soon about regulating traffic. Fares used to be thirty dollars and more for this trip. So many steamers are working the route, we paid less than a tenth of that. And for a stateroom."

Lana nodded, thinking river travel was the first real bargain she had discovered since her arrival.

Around them flowed wild, excited talk about gold strikes and riches.

"Fellow panned fifty thousand dollars in gold dust over on Sullivan's Creek," claimed one bearded man in a red flannel shirt as he walked behind them.

"That ain't nothing!" his companion said. "Thousand dollars a pan is what I hear they're getting off the south fork of the Yuba."

Each story she was able to pick out from the crowd grew more exaggerated. No one had tales to tell about failure. And Lana heard no mention of a young man who had tried to run to the sky. Poor Lucas McBride. She must be the only one on board to remember him.

Even Tony seemed preoccupied as he stood beside her, his eyes trained on the passing countryside. She thought again of the reason he had given for this journey.

I've got a few ghosts to bury.

The words came back to puzzle her. Maybe a woman was bothering him, and she wondered if an unhappy love affair might be the source of the veiled look of sad remembrance she could read on his face. The trouble was she had a difficult time imagining Tony not getting any woman he wanted.

Maxwell Shader had mentioned a name her first night in town—Jess Tucker. Tony had been visibly upset. She tried to remember the exact exchange of words but could not. Maybe this Tucker had won the woman Tony wanted. If so, she would like to get a look at the man.

Suddenly she became aware of a change around her—a charged feeling in the air. The scream of the *New World*'s whistle filled the air; it was followed by an answering cry from the port side of the steamer.

152

"A race!" someone yelled, and the call was taken up by what seemed a hundred other passengers.

Shaken from his musings, Tony muttered something about "damned fools."

"What's going on?" asked Lana.

"It seems we've been challenged to a race. From the looks of where we are, it's probably all the way to Sacramento."

"Can these steamers go very fast?"

As if in answer, the boat gave a jerk.

"You're about to find out. Come on. If we're going to be caught in this madness, we might as well watch it from the forward deck."

Grabbing her hand, he pulled her through the throng of men crowding the walkway.

"Fire up!" was the call of the hour. And "Don't let the rascals beat us." In the short distance to their viewing post Lana heard at least a dozen bets placed.

On the port side they could see the rival steamer; in size it looked little different from the *New World*.

"How does anyone know which boat to pick?" Lana asked.

"Doesn't make much differnce," replied Tony. "Men will bet on most anything."

Boris joined them on the forward deck. "I see the day has begun, Countess," was his only comment. Like Lana, he was adapting to the unexpected.

Since there was nothing else she could do, Lana gave herself to the excitement. The *New World* slipped through the water like a dolphin, but she was able to gain little on the challenging ship, another side-wheeler named the *Gallant*.

Lana was alarmed at the closeness of the two ships; she could count the passengers on the deck of the *Gallant*, could almost read the challenge in their eyes.

No one else seemed concerned. Cries of "Fire up!" were the only words to be heard.

At times they were lost in the hissing of the steam and the howling of the piston. Smoke poured from the twin

153

stacks behind the wheelhouse, and the vessel creaked and labored in its valiant attempt at victory.

Gradually the *New World* began to ease ahead. Exclamations of excitement erupted. Without thinking, Lana clutched at Tony's sleeve and joined in the celebration.

"Get a good look at our stern," one of the passengers called across the water.

And that was exactly what the rival travelers were forced to do as the *New World* increased the distance between the ships. By the time her engines were cut back at the Sacramento dock, the *Gallant* was a hundred yards behind.

Around Tony and Lana, bets were settled and arguments began concerning the precise conditions of the wagers.

He grinned at her. "Sorry you didn't get some money down?"

"Americans!" was all she could say.

The town of Sacramento was a pleasant surprise. Unlike the hodgepodge of buildings in San Francisco and the labyrinthine streets and alleys, it had a uniformity that suggested order and planning. A levee had been built the length of the town to protect it from the river. Wide, straight streets were laid out at right angles and named by number or letters of the alphabet, J Street being the central street in town.

Most of the houses were wood, painted white, and trimmed in green. On the welcome walk to the Orleans Hotel at J and Second Streets, she saw no structure that was grand or glorious, but neither did she seen anything resembling the Gut Bucket Saloon.

Boris remained behind to arrange for delivery of their parcels.

As she strode alongside Tony, her sable coat once more tossed across her arm, she heard what sounded like a riot in the distance, and she began to question her quick and favorable judgment. Her opinion was amended completely when she got a close-up view of the chaotic scene in front

154

of the hotel.

The intersecting streets were teeming with four-horse coaches. She counted twenty before giving up. Drivers were bellowing to the crowds that it was time to get aboard and almost simultaneously swearing at each other for reasons Lana couldn't begin to fathom.

Tony guided her into the crowded lobby. "I'll see about a room where you can rest and wait until Boris gets here with the samovar," he said blandly.

"And what will you be doing?" For all his solicitude, Lana didn't trust him in the least to keep her well informed.

"Seeing about transportation to Hangtown."

For a moment she caught that same distant distress in his eyes that she had seen on the steamer, then it was gone, so quickly that she wondered if she had imagined it.

Lana looked back toward the street. "Where are all those conveyances bound?"

"Mining towns. The Orleans is Sacramento's staging house."

"But you said we will be going by horseback."

Tony shrugged. "I'll get you to the cabin all right."

He seemed distracted as he talked, half listening to her and his own replies. Then his mood changed. "If we're going to do this, I might as well get started," he said abruptly. "Get some breakfast. I'll be right back."

Last night's meal on the *New World* had been far from adequate and Lana realized she was ravenous. While she was waiting for both Boris and an available table, she stood for a few minutes beside one of the steamer's passengers, the woman with the feathered hat. The plume was drooping a little this morning, but her cheeks were as rouged as they had been onboard. She introduced herself as Carmen.

"You're the woman with that good-looking man. You two married? Didn't think so. He don't look married." She eyed Lana's sable coat. "Where you two heading, honey?"

"Hangtown."

Carmen's eyes widened, and Lana admired the way she

155

could lift her kohl-thickened eyelashes so gracefully. They appeared to weigh a pound each.

"That place is too rough for me. I'm heading for Coloma."

Lana decided not to ask for particulars about her destination, instead concentrating on the journey. "Have you ridden one of these stages before?"

The question seemed innocent enough, but it unloosed an onslaught of colorful language that Lana hadn't heard since her visit to the Barbary Coast. Throughout Carmen's discourse she was led to understand the coaches, unsprung and uncomfortable, were stuffed with coarse, cigar-smoking Yankees and tobacco-chewing cowboys, neither of whom knew spit about how to treat a lady.

Between the two of them, the cowboys were the worst. They kept poking folks with their rifles, and they didn't give a hoot in hell where they expectorated their tobacco juice.

And the passengers weren't the worst part. The route was dusty on the plains and arduous in the mountains, where everyone but the driver was required to get out and walk on the uphill roads. The men entertained themselves with crude suggestions as to how they and Carmen might pass the time.

Lana gathered that the insulting part of the suggestions had been the omission of financial remuneration.

"I ain't going up in those frosty hills for my health," the woman concluded before disappearing into the crowd.

Lana was left with much to ponder as Boris joined her in the hotel restaurant; they were just completing their meal when Tony returned.

"All set," he reported as he pulled up a chair and signaled for the waiter. "We've got rooms here for the night. I had to make arrangements for travel in the morning. The coaches you saw were already filled."

"I suppose one more day won't hurt," Lana said.

"Right. You'll leave at dawn."

Immediately suspicious, Lana set her folded napkin beside her plate. "What do you mean?"

156

Tony forced her to wait while he placed his order.

"Just what I said. You and Boris will go by stage and meet me in Hangtown. I'll be riding up."

Lana stared at him in disbelief, forcing herself to silence while his coffee was served.

"Countess—" Boris began.

"I'll handle this," she said, more curtly than she had intended.

"In that case," he said, standing with dignity, "I shall make sure the local ruffians have not absconded with the bags I left at the desk." He turned to Tony. "Mr. Diamond, I feel confident the travel arrangements you made are satisfactory. It is necessary, sometimes, for some of us to adjust to the unexpected."

There was no doubt in Lana's mind that Boris trusted Tony completely. She felt abandoned. Between the two men, she was getting a ferocious headache. She decided to attack them one at a time and waited until Boris was gone before speaking.

"Separate travel arrangements were not at all what we discussed," she said. "I hired you to guide me. Not send me on my way."

Tony's eyes glittered dangerously. "If you're thinking about that money bag you left in my room, think again. Your winnings were deposited in your name. You didn't hire me to do anything. I agreed, although only God knows why, to let you accompany me."

A cry of protest sounded in Lana's throat. How could she ever have let this man . . .

"Have you forgotten so soon? You changed your mind about bringing me right after you got me in bed," she hissed and was immediately sorry. She didn't care at all for the smile that curled his lips.

"That's right. So I did. It slipped my mind."

It was casually said, as though the seduction of an innocent woman was an everyday occurrence for him, and one not always pleasing. The thought stung. Not even the count had been so insulting.

Suddenly Lana was aware of the quietness around them,

157

and her shame increased. She had wanted a return to their arguments, but nothing like this. She wasn't prepared for the hurt he could now inflict.

Still, she knew how to put on an aristocratic countenance, even when confronted with such scorn. She stood, eyes flashing and head high, and waited for Tony to do the same.

"Lana—"

"Please don't interrupt your meal on my account. I'll be in my room. Perhaps we can have tea later, Mr. Diamond, and discuss our plans."

This time she draped her coat over her shoulders; it made a much better impression when she wore it, and it twirled so dramatically when she turned.

For Lana, impressions were very important. They allowed her to keep her pride.

In late afternoon a knock on her hotel room door stirred Lana from a restless nap. "Waiter," was the muffled report from the hall.

Smoothing her wrinkled gown, she let him in and was surprised to see a full tea service on the cart, along with a tray of finger sandwiches and another of small, frosted cakes. He rolled the cart in front of the small settee at one end of the spacious room.

"All paid for, miss," the waiter said when she reached for her reticule.

Lana nodded. Somehow, she vowed, she would force Tony to accept recompense for every penny of her expenses, with an additional percentage added as salary. In no respect was she a recipient of charity, and furthermore, she didn't care how rich he was or how much he disliked being *hired.* She resented the fact that while he was filled with pride, she was supposed to have none at all.

The waiter was just leaving when the object of her thoughts appeared in the still open doorway. "May I come in? I beieve I was invited for tea."

Her mask of nobility slipped into place.

"Of course," she said, gesturing to the settee. "Let me pour you a cup." She forced herself to settle beside him, ignoring the watchful look in his eyes. He was dressed in black shirt and trousers and black riding boots, and when he stretched his legs out in front of him, they seemed to go on forever.

She turned her attention to her task. "Sugar?" she asked coolly.

"I beg your pardon? Oh, for the tea. No, thank you."

He took the cup with as much composure as she extended it, but he set it down untouched.

"Lana, about this morning."

"Yes, the arrangements." She was not about to let him apologize for his insults and so easily assuage his conscience—if he had one. "Surely you don't plan to go riding off into the distance and leave me and Boris to that dreadful stagecoach. We all go together. If that wasn't your understanding, it was mine."

"I'm going crosscountry. I've decided you would never make it, and neither would your friend."

Lana sipped at her tea and bit into a sandwich, knowing each dainty gesture was driving him to exasperation.

"I hope this afternoon isn't going to turn into another of those arguments where you present one side and I the other," she said.

"You don't have a side."

Talking to Tony was like talking to the wall.

She looked him straight in the eye. "When I was six years old, my father put me on horseback and taught me to ride. He was a hard taskmaster. If I fell off, and I most certainly did, I was made to scramble right back on. By the time I was eight, I was riding for miles about the countryside during all but the harshest weather. At ten, I could reach every village in the province. I was not a countess then, you see, and felt freer to do as I chose. Boris often accompanied me."

"But—"

"During the years of my marriage, I was happiest riding. For reasons which are not of importance, the count

159

sold off most of our stable and I have dearly missed what I so long enjoyed." Lana began to lose her composure, and she placed her shaking cup on the table. "The thought of confinement in a stagecoach, wondering what you are up to—"

"Is that what all this is about? What I'm up to?"

"What this is all about concerns agreements and trust. I thought we had the former, and since you claim otherwise, I no longer have the latter."

Tony rose abruptly and moved away from the settee. "Bringing you along was the stupidest thing I ever did. You had me so turned around there for a while, I didn't think straight."

"I had you turned around, did I?" She laughed without humor. "You've hidden it well enough."

"Lady, you don't know how hard I've been trying to be polite. And in case you think I didn't like what happened between us, you came very close to getting dragged into my stateroom last night. That's why I decided to put you on the stage."

Lana jumped to her feet. "How dare you!"

"I don't dare a damned thing now. I know why the count gave up on you. You're just too much trouble to court."

She came around the table and went for his eyes. He caught her wrists and pulled her hard against him. "You want to fight?" He twisted her arms behind her, still gripping her wrists in one hand. "That I'm ready for."

His free hand held her throat, and his thumb rested against her pulse. "Excited, Countess?"

"Repulsed!" She could feel his thighs tight against hers, and she swallowed hard.

He smiled, and there were flecks of light in his dark eyes.

"I have a better idea than a fight. You claimed to know everything about lovemaking that you wanted to know. Maybe it's time right now to teach you you're wrong."

She held herself still. "You have an exaggerated opinion of your abilities. I was not so thrilled the first time."

If she wanted to discourage him, she had chosen the

wrong thing to say.

He trapped her face with his hand, and his mouth moved brutally over hers. She writhed in his embrace, struggling to free herself, to break away from his harsh kiss, but she was caught.

His tongue demanded entrance, and he tasted deeply of her. His hand left her face to stroke her breasts; through her gown she could feel every movement; there was no brutality to this touch, except in the cruel way her body responded to him despite her rage.

He broke the kiss, ensnaring her instead with eyes that burned with desire. "I want you and I'll have you. And you want me." It was a statement, not a command, as though he could feel the hot blood coursing through her veins, could sense the madness of passion that had consumed her the moment he crushed her to his embrace.

Tony had told her they had much to learn about each other, and she knew now he had spoken the truth.

She had lied with her body when she fought him, lied with her lips when she denied her need. She would not whimper for release any more than she could utter imprecations against him.

"Let go of my hands," she ordered, "and you will find what I want."

Tony stared down at her for a minute, then threw back his head and laughed. "Countess, you are a woman as demanding as I am." The laughter died. "And you drive me wild."

Her loosened hands wound themselves in the thick, black hair at his neck and her lips opened to him. His own hands moved in her dark locks, freeing them, and he stroked her unbound hair while his kiss deepened.

This time there was no innocence of discovery, no wondering about the discomfort when their bodies joined. Lana let the pleasure of desire wash over her and reveled that such feelings were stronger this time than the first.

Tony's fingers worked at the buttons of her gown, then pressed against her bared flesh. She was caught in an insane desire for him to tear her clothes from her body and

161

ravish her. No gentle caresses would satisfy her today. Her blood pulsed hot and fast in her veins, and she thought she would explode with the urgency of her need.

Tony broke the kiss, his breath coming quick and shallow. "Say you want me," he ordered huskily. "I want to hear it."

"I want you," she whispered against his lips and, emboldened, gave her own order. "Now you tell me."

A guttural sound issued from deep in his throat. Taking one of her hands in his, he dragged her fingers down his shirt and trousers and pressed them against the hard evidence of his arousal. Even through the thick cloth, she could feel his tight swelling.

"Does this tell you what you do to me?" he asked, his breath warm against her hair.

She could feel the heat of his passion against her hand, and her own desire became an unbearable torture. While she caressed him, unable to abandon the compelling wonder of his manhood, his hands played against the ripe fullness of her breasts. His tongue licked at the hollow of her throat, and she felt her pulse pound against him.

She bent her head and brushed her lips against his ear, circling it with her tongue. She found herself smiling at his moan of pleasure. When he lifted her into his arms and carried her to the bed, she moved her lips to his cheek and throat, savoring the taste of him and the roughness of his bristled face.

Lana had never known such wild abandon. She had lived with shame and self-loathing for most of her adult life, had told herself she was not a real woman with a real woman's needs.

Tony taught her otherwise.

They undressed, quickly and without coyness, and fell upon the bed in each other's arms. Her dark hair spilled across the white pillow, and he wound his fingers in the curls as he kissed her eyes, her cheeks, her throat. Each touch thrilled and made her yearn for more.

Their needs were primal. Nothing tame or subtle would satisfy. And what made those needs all the more glorious

162

was the fact that they were shared.

Tony knew her better than she knew herself as his hungry lips and hands explored, unerringly finding the hidden, sensitive places on her body that could be aroused. Her passion grew until she thought at last there could be nothing else. He showed her she was wrong.

She followed his lead, letting her hands roam his body as his had done over hers, lingering when she felt him grow tense and when a low cry sounded in his throat. His skin was tight over sinewed muscles. There was nothing soft about him, nothing in excess save the mindless waves of ecstasy he sent coursing through her.

This time when she parted her legs to him, she was ready, moist, and warm. He slipped quickly inside. When she felt his hardness within her, when his thrusts quickened, she clung tightly to him. Dark, velvet rapture enveloped her, and then against that darkness came the explosion of a thousand stars.

She cried out his name, and he whispered hers as his body shuddered with the same explosion. Her hands raked across his back. Slowly the shudders subsided, and her heartbeat slowed to a hard pounding that was almost painful. Still she held him tightly. She felt depraved and glorified all at one time, but for now she would think only of joy.

Tony was the only reality in the world, and with the wild desires he had let loose in her, she didn't know how she could ever let him go.

Chapter Fifteen

Before dawn the next morning Tony sat in the Orleans restaurant, a cup of coffee in front of him, and tried to figure out just what in the hell he thought he was doing. This journey into his past was hard enough, but to bring the Countess Svetlana Alexandrovna along bordered on the insane.

Especially since he could think of little else but her—not even Jess—and more especially since he couldn't keep his hands off her. Maybe he shouldn't have changed the stagecoach plans.

Lana had puzzled Tony from the beginning, and he had misfigured her down the line. He had labeled her everything from ice queen to harlot, but still he hadn't been able to stay away.

No man could, not after once holding her in his arms. In his mind flashed an image of Lana lying naked in the bed, of her dark hair spilled across the pillow, of full breasts and gently flared hips, of long, slender legs stretched out beside him. Those legs had wrapped around him and pulled him down into dark rapture. Tony stirred restlessly, his physical discomfort increasing, but he made no move to brush aside his thoughts.

Lana had been shy and bold, exploring him as he explored her, intriguing surprise lighting her eyes as she touched his body—everywhere. Remembering that light and the small smile that had sometimes tugged at her lips

165

came close to being painful. Making love to Lana was like making love for the first time.

The more he learned about her, the less he knew; the more he made love to her, the more he wanted to be with her all the time. What he had here was an impossible situation, considering the days that lay ahead.

She had slept in his arms yesterday afternoon as though all was at peace between them, but the time had been brief. Upon awakening, she was as skittish as a colt. It was as though she were learning things about herself she couldn't handle and didn't know whom to blame. She settled on him.

She could be right.

Exasperated, he stared at the doors leading into the Orleans Hotel lobby. His body slowly relaxed. A couple of red-shirted miners entered to join the dozen men already in the restaurant. Most gold seekers couldn't afford a place like the Orleans—they settled in makeshift camps near the river—but there were enough to keep the hotel in business.

Maybe he should have taken the countess to one of those camps instead of the Orleans and given her one night of sleeping on the hard ground, and a couple of his meals cooked over an open fire, a skill that Tony had never mastered. The shock might have convinced her to let him make the journey alone . . .

But then neither of them would have had their love in the afternoon. And it was too late to question his judgment now.

Any minute she and Boris would be coming down from their rooms. The three mounts he had hired at an exorbitant fee were waiting at the stable. The sun would be up soon, and it was time they were heading out.

Tony didn't know how to greet her. She had hated his solicitude in San Francisco—he had seen it in her flashing dark eyes—but he had been torn by guilt about being the first. Without knowing what was happening until he couldn't stop, he had unlocked the passions she kept hidden from even herself. Those passions were a precious gift to a man, and once aroused she had given them freely, with no coy accusations afterwards that he had forced her to his will.

When they had awakened after the second time, she had given him no chance to play the gentleman. He had tried to apologize for his angry crack about the count giving up on her, but she had brushed his words aside.

"Count Dubretsky and I had reasons for our particular relationship," she had said, her eyes holding steady with his, all signs of wondrous surprise gone. "And those reasons are none of your concern."

Tony was a little slow sometimes; he should have caught on earlier that she didn't want to discuss her late husband.

"I'm not fragile, Tony," she had snapped later over supper at this very same table where he waited for her now. "Feel free to argue with me whenever you like. You make me nervous with all this gentlemanly talk. It isn't like you."

Now that was telling him straight.

Altogether, the countess was an amazing woman. She was still unnerved by whatever it was that was happening between them, no matter how strong she claimed to be, but outside of bed she covered it by arguing with him on every issue, and she was good at it. He had a hard time getting in the last word. What he dreaded was the moment she found out that she wasn't the only one in this strange scouting party who had a special interest in finding brother Nick.

Tony shook his head. One fact emerged from all the rest. Lana could light a torch in him that seared away thoughts of anyone else. If only they didn't go for each other's throats everytime they disagreed, she would be the perfect woman.

She was beautiful with those ripe-plum eyes and fine face he never got tired of stroking, and there was a delicate strength to her long-limbed figure. Tony grinned. Even her bones seemed aristocratic.

As important as anything else, she was caring—she had shown that with the discomforts she was enduring to find her brother and, even more, with her sympathy for that poor kid McBride. She had gone so far as an attempt to shield him from arrest.

Lana would fight the devil for what she believed in. She had proven that often enough with him. Except for a certain exasperating stubbornness, he couldn't think of a single flaw. Count Whoever-he-was must have been a real jackass.

It was a good thing for both of them she was leaving soon for the old homeland, or he might have tried to prove he wasn't the tempter devil incarnate after all. And he wasn't an insensitive clod.

Tony was a drifter and there was no telling when he might start drifting again. He had made a lot of money—more than he had ever imagined he would—but financial success didn't necessarily give a man roots. And more important, he didn't want to get close to anyone ever again.

And Lana? She belonged to tradition, to rules of behavior, to a world of manners and culture that was a far cry from anything Tony had ever experienced. He could be smooth, all right; he socialized in the fanciest parlors in town. But he still had that Hangtown dirt under his fingernails, and he carried the stale whiskey odor and acrid smoke from a thousand saloons.

There was no danger that either of them would emerge from whatever it was they shared with a broken heart. It had never happened to Tony before, and he couldn't see her ladyship the countess really falling for a man like him.

But, by damn, she wasn't a lady in bed.

The door to the restaurant opened, and the conversation around Tony died. He looked up to see a sight he would never forget.

Lana, magnificent creature that she was, stood in the doorway, tall and slender, dark eyes challenging him to question her apparel for the journey. A riding habit the color of juniper leaves followed the gentle lines of her body and caressed the curve of her breasts. How he remembered those breasts, swollen and hard-tipped under his fingertips . . . his lips.

Her thick black hair was pulled back from her face into a mass of curls; resting just above the sweep of her eyebrows was a ridiculous little black hat, its matching feather arching into the air like a raven about to take flight. The hint of a smile graced her aristocratic face with its high cheekbones. Her skin was the color of ivory. Every inch of her was that same ivory, and he thought about how silken it felt to his touch.

Rising above the high collar of her jacket was a long, slender curve of neck. Her head was held at a slight angle as though she listened to a song lesser humans could not hear.

Tony felt a familiar tightening in response. If he sat here much longer contemplating the picture she presented, he would embarrass the both of them when he stood—either that or he would bound from the chair and drag her back to her room. Either choice was a most inappropriate beginning to what would surely be an arduous journey. And it would most assuredly prove to Lana for all time that he was nothing more than a lusty boor. He would plead guilty to only half of that charge.

At least there would be no time for temptation on the road. And even if there were, there was always the stern-faced Boris to protect his mistress. A high-principled and astute man was Boris. Tony liked him.

Grabbing up the holstered gun and hat resting in the chair beside him, he strode quickly across the room.

"Do I meet with your approval?" Lana asked when he joined them at the entrance to the restaurant. "You've had enough time to decide."

Tony hated it when she played the superior countess. With the eyes of the room pinned on them, Tony felt his blood boil, and he forgot all the kind thoughts he had been thinking—and the compliment that had been on his lips.

"Whether I approve or not, you've got the favor of every man watching. This journey is going to be hard enough without you throwing out taunts along the way." He gave her a quick perusal, from feather to boots and back to her

169

flashing eyes. "Where in the hell did you get an outfit like that?"

Her cheeks reddened. "Boris purchased it for me in San Francisco. I didn't realize I was supposed to wear a sack. You should have warned me." Her booted foot tapped impatiently on the wooden floor. "Since you didn't, I suggest we be on our way. I wouldn't want to embarrass you any longer than necessary."

With a flounce that only enhanced her provocative appearance, she picked up a single valise and turned toward the door.

Tony cursed himself for reacting the way he had, then cursed Lana for antagonizing him. The journey loomed longer and more difficult than ever. He nodded a greeting to Boris, who had changed from his usual black suit to a flannel shirt and coat and a pair of coarse woolen pants, garb very much like Tony's. His polished shoes had been exchanged for a pair of riding boots. Standing to the side with a large package in his hand, he looked very much ill at ease. Tony understood. The servant was at his best in drawing rooms, not out on the trail.

Strapping on his gun, Tony returned his attention to the countess. Something was wrong about the scene. It took him a moment to figure out what it was.

"You've only got one bag each. What happened to the rest?"

Lana glanced back at him from beneath that ridiculous hat. "Boris and I conferred and decided we needed only one change of clothes. The balance of our belongings has been left as payment against our bill."

"Ever the proud countess, aren't you? Don't tell me you're leaving the samovar behind."

Lana shook her head, setting the feather in motion. "I'm not that reasonable. The sable is wrapped around it in Boris's parcel. Inside, I believe, he has stored some personal items, along with the tea and tins of milk. It really does not take up much space at all." She nodded toward the door. "Shall we leave?"

Slapping his broad-brimmed hat low on his forehead,

170

Tony led the way.

At the stable, both Lana and Boris proved themselves able handlers of horses. Tony had chosen sturdy mounts, gelding bays for both him and Boris and a chestnut mare for Lana. She sat the sidesaddle just as he had figured she would, like a lady going for a ride in the park.

There was nothing ladylike about the way she headed out down the stage road that led across the valley and into the foothills east of Sacramento. Dawn lay just beyond the horizon; against the pink-edged sky the Sierras rose in majestic silhouette.

The countess rode all out, feather fluttering, for only a short distance. Away from the streetlights of town, the early morning darkness thickened fast, and she soon slowed down to a canter.

"Don't say it," she advised Tony when he caught up with her. "We've got a long ride ahead and I should pace the horse better. But it has been so long."

Close to her, Tony could make out the gleam of excitement in her eyes, and for once he declined to lecture. The jealousy he had experienced back at the Orleans seemed foolish now, and he could appreciate the thrill of the ride.

The few facts he knew about her slipped into a pattern. The count and countess, for all their pedigree, must not have possessed much money, and the count had been forced to sell off their horses.

Tony went a step further. Lana, reduced to shabby clothes, needed brother Nick to claim the family estate as his inheritance and help straighten out the finances at home. She was not a woman who would relish living in poverty.

For once he could almost feel sorry for her. With Tony and Lord Dundreary's Sydney Ducks on his trail, Nick had proven himself decidedly unable to manage his own affairs, much less those of his sister.

As night turned into day, they set a moderate pace across the valley and up into the hills. Groves of trees, mostly spruce and sugar pine, grew thicker the higher they rode, and the air took on the crispness of late autumn. Ahead of them, probably on tomorrow's trail, lay patches of snow which would thicken on beyond Hangtown.

There had been no reports of heavy winter storms in the area where they were headed, but it would take a miracle for the journey to end without at least one blizzard. Tony admittedly didn't know much about Russia, but he hoped that Lana had been right when she said the winters there had prepared her for the worst.

Tony wanted to guide them along the shorter back trails away from the main traffic to the mining towns, but he was unsure of their riding skills. Many a man had frozen with fear on a steep slope with a granite wall on one side of him and a hundred-foot drop on the other.

At the first such challenge they came to, he pulled to a halt and turned in his saddle to give warning. "Better stay close to the protected side, and don't look down. As I recall, there's a clearing around the bend up ahead where we can stop for a rest. You can enjoy the view there."

Lana's chin tilted dangerously. "Are you afraid we will panic?" She gave him no chance to answer. "Let's relieve his worries," she said over her shoulder to Boris.

"Whatever you wish, Countess."

Before Tony could protest, she reined her horse around his on the open side of the narrow trail, Boris close behind. The hooves of Lana's mare sent a dozen pebbles and rocks skittering over the edge and into the ravine far below.

Tony caught up with them at the clearing. "That's not the smartest thing you ever did," he said sharply. "You came damned close to finding out how dangerous this trail is."

"I knew exactly what I was doing," she threw back at him, her gloved hand stroking the neck of the mare.

"Maybe. Just don't get too sure of yourself and do something else stupid." He ignored the unladylike growl that came from her throat. "For all you knew there was a gang of outlaws waiting for you to round the bend. A lot of men in these mountains would rather find gold in someone's saddlebag than dig it out of the ground."

172

"It is not necessary to remind me repeatedly of my limitations. I'm not going to do anything foolish that would endanger any of us."

"Oh, no? What about a late-night visit to the Celestial Kingdom? It would take a foolhardy woman to do such a thing."

Tony saw Boris's eyebrows arch.

Lana shifted nervously in the saddle. "Shouldn't we be moving on?" she said.

Tony figured he had made his point, and once more they were under way. He had to give the Russians credit. Not once did they complain about the pace he set; only rarely did he stop to water the horses in a fast-running creek and to provide them with feed and a moment of rest. For his human charges, he offered jerky and cold biscuit, which was accepted without comment.

Back at the Orleans, Tony would have bet a goodly sum that Lana's headgear wouldn't last longer than the first gust of wind that greeted them at the top of a hill. He would have lost. The hat remained firmly in place, feather and all, although he did notice a curl or two of Lana's black hair had strayed down to the velvet collar of her green wool jacket.

Dusk came early in the foothills, and they were only a third of the way to Hangtown when he decided it was time to look for a place to camp for the night. The moon would be full, but he didn't want to take any foolish risks by traveling at night. A few hundred yards on up the narrow trail they came to another creek, this one not much more than a trickle, but it was sufficient for their needs.

He looked behind them. Through a break in the trees he could see the lights of Sacramento beginning to flicker. Looming farther to the west and lighted by the setting sun was the coastal range, which blocked the view to the sea.

"I assume we will be stopping here for the night," Lana said.

"Tired?" Tony asked.

There were smudges under her dark eyes, and Tony knew she must be stiff from the unaccustomed ride. But he

173

also knew she would never admit it.

"I was thinking of the horses," she replied.

"Of course." He looked in admiration at her. Again he thought that the countess was quite a woman. "Wait here and I'll see what's up ahead."

Without lingering for a rebuttal, he scouted the area and higher up the rise located a network of flumes and sluice boxes similar to the one he and Jess had constructed. With the spring thaw the narrow stream would be wide; at one time in the early prospecting days it must have carried the all-important gold down from the mountains.

Tony didn't stop at the creek. A weed-choked path led away from the main trail, and he followed it to a scattering of shanties located in a nearby draw. A few clapboard buildings, sturdier than the shanties, clung to the steep slope to the north, their wood sidings bare and splintered, their interiors dark.

The surrounding hills had long since been denuded of trees; only blackened stumps remained. They stood like sentinels guarding against unwelcome intruders. The wind whistled down from the surrounding elevations and echoed along the lone, rutted street of what once had been a mining town.

The dying sun washed the scene in a mysterious yellow glow, and the skin on Tony's neck bristled. One hand rested on his holstered gun. A shutter on one of the buildings banged against the siding, and Tony whipped the gun from its casing, then called himself a fool when he realized the source of the noise.

Soft from city living, that's what he was to let something as ordinary as a ghost town spook him. The foothills of the Sierras were dotted with such places.

Riding the length of the street and back again, he saw no movement, heard no sound that couldn't be attributed to the wind. The sun would be gone within the hour; if they holed up here for the night, at least they could have shelter from the cold air. He would break in the countess and her servant gradually before exposing them to a winter camp.

The shanties he rejected as too insubstantial to protect

174

them from a cold blast of wind or rain that could sweep down upon them during the night, and he headed toward the nearest of the clapboard structures, tethering the bay to one of the ugly stumps. The door hung crooked on its hinges and squealed like an injured animal as he opened it. A broken-legged table sat in the midst of dust and cobwebs in the middle of the single room, but the chairs were long gone.

Tony could almost hear the echoes of heated monte games in the musty air. The gamblers would most certainly have been there. Any mining town worthy of the name had its share of sharp-eyed strangers who swooped down to pan for gold in their own way, using cards and chips instead of shovels and picks. With the way the world worked, they seldom went away with empty pockets.

The uneasiness he had experienced down on the street returned, but he couldn't for the life of him figure its source. He decided to inspect the other shacks on the hill; if the feeling didn't go away, he would make camp closer to the stream and they could sleep outdoors. It was what he had originally planned, anyway.

The next two shacks were much like the first, close and cobwebbed, with little or no furniture. One had a couple of bunks built into one wall, but Tony couldn't see the countess reclining on either one of the stained straw mattresses. Besides, he wouldn't ask her.

He made up his mind to head back and make that camp beside the creek, but first he would inspect the last building deep in the draw. It was bigger than the others, even had a porch across its front. If someone were hiding somewhere, this last structure was the most likely place. There would be no rest for him until he determined that the ghost town really was abandoned.

His wary eyes darted back and forth as he made his way through the weeds and stumps of once lofty pines that had graced the hillside. He could smell trouble. Looking back over his shoulder, he spied a suspicious shadow beside the building he had just left, then decided it was only the wind ruffling the nearby brush.

175

Gun in hand, he approached the cabin slowly and stepped up on the porch, avoiding a broken plank directly in front of the closed door.

The floor of the porch creaked loudly, announcing his arrival, and he called out, "Anyone here?"

His only answer was the howl of the wind.

He began to feel foolish. Any minute he expected Lana to come riding down the street, the faithful retainer Boris in her wake. He could hear her ask if this skulking around in the dusk, gun in hand, wasn't another example of the American way of life. With a grunt of impatience, he yanked open the door, which squealed in protest.

As soon as he entered, he realized he had made a mistake. The air inside the darkened cabin was fresh, as though the windows and doors had been opened often, and he detected the faint, lingering scent of tobacco smoke.

He whirled, too late.

"Drop it," a voice growled.

Tony found himself looking down the twin barrels of a shotgun. Both hammers were cocked.

Behind him he heard the scratch of a lucifer stick. A lamp cast a shaky light into the room, and footsteps shuffled across the wooden floor. The unmistakable prod of a gun barrel pressed against his back.

Slowly Tony let the gun twirl in his hand and fall with a clatter to the floor. With a gunman in front and another behind, he realized he was trapped.

Chapter Sixteen

Lana paced along the stretch of bank beside the narrow creek, pivoted when she came to the bush that marked the farthermost edge of her route, and began the return trip. Her black leather boots came down hard against the rocky ground.

"What could have happened to him?" she asked the nearby Boris for the hundredth time.

"Mr. Diamond is a capable man," Boris said. It was an idea he had presented several times in response to her query.

"He wouldn't really have abandoned us," she said to the evening air.

Boris remained silent; the only response was a rustle of leaves in the trees on the far side of the stream.

Lana's gloved hand slapped against the divided skirt of her riding habit. Farther down the bank the chestnut mare, tethered beside Boris's gelding, jerked her head at the sound, then went back to cropping a patch of sweet Sierra grass.

"He's been gone close to an hour," she explained as though she were the only one who truly understood the situation. "It will soon be completely dark," she added, discounting the full moon that was on the rise. The silver light it shed was thus far lost in the still golden glow from the setting sun.

"Not completely dark, Countess." Boris sounded

maddeningly calm.

Lana sighed worriedly. "Unless in his know-it-all American way, he's erecting some kind of primitive cabin for us, he must be in trouble."

She stopped her pacing and stared at Boris, who stood at attention in the pathway along which they had been riding when Tony decided it was time to make camp.

"I am worried, *tovarisch*," she said, reverting to the pet name she had used as a child. Friend. Boris had always been that.

For all his silent insouciance, she could tell he was as worried as she. Definite creases had formed between his pale eyes, and his long fingers repeatedly brushed unseen lint from his trousers. Such subtle signs were equal to cries of woe from any other man.

It was Boris's distress as much as any other factor that sent a chill across her soul, and she reached a decision. "Get out the pistols."

"Countess, is that wise?"

"You know it's the only thing I can do. One way or another I'm riding after him, and I would be much better off armed. Besides, there are two weapons. One for you and one for me. I doubt that I could convince you to remain here."

"The countess's doubt is correct."

"Remember the hair trigger," she warned as he strode past her.

"I shall."

Boris's long legs carried him quickly to the gelding, where he removed the box strapped behind his saddle. Carefully he lifted the sable-wrapped samovar from its interior and reached inside. He pulled out a long oak case and, placing it on a large boulder, opened the lid. Resting against the green baize lining of the case were the French dueling pistols.

"I'll take the one that pulls to the right," said Lana. "I know how to compensate."

Boris merely nodded. She might have been telling him which wine she preferred with her meal.

178

He loaded the guns and waited as Lana selected hers. "Remember," he said, "the hair trigger."

"I will."

Lana also remembered the gun holster that Tony strapped to his thigh. A handy device, she thought, as she tried to figure out a way to carry the gun. When she had gone into Chinatown, she had been wearing a cloak with a deep pocket, but the riding habit Boris had found in a San Francisco shop had no such practical feature.

Then she thought a moment about Tony's thigh. Her breath quickened. Nothing must happen to that or any other part of his anatomy. She had been blaming him for the turmoil that seethed within her and for the depravity she had discovered in herself, but all she could remember now were his strength and his bravery and his intelligence and a thousand other traits that separated him from other men.

The same premonition of trouble she had felt on the dock in San Francisco returned to her now, only stronger than before because this time it dealt with Tony, not some vague image of what the journey would be like.

Aided by Boris, she settled into the saddle, the gun held carefully in her right hand. "Let's go quickly," she said.

Farther up the trail they found the flumes and sluice boxes right away. Lana recognized them from the description of placer mining Tony had provided as conversation during that strange noontime meal. Beef jerky, he had called it; she didn't think it would ever become a favorite at home.

In memory his voice caressed her, even with such strange-sounding words as sluice and flume and jerky. And then she remembered other words, whispered into her ear.

"Please be all right," she said softly into the air.

In the dim light they almost missed the path leading away from the main trail. It was Boris who spotted the signs left by Tony's bay.

"The front left shoe is loose," Boris exclaimed. "I noticed it when we were still in the valley. Notice how the

179

hoofprint is different from the rest?"

Lana looked at him with renewed respect. There seemed nothing Boris could not do.

Except perhaps engage in fisticuffs. She hoped whatever awaited them at the end of this particular path did not involve hand-to-hand combat. She cradled the comforting pistol against her body.

As they rode into the draw, she took in the gloomy scene. All was dark save for the light in a far cabin. None of the other buildings showed any signs of life, and she was reminded of deserted peasants' huts across the Russian countryside.

Tony's bay gelding was not in sight. It was a small thing, but it worried her. If by some chance he were inside the lighted cabin working to make it more comfortable for them, he probably would have tethered his horse to the front porch, near which grew ample stands of grass.

They pulled to a halt a short distance down the rutted road. The yellow light of day was almost completely gone by now, replaced by the gentler wash of the moon. Strange shadows were cast along their path and up the hillsides, but Lana could look at only the dim, flickering glow escaping from a lone, faraway window.

"He must be inside," she said, whispering as though the sound of her voice would echo against the hills.

"Allow me, Countess," Boris said, and he rode ahead.

"No!" She swallowed guiltily. Her cry had been much too loud.

Her heels urged the mare forward. "I suggest we ride a little farther, then leave the horses and go on foot. That way we can look into the window before announcing our arrival."

"I agree with everything, Countess, except the *we*."

She acquiesced with as much grace as she could muster, knowing it was better sometimes to yield to his judgment, then watched with held breath as her companion tied his horse to a stump and made his way the fifty yards to his destination. His long legs moved quickly, but try as she might Lana could not detect that he made a sound.

180

Avoiding the porch, he took advantage of his height to stare into the high window on the near side. She tied her horse beside his and stood waiting as he circled the cabin and disappeared from sight. It seemed a year before he emerged from the right, but his stride carried him quickly back to her side.

"Our fears were justified."

A sob caught in Lana's throat. "Is he—"

"Bound to a chair, but he seems in good health considering the circumstances. His horse is tied on the far side. Two men are inside with him. Unsavory characters, I must report. One is sitting just inside the door with a rifle leaning against his chair. The other is standing farther in the room, drinking some sort of amber liquid. American whiskey, I presume."

"We'll shoot our way in," Lana declared.

"Unwise. Begging your pardon, Countess. Might I suggest that while we converse we sequester ourselves and the horses in the shelter of one of the other buildings? In the event one of the men decides on a moonlit stroll."

Lana's respect for Boris took another forward leap. The breadth of the man's talents had gone untested on a Russian country estate. She was beginning to feel like a helpless fool.

But it was Lana who came up with the plan they eventually settled on. Surprise and precise timing were the primary elements upon which their success depended, but she and Boris had long functioned as a team.

At first he tried to argue with her, but she convinced him that they owed much to Tony. He would not have been captured by these outlaws—for surely that's what they were—if he hadn't been looking for a suitable camp for the night.

"You like him. Admit it. You said he was capable, but he's far more than that."

"It is true," Boris said, "that I have developed a sympathetic feeling for the gentleman."

Lana realized how deep that sympathy went. Boris labled few men of his acquaintance "gentleman."

181

"We might ride into the nearest town," she said, "but we haven't the vaguest notion where that might be. Even if we had a map, he could easily be . . . dead by the time we returned with help." Lana's voice caught. "This time I must insist you listen to me."

"Only," he answered, "because I think the plan has some merit. Please note that the window is without glass. We must be very quiet."

They checked their weapons, reminding each other needlessly that they would have time for only one shot apiece, and then Lana checked her hair and the rest of her appearance. When a cloud passed over the too bright moon, they began the long, stealthy walk toward the cabin. Their arrival wouldn't be a secret, but they didn't want to be discovered too soon.

Motioning for Boris to take up his post at the side of the cabin, Lana strode onto the porch, in her anxiety almost stepping through the broken plank. The gun was held tight in her right hand against the folds of her skirt.

She made no attempt to be quiet—a good thing since the porch creaked loudly—and she raised her left hand to knock firmly at the door. "Is there anyone inside?" she called. "I am the Countess Svetlana Alexandrovna of St. Petersburg and I am in terrible—"

The door was flung open. As her hand was raised to knock once again, she was thrown slightly off balance, and her request for assistance came to an unscheduled end.

Regaining her composure, she stared imperiously at one of the men Boris had labeled unsavory. An uglier, meaner face she had never seen in her life—beady, red-rimmed eyes and a twisted mouth surrounded by dirt and a stubbly beard. A rifle pointed directly at her breast.

"What the hell—" he snarled, then stopped as she stepped closer into the artificial light. "My gawd!"

"Do put that thing down, sir," Lana instructed, and with her left hand she pushed the barrel aside. "I mean you no harm."

The glare Tony was directing her way would have stopped a lesser woman, but she was in reality a countess and she had had years of using the position to her advantage. Besides, she was a woman, a fact Tony certainly could not have forgotten. Men, especially brutish ones like these two captors, never suspected that such a frail specimen of humanity could be a threat.

The other man, much like the first only fatter and more hirsute, was holding a rather ugly pistol in his hand.

"Please lower your weapon," she ordered in her haughtiest voice.

She had no chance to see if he would obey, for just then Tony decided to inject himself into her plan. Leaning back in the chair, he brought his legs up sharply against the table and sent it flying into the face of the far gunman. Incredulous, she watched him jump to his feet, hands free, and go for the one with the rifle.

As he wrestled him to the ground, a deafening shot came from the window where Boris had positioned himself, and the culprit who had been stunned by the table fell like a rock to the floor.

Dizzy from the explosion and the erupting violence around her, Lana watched in horror as Tony and the remaining outlaw scuffled, fists flying, along with dust and spurts of blood, first one and then the other seeming to gain the ascendency. Boris joined her in the doorway, but she knew there was nothing he could do—and prayed that he knew it, too.

At one point the gunman, staggered by a particularly vicious blow, grabbed at the chair and brought it crashing against Tony's head. Tony fell sideways at her feet, and she thought he must surely be unconscious.

"Your gun, Countess!" Boris yelled.

The shouted reminder, coming from such an unexpected source and from such a close range, startled Lana from the terror that had possessed her. Realizing she had a clear shot at the gunman, who had thrown himself at the rifle in the corner of the room, she raised the dueling pistol, took careful aim, and froze as she stared into the twin barrels of the rifle.

She felt Tony's hand reach up to cover hers. His finger

had only to touch the trigger for the gun to fire.

Both rifle and pistol exploded simultaneously, but the rifle missed its mark, the bullet winging over Lana's head and cutting her feather in half.

The gunman stared at the two of them, then with the rifle lowered, stared at the hole in his chest. A widening stain darkened his shirt. His eyes rolled back in his head and, like his partner before him, he fell heavily to the floor.

Tony pulled himself upright; in shock, the three of them stood still for a moment, the gunshots still echoing in the dusty air.

Then Tony moved quickly to first one body, then the other, before returning to the doorway. Lana knew without his saying a word that both the men were dead.

A trickle of blood trailed from a cut at Tony's temple, and she had an impulse to reach out to touch the wound. The fury burning in his eyes stopped her.

"Don't you ever, ever, *ever* do anything so stupid again!" he said, his voice quivering with anger.

Then he wrapped her tightly in his arms.

184

Chapter Seventeen

Under a full moon they buried the two outlaws—Parker and Chance were the only names Tony had heard—in shallow, unmarked graves behind the cabin.

"As soon as we get into town, I'll let whatever authorities are there know what happened," Tony said. "I don't imagine anyone will come after the bodies, however. This kind of thing is not too unusual. There have been many campsites in this part of the world that have turned into cemeteries."

Lana didn't doubt him in the least.

After a brief ceremony in which Tony intoned a few words about an afterlife—words more out of respect for her feelings, Lana suspected, than for the recently departed—the three of them set to work making the cabin with the bunks more habitable. The outside air had taken on a sharpness that foretold a winter blast might hit them during the night, and as Boris pointed out in his logical way, there was no reason to subject themselves to more discomfort than was absolutely necessary. The usable furniture from the other buildings had been assembled for their use.

Tony talked while they worked. Lana thought he was too harsh with himself when he described how he had been taken prisoner, but that was his way, she decided, when he was under stress. He had been harsh with her, too. At least for a minute.

Parker and Chance had been thugs and drifters who managed to cripple both their mounts. Tony was an unexpected but very welcome surprise, especially after they found the purse of gold hidden in his saddle blanket. The only reason they hadn't killed him outright was that they figured he could lead them to more. Their greed had done them in.

Lana tried to regret their passing, but she could not as she remembered the threat they had brought to Tony's life.

She watched him nail a board across an open patch of window. Through his shirt she could see the play of muscles across his back. At that moment he looked invincible . . . but she could too easily remember him bound to that chair with two gunmen standing over him. She pulled herself short. When she *thought* he was bound to the chair.

"How was it your hands were suddenly free?" she asked as she wielded a broom she had found hooked to the rear of the cabin. She coughed on the dust.

"Ever used one of those before?" Tony asked with a smile.

She decided not to tell him just how skilled she was at the domestic arts. He wouldn't believe her, anyway.

"You have not answered my question," she said.

"Those two bastards were not only mean, they were stupid. The knot was child's play. I was waiting for the right moment to attack when you knocked at the door."

Lana swept the broom in his direction, sending billows of dust around his once-dark trousers.

"Oh, sorry," she said, "I guess this really is difficult to do. Now, what were you saying? Oh, yes. Something about taking care of yourself. You could, of course, have handled the two armed men with no difficulty."

"None at all," he said.

"I will certainly keep that in mind the next time you are wounded and held at gunpoint."

In case he missed her message, she glanced at the wound across his temple, which had been cleaned and sprinkled with antiseptic from a kit packed in his bedroll, and was struck with contrition that she had swept dirt on him.

Tony shook his head. "And I remember when I used to win arguments against you."

"You remember more than I do."

Ignoring her, he gave a quick inspection of the crude window covering and announced it satisfactorily airtight. "You should be warm enough in here," he said, then went outside to fry the fresh beef he carried from Sacramento.

"Enjoy this," he ordered as the three of them sat around the campfire later and chewed on the tough meat. "The rest of the time it will be hardtack and biscuits, and beans if there is time to cook them."

Lana could not see that one meal was any better than the other, but she wisely kept quiet.

After supper, she watched as Boris called Tony aside. She wondered what had the two men so deep in conversation, then decided they were discussing how to keep her in line should another emergency arise.

Her vision was centered on Tony; she couldn't keep her eyes away from him. Broad-shouldered and slim-hipped, he warmed her far more than the fire. Even standing still, he emanated a graceful and quiet strength. His hair was unkempt, and his lean face was shadowed with a day's growth of beard. He must be close to exhaustion, yet all evening his movements had been smooth and supple without any signs of fatigue.

He looked more masculine and appealing than she could ever remember him, and she shuddered to think how close he had come to losing his life. After Sacramento, she had sworn to stay away from his embrace. He weakened her, she had decided, and made her dependent on the pleasures of the flesh. What a fool she had been to curse him for the feelings he had set free inside her. She was more alive than she had ever been.

Emboldened by the events of the day, she determined to tell him in a more personal way of her joy that he was unharmed . . . and of the unexpected changes he had brought to her life.

When the men returned to the fire, she let her eyes linger

on Tony. His returning gaze set her heart to pounding, and her toes curled in her boots.

"I would like to talk to you alone for a few minutes," she managed. "In the cabin."

She ignored the knowing look on Boris's face. For a change he could not know what she was thinking. She refused to wonder if he would approve.

Inside, a lone lantern cast flickering light on the splintered walls and sent out rays of heat. She glanced at the hat she had worn all day. Feather half-gone, it sat like a broken-winged bird on the table, a symbol of their close call with death.

She turned to face Tony and swallowed, irritated that she should suddenly feel so shy about what she wanted to say and do.

"It's awfully warm in here, don't you think?" she asked.

Tony's gaze never wavered from her face. "For hanging meat, yes. For human habitation, I'd say it's all right." His eyes glittered darkly. "Is that what you wanted to talk about? Or maybe"—his voice dropped to a suggestively low pitch—"you didn't want to talk at all."

Lana's knees almost buckled under her. Taking a deep breath, she ventured forth.

"I do not always make a great deal of sense when I'm around you," she said with a shake of her head, "either to myself or anyone else. That's because I do not understand completely what is happening to me . . . to us."

Tony tried to speak but she hurried on. "I came to California knowing myself and what I wanted, and a week later I learn I do not know myself at all."

"I'm having the same trouble, too," Tony said. "About you, that is. You could sit with ease on any throne, and yet I wouldn't be surprised to see you hike your skirts and invade a lion's den."

Lana studied her hands. "Nicholas and his safety were all I could think of, especially after I saw the violent land to which he had journeyed. And the ruby, of course. It was frequently in my mind."

Tony started. "The ruby?"

188

"You remember the Blood of Burma that Lord Dundreary claimed Nicholas lost to him? The jewel was not my brother's to gamble away. It belongs to me."

The dark look on Tony's face surprised her. "Do not be too harsh on him," she added quickly. "He did not know when he took it that my father had willed it to me. He assumed, as did I, that the family estate would take care of my needs. Papa viewed our respective inheritances differently."

"You should have told me before," he said sharply.

"Why? My tangled financial affairs were none of your concern, and they are not now," she said, unable to keep the pride from creeping back into her voice. "I wanted a more personal confession. Please do not stop me, Tony, from what I have to say. We Russians quietly brood. We're not given to revelations as readily as are Americans."

"Maybe I need to do a little confessing of my own."

"Later, when I am through. Unless I am embarrassing you."

Tony shook his head slowly. "Just surprising me."

Lana began to relax, and her lips curved into a smile. "Have you ever seen one of those hollow Russian dolls? They're carved out of wood and inside is a smaller doll, and inside that one an even smaller doll, and on and on. I'm a little like that. I keep finding another woman hidden inside me and wonder when I'll arrive at the end."

"Lana—"

She waved him to silence. "Please let me finish or I'll never get this said. About all I do know is that I'm more than I thought I was, not less. On the ride today, as unsettled as I was being so close to you, I found I noticed everything around me more. The air smelled cleaner, and the birds sang more sweetly than I can ever remember. And it's not just because it's American air and American birds. The change is in me."

She stepped close. "All of my senses are more awake, Tony, thanks to you." A rush of joy tingled within her, and she forgot her shyness. "I can show you how I feel in only one way."

189

She wrapped her arms around him and brushed her lips against his, lightly at first and then more firmly. Her tongue traced the edges of his mouth, then dipped inside to taste the moist, warm goodness of him.

Breaking the kiss, she brought her hands to his face and ran her fingers gently over the thin scar at his temple, then more firmly down his bristled, lean cheeks; all the while her eyes were trained on his parted lips. Magic lips that brought such a surge of feeling wherever they touched.

She glanced back at his eyes and was startled by the troubled look in their depths. She pulled free from his embrace.

"Do not worry that I am making any demands of you." She held her head proudly. "I know that these are only temporary pleasures, that we will at some time be finished with our business and go our separate ways." The words brought a heavy weight to her heart, but she knew she spoke no more than the truth. She touched her fingers to his lips. "If your confession is along those lines, it is not necessary for you to speak."

A low, guttural sound, half cry and half moan, sounded in Tony's throat. His hands reached out to caress her waist, then trailed down her hips to her buttocks. He pulled her hard against him, and she could feel the beginnings of his arousal.

"No," he whispered huskily. "Right now I don't want to speak at all."

"I'm sorry, Tony. We can't," she whispered, her hands pressed firmly against his chest. "Not tonight. I did not mean more than to talk. And to kiss you, of course. I certainly thought of that. But when we can . . . Oh, Tony. I was so afraid you were dead."

"And that mattered to you? Aside from any need you have of me as a guide to find Nick?"

The heat of his body mingled with the heat of hers. "It mattered to me. When I rode after you, Nicholas and the ruby were the last things on my mind."

As she drowned in the depths of his eyes, Lana wondered just how much Tony really did mean to her. Perhaps she had been fooling herself when she spoke so surely about leaving him, but she could not put her feelings into words. Buried inside, undiscovered, was another doll that held the truth of her emotions.

But she did know the physical burning that he set to flame. Once again she wrapped her arms around him and held tight. His lips and breath warmed her ear.

"If you're worried about Boris, we have his permission," he said huskily.

Lana pulled back and looked at him, wide-eyed. "His permission?"

A half smile tugged at Tony's lips.

"At least that's the way I interpreted our talk. It seems he liked the changes in you and says I'm good for you. And he plans to sleep in another cabin tonight."

Lana was both stunned and warmed by her old friend's presumptions.

"I'm beginning to think I don't know Boris any more than I know myself," she said. "You and I are to spend the night in here alone?" She glanced around the small room and saw that the mattresses had been pulled from the bunks. Across them were spread a couple of blankets. "I see that we are."

"Now what was that you were saying about showing me how you feel?" Tony asked. Gleams of light danced in the depths of his eyes as he reached out and began to unbutton the jacket of her riding habit.

Perhaps it was wrong to indulge herself in such ways when her mind was still unsettled about the depths of her feelings. But she could no more have stopped him at that moment than she could have flown to the moon, and she stood before him in silence while he slipped the jacket from her shoulders and tossed it aside. Next came the chemise that she wore next to her skin. His fingers worked in the pinnings of her hair, which soon tumbled to her bare shoulders. Trembling, she heard only his quickened breath.

She watched his hands stroke her breasts, brown skin against white, his thumbs rubbing at the tips until they were hardened and erect.

"You chose a poor comparison," Tony said huskily. "A wooden doll? Never. You are soft and warm, and your skin feels like silk to my touch."

Tentacles of pleasure enfolded her, and she felt the center of her womanhood begin to pulsate in anticipation of the rapture that only Tony could give.

Once again she pressed her hands against his chest, this time to feel his muscled strength, and she took pleasure in the pounding of his heart. She worked her way to the taut sinews beneath his clothes. He grew still as her fingers played with the buttons of his shirt. She tossed the garment beside her jacket and rubbed her breasts against his chest.

Again, white skin against brown. It was an incredibly sensual sight.

Her last inhibitions slipped from her as she let her hand trail to his belt, then lower to the hard arousal that she had caused. She was thrilled and proud and a little frightened by the size of him.

"You see what you do to me, Lana?" he said. "I can think of nothing but you."

She melted against him, willing herself to stand as he undressed her, and then himself. The heat of desire warmed her as no campfire could. They lay down on the blanket and he pulled her into his embrace.

"You're like wine in my blood," he said as he ran his fingers over her shoulders and down to the rise of her breasts. "A fine vintage wine. You should be lying on satin sheets, not this coarse wool."

"Satin?" Her eyes sparkled devilishly. "I have an idea. Just don't go anywhere."

"Foolish woman."

She forced herself out of his arms, surprised and at once pleased that she could move about in front of him without so much as a handkerchief to hide her nakedness. Grabbing for the sable coat thrown across the table next to the lamp, she knelt beside the double mattress. Tony rolled away to make room for the coat. With the fur

*We have 4 FREE BOOKS for you
as your introduction to
KENSINGTON CHOICE!
To get your FREE BOOKS, worth
up to $24.96, mail the card below.*

FREE BOOK CERTIFICATE

Yes! Please send me 4 Kensington Choice (the best of Zebra and Pinnacle Books) Historical Romances without cost or obligation (worth up to $24.96). As a Kensington Choice subscriber, I will then receive 4 brand-new romances to preview each month for 10 days FREE. I can return any books I decide not to keep and owe nothing. The publisher's prices for Kensington Choice romances range from $4.99-$6.99, but as a preferred subscriber I will get these books for only $4.20 per book or $16.80 for all four titles. There is no minimum number of books to buy and I may cancel my subscription at any time, plus there is no additional charge for postage and handling. No matter what I decide to do, my first 4 books are mine to keep, absolutely FREE!

Name _____

Address _____ Apt. _____

City _____ State _____ Zip _____

Telephone (___) _____

Signature _____

(If under 18, parent or guardian must sign)

Subscription subject to acceptance. Terms and prices subject to change.

DF0198

against their makeshift bed, the dark brown lining was exposed.

"There's some satin for the both of us," she said.

"Amazing," Tony said with a grin. "You satisfy every need."

She matched his smile. "I'm going to try."

Which is exactly what she did, letting her imagination take flight as she showed him the passions he had freed in her, the years of self-doubt and loneliness fading into nothingness. Her hands caressed and stroked, her lips brushed against his lips, his throat, his chest, lingered in the crook of his elbow before moving down to his fingers and palm.

He met her passion with equal desire, his hands as magical as his lips as he discovered every nerve ending in her body; she had never felt so alive. The cool, slick satin beneath them accented the heat of their bodies as they moved against one another, and Lana trembled with an insatiable hunger to melt inside his skin.

When at last their bodies joined, they moved as one being, her body merging with his until she did not know where they were separate. She became a part of him, and Tony was a part of her. Her own spiraling joy mingled with his; she knew the quickening of rapture, shared it with him, climaxed with him wrapped tightly in her arms, his lips and breath warm against her throat.

If this was depravity, so be it. It was also life, a celebration of joy and wonder. She wanted to cry out with happiness, but she thought he might think her insane. Surely other women didn't react to mating with such glorious abandon; otherwise, how could they stay out of bed?

Tony stayed inside her for a long time, at last moving only to enfold them both in the warmth of the coat. Wrapped in sable, her naked body pressed to his, she smiled to remember the stiff-necked countess who had descended into the maelstrom that was San Francisco little more than a week ago.

She was caught in another kind of maelstrom now, a

193

storm of pleasure and fulfillment. Perhaps she ought to be afraid of the lightning and fire, and maybe she would be later. But not tonight. With the wind howling around the tiny cabin, she found safety in Tony's arms.

When they awoke the next morning, this time she was not ashamed, not filled with a self-anger that she turned on him. She kissed him warmly and welcomed his equally fervent greeting.

They emerged to a wonderland of white. During the night the first snow of winter had come to the hills, a light sprinkling that obliterated the tawdriness of the abandoned town.

Boris, his face without expression, invited them to his cabin for breakfast. Awaiting them inside was the samovar, ribbons of steam drifting from it into the warm inside air.

"I was hoping, Countess," he said, barely able to keep the twinkle from his eyes, "that you and Mr. Diamond could take time for a cup of tea."

Chapter Eighteen

After breakfast, Tony announced he needed to ride on ahead to scout out the condition of the trail. Lana and Boris could remain behind to finish breaking camp and saddle their mounts.

"I promise not to investigate any abandoned buildings if you promise not to ride after me," he said, looking down at Lana from the bay. His hat was pulled low on his forehead and rested above the dark sweep of his brows. Above him was an expanse of gray sky.

Standing in the road in front of the cabin where they had spent the night, Lana agreed, but she still wasn't convinced that her attempted rescue had been a mistake.

He stared down at her long and hard. "We need to talk. Maybe tonight when we make camp."

Puzzled, she returned his gaze. "If that's what we need to do."

She watched him ride away. Tony *never* wanted to talk. Well, sometimes maybe. Lying beside her on the sable coat last night, he had said a few things that would have shocked her only the day before.

Things like, "Has anyone ever told you that you have sensual earlobes?" or "You hold me so tight and sweet inside you that I go mad," or "Sleep with your back against me. That way I can hold your breasts and wake up with you pressed hard against me." The memory of his words sent frissons of desire skittering through her, and

195

she caught her breath.

Remembering the stern look on his face as he had looked down at her this morning, she doubted he had been thinking of any such erotic utterances. Desire turned to puzzlement as she thought about the confession he needed to make. What did he need to tell her that she did not already know?

Such concern on her part was foolish. She did not know exactly how she felt about Tony, and she sensed that he was no surer about her. They took pleasure in one another; it was more than Lana had ever believed possible, yet she suspected that what they shared was growing into more . . . far more. She refused to put a name to it, but maybe he would tonight when they talked. In such a case any time she spent in fretting would be time wasted.

Wrapped in sable, her wounded hat replaced by the sturdier astrakhan, she felt warm and secure, but it wasn't the fur alone that kept out the cold. For the first time in years she felt like running and playing in the snow, scarce and powdery though it was, but she held herself in check. She had lost control enough already without making a complete fool of herself in front of the staid Boris, and she forced herself to the task of saddling both of the horses, which were tethered on the protected side of the cabin.

With her mind at peace, she worked quickly. She harbored no regrets about last night, no matter how licentious Tony might think her. If he were to leave her now never to return, she still would not regret it—though the thought brought her sharp pain. Since her marriage there had been few memories to look back on with pleasure. Last night would be one of those few.

The only thing she could not feel easy about was Boris. From her position on the slope of the hill, she watched him move about the campfire gathering the few utensils they carried with them. His face was as solemn as ever. When the horses were ready, she walked down to join him.

"My tasks are almost completed here, Countess," he said.

She looked in vain for the twinkle she had seen earlier in

his eyes, but he was all seriousness. Still, she was certain he knew exactly what had happened last night. Well, maybe not exactly. Even she could not believe some of the things she and Tony had done, and she had been an active participant throughout it all.

But her old friend would have a general idea. Boris the nanny, who had helped raise her from nursery toddler to a respectable and chaste young lady. Boris the friend, who had helped her elude the few visitors of the count with more varied sexual tastes than their host. Boris the protector, who had traveled to California to keep her from harm.

When even the samovar was packed and they were left with only the wait for Tony's return, she put the question to him directly. "Why did you do it?"

She had to give him credit. He didn't raise so much as one eyebrow, or pretend he didn't know what she meant.

"The countess is a happier person than she has been for many years," he said simply. "It is a happiness she deserves."

No talk about future events, about where this mad affair with Tony might lead, or whether she might be hurt. Boris the planner had become live-for-the-moment Boris. With the feel and scent of Tony still on her skin, Lana thought it was a wonderful way to be.

Tony returned to announce the trail passable, and they were immediately under way. The midnight snow had left the increasingly steep trail slippery, and travel was slowed, but they encountered no real difficulties . . . until lunch, when they stopped in a clearing where the horses could find grass and the riders could chew once again on jerky and cold biscuits. They paced and stretched their legs while they ate.

Tony took a long swallow of water from the canteen. "We're being followed," he said.

Startled, Lana looked back down the trail, its white surface now marred with the imprints of a dozen hooves.

"How can you tell?"

"A good mountain man just can." Tony looked at her

197

and shrugged. "And if that doesn't convince you, I got a glimpse of some horses behind us on one of the switchbacks an hour ago."

Lana refused to be worried. Tony was in charge. "What do you suggest we do?" she asked.

"We lay a trap. Could be nothing, but I don't like strangers at my back."

"No good mountain man would," she said, leveling a mocking glance at him.

Tony grinned. "You learn fast."

Boris said, "How may I be of assistance?"

"Keep the countess under control."

"I shall do what I am able."

Lana let the two men talk. She had no intention of interfering in Tony's plan—unless and until she determined it was necessary for her to do so.

"As I recall, the trail cuts back sharply to the right a few yards ahead," Tony said. "Right here is as good a place to catch them as any."

Lana studied the trail over which they had already ridden. "But what about the tracks?" Immediately she wished she could pull back her words. Tony gave her a look that said he knew what he was about.

"We'll ride on ahead and secure the horses," he explained as if to a child. "Then I'll double back and stop them as they ride by. Even if there's no problem, we'll put them ahead of us instead of behind."

"I would like to take part in this doubling back," Boris said. "I can be armed and perhaps of assistance."

Tony agreed, Lana smiled innocently as though she would not dream of asking to come along, too, and they put the plan into action. The trail was as Tony had remembered it. Leaving her with the three mounts securely tethered out of sight of any passersby, he and Boris set out on a smaller footpath that carried them back over the rise around which they had just ridden.

Lana waited for awhile in the quiet woods where the men had left her, then grew impatient. What if there were trouble? She still had the remaining dueling pistol, and

198

this time she swore not to be fainthearted if she needed to fire.

Maybe the trail would be too difficult for her to traverse. There was only one way to find out. Feeling somewhat like a scout, she edged from her seclusion, located the footpath farther up the trail, and made her cautious way along the clearly visible footprints left by the men. The higher she went, the thicker seemed the snow. The trees grew close together, their limbs heavy with the powdery whiteness.

At a high point on the rise, she stopped to listen to the call of a jay and thought what a paradise this seemed. The vista stretching out before her was glorious—white peaks and dark evergreens, interspersed with brown stretches of ground where the snow had not held. The mountains seemed to go on forever and she stole a precious moment to enjoy them. In Russia she would have been concerned about bears and wolves.

The thought stopped her. Tony had never mentioned such predators, but that did not mean they could not exist in the Sierra Nevadas. She knew for a fact he didn't tell her everything. Sobered by the remembrance, she wondered just what danger Tony and Boris might have headed in their direction.

With fingers curled tightly around her dueling pistol, she quickened her pace, slowing when the path took a downward turn. She rounded a particularly large and snow-laden bush and found herself looking down on the clearing where they had eaten lunch. Tony and Boris were nowhere in sight, but she was not surprised. Good mountain men would not expose themselves to possible danger if they could help it.

She pulled back behind the bush and waited. The minutes crept by, and she pulled her sable tight around her. She might be impatient, but at least she was not cold.

She sensed the approach of the riders before she saw or heard them, and congratulated herself on becoming a pretty good mountain man herself. Carefully she returned to her vantage point above the clearing.

There were three of them in hooded coats, riding single file. They looked burly and bearded, but she told herself the meanness they seemed to carry was probably the result of her imagination. The one in front appeared to be the broadest, and she decided probably the meanest, too.

Tony, gun in hand, suddenly materialized on the trail in front of them. Where he came from, Lana couldn't imagine.

"Good afternoon, gentlemen," he said. His voice drifted loud and clear up to her.

"What the 'ell!" the burly leader growled.

"Thought I might make it easier for you to catch me if I slowed down a little," Tony responded.

Lana couldn't see his expression for the wide-brimmed hat he wore, but she would bet there would be a half smile on his face.

"I share his sentiments."

Lana followed the distinctive sound of the voice and saw Boris standing to the rear of the small procession, the dueling pistol prominently displayed in his gloved hand. The three men could move neither way without encountering trouble.

"Listen, mate, you don't own this mountain," the leader said.

Lana caught her breath. From his accent she judged him to be English . . . or perhaps Australian. Could these be the Sydney Ducks that Lord Dundreary had hired to harm Nicholas?

Tony held his ground. "Let's say that for right now, I do. And I don't like men at my back."

"Then get yourself behind us, and we'll lead the way."

"You wouldn't have the vaguest idea where to look for Nick Case. I don't think Dundreary would pay much for failure."

The leader hesitated. "Ain't no concern of yours what Dundreary would do. If that's the guv'ner that hired us, and mind, I ain't saying it is."

Tony ignored the halfhearted denial. "Just what are you supposed to do? Bring back the ruby? Or Nick? Or maybe both?"

The Duck seemed to give up all ideas of pretense. "Oh, m'lord wants the bastard all right. Alive or dead, don't seem to make a difference."

"Mick," growled the rider behind him, "You goin' to jaw all day? If so, I'm takin' a leak."

"Same wi' me," said the third.

"Just drop your guns on the ground where you are," Tony advised. Mick hesitated, then did as he was told and the other two followed suit.

Under the watchful eyes of both Tony and Boris, the three Ducks reined their horses into the clearing and dismounted. They removed their protective hoods and unbuttoned their coats. When they proceeded to unfasten their trousers, Lana turned her head discreetly. She had suffered the same discomfort as they, but she had sought the privacy of a rather thick-leaved bush.

Boris gathered in the guns as Tony continued. "You've admitted to being after Nick. But what about the ruby? Knowing Dundreary as I do, I'd say he would never let it get away."

The one called Mick grinned. "And you'd be right. Blood o' Burma or some such nonsense is what he said. And we're to fetch it back to him."

"Whatever else he may be," Tony said, "Dundreary is no thief. He cannot have the ruby."

"And who says it's up to you, mate, what m'lord is after or who owns the bloody jewel?"

Tony paused and looked from man to man. Boris held his position at the edge of the clearing where it opened onto the trail.

"As rightful owner of the Blood," Tony announced, "I'd say it's very much up to me."

Lana inhaled sharply. What kind of subterfuge was Tony up to now?

"What lies you tells, mate. The guv'ner said we was to watch out for you."

Tony shrugged. "I've got witnesses. Nick is a rather careless young man. He lost all rights to the ruby to me in a

201

gambling game. He went back to the hotel to retrieve the jewel and ran into your employer. I can only guess what went through Nick's mind, but I'd say he was trying to win enough money from Dundreary to buy the ruby back from me. Unfortunately, he lost it a second time. And no one has seen him since.''

Lana sat back in the snow, stunned. An icy fist took hold of her heart. She had no doubt that Tony was telling the truth . . . probably for the first time since they met. He owned the ruby. *Her* ruby. No wonder he had been startled when she mentioned it last night. He had been after Nicholas—and the jewel—all along, from that first day at the Gut Bucket Saloon, to this journey into the mountains.

He had not wanted her to come along, but she had insisted. Horror piled upon horror in her mind. She had let him do so many other things . . . and worse, she had thrown herself at him. How he must have laughed. A little extra something for the journey . . . a willing Russian fool. Maybe he considered her as interest on her brother's debt.

All of Lana's self-doubts and recriminations returned in a rush. Whatever had led her to think she could, with any accuracy, judge a man? Or that one would treat her right?

She wanted to cry, but she held back the tears, letting rage burn them away. She shuddered. Hell truly had no fury to match hers. She had been lied to and seduced . . . and worse, she had reveled in the pleasure of his embrace.

Tony had needed to confess. Or so he had said. But he had not let that particular need interfere with his more immediate desires.

She forced herself to gaze back at the assembly below, and at Tony, who stood aside from the others. The pistol grew heavy in her hands. If she raised it . . . aimed carefully . . . one shot . . . then she would be avenged. She could not do it, and hated herself for having contemplated such a thing.

Tony Diamond had raised her spirits higher than they had ever been before, but he had also brought her lower than even the count. The hate that she felt for herself was wide and dark and deep enough to include him.

One thing and one thing alone had kept her going through the years. Pride, or at least the pretense of pride. She was still a countess, and Tony Diamond had proven himself once and for all an American peasant, without the peasant's dignity that comes with honest work.

Below the talk continued, but she had heard all that she could bear for one afternoon. Let the men work out whatever arrangements they wanted. Men were good at arrangements, usually at the expense of some stupid woman. But not Lana. Not ever again.

She did not remember the return trek across the rise or her arrival at the secluded place where the horses were hidden, but she suddenly found herself beside the mare. She packed away the gun lest she be tempted to use it when Tony came into view. A warning shot aimed close to his feet had a great appeal for her right now.

Her gloved hands stroked at the chestnut's mane. "For once," she whispered, "I know more than he does." The horse whinnied in approval. "He thinks me ignorant and infatuated with him. But I am neither."

She refused to acknowledge the heaviness of her heart.

By the time Boris and Tony came striding up the main trail, she had gotten herself under control. Her entire married life had prepared her for pretense, and she refused to let her emotions control her now.

"Did you find them?" she asked, looking first at Boris and then at Tony. "You've been gone for so long."

"We found them all right," Tony said. "And sent them on their way. They may show up later—it's hard to predict what such men will do—but I doubt it."

"Were they a threat to us?" she asked, her question directed to Boris. He must have heard Tony as clearly as she, and he knew how much the ruby meant to her. Surely he was not a part of Tony's lies.

"No, Countess," he said without inflection, "not to us."

She waited for Boris to continue, to register some displeasure with their duplicitous guide, but when he did not, she felt a crushing of her spirit as strong as when she had first heard Tony's wounding words. Boris admitted to liking Tony. Because he made her happy, her old friend had said. He wasn't making her happy now. Did Boris really believe she would sell herself and her future for a few stolen minutes in Tony's arms?

Somehow Tony must have convinced Boris to go along with his lies. She must give her old friend a chance to explain.

But not Tony. He had all the chances with her he was going to get.

"Then I suggest we be on our way," she said brightly. Too brightly, but neither of the men seemed to notice. Tony gave her a long look as he helped her into the saddle, but he had begun to do that lately. The deceiver probably could not believe his good fortune in finding such a gullible fool.

The rest of the afternoon's trek was made mostly in silence, and they made camp in a grove of evergreen and pine away from the trail. As he had done last night, Boris excused himself after supper, this time taking his bedroll where he could neither see nor hear them, saying he would build his own small fire for the night.

Lana cleared the rocks and pebbles from a place near the glowing coals of the campfire, the snow having long since melted, and spread out the protective rubber sheet and blanket that made up her bedroll. She decided against removing her wool riding habit. Last night Tony had done it for her. She would break his fingers if he tried tonight.

Tony tossed his hat to the ground by his bedroll, then moved close to stand beside her. "You're very quiet. Is something wrong?" He reached out to touch her face, and she pulled away.

"Nothing is wrong. Now."

Around them the night listened in silence, and she could hear only his steady, even breath.

"Want to tell me what you're getting at," he said, "or am I supposed to guess?"

Lana had planned to wait until Nicholas was found

before revealing what she knew. But she could not and forced herself to look into Tony's eyes. They were dark and glittering and puzzled.

"Remember those little dolls I mentioned earlier?" she asked, her chin held high. "The ones I keep finding within myself. I found another one. It's one I knew was there but had forgotten about. The one that has pride and self-respect. The one that is not a hedonist, but believes in truth and honor."

Tony's dark stare didn't waver. "That's quite a speech. Too bad I don't know what in the hell you're talking about."

"It is enough that I do. I hoped to keep quiet a while longer, but I find I cannot. I know why you're after Nicholas, and it has nothing to do with burying ghosts or helping me. Unless you consider an unpaid gambling debt a ghost."

"I see," Tony said flatly. "You followed me this afternoon."

It was a statement, not a question, and Lana could see no reason to respond.

"Don't you know that no one ever overhears anything good?" Tony asked.

"I consider the truth good news. At last I've heard it."

"And you immediately assumed the worst."

Lana was astonished to see anger in the depths of his eyes when she should have seen guilt. Tony was very good at throwing whatever arguments she gave him back onto her. But not this time, and not ever again.

"I did not have to assume anything. You explained it all very clearly for me. What I do not understand is how you convinced Boris that you are still a man of honor. Somehow you have him under your spell."

"But not you."

Lana took a step away from him. "Almost, Tony." Her voice grew smaller. "Almost." She swallowed hard. She would not, could not cry now. "I suppose that's what you wanted to talk about tonight. You would let me confess exactly how far down the primrose path I had strayed.

Fortunately for me, I ran into a thorn bush. It stopped me from making a complete fool of myself."

"You've painted me as quite the villain, haven't you?"

"A charming one, of course. There are too many recent memories for me to deny it. And you, no doubt, are too much of a cad not to mention them now."

"If you're talking about last night, you're damned right. You approached me, remember? And I never forced you into anything you didn't want to do."

Tony was in full rage, and she felt a shiver of fear.

"But you knew better than I, how I would respond each time you kissed me," she managed.

"Tell me this, Countess." He spat out the word. "If I'm such a bastard, why did I even tell you where Nick was hiding?"

"I can't explain why you do what you do. I don't think the way you do. But I warned you once I would follow you or hire someone who would. The Sydney Ducks managed to stay on your trail for quite a while, and they seemed rather boorish to me. Surely I could have found someone more professional to take the job."

"If you paid him the way you paid me, I'm sure you could."

Lana slapped him as hard as she could, sorry only that she had not removed her gloves.

Tony made no attempt to defend himself. He shrugged, his fingers raking through his thick, disheveled hair.

"I didn't mean that, Lana. Whatever differences lie between us, you never prostituted yourself to get what you wanted."

Lana winced at his words. "As opposed to you. Men can use their bodies for a purpose as well as a woman." She wrapped her arms tightly around her chest, as if the sable fur could infuse her with the courage that was fading much too fast.

"Understand this, Tony Diamond. The Blood of Burma is my birthright. It will never be yours, anymore than I will ever be yours again."

Tony's eyes locked with hers. "You said that once

206

before, Lana. Back in San Francisco. I wonder if you mean it now any more than you did then."

In answer, Lana could only turn her back and wait for him to leave. She had faced him with the truth and held her ground. The satisfaction she should have enjoyed tasted bitter in her mouth, and she felt close to collapse. She turned to find he had gathered up his bedroll and moved into the darkness of the surrounding woods.

There was nothing left for her but to get through the night. And the next day. And on until Nicholas was found. As much as she hated Tony right now, she knew he would not abandon her and Boris on this unmarked trail.

Huddled beneath her blanket and sable coat, she found sleep impossible. She had thrown out such proud words of hate, but at this moment she had never felt so alone.

A traitorous thought flashed into her mind. What if she had not followed Tony today? What if she hadn't overheard the truth? At this moment she would be wrapped in the comfort of his arms.

She brushed the image aside. He had questioned her resolve, but she could not . . . must not question it herself. If she did not know better, she would think she had fallen in love with the man, but such an idea was absurd. She would have to hold within her a little doll of insanity for such to be the case.

Chapter Nineteen

Protected from the wind by a thick juniper bush, Tony wrapped his bedroll around him and tried to fall asleep, repeating a litany about how he should have told Lana the complete truth from the beginning, then countered with arguments that she should not have been so quick to believe the worst.

He *had* won the ruby from Nick before Dundreary had been involved; he *had* been looking for the young Russian that afternoon in the Gut Bucket. And by damn, he had intended to claim his winnings; it was the only way to throw a scare into the fast-living young man. The only reason he had gotten into the poker game to begin with was because Nick was in danger of losing the jewel to a cardshark who was dealing from the bottom of the deck.

I did it to protect your brother.

He had wanted to tell her the truth last night. But she had looked at him with such warm, welcoming eyes. And he was human. Not immoral. Not a bastard. Just a man wanting a woman too damned much!

And so he had decided to wait until tonight to make his speech; the more he thought about it, the more he decided she wouldn't have believed a single word.

In the light of all she had told him, he could see now that her claim was stronger than either his or Dundreary's. He would like to tell her that sometime; most likely, she would suspect him of wanting to get her back in bed.

An hour later Tony was still shifting his body under the double blankets and trying in vain to find a more comfortable position. The hard-packed snow beneath him had little to do with his unrest. As usual, Lana was the cause. No matter how much rage she aroused in him, she also managed to arouse something else. The countess was right. He *did* want to get her back in bed. Fool that he was, here he was aching for her, a hundred physically disturbing memories keeping him from sleep.

They had made love three times—he amended the number upwards as he remembered the long, sweet hours in the ghost camp cabin—and he already knew more about Lana and her responses than about any of the women he had been with more often. Knew where she liked to be touched . . . knew where she liked to be kissed.

Damn! If he didn't stop this futile pursuit, his body would be rock-hard in a minute. Pleasing Lana had given him more satisfaction than he had ever received in his more selfish love affairs; remembering her without any hope of relief brought only pain.

She had as much as called him a hedonist without truth or honor. Strong words for a woman who only the night before had taken all he could give her and had begged for more. If she possessed a larger amount of that truth and honor she seemed to value, she would admit to a strong streak of hedonism in herself.

What he had better do was remember the haughty countess who had looked at him with contempt over the campfire, and forget the woman who had wrapped him in sable last night. Remember the angry words of hate she had flung at him, and forget the whispered phrases and soft sighs that had warmed him in the cabin.

The countess did a great deal of talking about discovering herself. Surely she knew by now the depths of her passion. Tony couldn't help but speculate once again about the strange marriage that had existed between her and the late count. Before Dubretsky ever had a chance to claim his conjugal rights, he must have disappointed Lana in some way—real or imagined—and she had kept him distant. Tony had already figured out that the count's estate was not a wealthy one. He could have misrepresented his holdings. If there was one thing the countess could not tolerate, it was misrepresentation.

Even though she had misrepresented herself as something far different from a virgin widow.

Tony had a lot of reasons for scorning the woman who had turned his life upside down. He had saved her from the angry Celestials and brought her along on this journey, when common sense told him he was making a mistake. For his troubles he had been given a verbal back of her hand tonight.

Yet when she had glared at him with such magnificent rage, sparks lighting those wonderful dark eyes, he wanted only to crush her against him and kiss the anger away. He knew he could do it, and if she threw her anger and contempt at him one more time, he just might prove it to her, too. There wouldn't be much of a relationship left between them, but hell, there wasn't much now.

A stiff belt of whiskey would do Tony a world of good; it was the one necessity he had left behind, believing in his ignorance that the journey to Hangtown would be short and sweet. He better not make any such mistakes again, or he would never make it back to San Francisco sane.

Hangtown. Lana had him so bumfuzzled that he had forgotten how much he hated the place. Forgotten about Jess and how he had met his death there. Forgotten how much he dreaded returning to the cabin that he and Jess had built.

With the wind whipping through the pine branches above him and the moonlight shimmering on the snow-covered ground, he had a lot of time to remember it now. Svetlana Alexandrovna had seen to that. Tony was a fool to let her get to him the way she had, but he wasn't the first man to lose control over a woman, and he wouldn't be the last.

But Lana would be the last for him. Some men weren't made for commitments; they hated too much when things went wrong. Tony was that way.

Sometimes he even confused Nick and Jess—thought about one, but it was the face of the other that popped in his mind. Both were fair-haired and convinced life was a game. They were wrong. The truth was, life was damned complicated.

Around midnight he heard boots crunching into the drifts of snow and rose up to see a figure moving through the trees in the direction of the campfire. He reached for the gun at his head, then paused. Even in the shadowy moonlight, he could recognize the familiar, long-legged figure of Boris, a bedroll tucked under one arm. He must have decided that all wasn't well between the two lovers and was moving closer to his mistress to provide her protection.

Boris was a good man. He gave Tony hope that all Russians weren't as unreasonable and headstrong as Nick and his sister. After the encounter with the Sydney Ducks, Boris had wanted an explanation about the ruby. Not that he would ever ask, but Tony had seen the questions in his eyes and had described the way the card game had gone.

No gambler would give up his winnings, Tony had explained. If Nicholas hadn't realized that yet, it was time he did. Maybe then he would quit risking things he didn't want to lose. Tony had even hinted at the protective attitude he felt toward Nick, if not the reason; unlike Lana, Boris had listened to Tony and seen his side.

Tony fell asleep sometime close to dawn; when he awakened, the sun was already visible through the trees. He jerked to his feet, and in seconds had boots and jacket on and the holstered pistol strapped firmly in place. He hurried to the campfire to find only cold ashes, Lana and Boris packed and waiting, and the horses saddled and fed.

"The countess thought it best to let you get your rest," Boris said.

Tony glanced at Lana, who stood holding the chestnut mare's reins, her black hair piled beneath the black astrakhan hat, her slender body wrapped in sable fur.

"How thoughtful of the countess," he said.

Nodding in mock gratitude toward Lana, Tony looked

for signs that Boris had talked to her about the poker game with Nick, softening signs that she understood Tony was in the right. He found nothing soft about the stiff way she held her body or the hard look on her face. This morning she was every inch the countess. Her eyes were like the ashes of last night's fire.

So be it, Tony thought. He could be just as stubborn as she.

He paused only to grab a couple of cold biscuits before starting out on the hard day's ride that would take them into Hangtown.

Placerville was the official name, he explained an hour later when they stopped to water the horses. He kicked at a rock beside the stream. "But you'll rarely hear it used."

"I assume there's a reason for that," said Lana, already mounted and ready to renew the ride. It was the closest she had come to conversation since last night.

Tony pulled himself back in the saddle. "Justice is quick if not fair in the mountains," he explained curtly, unable to keep the bitterness from his voice. "In Hangtown it's dispensed from a tree at the center of town."

He felt Lana's eyes on him, but when he turned in her direction, she quickly looked away.

They rode in the same order as yesterday, Tony in front and Boris bringing up the rear. The distance between his two charges gradually lengthened during the day, and Tony got the feeling that the Russian servant was dropping farther behind to give him and Lana a chance to talk things out. Boris would have to turn tail and race for Sacramento in order for that to occur.

By the time the sun was at its zenith, they had made it to the highest point on their day's route. From here most of the way into Hangtown was steeply downhill, curved, and dangerous, and Tony figured they needed the rest as much as the horses. After a brief search, he located a fast-moving stream not far from the trail.

"With any luck we'll be there in a few hours," he announced as he secured the horses, "long before dark, but it's a tricky ride. Boris, you build a fire and I'll catch us a rainbow trout. It's about the only thing I can cook worth a damn."

"We look forward to a new culinary experience," Boris said.

Lana made no comment, instead turning her attention to the timberland that stretched toward the east away from the creek.

Tony followed her gaze. The trees were high and wide and the carpet of snow beneath them unmarred except for an occasional animal track. With winter coming on, elk and deer would be rare now, as well as the mountain lions and wildcats that sometimes frequented the area. The most dangerous predators, the grizzlies, would be hibernating in their dens.

He watched as she took tentative steps across the pristine snow toward the trees. She was a graceful swath of black against the whiteness, and she somehow looked more fragile on foot than she had on the mare.

"Don't go far," Tony warned.

She cast a scornful look over her shoulder at him. So much for playing the watchful guide, Tony decided. She was after privacy, and she wasn't about to honor any restrictions from him.

From instinct, Tony checked the gun at his side, then glanced downstream to where the horses were tied. The double-barreled rifle sheathed against his saddle would be easy to reach. If Lana didn't get into more than routine trouble, he should be able to provide her ample protection.

"I shall construct the fire," Boris said and set out to gather a few of the tree branches that had fallen to the ground.

Tony concentrated on the fish. First he found the perfect stick, strong enough to pull in a three-pound trout and slender enough to give the fish some play. Attaching the hook and string he carried in his saddlebag, and using a piece of rolled biscuit as bait, he trolled for only a few minutes before meeting with success.

"Get the pan ready," he called over his shoulder as he flipped the fiesty trout onto the gravel bank, but there was no response. Reaching for the knife at his belt, he turned and looked past the infant fire to a broader set of footprints beside Lana's stretching around the trees and over a rise. After all his years of experience in caring for his mistress, Boris must have wanted to make sure she was all right.

A single high-pitched cry from the woods sent Tony on the run. Grabbing the rifle, he followed the clear tracks left by the pair. They wound through the mountain forest, down a gradual slope and up another.

"Lana!" he called out. There was no response, other than the echo of his voice through the pines.

The footprints moved deeper, and he heard himself cursing her for having wandered so far . . . just to spite him, probably. If it was privacy she was after, he would gladly give her all that she craved by distancing himself from her as soon as they got into town. He would be damned if she would offer provocation for him ever again. On the contrary, he was fast working himself up into a full rage.

The rage died at the top of the next rise. Lana stood fifty yards away, close to the edge of a ravine. She didn't react to Tony's arrival, didn't even seem aware of Boris, who was standing halfway between them, still as a post.

Her attention was riveted to the sight of an upright female grizzly towering eight feet in the air, her powerful forelegs circling ominously, the long, wide claws on each paw curled in Lana's direction. The bear had only to lumber a dozen steps forward and Lana would be in reach.

But for Lana to step backwards would be equally dangerous. Tony knew this ravine. It was narrow and rugged and deep.

"Don't move," Tony barked and prayed she heard him.

Slowly he raised the rifle and aimed for the delicate target just above the grizzly's snout. His finger touched the trigger . . . but before he could fire, the shaggy-furred beast dropped to the ground and loped toward Lana.

Boris was quicker. Reaching her before the threatening bear, he stretched his long arms forward and shoved her to the ground. He tried to stop his forward progress and place

215

himself in the path of danger in the place of his mistress, but his impetus carried him past her toward the fissure, and as Tony watched in helpless horror, Boris disappeared from sight.

Momentarily distracted by the intrusion, the bear stopped in her tracks. Once more she rose on her enormous hindlegs and towered as tall as the trees. Tony risked one shot. The explosion shattered the stillness, and the needles of the sugar pine under which he stood shook in anger at the noise.

At first he wasn't sure if his aim had been true. The bear seemed to waver, and Tony could swear she turned her small dark eyes in his direction.

He fired again, and the roar of the rifle joined the fading sounds of the first shot. After an eternity the grizzly's brown bulk swayed, then fell heavily to the soft snow, and she was still.

Freed by the death of the bear, Lana rose with a cry, eyes wide and dry and terrified, parted her lips as if to call out to Tony, then turned toward the ravine, her long sable fur darker against the snow than the fur of the bear.

"Stop!" Tony yelled. His boots crunched into the icy surface of the ground as he hurried toward her.

He caught up with her at the edge of the ravine. She clung to a small tree that grew at an angle over the chasm, its roots clinging defiantly to the soil and rocks. Her gaze was directed downward. Tony's eyes followed, and he saw Boris lying on a narrow ledge twenty feet below them, his left leg twisted awkwardly beneath him.

"What have I done?" she said, her voice little more than a whisper.

Tony shifted his gaze to her face. Eyes squeezed tightly shut, tears clinging to her lashes, she had such a look of despair that he wanted only to hold her tight in his arms.

But there was no time, and his embrace would do her no good.

He looked back once more into the abyss. A sheer granite wall dropped away from his feet, its striated surface leading down to a dry creek bed. The narrow ledge which had stopped Boris's descent—and, Tony prayed, saved his life—was halfway to the bottom.

"Boris!" he called, and the name echoed in the stillness below.

There was no answering sound, no sign of movement.

"He must be unconscious," Tony said, praying his words were not a lie.

Lana's eyes were open now, but she continued to cling to the slender trunk of the tree. Her hat was gone, and wisps of black hair rested against her colorless face. Her lips were pinched and tight.

"I'll need your help," Tony said sharply. "Don't turn coward on me now."

She swallowed once and stood free of the supporting sapling.

"Tell me what to do," she said, her eyes never wavering from the ledge.

"There's a rope tied to my saddle. Go get it."

He didn't have to repeat the order. She whirled away from the ravine and disappeared through the woods, returning faster than he would have believed possible. Only then did he realize she hadn't really gone very far away from the stream where they had stopped. The distance had seemed forever when he was hurrying in the direction of her scream.

Tony worked quickly, looping the rope around a smooth boulder which rested half-buried at the fissure's edge. When the rope's free end was lowered, it came to rest in a curl on the ledge beside Boris's motionless body.

"Good," Tony said, keeping his voice tight and calm. "It's long enough. Now for the second part."

He pulled the rope back to the top and directed a searching gaze at Lana, wondering how strong she really was. And wondering if he had the courage to endanger her life.

"You'll have to go after him," he said.

Doubt flickered in her eyes for only a moment, then gave way to a glint of resolve.

"Whatever is necessary," she said.

Tony was the one who could not rid himself of doubt. If there were any way other than to send her down to that ledge, he would have taken it. The thought of Lana suspended over the ravine, of her life dependent on a length of hemp and on his strength, tore at him.

He had failed someone once long ago; he could not fail again.

He explained the procedure. The brief words were quickly spoken. She nodded, tossed her coat aside, and waited while he tied the rope in a slipknot—almost like a hangman's knot. The thought rushed through his mind and was gone.

He slipped the circle of rope over her head and upraised arms, then tightened it around the snug-fitting riding habit at her waist, and showed her how to entwine the rope around her gloved hands to insure a more secure hold. Not once did she shiver in the biting cold, but her breath turned to vapor in the still Sierra air.

There was no time for a lesson in mountain climbing, and he made do with one command. "Listen to me as I lower you and do exactly as I say."

Her answer was a curt nod.

"Keep the bottom of your boots flat against the rock as though you were walking down. Don't let go of the rope, even though you have the added safety of the loop around your waist. I'll lower you slowly to the ledge. All you have to do is hold on, keep your eyes on the wall in front of you, and trust me."

Her eyes locked with his. "I do."

"Good. I'll remember that." Tony risked a brief smile, and was relieved to see a softening of her tightly held lips.

The first part of the rescue came exactly as he had hoped. Crouched on the ledge, her riding habit a splash of dark green against the gray rock, she ran quick hands over Boris's face and felt for a pulse at his throat. When she looked up, Tony could see the good news in her eyes.

"He's alive!"

Tony shared her feeling of relief.

"And," she added, "mercifully unconscious. I'm afraid

218

his leg might be broken."

Next came the part that filled him with fear, the moment of greatest danger for Lana as she transferred the safety rope from her body to Boris's. He should have had more faith in the countess. She performed her task just as though she had done such things all her life.

Pulling the inert body to the surface took a long while— much too long, to Tony's way of thinking. Sitting close to the edge, legs braced against the boulder around which the rope was looped, he was able to get a clear view of what was happening below. Each tug of the rope brought Boris closer. Despite the cold, sweat broke on Tony's brow, and he winced each time the Russian's weight brought him in contact with the rough surface of the granite wall.

When at last Tony had hauled him within reach, he secured the rope to the smooth trunk of a sturdy pine and used his hands to drag the still unconscious man to safety. He placed him on the sable coat he had spread out across the snow, careful to move his leg as little as possible.

The last—and for Tony, the most unnerving part of the rescue—was Lana's return. He didn't let himself think about the distant gravel bed at the base of the abyss . . . ignored each time her body brushed against the unrelenting granite . . . tried not to think of how vulnerable she was as she swayed at the end of the taut rope. Only when he was able to grip her shoulders and bring her up beside him did he let himself think of the dangers involved in what they had done.

She let him pull her to her feet and remove the rope; together they stepped away from the abyss. When she turned to look at him, he saw the terror in her eyes soften to the warmth of relief. There was a hint of triumph in those dark depths as well. With a gloved hand she wiped the beads of sweat from his brow.

"Well done," she said solemnly, color once more in her cheeks.

"I think that's what I should be saying," Tony replied. He didn't mind in the least that her voice sounded stronger than his. His eyes glittered darkly into hers. "Well done,

219

Countess. Now let's see about that broken leg. I don't suppose you can make a splint.''

Lana knelt beside her old friend and gingerly ran her hands over the calf of his left leg, then lifted her eyes to Tony.

"As a matter of fact," she said calmly, "I can. While you go get a knife, I will inspect the break. When you return, I will show you exactly what we need to do."

Chapter Twenty

Tony helped her with the splint, carving the rough boards from an old log he found in the woods, and tearing one of his shirts as binding. They concentrated on the spot just below Boris's knee where the leg was swollen and bruised.

While they worked, Tony insisted she wear his jacket. It embraced her with warmth, the way his arms had once done, and kept her calm.

By the time they were finished with their ministrations, Boris was awake. She knelt beside him as he lay on the satin lining of the sable coat.

Boris's pale eyes looked up at her, his skin paper-thin against the skeletal lines of his face. He looked older than his fifty years. Her calmness fled, and she blinked back tears. She had always depended upon his quiet strength and guidance . . . even if she seldom let him know it. She prayed she would be strong enough for him.

"Can you ever forgive me, *tovarisch?*" she asked, holding one of his hands in both of hers. "Tony says I must have disturbed the bear when she was searching for a place to dig her den."

"The countess does not need forgiveness," he said, his voice faint but steady. "I wish only to know that she escaped harm."

"Undeservedly she did," Lana said, encouraged by his composure. It would take more than a fall off a mountain to bring Boris to the level of other men. "But I'm afraid you have broken your leg," she added. "And there's a nasty bump on the back of your head that's going to hurt."

Boris smiled, then winced. "I confess to the countess that it already does."

Lana squeezed his hand.

Tony kneeled across from her. "The break is simple and clean, Boris. Had to cut your trousers to make sure. The skin is not broken, but the bone will take some time to mend. A doctor should look at it, but unfortunately the nearest one that I know of—if he's alive and sober—is in Hangtown. We can hope someone else has taken his place."

Lana looked up. "But how can we—" She stopped herself, unwilling to discuss the problems that faced them in front of her injured friend.

Boris attempted to sit, then fell back heavily to the ground, his eyes closed and the creases around his mouth deepened. "I will need some assistance to ride."

"That you will not do," Tony said emphatically. "We can make a travois out of blankets and a couple of thin logs so that you can travel without moving your leg. It must be kept straight. Then we'll get you into town."

He set to work felling and stripping a couple of young trees, explaining as he worked the Indian method of carrying their belongings behind their mounts. Lana brought back Boris's horse and the blankets that had served as his bedroll and helped Tony stretch them around the smooth logs and across the rope which had been used to form a crude net between the supporting shafts.

Moving Boris to the travois was the difficult part.

"Wish I had some whiskey to offer," Tony said. "I wanted some myself last night."

"I will think of iced vodka as you work," Boris said. He gave no indication of pain as Tony lifted first his shoulders and then his legs onto the blanket, but his face was as white as the snow and his gray hair hung lank about his head. Somewhere at the bottom of the ravine must lie the woolen cap he had worn.

222

Lana did what she could by moving the coat from under him and holding the blanket taut, all the while wanting to give voice to the cries he must be holding inside. She could not still the trembling of her hands.

Tony used Boris's belt to strap him in place. The blankets from Lana's bedroll were used to cover him.

Next came the roping of the travois to the back of Boris's gelding, a simple procedure it turned out under Tony's expert guidance. With him in attendance, Lana was able to locate her hat near the spot where she had first disturbed the grizzly.

"She must have been ready to dig between the roots and burrow in when you came along," Tony explained.

"She sent me running fast enough," Lana said, "stupidly toward the ravine." Her only consolation was that there were no cubs left motherless by the death of the bear.

With her sable coat once more pulled close to ward off the brisk afternoon air, she walked slowly beside Tony as he led the gelding back to the creek and the dying fire. Boris lay quietly on the travois.

The trout had somehow managed to flip himself back into the stream and swim to freedom. Tony swore the fish's survival was a good sign, even if he did have to sacrifice the hook and string that the fish took with him. Leading the way with Lana riding at the rear behind the travois, he began the arduous descent. Lana estimated they had only a few hours of daylight left.

The cutbacks were the worst. Tony dismounted and guided first his horse and Lana's and then the riderless gelding around the bend while Lana followed on foot, making sure the end of the travois did not come too close to the edge of the trail. They talked little during the journey and then only about their separate tasks.

Once while they were crossing a sloping plain, Boris cried out in pain.

"Stop!" Lana called out. Dropping to the ground to check on him, she found he was unconscious. Her feelings of desperation returned.

223

"We can't go on like this much longer," she said when Tony joined her. "He is strong and brave, but he is not a young man."

Tony nodded in agreement and shifted his hat lower on his forehead as he studied the terrain.

"This is the smoothest land we'll be crossing," he said, his dark eyes troubled. "He'll never make the final ascent without hurting like hell." He glanced at Lana. "Quit blaming yourself. What happened was an accident."

Lana bit at her lower lip. Tony had read her mind.

"There used to be a fairly active mining camp in one of the draws," he continued. "It was well off the trail, but the route was fairly flat and straight. Nugget Bar it was called. I think it's best if we ride there and try to get help."

Lana readily agreed, and the curious band of three—the *troika*, she labeled them—set out cross-country. Close to dusk they found the camp, located in a valley a few miles off the main trail beside one of the hundreds of tributary streams that veined the western Sierras. The surrounding hills had been denuded of trees, leaving only stumps and a few cabins. She was reminded of the ghost town where they had stayed two nights ago. Light snow covered much of the ground, but the stream, not yet frozen, moved quickly over its rocky bed.

A dozen men in heavy jackets stood or scurried about near the sluice boxes on both banks of the creek. One by one they stopped their work to watch the strange procession entering the camp.

As Lana reined her horse to a halt beside Tony's gelding, she turned her attention away from Boris and directed it toward the miners. She caught her breath. The men were Chinese.

"Is it safe here?" she asked, careful to keep her voice low.

"Safer than with most whites, I imagine," Tony said. "I just hope they speak English."

He nodded to one of the pigtailed men who stood silently watcing them. "Good day."

The Chinaman bowed from the waist. "Welcome to our most humble camp."

Lana shifted nervously in the saddle. She had been welcomed into the fan-tan parlor, too, but the good will had lasted only until she started to win.

She turned her eyes to Tony. For all the hurt he had dealt her, he was still the man she could depend on in time of trouble. Terrified as she had been while suspended over that canyon of open space, she had trusted him to lift her to safety. And he had guided them through the long afternoon down a treacherous trail. She trusted him now more than ever.

"We have an injured man with us," Tony said. "We need your help."

The Chinaman slipped one hand and then the other into the opening of the opposite sleeve of his jacket and looked at them in silence for a moment. "It is not often," he said in clipped English, "that the white man asks the aid of a Celestial."

"The white man could learn much from you," Tony said. "When he gives up on a claim, you come in and find gold dust that he has overlooked. You work hard, long hours and with much care. And you have learned your English well."

"I toiled as a slave in a mining camp when I first arrived. It was expected that I understand the commands if it was my desire to live."

Lana swallowed and kept quiet.

Beside her, Tony seemed as calm as he had ever been. He introduced himself and learned the Chinese was called Sung Lee.

"Mr. Lee, we have no commands to give. Only a request that you provide shelter for a brave man."

As if on cue, Boris moaned softly behind them. Lana could be still no longer. Dismounting, she handed the reins to Tony and hurried back to make sure that their patient was as comfortable as possible. She found that with the travois finally at rest, Boris was slowly returning to consciousness.

The sound of shuffling feet surrounded her, and she looked up into the faces of a half-dozen Celestials who were gathering around the makeshift bed. "Do you speak English?" she asked. They looked blankly at her. The only Chinese words that Lana knew were the numbers one through four, and she doubted they would do her much good right now.

She pulled the sable coat protectively against her body, then lifted the blanket where it covered Boris's leg. With a gesture toward the split trousers, she looked up, hoping to see an understanding light in their eyes, but she was met with nothing other than blank stares. Like the Celestials in the gambling den, they did not reveal what they were thinking.

At last one man crouched beside her. He removed a glove from his right hand and ran his fingers over the hard, swollen skin beneath the splint.

"Ah," he said, more an articulated breath than a word, but Lana took it to mean he understood. With uncommon gentleness he tucked the blanket once more in place and rejoined the others. They chattered in their strange-sounding tongue.

Boris's pale gray eyes fluttered open for a moment, then closed. He either accepted the cluster of Chinamen around him, or he was too much in pain to see them. Lana and Tony had already decided he had suffered a mild concussion in the fall. In the background she could hear Tony and the English-speaking Celestial talking, but she remained where she was in case Boris should open his eyes again.

At last Tony knelt beside her, and the Celestials moved away.

"We're in luck," he said with a smile, and Lana's heart lifted. "We will remain in camp for the night. Early in the morning I'll ride into town and investigate getting a doctor back out here. Once Boris is taken care of, I can see about finding Nick."

Lana started, the sound of her brother's name on Tony's lips bringing back all of the troubles between them. In the excitement and near tragedy of the afternoon, she had forgotten he was as eager to find Nicholas as she, but the memory of his disclosure to the Sydney Ducks came back in a rush.

She did not want to think about Nicholas right now, did not want the troubles between her and Tony to intrude. Tony had saved her and Boris from a frightful death. That was all she should be considering now, and she bent her head, unwilling for him to see the look of dismay that must surely be visible on her face.

"What's wrong?" he asked. "Don't you trust me to go into town alone?"

Always he seemed to read her mind! She stared up at him. He was so close she could count the bristles on his cheeks. She stood and distanced herself from him. "I can't help myself, Tony. I know you need to go after medical help." She glanced down at Boris, then forced herself to look at Tony again. "I ask only that you hold off the search for my brother until I can join you."

Anger flared in Tony's eyes, and he rose to face her. They stood apart from the travois, and he kept his voice low and harsh. "Until you can watch me. Isn't that what you really mean?"

The words of trust she had said at the edge of the ravine seemed to hang in the air between them . . . but try as she might, she could not welcome them into her heart. Too long and too well had she been trained in the ways of men.

After all Tony had done today, she should have faith in him, and yet she could not ignore the doubts that ate at her mind. He had not been completely honest with her before; he could lie to her again.

She stood firm under his glare. "I want to be present when Nicholas is found. You may interpret that in any way you choose."

"Thank you for your permission. Excuse me, Countess. I'll be arranging to have Boris moved into one of the cabins."

Boris stirred restlessly, and Lana hurried to his side. Crouched on the ground beside the travois, she pushed aside the feeling of loneliness that swept over her and concentrated on her old friend.

"Countess."

The faintly issued word brought her relief. A silent Boris was a frightening thing, and she took his hand in hers. "We have a place to stay for the night," she said, "and a plan to get you better care than I can give."

"You must listen to what I have to say." The words came out more clearly than she would have expected.

She managed a weak smile. "Since when did I ever not do that? You must save your strength."

"Humor an old man."

Lana started. He had never before described himself in such a way.

"Tell me," he continued, "what took place. My memory fails."

Lana glanced up to see a pair of Celestials carrying a long, narrow bed in the direction of a nearby cabin; Tony was behind them with a load of wood.

"We'll have you inside soon," she said. "And there's nothing wrong with your memory. You were unconscious most of the time."

The implacable look in his eyes told her he would not rest until the truth was revealed, and she quickly described what had happened, dwelling mostly on her stupidity and Tony's unfailing strength. Boris's eyes remained closed while she spoke. When she was done, he looked up and smiled.

"That was a courageous thing that you did today." His voice was low but there was no quaver that she could detect.

"It was a stupid thing I did today. I was thinking of other things and did not even see the bear." Her voice broke for a moment. "What *you* did was the bravest thing I have ever seen."

"Are we to argue, Countess, over who was stupid and who was brave?" He sighed and closed his eyes for a moment. "I do not have strength for that when there is much I want to say."

Lana brushed a strand of gray hair away from his face and pulled the blanket close around his throat. "I will be quiet and listen."

Boris's thin lips twitched, and his eyes once again held the sparkle that signified he had the upper hand. "Your attention is the one advantage of a broken leg, Countess. I will remember it the next time I wish to speak."

True to her word, Lana kept quiet and waited for him to gather his strength.

"You are wrong about him, Countess."

She had no doubt as to the identity of *him*.

"You heard us talking just now?" she asked.

Boris gave a weak nod. "What he does is the right thing. He has explained to me his purpose, and I agree with him."

"I want to believe as you do, *tovarisch*. Tony is brave and strong and has taken care of us well. But that does not mean he cannot lie. Did he not win the Blood in a gambling game shortly before Nicholas disappeared? And did he not keep the game a secret?"

"Such are the facts. But facts can be misleading. Believe what he tells you. Do as he says."

Lana's eyes widened in surprise. Boris had never once in his life openly ordered her to do anything. He preferred the indirect approach.

Boris ended his speech by closing his eyes, his breath even and deep. If he were not asleep, he was doing an excellent job of pretense.

Do as he says.

The words could have been prompted directly by Tony. They threw Lana in a quandary. Boris had made the one request she could not honor, at a time when she could not refuse.

Standing aside, she watched as their Chinese hosts unfastened the travois from the saddle and moved Boris into the nearest cabin. Tony was standing nearby while they worked. Once his eyes caught hers, but, coward that she was, she looked away. Wouldn't he just love to know what Boris had said?

Inside, the cabin was aglow with the light from a small fire in the corner fireplace, and Lana was pleased to see

229

that the bed was long enough to support Boris's long frame. In a short while they were provided with a thin, herbal broth that tasted delicious to Lana after Tony's offerings of fried beef and jerky. Stretched out on a cot in the airtight cabin, Boris managed to eat the two bowls of steaming soup she served him, and she was relieved to see the color return to his thin face.

What did not please her was the request he made after the meal.

"Countess, please ask that Mr. Diamond come inside."

He knew she could not refuse him.

When Tony was standing in the small room, Boris had once last instruction for her. "I wish to speak to him alone."

Tony shrugged as if to say he was as puzzled as she. Grabbing up her coat, she strode outside to the clean mountain air and counted the stars as they broke into the wide, dark sky. The moon was obscured by a tall Sierra peak. With the Chinese scattered inside the other cabins, she confined her pacing to a narrow stretch of gravel beside the stream. Her cheeks stung from the cold, and she shoved her gloveless hands up the sleeves of her coat as she had seen the Chinese do.

What could Boris be up to? Surely he was not asking that Tony take care of her. She would die from shame.

At last she heard the crunch of boots on gravel behind her, and she whirled to see the tall, lean figure of Tony moving her way. In the dark she could not make out his expression or the look in his eyes, yet she sensed that he was in a somber mood.

"Is Boris all right?"

"Better than I would have believed possible. Whatever Sung Lee put into that soup, it seemed to give him strength. Certainly enough to talk more than I would have thought wise."

"You should not have let him."

"Have you managed to stop Boris when he has his mind set on anything?"

Lana conceded he had a point. "What"—she hesitated

230

—"did he say? Or did he send word I am not to ask?"

She could almost hear Tony smile. "You can ask. We talked about you."

She caught her breath, unsure if she wanted him to go on.

"He is very proud of you," Tony continued. "And he has a right. He told of how the count mistreated his serfs and of the hate they gave him in return. After his death, you took advantage of a Czarist decree and gave them their freedom. Yet almost every one of them chose to remain on the estate and work for you."

"They . . . had no place else to go," she stammered, unused to the kind words.

"I think you're too modest. You began lessons in reading and arithmetic. You worked beside them. You even helped set a broken leg out in the fields. He pointed out the good training that particular task had been."

Lana smiled. "Boris always was a practical man."

"And you, it seems, are a very practical woman. In San Francisco I had wondered about the firmness of your hands. It was the one thing about you that did not seem aristocratic."

"What I did, I did to survive. You make me sound like a saint."

"That seems to be Boris's opinion."

Driven to ask one last question, Lana looked down at the moving water close to her feet. "Did he mention . . . anything particular about the count?"

She could hear Tony's deep, even breathing, and twisted her hands nervously as she waited for him to speak.

"Only to say that anything else I wanted to know should come from you."

"I see," she said, her sigh audible in the still night air. "Then that is all."

"Not quite. If he finds himself feeling as strong tomorrow as he suspects he will be, you are under orders to accompany me into town."

"Orders? Was that his word?"

"Not exactly. You know how he is. He took a little

longer to phrase it, but I got his meaning."

"I will not leave him."

"And I was under the impression you didn't want me to ride in alone."

He hurried on, giving her no chance to respond. "Our Chinese hosts have assured me they will care for him. He is concerned about finding Nick. He is afraid that if you're not with me, your brother will see me and run away in panic."

"But Nicholas is at the cabin," said Lana in protest.

"I have assumed that he is. But what if he couldn't find it? A Hangtown hotel might do just as well. I am to remind you the time runs out at home. He said I was to mention Cousin Rudolph. You would understand."

"And so do you," she said, remembering how much she had revealed to Tony a lifetime ago in his hotel room. If Nicholas didn't return within the year, they could all say farewell to the Kasatsky lands. Lana shuddered at the thought.

"There are two things more," Tony said.

"Only two? Boris must indeed be tired."

Tony's lips twitched. "You may have other things to say when you hear them. First, you are entrusted to my care—don't say it, I tried to talk him out of it. He seemed to think I would do an adequate job."

"He doesn't know you the way I do."

"Few people do."

His deep voice caressed her in the dark, and her blush came and went unseen.

"And the second thing?" she managed. "You said there were two things more."

"Oh, yes. He insists that we leave the samovar. He is convinced that the Chinese will not be able to brew a proper cup of tea."

Chapter Twenty-One

Boris awoke before dawn the next morning in what was for him a cantankerous mood. Even though he did not complain overtly, Lana understood the signs and began to feel sorry for the Chinese who had promised to care for him.

The tea was not quite hot enough. She knew because he took only one sip and said he would have a cup later when perhaps the water could be boiled.

And even though the fire was little more than glowing coals, the room was too warm. Evidence of this came when he fanned himself with the edge of the blanket, bringing Lana quickly to his side to feel for a fever. His brow was as cool as the look in his eyes.

The things he should have complained about—his aching head and body and what must surely be a very painful leg—went unmentioned. She honored his courage by not mentioning them, but she took a moment to make sure the splint was still firmly in place.

She left when Tony came in to take care of the patient's ablutions, then met him at the door.

"There's fresh water inside for you. I'll be ready to leave as soon as you are," he announced. He sounded no happier about the traveling arrangements than she.

Lana hurried through the doorway past him, taking care not to brush against him lest he misinterpret her touch as something more than accidental. She could have no lascivious thoughts about him now—or at least she had to try. During yesterday's near tragedy, they had worked as one, but today their differences were as sharp and clear as ever. For a while an unspoken truce had been called between them, but Lana sensed the war of wills was once more in full force.

With Boris's eyes discreetly closed, she bathed awkwardly in the shallow tub that Tony had found behind the cabin. For her ride into Hangtown, she wore the second riding habit Boris had purchased for her, a scarlet wool jacket and divided skirt even closer-fitting than the green.

"I never realized you preferred such colorful women's clothes," she commented when she was dressed.

"I grew weary of gray."

Boris declined additional comment on his selections, but she was well aware of his purpose. He was wrapping her in attractive finery the way he might a Christmas package. It was as though she were a gift, with the only recipient she could think of a dark-eyed, devious Californian who had somehow caught the favor of her old friend.

She had to give Boris credit for his taste in clothes. She had only the one bright gown, the one she wore her first night in San Francisco, and gray had begun to bore her, too. Only she had not made the effort to do something about it.

Deep in her heart she knew she presented an attractive picture. And she was glad. Let Tony know that she did not plan to waste away into dowdiness, dependent upon him for male attention. Not that she wanted any, but that was beside the point.

At last, with him waiting outside beside their saddled mounts, she could put off the inevitable no longer. She covered herself with the sable coat and placed the astrakhan hat over the hair she had piled on top of her head.

She allowed herself one show of sentiment: a hastily brushed kiss on Boris's cheek.

"*Do svidaniya, tovarisch,*" she said softly. "We will be

234

together soon. And," she added with a smile, "I have left you one of the dueling pistols. For a feeling of security, of course, nothing more. The way you made sure I had that old faded blanket when I was a little girl. The gun, by the way, does *not* pull to the right."

Boris responded with a smile, faint and quickly gone, but it was enough to give her the courage to leave.

Valise in hand, she took time to thank the Celestials, not caring whether they understood her or not, and once more took to the trail, for a while riding beside Tony instead of in her usual post to the rear. She assured herself it was not a pleasure to gaze incessantly at the coat that hugged his broad back or at the curl of black hair beneath his hat.

Or, she thought wryly, to watch for the frequent times when the gelding lifted a none-too-delicate tail and relieved himself, necessitating a more careful reining of her own mount. Somehow the actions of Tony's horse seemed symbolic, but she did not let herself analyze that particular thought too long.

Overhead the sky was leaden gray, and she wondered if another storm might not be on the way. Beyond the mountain meadow through which they rode stretched the snow-covered Sierras. They might have been a beautiful sight, but Lana decided she was tired of beauty. Right now she would prefer a stuffy drawing room and a pot of tea.

Soon after they were under way, Tony glanced briefly at the splash of red wool that brushed against her boots below the black fur.

"Another new dress, Countess?" he asked mockingly. "I'm partial to red, but then I can't believe you wore it for me."

Her eyes darted to his. "Most certainly not. I never thought of such a thing," she said, knowing she spoke a lie.

Really seeing him for the first time this morning, she was struck by how ruggedly handsome he was, with his hat pulled low over a sweep of dark brows, and his face lean and weathered by the winter wind. There was something almost illicit about their riding together alone

235

in the empty vastness of the mountain valley, and her heart quickened its beat.

She forced her eyes back to the trail. "When will we arrive?"

"Shortly after noon, as best I can estimate. Provided we don't encounter any other emergencies."

"I'm not planning on one," she said, tightening her grip on the reins. The mare responded with a jerk of her head.

Tony was quick with a rejoinder. "That's good news."

She warned herself to keep quiet, but the perverse side of her nature was in control.

"As I recall," she said sweetly, "you were the one who rode into the ghost town."

"True, but as I recall that particular delay wasn't a total waste of time. Don't you agree?"

Lana's gaze flew back to her adversary's face. "You, sir, are no gentleman!"

"Surely you're not realizing that just now?"

She would have sacrificed her fur-lined gloves to have Boris eavesdropping on their conversation right now. Since that was impossible—and he would never believe her if she repeated every one of Tony's words—she shut up and concentrated on making good time.

When the trail narrowed and began to snake downward along the edge of a Sierra mountain, she found herself once more bringing up the rear. Thinking over his rude comments, she stuck an unladylike tongue out in his direction and remembered when she was a hoydenish child how her mother had warned her she should not do that in the wintertime, else her tongue might freeze.

What would her mother think of Tony Diamond?

It was a thought worth pursuing. In his younger years, her father had not been unlike Tony. Dashingly handsome he had been, and rugged from the hours spent outdoors in the service of the Imperial Guard. Her mother, daughter of an English diplomat to the court of the Czar, had fallen deeply in love with the tall, dark Russian.

"Never once," she told Lana shortly before her death at

age thirty-five, "have I regretted not returning to England. My home is with your father. When you find your own love, you will feel the same."

Lana's heart grew heavy in her breast. "Stay in California with Tony?" she whispered, her words muffled by the wind and the horses' hooves striking the hard ground. "No, Mama. Tony may seem much like Papa, but it is not love we share. And he would not ask me."

Lana's home was on her estate, her life's work caring for the peasants who depended upon her. Once she got her hands on that ruby—and she would, oh she most definitely would—then she could book passage for herself and Nicholas and Boris on the first available ship. If at some time in the distant years she met a fellow countryman who was willing to share her life and work beside her . . .

She brushed the thought from her mind. Between Tony and the count, she had had all the heartbreak she could stand. She was through with men.

They rode quietly for a long while, not speaking much even during a stop to water and rest the horses. Just when Lana realized that something was different, she was not sure. Maybe it was the way Tony's shoulders seemed to hunch over the saddle when he usually rode with a straight back, or maybe it was just that she had grown sensitive to his moods. When the trail widened on a long downward stretch, she pulled beside him. He seemed not to know she was there.

She was struck with the memory of Tony's ghosts. Hangtown must be near.

They came to a fork in the steep, winding trail, and Tony reined to a halt. He gestured to the left, where a smaller path sloped downward through the snow-covered pines.

"The cabin is in that direction," he said. "We'll come back this way after we locate Doc."

Lana felt a thrill of anticipation. Nicholas seemed so close at that moment she could almost hear his laughter, almost see the bright smile on his fair and boyish face. Would he have changed because of his troubles? Not

Nicholas. He never seemed to change, not even when he had gone through those terrible fights with Papa over her marriage. To Lana he had always presented a sunny radiance. She had missed him more than words could describe.

She looked at the path, faint but visible where it had been cut through the brush. "I thought you said it was difficult to get to," she said.

"It is. What you're looking at only goes down to a ravine. The rest of the way is unmarked . . . unless you know what signs to look for."

When she looked back at Tony, she knew her eyes were shining but she did not care. "Let us hurry, Tony. There is much that has to be done."

So happy was she that she almost missed the dark look of despair that shadowed Tony's face.

The look was gone almost as soon as she saw it, but he could not lighten the tone of his voice.

"Of course, Countess," he said. "There is much that we both have to do."

Her joy died as quickly as it had been born. How quickly and completely he could wrap her in his troubles, even though she knew not what those troubles were. No matter how much she viewed him as a foe, right now she wanted to reach out and offer him the comfort that in her woman's heart she knew she could give. But she feared rejection. And she feared he would misunderstand, taking her caring for pity or, worse, a sudden blossoming of the lust that she had too often shown him before.

A sudden chill rushed through her, and she pulled her coat tight. With the passing of morning the sky had darkened to a deeper gray, and there was a distinct drop in the temperature that ate into her bones.

She dug her heels sharply into the mare and spurred her into the lead. Without a backward glance, she rounded a bend and came to an abrupt halt. A man was riding up the trail toward her, hat low on his head, fair hair brushing against the collar of his coat. When his mount, a black, neared, he lifted his eyes from the ground, and his eyes

238

widened in surprise.

"Svetlana!"

"Nicholas!"

She was too taken by surprise to feel anything but astonishment.

She heard Tony's horse halt behind her.

"Hello, Nick."

"What in the hell . . ." Nicholas stopped, staring first at Tony, then back at her.

"We've ridden a long way to find you," Tony said. "You should be able to greet us more warmly than that."

The horse that Nicholas rode skittered about nervously on the narrow trail, and he pulled back sharply on the reins until he was once more in control. His blue eyes, still wide in astonishment, settled on Lana. "You're supposed to be in Russia!"

"Obviously I'm not," Lana said, her own surprise at last giving way to irritation. She agreed with Tony. A warmer greeting should have been offered her after the long months of separation. "I've come to take you home."

He shook his head. "I don't understand."

"If you listen a moment," Tony said, "your sister will explain."

Nicholas's attention suddenly became focused on Tony. "I don't have to guess why you are here. You shouldn't have come. I'm taking care of my own problems."

"None too well!" Tony said sharply.

"You'd like to believe I'm not," Nicholas rejoined. "That way you can get what you want."

He turned his attention once more to his sister and, pulling his mount close beside hers, lapsed into Russian. "I know not why you are here, but I am glad. We must talk, later when we can be alone." His eyes softened. "I will find you, Svetlana, and you will reveal all. About Papa and home, too?"

He smiled, a flash of summer obliterating his winter frown, and Lana was reminded of when he was a little boy.

The mare's head bobbed, but Lana held tight to the reins. "About Papa—" She stopped. "Yes, we must talk.

Please ride with us into town."

Nicholas turned deeply troubled eyes past her and fastened his gaze on Tony, who sat quietly on his mount behind Lana. "I cannot. There are things I must do before I face *him* again."

"Let me help you."

He looked at her once again. "I couldn't help you back in Russia when Papa forced you into marriage. I will not ask for your help now. Have faith. It warms my heart to see you again."

Nicholas pulled back on the reins as though he planned to turn the black horse and join them.

"Nick." Tony's voice cut through the cold air. "I wouldn't do anything foolish if I—"

The warning ended abruptly when Nicholas lashed suddenly with his crop against the black's flank and jerked the reins sharply to the right. The horse pivoted in place, eyes rolling in his dark head, and with Nicholas leaning back in the saddle plunged down the steep embankment near the trail that led in the direction of Tony's cabin, hooves throwing up snow. He seemed to slide more than gallop through the brush and trees.

Lana's mare, as startled as her rider, reared and took off down the trail.

"Tony!" Lana cried out, pulling back hard on the reins, but the mare paid her no mind. She bounced precariously in the sidesaddle; in desperation she gripped at the reins and pommel. The hard ground seemed to be coming up at her on the downward path, and the jagged granite wall to her right seemed as threatening as the sharp drop to her left.

Out of nowhere Tony's gelding thundered between her and the yawning chasm. Strong hands covered hers and jerked back sharply on the reins. Side by side the gelding and mare raced toward the sharp cutback which was all that Lana could see of the trail.

The slowing was barely perceptible, and then the horses stopped as suddenly as the race had begun. Lana was flung forward, then settled back in the saddle with a jerk. Unable to think or speak, she could only gasp for breath and squeeze her eyes closed to the sharp drop-off not three feet from where the horses had ground to a halt.

Not trusting herself to speak, she opened her eyes and looked at Tony. He glared back at her, rage etched on his face, and she forgot whatever she had planned to say.

"A rather dangerous plan, Countess."

She stared at him in disbelief and found her voice. "You think Nicholas and I *planned* that?"

He breathed deeply for a moment. "I assume all that gibberish was not just brother and sister hellos."

The gelding snorted, his proud head jerking against the reins, and he stamped at the ground. The mare responded with an answering snort, and tried to skitter backwards on the trail away from him.

"Somewhere in all that obvious affection," Tony added, "Nick must have also told you good-bye."

Tony's fury was like a tight wire close to the breaking point, and Lana's own anger took hold. "You're free to follow and ask him what he said."

"He's long gone by now; I don't suppose you'd care to reveal any other plans you two might have made."

She ran a shaking gloved hand over the mane and neck of the mare, soothing the horse since she couldn't soothe herself. "I think I need to stand for a while. If my legs will hold me."

Tony nodded. Dismounting, he helped her to the ground. She pulled away while he ground-tethered the horses to the edge of the trail.

She gazed around her at the granite wall and trees and sky. Except for a hawk circling overhead, all was silent and still, as though the near violence on the trail had stunned the world.

With her hands gripped tightly together, she turned her back to Tony. "He said there were things he needed to take care of," she said at last, then added, "without you. He seems afraid of what you might do."

"That seems to be a family trait."

Still shaken and close to tears, Lana took a moment to

respond. Why she should want Tony to understand, she did not know. But it seemed desperately important that he know the reason Nicholas had run from him.

"He's young and proud," she said, her eyes trained on the ground. "He left Russia to escape the dictatorial hand of Papa. He wants to prove something to himself." She remembered a young girl's pixie face and round blue eyes shining with love. "And maybe prove something to Elizabeth Dundreary, too. I do not know how he feels about her."

"After only a few minutes of conversation, you seem to know a great deal about Nick."

She turned to face him. "He's my family, Tony. Other than Boris, he is all I have in the world. You do not understand." Tony was standing closer than she thought, his lean face solemn, and she caught her breath.

"Ah, I see what you mean now," he said. "Since I don't have a family, I couldn't know what it's like to be close to someone."

"I do not think you will let anyone get close to you, Tony. And please do not say anything about what has happened between us. I do not mean that kind of close."

Tony stared at her for a long time. "I wonder if you know how right you are?" He reached out and fingered the hair that had worked loose from under her hat. She did not pull away.

"You're a beautiful and intelligent woman, Lana. It's too bad things just can't work out for us. Too many obstacles keep getting in the way. Too many memories we can't forget."

Lana remembered the tenderness she had felt toward Tony just before she rounded the bend and spied her brother. She had wanted to offer him consolation for whatever worries ate at his mind. How glad she was that she had not, for she saw now he would only have rejected her. A desolation swept over Lana unlike anything she had felt before, but she kept her head high.

"I'm all right now, Tony. We need to ride on into town and find the doctor for Boris. We let Nicholas get away,

and we're not doing much good for each other, but at least
we can help that dear man."

The cluster of buildings that was officially called
Placerville stretched along a hollow formed by one of the
Sierras' thousand creeks. It was by this creek that the town
had sprung in the early days of the gold strike.

Neither Lana nor Tony spoke the remaining mile into
the hollow, not even when they arrived at the edge of town.
Lana's thoughts were torn between seeing her brother
again so briefly after so long a time and wondering what
worries were eating at Tony. She could not put those
worries out of her mind.

Nicholas would find her again—he had promised, and
for all his rapscallion ways he had never broken his word.
Until she heard from him, she could do nothing but wait.

And Tony? She doubted he would ever confess his
troubles . . . certainly not after today. He had the misguided idea she had betrayed him and helped Nicholas get
away.

Hangtown, she discovered, was nothing more than a
single rutted thoroughfare running between high steep
hills. A few side streets cut up the hillsides. Snow, turned
to brown slush by the traffic, filled the ruts and banked
against the high curbs of the plank sidewalks.

Lana was amazed to see men digging in the center of the
main street, some of the holes six feet deep, while their
partners were either bailing water or washing the mud
through a wooden-framed sieve. She corrected herself
again. Through a rocker. Back when they were speaking
civilly two days ago, Tony had had a long time to explain
the various ways men looked for gold.

But on a winter's day? And in the middle of town?
America was crazier than she had thought.

Reluctantly she turned her attention away from the men
and onto the architecture. Clapboard houses and log
cabins lined the route. In the window of one sturdy, cared-
for shack hung a Wells Fargo sign; but most of the

243

buildings were unpainted, and in the gloom of winter looked gray and worn.

As oppressive as the scene appeared, it was made worse by the braying of mules and the shouts of men, and by the stench which hung in the air. Too many people and animals were crowded into too small a space.

All in all, she thought with a sigh, it was a far cry from St. Petersburg. She almost missed the Gut Bucket Saloon.

As they made their way down the street, Tony still in the lead, Lana found herself the center of unwanted attention. Slowly the shouts around her died, and even the mules ceased to bray. Or so it seemed to her. She wondered if the town had been this quiet since the discovery of gold.

It must be the coat, she told herself, or the way she sat her horse. But of course neither was true. The Hangtown men were looking at her the way they must have looked at a three-pound nugget . . . in amazement and in covetous desire.

Tony hastened the gelding's pace as they passed the town's lone tree, a towering oak that stood by one of the side streets.

Here was where justice was dispensed, he had told her. She shuddered and looked away. In Russia, a man was sentenced to Siberia, but in most cases he kept his life.

Tony didn't slow down until he came to a two-story building which bore a sign reading simply HOTEL. They both dismounted and tied their horses to a splintered post. Taking a cue from him when he thrust his bedroll under one arm, she grabbed for her valise.

"Tony Diamond!" a man called from the opposite side of the street. "Wait up there a minute."

She turned to see a short, barrel-chested man with a balding head and a beard of gray making his cautious way across the street.

Tony muttered an obscenity under his breath as he shifted toward the sound.

"I'll be damned," the man said when he joined them on the sidewalk. "It really is you." He scratched at his beard, threw Lana a quick look, then caught himself and stared at her in open amazement. "I'll be double damned!" he exclaimed.

There was something openly innocent about his profanity, not repulsive as the looks from the other men had been, and Lana found herself smiling at him.

"Hello, Dusty John," Tony said with resignation. "May I present the Countess Svetlana Alexandrovna?"

Lana thougt he could just as easily have omitted her title and full name here in Hangtown, but she didn't complain. At least he was being halfway polite.

"A real countess?" Dusty John's face was aglow with pleasure as he looked at her. "I'll be damned. Pardon my manners and language, but I never met no royalty before." He glanced at Tony. "'Cept maybe for that woman what called herself a duchess. Remember her, Tony? Come to think of it, she sure had a bodacious number of what she called dukes visitin' her out at that shack she called a palace. Nope, not the same thing at all."

"What a liar you are, John," Tony said, a half smile on his lips. "You knew exactly what the duchess was up to. First hand, I imagine. How have you been?"

"Still lookin' for a strike. Still turnin' up nothing but dust and rocks." He glanced at Lana. "That's how I got the moniker." He looked back at Tony. "What brings you to this god-forsaken place? Never expected to see you here again."

"Business," Tony said, the smile gone. "Is Doc still around? And more important, is he sober?"

"He's here all right, and as sober as he can manage. Been on the wagon awhile now. Made him grumpy as hell, but I guess we can't have everything around here."

Tony nodded in satisfaction. "Look, John, maybe we can get together later for a drink. Right now the countess is tired and I need to see about getting her a room. And see about finding Doc. There's an injured man back at one of the camps I want him to tend to."

"Sure thing, Tony. Let me know if I can help. I'll be at the Fat Lady if you get thirsty. *Still* can't get over seeing you again."

245

They left him on the sidewalk shaking his head.

Lana had to hurry to keep up with Tony as he strode inside, and she put Dusty John from her mind. The lobby consisted of one desk, one grizzly-faced clerk, and no chairs. There was no sign of a nearby restaurant or gambling hall, nothing to remind her of the Ace Hotel. Except for the rooms upstairs. Lana felt the closeness of the inside air as she remembered too well what Tony could do in such a place.

He talked for several minutes with the clerk, then directed his long stride toward the stairs. She was tempted to demand she be told what he was up to, and would have if she thought he would respond. She would not have been at all surprised to find he had rented only one room. If he thought for a minute . . .

He stopped before a door at the end of a dingy hall, inserted the key, and walked inside. She remained where she stood.

It took only five seconds by her reckoning for him to stick his head out the door. "We can talk wherever you choose," he said calmly. "In privacy or not. I promise it won't take long."

Against her better judgment, Lana edged past him into a room even smaller than the lobby downstairs. There was barely room for a bed, one table, and a kerosene lamp. A single window let in the gray winter light.

Tony stood between her and escape. Close. Much too close. "I want you to stay here while I go find Doc and direct him out to the camp," he said.

She set her valise by the table and, removing her hat, tossed it on the bed. "Won't he have trouble locating it?"

"Everyone who's been in Hangtown long will know about the Nugget Bar. It brought in quite a lode for a while."

"I assume you'll be returning to the hotel."

Tony eyed her carefully. "And what do you assume I'll be doing when I return?" His voice was deep and low.

"You won't be welcome in here. You said we had our

246

differences, remember?"

"I wasn't talking about in bed." He tossed his hat on the blanket beside hers, and his bedroll fell to the floor. "Countess, don't you know at least a little about yourself?"

"I—"

Firm hands gripped her arms, and her words were swallowed as his lips covered hers. He crushed her to his chest. The suddenness of his action took her by surprise, and it was a moment before she could react, before she could pound her fists against him and try to twist away.

He ignored her feeble attempts to be free. His kiss deepened, and expending very little effort he managed to slip the coat from her shoulders; it fell to the floor.

In that brief moment when his hold relaxed, she jerked free. "No, Tony, no!"

He paid no attention. His arms once more encircled her, with one hand pressed tightly against her back, he ran the other palm from her hip to her breast, his thumb playing at the fast-hardening tip. Through her clothing she could feel the arousing pressure everywhere he touched.

Lana lost control, feeling as though the rational side of her were outside her body, unable to interfere and quell her desires. Her hands unfolded and she entwined her fingers in his hair. His hand moved lower down her spine until he was able to press her tight against him. His thigh shifted between her legs, rubbed back and forth, and she exploded with need.

Breaking the kiss, she buried her face in the crook of his shoulder. "Tony . . . oh, Tony," she whispered.

He drew still, his leg shifting away from her, but he continued to hold her tight, both hands pressed to her back.

"My God, Lana, you make me forget everything but you." The words burned into her ear.

The moment of passion had passed; Tony's embrace was not one of affection for her. His thoughts were turned upon himself.

An icy fist clutched at her heart. "Should I apologize?" she asked, looking up at him. She felt as though a great weight were crushing down on her, the weight of her humiliation that she could so quickly respond to him.

She looked deep into his eyes and seemed to see inside his soul. Dark, brooding thoughts stirred him, but they were thoughts he would not share. Forgetting his lies, she had offered herself to him when she swore she would not, and he had rejected her.

Stunned by the pain of that rejection, she thrust herself away. He did not try to stop her as she sat on the edge of the bed.

Her fingers rested against her lips, as though she could hold back the harsh words of recrimination she wanted to fling at him, but she knew that no matter what she said, she did not have the power to hurt him as he did her. He had done far worse than bring her pain; he had shattered the last vestiges of her pride.

Tony had built a wall between them; the only way he could scale that wall was through the lust that they shared. For him today that lust had not been enough.

She looked up into his eyes and thought she saw regret. But she must be wrong. There was no trace of sorrow in his voice.

"I have to give you thanks for one thing, Lana. For two years I've thought about what returning here would be like. For two years I've sworn I would never subject myself to finding out. And when I finally do, I'm so wrapped up in you, that I forget my real troubles."

He reached past her for his hat and cradled the bedroll under his arm. "Now I'm going out to find the Doc and then get a bottle. I'll be in the room next door. I don't think Nick will be coming after you today. He'll most likely wait until tomorrow or later when he thinks I might be careless. That window is nailed shut and the clerk is getting a guard to watch the lobby in case he tries a more direct approach."

Her fingers brushed at the strands of hair that had loosened around her face. "And what if I simply walk down to meet him?"

248

Tony reached in his pocket and pulled out a key. "Unless you're good at picking locks, I don't imagine you'll be doing that."

"You're going to lock me in?" she asked in amazement.

"I most certainly am. About the only way I'm going to get through the rest of this day is to get roaring drunk. And for once I want to be sure that I know where you are."

Chapter Twenty-Two

Lana had no idea how long she sat on the edge of the bed before deciding what to do. She knew only that by the time she finally stirred, the gray light drifting into the hotel room seemed a little gloomier and carried far less heat than when she had arrived.

She had reached her decision slowly, a process of reluctant acceptance, self-appraisal, and at last a plan.

The first conclusion had been so obvious that she wondered why she had not realized it long ago. But that didn't make it easy to accept. A woman could run a long time and a long way to put distance between her and a man, but she could never run far enough or fast enough to get away from herself.

This afternoon she had taunted Tony and he had kissed her; in an explosion of need, they had clung together for a precious moment. The moment had shattered, but still she had wanted him. In the face of rejection . . . knowing she could meet with only heartbreak . . . she had wanted him. How could she regret feeling the way she did? She might as well regret her need for air.

At last Lana had arrived at that last small doll holding the secret to her heart. She loved Tony. Unwisely. Passionately. And, she sensed, forever. That she loved a man who did not return her love did not alter the facts. That it would be an unhappy love did not weaken its hold on her.

The second conclusion had been even harder to accept, since it involved placing blame on herself. A woman in love thought of her man. And Lana had been thinking of herself . . . of how she was lied to, how she was misunderstood and mistreated, how her own problems could be solved.

But Tony had problems, too. Torment had been in his eyes. He had hinted at what they might be before, and she had been wrong to ignore what he said.

She could figure out a few things that those problems probably did not involve. For one thing, money was not the issue; she had seen ample evidence of his wealth, from the opulence of the Ace Hotel to the way he had refused her gold. Health? She had never met a more able man than he, and she had put him to a test or two.

And she knew in her heart it was not woman trouble. She would swear that when she had lain with him she thought of no one but her. He may not have given his heart to her, but neither had he given it to anyone else.

Something in the past was troubling him—ghosts, he called them—and she had to help him bury them if she could. The next move was up to her, and it did not take too much thinking to know what that move must be. But first she had to get out of the hotel.

She looked at the closed door that led to the hall and smiled. Dear, misguided Tony. He knew so much about how to arouse her, what to say that would anger her or make her laugh. But she had her secrets, too. For one thing, she knew how to pick a lock.

It was another skill she owed to the count, and right now she rated it right up there in importance with gambling. He had not taught her directly. What he had done was lock her in her room one night when he thought she might prove too much competition for the particular gentleman he had coming to call.

Furious, she had taken out one of her hairpins and set to work. It had taken her two hours and a dozen more pins to complete the task; when she was done she hadn't even left the room. But she could if she had wanted to. That had been her solitary goal.

The next time he tried it, she cut the time to one fourth of the original. The secret lay in the way the pin was bent and the angle at which it entered the narrow opening where the key was supposed to fit.

It was after this second time that she met him outside the drawing room and informed him she had no interest in joining him or his guest. He never locked her in again.

Surely lock-picking was a skill one did not forget, like riding a horse. It took her half an hour by her estimation to find out she was right. When the handle turned in her hand and the door creaked ajar, she almost whooped with joy. Except that her goal was not really reached; her work had just begun.

She closed the door once again and set herself to smoothing her hair and donning her hat, gloves, and coat. Her fingers trembled as she worked; for all her convictions that she was doing what she must, she had no idea that everything would turn out right. What if Tony did not understand? He could very well hold her in deeper contempt than he already did.

But she had made up her mind, right or wrong, to help him. She could not return to Russia without knowing she had done all that she could.

From the valise she took one special item—the second dueling pistol—and thrust it in a pocket of her jacket. It hung awkwardly against her hip, but she did not consider leaving it behind. She had learned a great deal since her visit to the Gut Bucket Saloon. In California she did not go too many places unarmed.

At last she was satisfied she was as prepared as she would ever be. The scarlet riding habit showed above the fur at her throat and down the opening of the sable. If she did say so herself, with her ivory skin in contrast to her clothes, she made a striking picture in red and black.

This confidence in her looks was something she owed to Tony. Mama and Papa had always called her beautiful, but the count had taught her otherwise. Tony made her feel beautiful again.

Thinking that he might make a quick check of her door, she took care to lock it from the outside, thrust the hairpin key in the pocket holding the gun, and tiptoed past his room. The temptation to knock and see if he really were inside drinking did not occur to her. She had something else to do first.

In the lobby she spotted the desk clerk in conversation with a brown-skinned man she took to be Spanish. She decided he must be the guard who was watching for Nicholas. Praying that Tony had not put him on watch for her, too, she did the only thing possible. She walked calmly to the front door and went outside. There came no shouts or the sounds of pursuit, and she turned her attention to the street.

Sunlight was fading fast, but in November in the mountains the dimness didn't mean the day was close to an end. The air was heavy with a damp cold, and she was certain a storm was on the way.

Down the street along which they had ridden earlier, torches flickered in the gloom, and she turned in their direction. There was still traffic in the streets but few pedestrians were about and she was able to walk down the plank sidewalk unmolested. She stopped the first man who paid her much attention . . . or at least *she* stopped. He was already at a standstill and gawking at her.

A grizzled old man in an oversized coat and rubber boots, he pushed back his misshapen felt hat but made no move to speak.

"Excuse me, sir," she said. "Could you direct me to the Fat Lady Saloon?"

He cleared his throat and spat through sunken lips into the banked, stained snow at the edge of the street. "Beggin' your pardon, ma'am, but are you sure you want to go in there?"

Lana brushed one hand against the bulk of the hidden gun. "I am sure."

His round, brown eyes blinked twice. "It's down aways. You can't miss it, but once you get a good look at it, you'll wish you'd gone on by. Full of loud drunks by this time of

254

day." He hesitated. "You sure you know what you're doing?"

"Most definitely." Her words were not a complete lie.

"In that case," the man said with a toothless grin, "guess I'll just follow along behind and see what happens. Town's grown kinda quiet like with winter comin' on."

There was something comforting about the old fellow following her. Not that he would do her much good if she got into trouble—not that he had even offered to try—but somehow he seemed like a friend.

She paused until he was beside her. "What is your name, sir?"

He blinked again. "I'm called Cooter. Only name I need nowadays."

"Well, Mr. Cooter, I would be honored to have you with me."

This time he blinked three times, and she could have sworn he blushed. But he insisted on walking behind.

"Hold up," he called in the middle of the next block. "Don't go looking for nothing fancy, 'cause you've arrived."

The Fat Lady Saloon was a one-story, unpainted clapboard building that looked much like the rest of the town's architecture, only it boasted a pair of swinging doors. She paused in front of them and looked in. As tall as she was, she could easily see into the smoke-filled room. Crude tables were scattered around a sawdust-covered floor; most of the customers stood around the rough-hewn bar. If there was a woman inside, Lana could not tell her from the men.

The basis for the saloon's name was readily visible. On the plank wall behind the bar hung a painting of an overly endowed nude stretched full length on what appeared to be a poster bed. Her long locks of golden hair spread across the right end of the canvas, but the lady herself took up most of the rest. A second patch of gold had been crudely painted between her voluptuous thighs. To Lana the pubic hair looked suspiciously like a triangular nugget, and she wondered if maybe the artist had been saying that

255

each man looked for gold in his own way.

What a thought! Before America, such an idea never would have occurred to her. Still, she had to give the artist some credit. He might never be represented at the Hermitage Museum in St. Petersburg, but there was a lively eroticism about the work that fit in with the saloon in which it was hung.

Her dark eyes darted around the room, and she heaved a sigh of relief. Tony was not inside. She wasn't ready to see him yet. Not quite.

The object of her search was at a table at the far end from the doors; with a vow that she would not let her courage fail her, she stepped inside. Cooter was close behind.

The room quietened as if she had ordered the men to cease talking. Too well she remembered the way she had tried to slip into the Gut Bucket. It seemed a long time ago.

Despite the outside cold at her back, she felt sweat forming in the curve of her spine. She knew what it signified—abject fear. Boris would be ashamed of her. Even Tony would not be too proud. Standing tall and self-assured, once again the aristocrat, she let her eyes drift around the room. "I am the Countess Svetlana Alexandrovna of St. Petersburg, Russia," she informed the onlookers, "and I have come on a matter of much importance to me."

A hoarse laugh came from near the bar, but it took only a flash of her dark eyes in that direction for the laughter to cease. Reaching under her coat, she pulled out the dueling pistol. A quick stir rippled across the room, followed by a silence even deeper than before.

"This pistol pulls a little to the right, but I know how to compensate," she said, waving it in the air. A couple of men ducked low in their chairs. "And I warn you, it has a hair trigger. In case someone decides to test my nerve. I wish to speak to Mr. Dusty John, who, I believe, is sitting at the back. I shall depend on you all to see that we are not disturbed."

"And I'll be watching here at the door to tell those that ain't here yet that by Gawd they better behave," Cooter announced in a high-pitched voice.

She walked to the back to greet an openmouthed Dusty John, her head held high and her stride long and graceful. It was a good thing no one knew the weak condition of her knees.

Dusty John rose to his feet, whisked the hat from his head, and brushed the seat of the empty chair beside him with the brim. "Proud to have you join me, Countess," he said, "but you wasn't the one I was expecting."

She sat, shifted her chair until her back was to the wall, and, as she rested the pistol on the table, gestured for him to sit close beside her. "I don't think Tony will be joining us. Mr. John, you and I need to talk. I must know everything you can tell me about what happened here two years ago."

"He ain't told you, huh? Not that I'm surprised. Course I don't know the way of things between you two."

"He's helping me find my brother."

"Oh. I was thinking it was something more." Dusty John scratched at his beard. "You sure you want to know? It ain't a pretty tale for the likes of you."

"I am not used to pretty tales, Mr. John. And I did not think this would be one."

"If you're sure." He gestured to the bartender. "I'm sticking to beer, but how about a brandy for you? Or at least what's called brandy at the Lady. We kinda take it on faith that Billy Boy's selling what he says he is. He don't usually serve at the tables, but I'm bettin' today he will."

Billy Boy proved Dusty John correct, and Lana took a sip of the mysterious liquid, its warmth trickling all the way down to her stomach and spreading outward along the way. She set the glass aside, glanced around the room to see that the other patrons had turned their attention to pursuits other than watching her, and announced, "I'm ready."

Dusty John took a long swallow of beer and wiped the foam from his hairy lip. "It ain't no secret, not from anyone that was around here a couple of years ago. And there's plenty of those like me still hanging around, stupid enough to keep trying for a strike. Tony ever mentioned a man called Jess Tucker?"

"He was his partner and close friend."

"The closest I ever seen. Jess wasn't like Tony. He was kinda wildlike. Women and cards and sometimes too much whiskey. Not that Tony didn't take his turn at each—beggin' your pardon about the women, but that is the truth. Only Tony was always touched with moderation. Not so Jess." He cleared his throat. "Tell me if I'm boring you, ma'am, or going into detail too much."

"You're not. Please keep on."

"Nobody ever did know where Tony and Jess made their strike, but once Jess come into town drinking and bragging and got himself a redheaded whore. The next time we seen him a week later he was aimin' to find her, swore she turned a robber onto him and Tony, and they lost everything they'd worked so hard to get."

"He didn't locate her, did he?"

Dusty John shook his head. "Time was, people didn't even bother to hide their findings. Leave it out on the table, they could, and the door unlocked. When they got back from wherever they had an itching to go, there would be the gold. Those times are gone." He sighed. "Not that that has to do with the story, but I sure do hate the way things change."

"But if the times are bad, then change can be good."

"Never thought about it that way." He signaled for another beer, but Lana declined a second brandy.

"Anyway," Dusty John said, "when Jess rode in all het-up about the robbery and finding that whore, there was no reasoning with him. Blamed himself for blabbing, he said, and took more whiskey faster than any man oughter. Shot up the place. A few troublemakers joined in—seems to me we've always got 'em—and for a while around here there was bullets flying like hail in a thunderstorm."

Lana waited for him to take another drink. The story was calling up unpleasant memories for him, and his hand was shaking as he lifted the glass.

At last he began again. "All that wasted powder," he said with a shake of his head. "Trouble was, one of those bullets caught an old feller right between the eyes. Parson, we called him, 'cause he was always marching up and down the street reading from the Good Book, that long frock of his dragging in the mud. Harmless he was, but I guess some of us figured our souls wasn't completely damned since we didn't run him out of town."

"How terrible," Lana said.

"Sure was. Parson was deader 'n one of my claims. A couple of the men swore it was Tucker's bullet that got him, and there weren't no one to say nay. Justice is swift around here. No jail to put a man in. You get a man like Max Shader, a little preacher in him, too, and a lot of judge, and you got instant trial, conviction, and sentencing. That old oak down the way has seen many an execution."

"Was Shader an official of some kind?"

"Too fancy a name for him. He hung around here a lot then, doing some prospecting but often just butting in. Lots of folks were glad to see him take over an unpopular job."

"I met him in San Francisco. He's forming a vigilante committee there now."

"Old dogs keep bitin' the same old fleas, don't they? Don't suppose that committee sits too well with Tony."

"No," she said, "it doesn't sit well at all."

For some reason she remembered Lucas McBride, the young man who had died trying to get away from Shader's men. She knew a little of how Tony felt.

"The story gets real ugly here, ma'am. You take the rest of that brandy, and I'll try to let you know just how bad it was."

Lana settled back in her chair and let his words take over, forgetting the gun on the table and the strangers around her. Dusty John told the story well. The main street of Hangtown had not looked much different from the way it did today, mules braying and holes dug in the street, only there were more men crowded around the oak. Somehow word always spread when there was going to be a hanging, and they were standing around, waiting for Jess Tucker's final words.

Jess was already on horseback, the noose around his neck, when Tony rode into the edge of town. The Parson's body was still warm in the back of the hillside shack that was used from time to time as a funeral parlor. Shader, Bible in hand, stood on the sidewalk beside the oak and pronounced sentence.

"By the authority invested in me by the good citizens of this town," Shader intoned, "I hereby order that one Jess Tucker, found guilty of the murder of—"

"Get on with it, Shader," came a voice from the crowd. "I got work to do."

"—of one Parson, identity otherwise unknown," Shader continued, unwilling to give up his moment of fame. "Where was I? Oh, yes, Jess Tucker shall be hanged by the neck until dead."

Shader opened the Bible. "I'll try to find an appropriate passage. You got any last words, Tucker?"

If he did, Jess never got a chance to say them. Hearing the hoofbeats of Tony's horse as it pounded down the street, Shader yelled, "Hit that horse and get the hanging over with."

The man who served as executioner, a volunteer who had struck it rich, then lost all his gold in a three-card monte game, did as Shader demanded. Jess's horse took off, leaving him twisting in the cold evening air.

"No!"

Tony's anguished cry echoed down the street, and his horse thundered to a halt beside the tree. Dropping the reins, he grabbed at Jess's legs and tried to lift the weight of the body and relieve the pull of the rope.

Tony must have been the only one there who didn't know that Jess was already dead. His neck had been broken the instant he fell from the moving horse and the noose jerked tight. The men lucky enough to be close by later said they heard the snap loud and clear.

"I've got you, Jess," Tony said as he clutched at Jess's trousers. "You'll be all right." Nobody told him he was talking to a dead man.

Tony's eyes darted to Shader. Cold eyes that could lacerate a man sure as a whip. "Cut him down, Max, or I'll kill you here and now," he ordered.

Shader snapped the Bible closed. "You're too late,

Diamond. Justice has been served."

"Cut him down."

Shader shifted nervously, then gestured to the executioner. "Get the ladder and do as he says."

The crowd backed slowly away as the ladder was brought. Tony sat silently on his horse and waited, still supporting Jess's weight. When the rope was cut, the body fell limply into Tony's arms, the noose still hanging around the bent neck.

Most of the miners and gamblers who had crowded onto the street, and the few whores who drifted out of the back rooms, claimed they had never seen such a sad sight, Tony cradling his friend in his arms. And they were afraid, too. Tony had a light in his eyes that they didn't like. A kind of wild fury that could lash out at any of them for not stopping the execution. They gave him plenty of room to ride out of town.

"For once," Dusty John said, ending his story, "Max Shader kept his mouth shut. No preaching about how folks ought to be getting that body back or how Jess ought to be buried in an unmarked grave."

His voice faded into the silence and Lana opened her eyes, surprised to see not the crowded street of Hangtown but the smoky interior of the saloon. A moment passed before she could speak.

"Did Tony ever return to town?"

"A couple of days later, after he buried Jess wherever they had that claim. No one ever could find it. Excepting the robber, of course. Tony came in roaring drunk and tried to cut down the tree. Couple of men stopped him, but you can see the scars on that trunk to this very day."

Lana played with the half glass of brandy. Tony bore scars, too, but they were the deep kind. He would not let anyone get close, but he was sensitive to every hurt, himself.

"What did Jess Tucker look like?" she asked.

"Fair-haired, as I recall. The ladies sure liked him. Said he had a nice smile. I wouldn't know about that. His only trouble was, he drank too much, and when he drank he got mean."

261

"Did you know the men who said he killed the Parson?"

"A couple of drifters. They skedaddled on out of town that very night. But no one had no doubt about what they claimed. Nobody but Tony, of course. Demanded to see them on that trip back to town. His doubt was what you would expect. Mostly, I think, he blamed himself for what happened. He shoulda kept better watch over the kid, 'cause that's all Jess really was. Or he shoulda got here faster the day of the hanging. Not that he could have stopped it. The whole town was behind Shader, considering how popular the Parson was."

"Do you have any idea how Shader ended up in San Francisco?"

"Hit a strike not long after. Can't speak for anyone else, but I was glad to see him get out of town."

Lana smiled bleakly and thanked him for his time. She kept the pistol in her hand as she walked out of the saloon. No one made a move to stop her.

All right, she asked herself, what was she to do now? Tony bore a heavy burden, but it was one he had put on his own shoulders. In his mind, he had let Jess Tucker die.

Night had fallen, and she turned her steps toward the hotel, gun in hand and Cooter close behind. Many people had to live with worries. They could not always live the life they wanted; no matter how tough they were, they could not exist alone.

Maybe it was about time Tony was made aware of a few facts of life. He had to be, if she was ever to have a chance to show him how she felt.

Confronting him was something she had to do. He had left her without pride, but maybe pride was a luxury a woman in love could not afford. She had never been in love before, so everything she was doing now was by instinct. Her instincts could be wrong.

Pushing doubts from her mind, she stopped outside the hotel to thank Cooter for his help, then headed determinedly for the lobby stairs.

Chapter Twenty-Three

Stripped down to nothing but trousers, Tony stretched his long legs toward the foot of the bed. Black wool pulled tight against his groin, and his bare feet pressed against the footboard. The hat he had tossed on the post loomed out of the shadows of the small hotel room, as did the holstered pistol beneath it.

He snorted in disgust. Both hat and holster were too damned easy to make out. By now he should be seeing double of everything.

Tony sank a fist into the pillows propped under his head and glanced at the half-empty bottle on the bedside table. In the light from the kerosene lamp beside it, the liquor was the amber color of whiskey. It had tasted like whiskey. But it hadn't done its job. Billy Bob at the Fat Lady must be selling watered goods. It was getting so that a man couldn't depend on anything anymore.

Outside, the November wind whistled; inside, the close hotel air carried the cutting edge of that cold, but Tony made no move to cover himself with the wool blanket beneath him.

Without warning, a scene played itself in relief across Tony's mind, and not for the first time today. The image was one he had carried with him for two years, only it was sharper now that he had returned to the site of its origin. The limp figure of Jess Tucker was swinging from an oak tree; galloping toward that figure down a crowd-lined street was a desperate rider, whip flailing, horse kicking up dirt. Only when he reached his destination, he found he had arrived too late.

Tony grabbed his whiskey, then set it down hard. The liquor sloshed against the sides of the bottle. There wasn' much point in drinking. Even if he managed to forge about Jess, he would only be troubled by another image this one of the black-haired woman lying in a bed simila: to his and only a wall's thickness away.

He rubbed the pads of his fingers against his chest. He'c rather have another hand working at that particula: job . . . a pair of lips tracking the fingers . . . the firn nipples of soft breasts brushing against him . . .

Damn! He was a fool. He didn't learn his lessons well The Countess Svetlana had cast him as the villain in thei: little story and chosen to protect her brother from the avarice she had decided was Tony's prime reason for stalking him. He had come close to tossing her on the bec and giving her what they both wanted. Why in hell he hadn't was a fact that escaped him right now.

Except that for all her difficult ways the countes: deserved more than a quick romp before being imprisonec in her room. Tony still had to deal with his ghosts. Jes: seemed as real to him, and at the same time as lost, as he had ever been. Trying to cut down that tree two years ago had been stupid; he should have been looking for the mer who claimed Jess had killed the Parson, or tried harder tc find the thief who had sent Jess on his last drunken spree

The shadows against the far wall became the shadow o: a body hanging from the thick branch of a tree, a body twisting in the wind. Tony leaned over and turned dowr the wick of the bedside lamp. Darkness enveloped him and a chill whispered across his soul. Maybe he would give the whiskey one more try.

He was fumbling for the bottle when he heard a fain: knock at the door. He sat up to reach for his gun, ther paused when he heard the soft woman's voice drifting ir through the door.

"Tony?"

He should have known she could escape from her

264

enforced prison.

"The door's unlocked," he said as he stretched back on the bed.

Lana slipped inside. In the slash of light that briefly fell across her from the hall he saw she was wearing the sable coat; what surprised him was the cascade of loose, thick hair that fell against her shoulders. He had never known her to wear her hair down out of bed.

He got no chance for further detail. Her face had been in shadows, and then as she closed the door behind her, once more the room was plunged into the depths of night.

Tony's heart pounded as he pictured her fur-clad figure leaning against his door. In the dark he could hear her uneven breath. He waited for her to speak. He had to wait a while.

"I need to talk to you," she said at last.

Tony had a few things he could say about needs, but he kept quiet.

"Are you drunk?" she asked. "I can return if you are."

Tony smiled to himself. The countess liked to put things straight.

"No, I'm not drunk," he said. And then, "Don't go."

When she didn't respond right away, he said, "Did someone bring you a key?"

"I haven't seen Nicholas, if that's what you mean. I let myself out. With a hairpin."

"My mistake. I should have taken them from you."

He could almost see her answering smile.

"Did you find the doctor all right?" she asked.

"He should be checking on Boris right now."

"Good."

He sensed her hesitation and fumbled about the bedside table for a lucifer stick.

"Please, no light," she said. Again came the quiet, and at last a sigh. It drifted across the room and settled on Tony like a warm breeze. "I've been in my room trying to decide what I wanted to say. And it's not about Nicholas or Boris or the Blood of Burma or whiskey or anything else that you could even imagine. It's not even about us."

Her voice held so many layers of meaning—of tensions

265

and doubts and even tenderness—that he found himself holding absolutely still, lest she turn and run.

"It's about me, Tony," she said hesitantly. When she spoke again, her voice had grown stronger. "And about dealing with unpleasant truths. That's what you're trying to do. Please don't deny it."

"This seems a night for dealing with a lot of things," he said.

If she heard him, she gave no sign. "Boris told you a lot of things about me and the work I have been doing with my people. He made me sound so wonderful, as though I were some kind of saint. I am not. I did those things for myself as well as the workers on the estate. I needed to feel wanted. And I wanted to feel . . . . clean."

"Lana—"

"If I stop now, I might not start again. What I have to say, I have told no one. Boris observed some of it first hand. Nicholas suspected, which is why he quarreled with Papa and ran away. Papa was so sure he had seen to his daughter's future with sufficient parental efficiency. Count Stefan Dubretsky owned a neighboring estate and was known for his hunting prowess. A manly man, Papa called him. The fact that he was twice my age was of no concern. In my country, many girls marry much older men. The truth was that after Mama died, Papa didn't really know what to do with me. To have me settled and the bearer of a title must have been the answer to his prayers."

"And what about your prayers?"

Lana's sharp laugh was at odds with the tenuous sound of her voice moments before. "A dutiful daughter is not supposed to have foolish dreams of love. If I did, it was only because I had lived a dreamlike life. Riding at will about the province, a loving brother as my companion and a doting servant to cushion my falls. Visiting the Czar before the Czarina became so ill and he became the rigid ruler he is today. Until the death of my mother when I was entering adolescence, I remember only happy times. After her death, there was sadness, of course, and Papa kept himself apart. When I took to reading, it was natural that I sought love in the written word."

Tony pictured her as she must have appeared in those years, the dew of youth on her cheeks, her dark eyes starry with dreams, and he felt a tenderness he had never before experienced.

This time when she spoke her voice was harsh and flat. "I did not find love with the count."

"I've already decided he must have been a bastard. As well as a fool."

"He was . . . different. I went into my marriage intending to honor its vows. A dutiful daughter turned into a dutiful wife. Stefan—it's strange but I haven't said that name since he died. He came into my bedchamber late that first night . . . he pulled at my gown . . .

"I was so innocent. The books had not told me what to expect, but I was a country girl and I had seen the animals mate. I was also obedient and I hid my fright. He fell hard on top of me, and I remember wondering why he didn't remove his trousers completely. His breath was sour in my face, and his hands were rough and cruel. His knee thrust my legs apart, and his body seemed to rut against mine. Like the animals I had seen in the field, only we faced one another."

Her voice grew small and seemed to come from a distance.

"I thought maybe he might have an easier time, and so would I, if I turned over and he came at me from behind. But he gave me no chance to speak . . . no chance even to move. He seemed . . . disinterested in me even as he lay between my legs. At last he cursed me and fled from my room. You see how ignorant I was. For a long time I did not realize my failure was really his. He did not like . . . women."

Tony's hands tightened into fists. He could feel her pain deep inside him, like a knife twisting in his gut.

"He told you?"

"It was not necessary. Men visited him from St. Petersburg. I walked in on him once. And then there was the occasional youth on the estate."

"And what was his dutiful wife supposed to be doing all

267

this while?"

"Using the peasant youths. He suggested it once when he was drunk. I chose, instead, a life of abstinence."

Too well did Tony remember the harsh judgments he had made of Lana and her use of men, and he held himself in revulsion as much as he did the count. Wanting to embrace her until all her painful memories faded, he resisted. She was not yet cleansed of the poisonous images that ate at her.

He listened as she described the count's final assault, an attempt for a son and heir to inherit and perhaps save the crumbling Dubretsky estate.

"The mating was as hapless as before," she said. "Only this time he was almost five years older and his body dissipated with overindulgences of many kinds. He collapsed on top of me, and when he did not move I thought for one terrifying minute that I would suffocate under his weight. It was his heart, of course, although the doctor gave hints that I was to blame. A young wife, I was told, can drive an old husband right to his grave."

Lana laughed, a quick, bitter sound that Tony had never before heard issue from her. "The good doctor did not know I was without passion. The desires I had felt as a young girl when I read of brave men and beautiful women—desires I had not understood—did not return once during the years of my marriage."

"And then old Tony comes along and drags you into bed."

"You have nothing for which to apologize. Until you, I had no idea that I was like other women."

"You're not."

"Do not say that, Tony. It is important for me to know that I have the passions of life. That I have gone through my own private hell and emerged a whole woman. It is important for you to know it, too. I spoke to you first of unpleasant truths. I live with the memory of them." Lana took a long, even breath before adding, "And so must you."

The words caressed Tony in the dark. "You know about Jess Tucker." He didn't even bother to ask her how.

"I know."

Suddenly, just as Lana must have planned, the pain of Jess's hanging eased in his heart. He had carried the burden of that pain for two years—in flashes of remembrance, in dreams that assaulted him in the night. But Lana had been wed to the bastard Dubretsky more than twice as long. Daily she had been faced with the horrors of that liaison from which only death could release her. He wondered how often she must have prayed that that death would be hers.

"Please," she said softly, "could we have the light?"

Tony sat on the edge of the bed, hands trembling as he struck the match to the wick. His eyes shifted to Lana, who stood just as he had pictured her, black hair thick against the black fur of her coat, her face pale, her eyes round and dark and deep as the night.

"You pushed me away earlier, Tony. As though there was no consolation in this world for you. As though I could not offer it. For a moment as I stared at the hard look of denial in your eyes, I remembered that my husband, too, had not wanted me."

She slipped the coat from her shoulders and it fell silently to the wooden floor. She stood before him naked.

"Until you," she whispered, "I doubted that any man would. At least a man whose desires I would share."

Tony caught his breath at the magnificent, unashamed woman who offered herself to him. His eyes lowered to her bare feet, then slowly trailed upwards along the path of slender, long legs that seemed to go on forever. His gaze lingered on the triangular patch of dark hair nestled between her thighs as he remembered the treasure buried beneath.

Her hips flared out gracefully, then nipped in to a narrow waist he could span with two hands. Her arms hung loosely at her sides—arms that looked almost frail but could embrace him so tightly that he forgot the world.

Her dark-tipped breasts were full and welcoming. He wanted to wet them with his tongue, to make them glisten in the flickering light.

Her neck was arched slightly, her head tilted as if once

again she were listening to a song that no one else could hear. Her finely sculpted face with its ripe-plum eyes and high cheekbones was framed by a mane of thick, black hair, a color darkened to midnight by the ivory smoothness of her skin and the blush on her cheeks.

Her full lips were parted. He wanted to bite on that sensuous lower lip, to draw a drop of her blood, to touch it with his tongue and make her a part of him. As if she read his mind, she caught the lip between her fine white teeth.

Tony's body was rock-hard in response to hers, his own blood flowing hot and thick in his veins, and he stood to face her. "You think I did not want you earlier in your room?" His voice was husky and low, and he halved the distance between them. "And do not now?"

Lana looked up at him, unblinking. "I am not the haughty countess tonight, Tony. If you tell me to leave so that you can be with your thoughts, I will. But it will not be an easy thing for me to do." A smile tugged at her lips. "And in truth, I believe you will not ask me to go."

Tony moved closer until the tips of her breasts were almost brushing against his chest. "And I say your getting out that door will be impossible." He reached out to take a dozen loose strands of hair between his fingers. He rubbed them gently. They felt like silk.

He cupped her cheek with his hand, the pad of his thumb stroking her mouth. She turned to kiss his palm. The ball of his foot rubbed against her ankle and down the length of her foot; he felt her toes curl beneath his.

When she swayed as though she might collapse, he took her hand and led her toward the bed. She sat on the edge, and he knelt in front of her.

His hands covered her knees, his fingers splayed wide. "A woman is a beautiful, mysterious creature." His thumb stroked the tender skin of her inner thigh. "A man's body is coarse and vulgar and obvious. Not subtle and supple like a woman's."

She started to speak, but he leaned forward and brushed his lips against hers to silence her. "A man becomes a true man only when he accepts the wonder of a woman and the power of her. And the deep mystery that can drown

270

him in a world of magic unlike anything existing elsewhere in the universe."

He bent his head to kiss her thigh, his hands feathering upward toward the dark, taunting patch of hair at the base of her abdomen. Her hands tunneled in his hair, and he wondered if she would try to stop him, knowing at the same time that he would not be denied.

His lips inched closer to her womanly treasure. Her hands stroked down to his shoulders, her fingers pressing tightly against the taut muscls of his back. She seemed to push him away, then with an audible sigh held him tight against her.

He parted her legs and she lay backward on the bed, stretched out in front of him, her feet resting lightly against the floor on either side of him. There was trust and desire and the edge of hesitation mixed in her movements as he did things to her that he had never done. His tongue sought the trembling folds of flesh that beckoned him. She moaned. He left a moist trail deeper, deeper as his hands stroked her legs, her hips, and moved higher to cup both her breasts. Beneath his lips he felt her muscles tighten. Her hips rose to meet his questing tongue.

When he found the hard bud of her desire, she cried his name. He was relentless, wanting to bury himself in her, lips and teeth and tongue moving in concert as her hands kneaded his bare shoulders and her fingernails raked across his upper back.

"No!" she said and then a softer "Yes, yes," as violent tremors shook her body. Her hands gripped his arms and tugged hard at him, pulling him upwards. He burned hot and hungry kisses against the fine pubic hair, across her abdomen, and over the soft rise of her breasts, his tongue lingering on the tips until they were damp and hard and deeply pink.

Her pulse pounded at her throat as he continued his torturous way upward. At last he stretched out on top of her and covered her open lips with his. He shifted their bodies until they were stretched side by side on the bed, one trousered leg between hers. His tongue stroked hers, the roof of her mouth, her teeth, returned to dance against her

271

tongue. He couldn't get enough of her. He had not lied. She was beautiful and magical and he could drown in the subtle mysery of her.

He felt her hands pull frantically at the buckle of his belt. He separated their bodies only long enough to unfasten the catch and rake the clothes from his body. When he leaned over her once again, her palm rubbed hard against his chest, circled his nipples, and massaged its way down the length of his torso, circled in the thickening hair between his thighs, and at last held his manhood in her hand.

Her fingers stroked the tight, throbbing shaft as she pressed her lips against his neck. "A man is a magical thing, too," she whispered, her breath hot and ragged.

Tony felt the coils of passion tighten. He wanted to climax inside her. She sensed his need and, parting her legs, guided him to his desire. He thrust deep, again and again, his arms embracing her as she embraced him, her breasts spread against his chest. Her head was tucked into the crook of his shoulder, her lips hot against his throat.

He held back, in thrall with her escalating response, until he knew she was at the edge of ecstasy. He bent his head to hers and kissed her as they peaked together, wild tremors raking both their bodies.

With the last vestiges of climax skittering through him, Tony broke the kiss and opened his eyes to watch the play of passions across her lovely face. Damp hair clung to her brow, and her thick lashes pressed against cheeks grown flushed with the heat of satisfaction. He had never gazed upon a more erotic sight.

She opened her eyes to gaze up into his, and he felt himself drowning in their dark, liquid depths. Their sweat-slick bodies clung tightly together as if each were afraid to move and shatter the perfection of the moment.

At last Lana smiled, a faint curving of her lips that was visible only when the watcher was one who awaited the slightest change in her expression, the least nuance that would tell him how she felt.

"It's winter outside," she said. "Why is it that I feel the

heat of summer?" Her thumb caught a trickle of moisture at his throat. "Why do I have this urge to open the window and let in the cooling air?"

Stretching out beside her, Tony stroked the dark tendrils away from her face. "I think it's called friction. Two bodies rubbing together can cause much heat."

"And so they can." Deep in her velvet eyes registered still another shift in her mood, this one more solemn. "You didn't reject me," she said.

Tony's heart pounded at the hint of vulnerability in the once proud countess, and he was suffused with another kind of warmth, a deeply satisfying sense that she belonged in his arms.

"I didn't know how much I needed you," he said, unashamed that his own voice was as ragged as hers had been. "You know something, my hot-blooded Russian?" He feathered a kiss across her lips, then lifted his head once again. "You're smarter than I am. You knew things that old Tony should have known but didn't. I was lying in here feeling sorry for myself, grabbing for weak whiskey, and there you were picking the lock to come join me."

Her smile returned. "Women have always been more practical than men. But you learn fast. I imagine you'll catch up with me."

Tony watched her smile die, and he caught his breath. He didn't want anything to bother her now, to bring back any pain.

"As long as you're giving me credit for intelligence," she said earnestly, "then add truthfulness as well. I didn't get between you and Nicholas today. I tried to talk him out of leaving, but he moved so suddenly that I could do nothing."

"It's not necessary—"

"Oh, but it is. To me, if not to you. Because I would have helped him if he had asked me. Until he left, Nicholas was my champion and my joy. His leaving came in part because he could not help me. He tried to talk to me about the count, but for me it was too late, and Papa would not listen. When their quarrels turned ugly, my brother saw only one thing to do."

"Nick was ever an impulsive youth."

"There we agree. Would you like to know the worst part about this afternoon on the trail? After all my bragging about riding, I couldn't even control my horse. I could have killed us both."

Tony brushed his lips against the edges of her mouth. "Saving you has become a part of my day's duties. Didn't you realize that?"

"No. But it's rather a nice feeling. No one outside my family has ever really cared."

Tony shook his head in disbelief. Lana didn't yet know how special she was, a failure he needed to correct.

"You must have nothing but fools in your country. You have more passion and loving goodness in you than any other woman I've ever met."

Lana's thick lashes rested against her cheeks. "Keep talking," she said softly.

"And your body is always tight and wet and waiting for me. I fit inside just right."

"Oh." The word was half sigh, half moan.

"You are very special," Tony said, pressing his lips against her closed eyes. "Don't ever think anything else."

She lifted her lashes to gaze up at him. "You're rather special in your own coarse and vulgar way," she said, her face flushed with pleasure and arousal from his blunt words. She bit at her lower lip. "And what else is a man? Oh yes, obvious. Now that I'll go along with, if not the first two." She ran her fingers down the curls of hair that bisected his chest, lingered at the base of his abdomen, then stroked down his thigh before reversing her route.

"For instance, it's difficult sometimes for a man to know what a woman wants. But a woman?" She stroked higher, caressing his slick, hard shaft. "She's given a rather obvious clue."

Tony's body was responding as she must have known it would; he let her tell him how wondrous and magical a creature was man.

274

Chapter Twenty-Four

In an upstairs bedroom of Maxwell Shader's San Francisco home, Isabel Wright lay still beneath him while he took his satisfaction. She had never complained about these times. If she seldom received the same satisfaction from him, at least she was lying atop silk sheets on a feather mattress, which was a hell of a lot better than some of the places she had lain.

Even if the man for whom she had to spread her legs disgusted her.

Max seemed to be having a difficult time tonight . . . breathing labored and sweating like a pig. If she expected to get him off her before dawn, she would have to give him a little inspiration. Wrapping her substantial thighs around his hips and locking her ankles against his buttocks, she gripped the silk sheets and began to moan and thrash her head back and forth.

He responded as she knew he would, his body stiffening and his plunges becoming deeper and faster. He liked to think she enjoyed him, even though he never did anything to make sure she did. But she knew him well. The more she moaned, whether in pain or pleasure, the more he felt like a man.

She might be enjoying this for real if someone else were thrusting himself in her. She thought of a lean body and long, strong legs, of firm hands that knew where to touch a woman. Tony Diamond had such hands. She had heard talk. Men thought women didn't talk, but they did.

Max yelped once, twice, and with great deliberation Isabel embraced him, but only to rake her fingernails across his back. He didn't like being marked in any way, but that didn't stop her. He had left his mark on her more than a few times.

He shuddered, took great gulps of air, then lay still, his damp body heavy against hers.

Unlocking her legs and resting her arms beside her, she shut her eyes to him as he rolled away. Max was developing rolls of fat around his middle that he couldn't disguise with a corset in bed. With his thinning, gray-streaked hair plastered sweatily to his head and his face flushed from exertion, he was not a pretty sight.

What would Tony Diamond look like after sex? Conjuring up provocative images—sweat, after all, didn't have to be repulsive—Isabel licked her lips and felt a tingling warmth between her thighs. At least some parts of her weren't dead yet.

While Isabel engaged in her private fantasies, Max sat on the side of the bed and grabbed for a towel, rubbing at his chest and abdomen and between his legs. He always wiped himself clean after lying with her, as though she had soiled him in some way.

Maxwell Shader, gentleman about town. What a laugh. Max the pig was closer to the truth.

Isabel squeezed her eyes closed. For all her stoicism and practical nature, she was building up a lot of resentment. Someday she would explode. Max better watch himself. She could do him a great deal of harm.

A knock on the door ended her musings.

"You have a visitor, sir," came the voice of Max's pride and joy, the white-gloved butler that Isabel had witnessed laughing at his employer behind his back.

"Damned late for a caller," Max growled.

"He refused to give his name, sir," said the butler from the hallway. "I took the liberty of asking him to wait in the parlor. I did not think you would want such a man loitering at the front door."

276

Without so much as a glance at Isabel, Max pulled on shirt and trousers and thrust sockless feet into his shoes. Fingers raked through his damp hair, and he snapped his suspenders in place. As he exited, Isabel wished the elite of San Francisco could get a look at one of their leaders now.

Not that he would be a leader long. Isabel was very much aware that things weren't going well with him. For one thing, he used her far less often. She knew enough from her days of working in the gold field towns that impotence was a sign of failure elsewhere in a man's life.

But, in helping him with his business as he sometimes asked—it made her look respectable, he claimed, and gave her a reason for so often being around—she had also taken to snooping, reading his correspondence and his ledgers every time she got the chance, and eavesdropping when callers looked particulary suspicious. During the past few months she had added to her store of knowledge which had begun two years ago when the two of them first met.

Max had trouble picking out good investments from bad. In a city that seemed to offer opportunities to everyone, he had started out with a fortune in gold and was in danger of going broke. He backed losers and thieves— losers who misled him into unwise purchases and thieves who stole what little he managed to earn.

And always because he was trying to beat the odds.

"This vigilante committee," he had bragged once, "is going to give me connections. Introduce me to people who talk my language, business people and politicians."

"How will that do you any good?" Isabel liked to encourage his talk.

"I might take on a partner in one or two enterprises, importing maybe. Might even open a bank. That's what I would really like to own. A bank."

Wouldn't we all, Isabel had come close to retorting.

"I may even run for office."

San Francisco might as well throw away its city charter if that ever happened, she thought.

She didn't think the deals he had hoped for were coming through. The committee wasn't attracting quite the level of attention he wanted; too many people seemed to think that given some support, the police and sheriff could eventually take care of the city's problems.

Pulling on her clothes as haphazardly and quickly as Max, she padded barefoot into the hall, her auburn hair loose and tangled, made sure the snooping butler was nowhere in sight, and headed for the stairs. She didn't stop at the parlor door where Max was ensconced with his late-night visitor; instead, she went to the adjoining music room.

What a joke the room was. Max knew as much about music as he did about making love. But the room, with its piano and harp, had come with the Russian Hill house and in his mind ranked in importance right behind the butler's white gloves.

Isabel liked it almost as much as Max did, but for a far more practical reason than any culture it might further. If she moved the rather garish landscape painting that hung on the connecting wall, she had access to a small peephole that had been bored by a previous owner of the house. She could see and hear everything in the next room.

As long as the music room was lit by no more than the wall lamp beside the door, there was little chance of someone's detecting her on the other side, not unless that someone knew where to look. The peephole opening was in another painting, this one a cluster of pansies and columbines that Max had probably never given a glance. Like the landscape, it had come with the house.

The visitor stood beside Max in front of the fireplace, facing her way. He wasn't much to look at—tall and burly, wearing shabby coat and trousers and a battered hat pulled low over his eyes. What little she could see of his face was covered with a black beard.

"I spotted him," the man was saying, "plain as day walking right down the street in the middle of Sacramento. He was with a woman—looked like a queen or something with her nose in the air. There was a servant, too, looking snootier than she did."

Isabel didn't know anything about the servant, but she

278

would bet the money she had been skimming off Max that he could identify the other two.

"I knew they were headed there, fool," Max growled, reaching for the brandy bottle and pouring a stiff drink. He didn't offer one to the other man. "You shouldn't have come here just to tell me that."

"I ain't finished. He left the man and woman at the Orleans and went to the stage office. Heard him myself buying a couple of tickets for Hangtown. He got a horse for himself at the livery stable."

Max lowered his glass. Isabel could almost hear his mind creaking from gear to gear.

"Any idea where he might be headed?"

"Diamond didn't leave no itinerary." The caller dragged out each syllable in disgust.

Max drank down the brandy and paced in front of the dying fire for a few moments, his short legs moving fast, his glance never lifting from the hearth rug. He stopped once to refill his glass.

"Where's your partner?" he asked at last.

"Him and me went different ways more'n a year ago." The bearded face, still directed toward the flowers, split into a yellow-toothed grin. "Fool's probably still up in the hills somewhere looking for gold. Ernie never did have no sense."

"Damn!" Max took up his pacing once again, pausing once with his back to the visitor. Light from a nearby lamp illuminated his expression, and Isabel almost gasped out loud. Fear was unmistakable on his face.

She had seen Max a lot of ways—arrogant, mean, drunk, conniving . . . and even generous a time or two when she had done something special to please him, although those times hadn't come lately. But she had never seen him afraid.

He whirled in place. "I guess there's only one thing to do," he said. "You can make the arrangements for me."

To Isabel's chagrin, he directed the man out into the hall. Rushing to the door, she opened it a fraction and peered outside, but all she could see were the two of them

279

hunched together and moving slowly away from her.

Closing the door, she leaned against it and tried t
think. Max hated Tony Diamond and made no secret of i
at least with her. And he was jealous of him, as any man i
his right mind would be.

But fear him? Max had put something over on him once
and always acted as though he could do so again.

Max and Tony went all the way back to Hangtown
where Max had overseen the hanging of Tony's friend. Sh
knew a thing or two about the hanging that Tony woul
probably like to know. As well as the events that ha
preceded it. Thus far she had figured she was better o
with Max, mean as he was, than she would be telling wha
she knew.

But time seemed to be running out for Max . . . an
a girl had to protect herself. The difficulty lay in stayin
clear of the law.

Just then the door was shoved open and Isabel wa
catapulted into the center of the room. Startled, sh
whirled and looked into Max's smiling face.

The smile wasn't pleasant and it showed no trace o
humor.

"I trust you saw and heard enough to pique you
interest, dear Isabel," he said. Turning up the wall lamp
he closed the door behind him and stepped close. His gaz
never left her face.

She swallowed hard. "I don't know what you're talkin
about."

"Come, come, Isabel. Give me credit for more sense
You really ought to see what your eye looks like dartin
about the center of that pansy. It gave me quite a start th
first time I noticed it."

Isabel had regained control. "I didn't give you enoug
credit, Max."

"You seldom do."

She feathered the thick red curls off her neck. "I onl
wanted to keep up with things so that I might help you
Your good fortune is linked with mine, and has been fo
some time. After all," she said, "we both know too much

about each other. We can't afford to be anything less than friends."

Isabel stared at him, unblinking. She had never threatened him before, but Max wasn't entirely stupid. He would know what she meant.

Moving closer, he grabbed a lock of hair and pulled her hard against him. "You play a dangerous game, Belle."

Isabel held very still. He hadn't called her by her old name in almost two years.

His free hand began to work at the closure of his waistband.

"Upstairs didn't really do anything for me anymore than it did for you. Could it be, whore, that there's only one way you can do me any good?"

Max would have to burn in hell before she was satisfied, but Isabel was too wise to give voice to her thoughts.

"It could be," she said, licking her lips with her tongue.

"Then show me I shouldn't get rid of you. Or punish you in any way."

"Of course, Max," she said, forcing a huskiness into her voice. She could do something about her resentments later . . . if Max gave her the chance. In the meantime . . .

In meek obedience, she dropped to her knees in front of him and helped him with the fastenings of his pants.

Across town, Elizabeth Dundreary paced back and forth in her third-floor room at the Ace Hotel, listening for sounds to indicate her father had returned to his adjoining room. He was up to something other than visiting the El Dorado gaming hall this late at night. She had noticed it in his eyes at dinner tonight when he received a message he declined to share with her. She hadn't seen such a scowl on his face since the day she talked too much, and in a temper he hired the Sydney Ducks to find Nicky Case.

Papa seldom confided in her. She knew she looked like a naive young miss without a thought in the world beyond her yellow curls and latest dress. It wasn't her fault she was cursed with a dimpled face and diminutive figure; she could still outthink her father most of the time.

That was the reason she had been able to see Nicky as often as she had. When Papa thought she was at dancing class or taking tea with one of her new friends, in reality she had been pursuing the man of her dreams. Her deception had bothered her a great deal at first, but Papa was so set in his ways and would listen to none of her requests.

She had fluttered around Nicky each time she saw him at the hotel; she let him think he was seeking her. They had shared long walks on the wild San Francisco streets. He really was a most wonderful gentleman—thoughtful and charming, and he made her laugh.

The last time she had caught him was one afternoon outside the double doors downstairs after what had been for him an unfortunate session at the roulette wheel. She had consoled him . . . they had gone to his hotel room . . . one thing led to another . . . and she had been ruined.

Wonderfully ruined. Gloriously ruined. Irrevocably ruined. And not just once, but three times, and all in the space of an hour. Nicky had been apologetic after the first time, and after the next two he swore he had been taking precautions . . . Her sensibilities were such that she couldn't ask him exactly what he meant; she understood only that she would not be with child.

Nicky was truly the man of her dreams to be so considerate. He would do the right thing by her. She was convinced of it, even though words of devotion had never passed between them. And if Papa thought he could harm one golden hair on her lover's head, he was very much mistaken.

Which was why she was so worried. Clutching at the skirt of her yellow chambray dress, she continued to pace. She simply had to find out what was going on.

Footsteps in the hall halted hers. Next came the unmistakable sounds of a key in a lock, a creak, and then a slam. Papa had returned. She began immediately to knock on the inside adjoining door between their rooms.

"Papa, we must talk," she said urgently through the panel.

The door opened to reveal Lord Alfred Dundreary, not in the evening clothes and cloak he usually wore for nights on the town, but rather what he called his serviceable tweed, a new fabric he had found on their last journey to Scotland.

"Elizabeth," he grumped, "what are you doing up so late?"

"I couldn't sleep from worrying about you." She smiled prettily.

"Hmmph!"

He turned back into his room, and Elizabeth followed.

"You were upset at dinner. I know you have no one with whom to share your worries. Except me. Please let me help."

"Nothing you should worry about, child. Those cursed Australians have let me down."

Elizabeth bit her lip to hold back a smile. "The Ducks didn't find Nicky?"

"They were on his trail. Only trouble is . . ." He looked at his daughter, his forehead furrowed above bushy gray brows. "Might as well tell you the truth. That scoundrel—"

"Nicky?"

"Biggest scoundrel I know. Can't forget how he took advantage of my little girl. Now I find he gambled with that ruby when it wasn't even his. At least those Sydney fools learned that much. Case lost it to Tony Diamond first, then turned around and lost it to me."

Elizabeth's heart sank. Sometimes keeping faith in her absent hero was a difficult task.

Dundreary cleared his throat. "Don't get me wrong, child. I'm thinking of you as much as I am that jewel."

Elizabeth lowered her eyes demurely.

"Fellow ought to be shot! Told those Australians as much. They shouldn't have come back here without him."

Elizabeth looked up in alarm. "You're not sending them out to search again, are you?"

"Half a mind to. Told 'em I would make a decision by tomorrow. Nick Case is nothing more than a rake."

Elizabeth was under no delusion about what Papa would decide, and her own temper flared. "You're too harsh on him, Papa. I've tried to tell you nothing happened that I did not invite. And besides, he comes from a good family. That ought to count for something."

"Impossible!"

"Remember the Countess Alexandrovna that you liked so much?"

"Ah, yes. Fine-looking woman. Went somewhere on a journey, as I recall, about a week ago. Just because she's a fellow countryman of this Case—"

"She's his sister." Elizabeth batted her eyes.

"What?"

"His sister. She told me just before she left, and she promised that things with Nicky would be all right."

Dundreary collapsed into a chair, hands resting on his tweed-covered stomach.

"I planned to tell you about Nicky and the countess when they were both here, Papa," she added.

For once Elizabeth saw her bombastic father speechless. But not for long.

"Hmmph! Should have figured that one out." His fingers drummed on the arms of the chair. "Both Russian. Don't look much alike, one fair and the other dark, but that don't necessarily mean much. Your mother was dark-headed, too, but look at you."

Elizabeth knelt in front of him and stilled one of his hands with her own. "And yet you say I am like her in many ways. Well, Nicky is like his sister. Kind and good. Why won't you believe me?" Gone were all attempts at girlish pretense. She spoke from her heart.

Dundreary's scowl softened as he looked down at her. "You're young, child. Innocent in the ways of the world. Nick Case dallied with you and ran up large gambling debts. Both unconscionable acts. If he is a man of honor, then he must be made to do the right thing."

"Are you thinking of marriage?" Elizabeth asked, wide-eyed. It could be that something good would come out of all this near disaster.

"Most certainly not! The debt absolutely must be paid. As for you, I want only to make it clear that he is never to come near you again. Or any other innocent young girl, for that matter."

Elizabeth's hope died as quickly as it had been born. Papa was impossible! She stood and put distance between them, letting him know by a scowl as fierce as his that she could not accept his judgment. She knew full well that on her cursed face the scowl wouldn't be very intimidating, but Papa would get the message.

"I want your promise, Papa, that you will leave Nicky alone when he returns. In return"—her voice caught for a moment—"I promise not to see him again."

Dundreary shook his head—slowly and sadly, Elizabeth thought.

"Can't do that, my dear. The man must be taught a lesson. I can promise only to have the Australians await him here in San Francisco instead of in the mountains."

"But he might return with the countess," argued Elizabeth, quickly becoming desperate. "They could do her harm, too."

"I will, of course, instruct them to concern themselves only with her brother. And to use only the physical force absolutely necessary to bring him to me. But the debt is a matter of family honor, a fact that the countess no doubt understands. She will also understand the harsh methods to which I have been forced."

Dundreary stood and stared ponderously at his daughter. "We are in a wild, uncivilized country, Elizabeth, and must resort to uncivilized means to see that justice is served."

Elizabeth could only stare at him in dismay. Papa was such an innocent. He might think he could instruct those ruffians in the fine points of performing their tasks, but she very much doubted that they would understand.

Chapter Twenty-Five

Lana soaked up the last drop of syrup on her plate with the last bite of flapjack, debated whether she was really still hungry after the biscuits, bacon, and eggs that had preceded this last course, then set down her fork.

"Enough," she said with a satisfied sigh.

"Now that's a word I didn't hear last night."

She looked slyly at Tony, who sat opposite her in the small Hangtown cafe. Her eyes trailed down his lean face to the wiry dark curls barely visible in the open throat of his shirt. "I must have a greater appetite for some things than I do for others," she said at last.

Tony glanced at the scattered dishes that rested on the table between them. "I'd say we both have all sorts of appetites."

Finishing his third cup of coffee, he shifted back in the chair opposite her, his long legs stretched out beneath the table until his boots touched hers, his gaze settled on her face. Thick, black hair swept low across his forehead, and there was a rough, sleepy look deep in his dark eyes that said he had spent a good night . . . and that the goodness had nothing to do with rest.

Remembering a few of the details, Lana found the one-room cafe suddenly warm, and she loosened the collar of her scarlet jacket. As far as she was concerned, the early morning hours had almost equaled the night, otherwise they would have made it to the cafe sooner, before the other

287

customers had left.

Tony grinned, and her heart skipped a beat. Love overflowed in her heart, so much that she almost spoke the words out loud that would tell him how she felt. But in their hours of wakefulness, hours she had spent in his arms, they had spoken no words of love, and Lana would not pressure him with avowals that he might not welcome.

"I found out a few things about Nick yesterday," he said. "After I left you securely locked in your room."

Lana ignored his sarcasm. "What did you learn?" she asked, glad that they could speak about Nicholas so casually.

"He'd been into town for supplies when we met him on the trail. And he'd stopped for a spell at the poker tables. It was his second trip away from the cabin."

"How was his luck?"

"Not bad. Not as good as yours, of course."

"I've been lucky in several ways," she said, and meant it.

Tony's eyes glittered. "You're quite a woman. Have I ever told you that?"

"You were speaking of Nicholas, I believe."

"Right. When we saw him, there must have been only one destination in his mind."

Lana grew solemn as her eyes stared blankly at the cluttered table. She folded her hands together at the edge, recalling how determined Nicholas had been to get away.

"The cabin, of course," she said. "And I suppose you want to go there, too."

She watched his eyes for signs of distress, wondering if he were quite ready to return to another place that held so many memories for him. She hoped he would say no, both for her sake and for his. Another night or two spent in Tony's hotel room might strengthen the fragile bonds between them.

She shook away the thought. Her purpose was to find Nicholas, not play out the fantasies that had suddenly crowded into her mind.

"You do want to go there, don't you?" she asked.

"I want to do what's right for you." Shoving the dishes

288

aside, Tony leaned forward to cover her hands with his. His thumb rubbed against her wrist. "Your heart is pounding."

"It must be the altitude," she said, locking her eyes with his. "It's been doing that since last night."

He lifted her other hand and placed it against his wrist. "It must be. I think mine is doing the same thing."

"Did you know," she said, unwilling to let go of the mood between them, "that your hands are rougher than they were in San Francisco? You must hold tight to the reins."

He took one of her hands between both of his and rubbed gently. "Are they too rough?"

The tingling that began in Lana's toes traveled up to her face and skittered down her spine.

"They have an interesting texture," she managed, then bit at her lower lip.

"We must discuss this again sometime when you can show me exactly what you mean."

Lana swallowed. "In the meantime, we better concentrate on—"

"Mornin', ma'am!"

The rasping, cheery greeting brought an end to Lana's reply. Pulling her hand free, she looked away from Tony and into the grizzled face of Cooter, her escort to the Fat Lady Saloon. He stood close beside her in the same oversized jacket and rubber boots he had worn last night. Lifting his misshapen felt hat, he grinned a toothless grin.

"Good morning," she said.

Cooter kept his eyes on Lana, giving Tony not so much as a single glance. "Anytime you need help again, just call on old Cooter here. Be glad to oblige. Folks are still talking about you and that gun."

Lana cleared her throat, well aware of the curious eyes resting on her from across the table.

"Thank you for the offer."

Cooter slapped the hat back on his head. "As I said, anytime. Saw you sittin' in here and wanted to let you know." Still grinning, he turned and made for the cafe door, his boots shuffling noisily against the wooden floor.

Lana turned back to Tony with a shrug. "There are some very interesting residents of Hangtown. Very friendly."

"Always seemed a little withdrawn to me. I'd like to hear how you and Cooter met. And maybe something about the gun."

"It was all very innocent and safe," she said with a wave of her hand, then hurried on. "Now about the cabin . . ."

Tony eyed her speculatively. "The cabin. Of course. We'll need to get some supplies of our own. In case Nick isn't waiting for us with supper on the stove."

Lana laughed, unable to picture her brother engaged in anything so domestic. "I'm surprised he hasn't starved to death staying out there by himself." A sudden thought struck her. "You don't suppose he's not alone, do you?"

"You're thinking he might have a woman with him? I suppose he could."

Lana dismissed the thought. "Forget I mentioned it. He has other worries on his mind. And I can't help thinking he just might hold some affection for Elizabeth Dundreary. Nicholas is no saint, but as far as I know he has never ruined an innocent girl."

"You love your brother very much, don't you?"

"I told you last night, Tony, how I feel about him."

"Your champion and your joy." The words came out as though they had been at the front of Tony's mind since she had said them. Before she could respond, he grabbed for his hat and coat resting beside her sable on the chair between them. "Shall we go get those supplies?" he asked. "We'll get you to him as fast as we can."

If Lana didn't know better, she would think Tony was jealous of her affection for Nicholas. The thought led to interesting speculation . . . and foolish speculation as well. There was no need to wonder if Tony loved her. If he did, he could have told her last night. Tony wasn't a man to keep his thoughts to himself.

Outside the leaden sky pressed low on the clapboard buildings of Hangtown, and for all its stillness, the air was bitterly cold. Along the sidewalk, men loitered, some glancing their way, most looking down into the patches of dirty snow as if they could find what they sought at their feet. Lana figured there would be no prospecting today for the ones who operated out of town.

They turned in the direction of the hotel and ran into Dusty John.

"Good morning, Countess," he said with a knowing nod, then almost as an aside, "Tony, how are you?"

"Good morning, John," Tony said. He looked at Lana, a question in his eyes. "Another friend?"

She nodded innocently. "As I said, it's a friendly town."

"Apparently so." He tugged at the brim of his felt hat to settle it low on his forehead. The position accented the thickness of his black brows and the depths of his eyes.

The prospector glanced from Tony to Lana and back to Tony again. "No need to tell me how you are," he said to him. "You don't seem wrapped in baling wire this morning."

Tony slowly looked away from her to settle a curious glance on Dusty John. "And I did yesterday?"

John scratched at his beard. "Tight, son. Real tight. Leave it to a woman to take care of a man's troubles. A good woman, that is."

"Either she takes care of them," Lana said, giving a sidelong look at Tony, "or she causes more."

Dusty John cackled. "Mighty right, Countess. Mighty right." He hit Tony in the arm with his fist. "Take care of her, you hear? Maybe see you two later at the Fat Lady." He grinned, then turned and strode off down the sidewalk, winding in and out among the loitering men.

Lana cleared her throat and pulled the sable tight around her. Lord, but Tony had penetrating eyes. And, she noticed with pleasure, a very forceful pair of lips. She had noticed them the first time she saw him. He had manly lips, not at all feminine. They went with his strong chin. And the rest of his face. He had been put together very well.

She especially liked the way his nostrils flared when he was trying to figure her out. They had flared a lot since the

291

two of them had met.

He bent his head to hers. "You keep looking at me like that, Svetlana Alexandrovna, and we'll never make it to the cabin."

That didn't seem at all a bad idea to her . . . except that they couldn't postpone any longer the confrontation with Nicholas. The more she looked at Tony, the more she realized that her love for him was forever. And there was trouble between the two most important men in her life.

She lifted the high wool hat she had been carrying and shoved it on her head. "Just tell me what to do. You are in charge."

Tony choked. "I'll remind you of that."

He led her to the general store halfway to the hotel and began giving orders to the clerk the way he sometimes did to her. She was relieved to see the clerk minded better, or else they would never get their supplies.

Feed for the horses came first, then flour, sugar, salt, coffee, beans, a package of fresh beef that Lana promised herself Tony wouldn't touch until she had prepared it . . . and the inevitable jerky. She planned to ask him sometime if he really found it palatable. If so, the man had no taste.

He surprised her by going back to the dry goods and rummaging through a stack of trousers and shirts. Every now and then he looked over at her, then rummaged some more. At last he settled on a pair of britches and a red flannel shirt.

"We may be at the cabin for a while," he said as he paid for the supplies. Lana was shocked at the amount of the bill. If Tony kept spending money like this, she would have to find another faro game.

"Deliver everything to the stable," he told the clerk, then once more led her out to the street. "The Fat Lady is next."

He seemed not at all surprised when she turned in the right direction and paused before the swinging doors. Nor did his eyebrows lift so much as a fraction when Billy Bob nodded at Lana instead of him. He did look bemused, however, when a couple of men at one of the front tables shifted their chairs away from the bar and stared warily at her.

"I know," Tony said without expression. "You'll tell me later."

To the bartender he said, "I'd like some real whiskey, if you know what I mean, Billy Bob, and a bottle of your best brandy."

"Yes, sir!" Billy Bob snapped. He nodded at Lana. "Morning, ma'am. The same brand all right?"

Lana swallowed. "That will be fine." She hadn't planned to tell Tony all of the particulars concerning her foray last night, but she was fast changing her mind.

They left town within the hour, this time with a pack mule in tow, and retraced their route up the steep incline that led to the fork in the mountain trail. When they came to the bend where Lana had almost gone over the edge— with Tony at her side—she couldn't keep from glancing down the sharp drop-off. Jagged granite rocks broke the line of snow, with an occasional tree or brush blocking what might have been the downward path of their narrowly averted fall.

She settled back in the saddle and urged her mare up the winding trail. Waiting where the smaller trail forked off into the thick pines were Tony and the pack mule.

"Stay close behind," Tony warned. "Part of the way is difficult."

His hat still sat low over his eyes, but she could see the solemnity of his gaze. Yesterday his look had been one of despair as he contemplated returning to the cabin he and Jess had built. It seemed to her that he had come a long way in burying his ghosts.

They both looked for tracks that Nicholas might have left, picking out a few at the base of the hill where the trail flattened and ran along the bed of a frozen creek. When a light snow began to fall, she knew that all signs of the path her brother had taken would soon be gone.

Just as Tony had told her yesterday, the well-formed but narrow trail ended at the base of a ravine, and they began to make their way once more upward, eastward it seemed to her, through the thick pines and the green-crowned trees that Tony told her were madrones.

The horses worked hard, and Tony and Lana stopped often to let them rest. Even at this high altitude and with the snow settling silently around them, the animals were covered in sweat. Always they moved deeper into the wilderness of ravines and peaks and frozen streams.

"We're really heading back in the general direction of Hangtown," he explained once. "But this is the only possible way to get where we're going. Jess and I scouted this area thoroughly the spring we settled in."

Pine and madrone turned to fir but always they stayed well below the timberline. There was no sun by which to judge the time, but Lana figured it must be getting late afternoon, and she wondered how much farther they had to go, and how much higher in the mountains.

She should have trusted Tony.

"We're almost there," he said.

He nodded to the left toward a seemingly impenetrable wall of granite, then reined the gelding across a flat, shallow patch of virgin snow in that direction. As Lana rode close, she saw a fissure in the granite that had not been visible from more than a few feet away, given the jagged way the rock was formed.

She glanced at the fast-disappearing tracks behind them. When she turned once more to follow, Tony, gelding, and pack mule had disappeared.

"Tony!" Her call for help was instinctive.

There was no answer, and she flicked the reins of the mare, urging her toward the narrow fissure. Closer still, she realized the opening was wider than she had first realized and seemed to lead into a cave. Waiting inside for her was Tony.

"I said keep close," he reminded her. She gave him no argument.

They rode deeper into the darkness, the air warm compared to the frozen outside. Lana blinked at what appeared to be a light in the distance, and for the second time she altered her assessment of their route. What had first appeared to be a cave was actually a natural tunnel that cut downward through the mountain. On the far side they exited into an enclosed valley, across the center of which wound still another frozen creek.

Wedged high against one of the slopes at the far end of the valley was a small wooden structure. It was the first man-made object they'd seen since leaving Hangtown and if it lacked a ribbon of smoke curling out of the chimney and a welcoming wave from a fair-haired brother, still it was a beautiful sight.

She glanced at Tony and let out a sigh of relief. The lines of his face were relaxed, and his lips were settled in the hint of a smile. He seemed as glad to arrive at the cabin as she.

"Did you ever give the place a name?" she ventured.

He turned to her, and she saw the smile had traveled to his eyes. "Never did. Maybe you can think of one while we're here."

"I'll give it some thought." Her gaze settled on those manly lips. "But I might need some inspiration."

"I'll see what I can do."

They made their way along the path cut by the creek.

"In spring," Tony explained, "the water roars over the precipice and comes close to flooding the valley sometimes. That's why we built the cabin so far up the hill. And there's another cave near there that we turned into a stable during the bitter cold. Keeps the horses nice and warm."

The farther they rode into the valley, the thicker fell the snow, as if challenging them to make the last hundred yards. The horses and pack mule labored through the deepening drifts. Neither Lana nor Tony spoke until they came to the cave halfway up the far rise. The enclosure proved to be twenty feet wide and twice as deep. Compared to the outside air, it was cozily warm.

Protected from the storm, Lana tossed her valise to the ground, unsaddled the mare, and proceeded to rub her down. Tony did the same with the gelding and mule, then spread out some of the precious feed.

"We'll melt down some snow for them. There used to be

a trough in here somewhere. Jess's idea." Tony stomped around the dark interior. "Here it is," he called. "We'll find out soon enough if it'll hold water."

Loaded down with supplies, they sloughed through the drifts toward the cabin some fifty yards away. The door, still tight in its frame, creaked as Tony pulled it open and gestured for Lana to go inside.

She knew as soon as she entered that Nicholas had been there, but how recently she couldn't tell. The dust and cobwebs of the years were not there; neither was the stale air that should have assailed them. It had been Nicholas, all right, who had made the small cabin habitable. She couldn't have explained to a stranger how she knew, but she did. She felt his presence in the room.

Against the back wall, the one wedged against the hill, were two bunks, end to end. On one was a rumpled blanket, as though a sleeper had just been disturbed. To the right was a long stone fireplace which covered most of the wall. On one side of the hearth was a stack of cut wood, on the other a low shelf holding cups and plates and a cast-iron skillet. A blackened pot hung from a nail above the shelf. A rough-hewn table, flanked by two benches, occupied the center of the room.

Lana walked toward the fireplace. Bending, she took off her glove and fingered the gray-white ashes; they were cold.

She looked back over her shoulder at Tony. "He's been here, but I don't think for several days."

"He'll come back."

Lana stood and removed the sable coat, tossing it onto the nearest bunk. "What makes you so sure?"

"You're here. If he doesn't know it now, he'll figure it out soon enough."

At that moment the whistling of the wind became a roar and it seemed to reach down the chimney for them. Through the single, rattling window at the opposite end of the room she could make out only a white blanket of snow.

She shivered more from the sight and sound than from

the cold. It seemed the most natural thing in the world to turn to Tony for reassurance. "The storm is getting worse."

His eyes didn't waver from hers. "I'd better see to a fire and water the horses."

Her breath caught in her throat. "We could be here for days."

"I know. It's why I laid in so many supplies."

Lana turned her gaze back to the swirling world of white outside the window. "Maybe we should have stayed in the hotel."

Tony shook his head. "Too many people around stirring up too many memories. And I figured I could handle those memories better out here."

"Any other reason?"

Tony shrugged. "Could be. As soon as we get settled in, Countess, maybe you could help me figure out how we might pass the time."

to, until he seemed the most natural thing in the world to keep to their reservations. "The scene is rather worn..."

His eyes didn't move, but when... "and here, are you for one more the figure."

"The breath came in a bad mutter... We could be like an deep..."

"I found it's why I hate to so idiotic simplistic."

Lana turned her eyes back up in wonderments of when outside the window. "Maybe we should have stayed in the hotel."

Zoey shook his head. "That many people around getting up too many reviewing... And I figured I could handle these problems better out here."

"So what now?"

Lori shrugged. "I guess. As soon as we get settled in. Chances, maybe you could help me figure out how we must pass all this."

Chapter Twenty-Six

In the dark surrounding the cabin a winter storm raged, but Tony, stretched out in front of the hearth beside Lana, was hardly aware of it. He had other things on his mind.

Propped on one elbow, he reached across her and ran a langorous palm across her bare flesh—from the inside curve of her bent knee to the outside of her thigh, slowing as he passed her hip, then coming to rest against the gentle rise of her breast where it began to form just under her arm.

"Now just what did you mean in the cafe this morning about the texture of my hand?" he asked.

Lana snuggled against the black downy pelt of sable that lay beneath their naked bodies, and in the process managed to settle closer to him. Under the coat were a couple of wool blankets and the side-by-side mattresses from the two bunks.

Her smile was feline as she looked up at him. The wildness of her long, loose hair gave emphasis to the delicate lines of her face. Light from the fire flickered across her body, causing enticing shadows in its long curves and subtle valleys, and was reflected in her ripe-plum eyes.

"You mean the roughness," she said, her voice pleasantly ragged to his ears. "It's difficult to put into words." Her tongue played along her lips. "When you . . . do that with your palm somehow it sort of catches against the skin. Lingers instead of slipping on by. Sets the nerves to tingling."

She feathered the pad of her finger against Tony's bristled chin and down the taut curve of his neck, stopping when she reached the hollow of his throat. "You know what I mean by tingling nerves?"

"I think I do." Tony's thumb brushed against the tip of her breast. "Sort of like that."

Lana caught her breath. "Sort of."

Tony resisted the urge to pull her under him and plunge deep into her welcoming warmth. Not that he wasn't able to. His body stayed ready for Lana; she had made him a strong and willing man.

But they had just finished a long and thorough, and very spontaneous lovemaking. Mute testimony to the suddenness of their passion was in the scattered clothes that lay on the cabin floor around them and in the half-eaten meal still on the table. As both agreed, they had appetites of many kinds.

Tony still couldn't believe what a glorious woman Lana was. Beautiful. Sensitive. Passionate. And surprising. He had always thought he preferred predictable women. Lana had changed his mind.

For the past two years he had been warning himself not to get close to anyone. With Lana, the closeness came naturally. And felt right. Even when they fought—and he was under no illusions that all their disagreements were behind them—he never really wanted to put distance between them, not on a permanent basis.

He moved his hand to cup her breast, a gesture of possession, and was rewarded by a soft moan from deep in her throat.

Outside, the night wind gathered in force and lashed at the small cabin. The door shook in its frame.

Lana's hand fanned out across Tony's chest, and his muscles tightened under her gentle touch.

"The storm is getting worse," she said softly.

"Worried about Nick?"

"He's a Russian, too, remember? He knows about winter storms."

"Then worried about us, maybe. Jess and I spent one winter here. The place is airtight enough."

The warmth in her eyes deepened. "I'm not worried at all. The cabin is like you, Tony. Sturdy and strong and dependable."

"Don't credit me with more than I can deliver."

"You haven't disappointed me yet," she whispered.

"I could say the same thing about you."

Tony slipped his hand to her waist, then let his eyes move from the thick hair spread across the sable to the curve of her breasts to the black patch nestled against her ivory thighs, and on to the bare foot that was resting on top of his. "If I can't get to more firewood after a day or two, though, you might have to put on some clothes."

Lana sighed. "I knew the place couldn't be perfect."

Tony nestled her closer to him until he felt the length of her body pressed against the length of his, soft flesh against hard musculature. His body took notice of each place that they touched.

"You sound complacent," he said, knowing his rough-edged voice sounded far from the same. "Mind telling me what happened to the haughty countess I met in the Gut Bucket Saloon?"

"You took her to bed, that's what."

"Ah, yes. I knew something like that had happened."

Lana's hand curled into a fist and she struck him in the chest. "And what happened to the arrogant Californian who challenged me at every turn?"

"You taught him better things to do than fight."

Her voice grew small. "I rather miss him in a way."

Suddenly she wrapped her arms around his chest and clung tightly, her head bent beneath his chin. "Thank you, Tony." Her voice was muffled, and for a moment Tony couldn't believe he heard her right.

"What are you talking about?" he whispered into her hair.

"For helping me to know myself. For helping me to be unafraid."

"You afraid? The woman who faced a room of

gambling Celestials? The woman who invaded a ghost town shack occupied by two armed desperados with nothing more than a single-shot dueling pistol?"

She nodded, the long tendrils of her hair riffling against his chest. "The same. I wasn't terrified by them. They were just men." She paused. "No offense intended."

"None taken."

"I was afraid of myself. Or of life. I suppose it amounts to the same thing."

Tony buried his hand in her hair, then stroked the length of her back with his thumb, beginning with the base of her neck and moving slowly down, ridge by ridge, to the base of her spine. His hand spread across her buttocks as he pulled her tight against him, his rigid sex pressed against her abdomen.

"Were you afraid of that?"

"I . . . didn't realize its power." She shifted her hips provocatively, then lifted her head until their lips were separated by no more than a whisper. Her eyes smoldered into his. "I didn't realize my power, either. Am I driving you a little crazy right now?"

Tony had to force himself to think, and his voice came out ragged and rushed. "Not so crazy I don't know what to do."

"So what's taking you so long?"

"Saucy wench. Is it an arrogant Californian you want to order you about? An arrogant Californian you've got."

Her only response was a grin.

"I can see I've got you terrified. Well, Countess, you can begin by lying back and making yourself available."

She bit her lip. "Is that an order?"

"Damned right it is."

"Let me know if I do anything wrong," she said, reclining against the fur and closing her eyes.

Tony smiled. She wasn't doing a thing about which he could complain, and he moved a hand between her thighs in search of the moist treasure that awaited him. One finger slipped inside her, then another. He stroked in and out, watching the passions play on her face, the captured

302

breath, the fluttering eyes. When perspiration beaded on her upper lip, he leaned down to lick it with his tongue.

"Now tell me that you like it," he whispered into her mouth.

"I . . . like it." Her words came out tremulous and slow.

She caught his lips with hers and clung tightly to him, her breasts flattened against his chest, her tongue dancing with his.

She broke the kiss. "Now, Tony, now," she whispered breathlessly into his mouth.

"Is that an order?" His palm pressed against her mound and rubbed slowly back and forth. "For a while, we'll do what I want."

Her head dropped back, and a grating moan sounded in her throat.

Tony was merciless. Palm and fingers rubbed against her, spreading her woman's secretions into the secret, yielding folds of her body. Her breathing became a shallow pant, her face flushed with a glow of dawning rapture.

"I want to watch you," he whispered huskily. He echoed her words of a moment ago, only with a meaning of his own. "Now, Lana, now."

His probing fingers played against her body in rhythm with the thrust of her hips, the short gasps that escaped her lips. Her eyes were squeezed shut, thick lashes resting against pink cheeks. He leaned down to brush his face against her swollen breasts and take one dark pink tip between his lips and teeth.

Her pleasure became his sweet torture; when waves of rapture washed over her, he watched the heat of passion tighten the lines of her face and took that rapture as his own.

Bending against his body, she clung to him, her face pressed to his damp chest, her breath a burning whisper against his skin. When at last she lifted her head and looked into his eyes, he saw all that he had wanted to see.

"You are a cruel taskmaster," she said, her lips forming a tentative smile.

He felt her fingers trail against his hip and move in delicate, enticing strokes to his abdomen.

"Not waiting for orders?" Tony asked.

"I am here to serve as best I can."

When she took him in her hand, he made a move to stop her. Pressing his lips against her neck, he whispered words of encouragement, guided her in what pleasured him, and when he could take the torture no longer, shifted his weight on top of her and plunged into her dark, welcoming depth.

In response her legs wrapped around his waist and her hips lifted to welcome each quickening thrust. He was lost in a world of velvet darkness, a rush of sensation unlike all others, intense and violent and beautiful. A cry tore from his throat at the moment of climax; he heard an answering cry.

Even as the shudders subsided and their gasps for air turned to soft, pleasurable sighs, Tony could not let her go, and he kept her wrapped in his embrace. Somehow the spirit of the Countess Svetlana Alexandrovna of St. Petersburg had worked its way beneath the skin of a California hustler—for that's how Tony saw himself— and had become a part of him, her breath his breath, her blood his blood, her joy his. The goodness that he saw in her became his goodness and made him a better man.

And he would tell her so, once the troubles with her brother and the misunderstanding about that damned ruby were settled. He didn't want to claim sainthood just yet. When Nick showed up again, Tony would take the Blood of Burma that was rightfully his, then place it in Lana's hand. Lana's firm yet womanly, long-fingered hand. She would curl those fingers around the jewel and realize the truth. He wanted nothing more than her.

Tony could see the scene playing out in no other way. From the opposite side of the world Lana had come to him; with a momentary anguish that cut into his contentment, he wondered how he could ever let her go.

*　　　*　　　*

The second afternoon of their snowbound stay in the cabin, Lana, wearing her scarlet riding habit and with her hair swept up into a chignon at the top of her head, met Tony at the door. He was carrying a load of logs and there were chips of wood clinging to the tightly curled threads of his black wool coat. His lean face held the shadow of bristles that he got every day about this time. The snow had stopped falling and she estimated the temperature outside had dropped to near zero, yet the black hair at his neck was damp with perspiration.

She took off his hat and tossed it onto the table, noticing the same spiked locks clinging to his forehead. He claimed to need a haircut, but thus far she had declined to perform that particular service—no matter how arrogant and demanding he became. Other services, gladly, but not that one. She rather liked the way the dark waves brushed against his collar and the way they curled around her fingers when she encircled his neck and pulled him close for a kiss.

She stepped aside and watched as his long stride took him to the few remaining stacks of firewood beside the hearth.

"Are the horses all right?" she asked, her eyes on the strong hands that placed the logs in neat stacks.

"Restless, but watered and fed." He added several pieces of the new wood to the fire.

"So am I," she said.

He glanced over his shoulder, his dark brows raised in question. "Watered and fed?"

"No, foolish man. Restless."

He grinned, and Lana's heart skipped a beat. He stood to face her. Removing his coat, he tossed it on the table beside his hat. "Anything I can help with?"

Lana let her eyes drift down from his face to the hint of chest hair at his throat, to the breadth of his chest and the flat abdomen, down the length of his strong legs, and back up again to where the stretch of his pants cupped his manhood.

She licked her lower lip. "You help?" She moved a

305

reluctant gaze back to his face. "Most definitely. I've decided it's my turn."

Tony's eyes narrowed. "To do what?"

"To give the orders. As I remember it, you were giving them last night."

"And you responded very well." His eyes took in the arrangement of hair that she had been working on and the smooth fit of her clothes. He didn't stop until he had moved down to her booted feet and back up to her face. "Playing games, Countess?"

"In a way."

Lana felt herself blush. She had never in her life done anything so wantonly brazen, not even with Tony. Her visit to his Hangtown hotel room had been motivated by a need to help him, but not now.

Her blush faded into a different kind of glow. She wanted to be silly and sensual and to immerse herself in the pleasures of the flesh. In this mountain isolation she felt the restrictions of the past lift from her, and she was giddy with the release.

"I'm yours to command," Tony said, his rough-edged voice wrapping around her like an embrace.

Lana flicked insolent eyes at him. "It's about time. First, I would like a bath. I trust there's some sort of receptacle around here somewhere. Thus far you've been so well equipped."

"A personal comment, Countess, or were you speaking about the cabin?"

"Whatever," she said with a wave of her hand.

She freed the top button of her jacket, then stopped. Tony was standing close, his eyes locked on her fingers.

"The water, remember?" she said.

"Of course." He brushed against her as he moved past to go outside.

"Your coat," she reminded him as he opened the door.

"I'm warm enough. Besides, I won't be long."

She delayed undressing until he had returned with a shallow tub half filled with snow. The tub bore the signs of rust in its seams.

"It's not porcelain, of course," he said with a shrug, "but I cleaned it out as best I could."

As he placed the tub in front of the roaring flames, she watched the rippling movement of muscles beneath his shirt. He turned to face her. "That ought to be ready before long. The fire is pretty hot."

The fire wasn't the only thing, Lana thought.

"I am reminded of an old Russian tale," she said, her fingers once again resting on the buttons of her jacket. "It's called the Snow Maiden and tells of a barren couple who are given a snow girl brought to life as their child. She mates with a man and then melts." Lana blinked innocently at him. "You have called me cold before—"

"It's been a long time."

"I wanted to ask only this. Do you think the same thing might happen to me?"

Tony shrugged. "Let's just keep experimenting and find out, shall we?"

"I thought perhaps you might say that."

Lana took her time undressing, letting Tony watch. It was still strange to her to be so intimate with a man, yet there was no shame in what she did. It was as though she was being repaid in pleasure for all the lonely years of her marriage.

But it was more than pleasure, or even passion, that she received. It was a feeling of belonging, of rightness, a sense of having at last come home.

Which of course was absurd. She might not melt like the maiden in the folktale, but the snow outside most certainly would. And then the world would intrude.

With his sleeves rolled to his elbows, Tony sat cross-legged on the floor by the tub, occasionally testing one hand in its fast melting contents as he watched first her jacket and then her divided skirt join his jacket and hat on the table. Then came the chemise, and Tony, his eyes on her bared breasts, sank one wrist into the cold water.

"Any particular reason you're doing that?" Lana asked.

He merely shrugged.

The remaining undergarment was one she had altered to accommodate the divided skirt, a petticoat slashed in two and then sewn up like two loose pants legs. With the lone hook unfastened at her waist, it slipped easily down her hips and pooled at her feet.

Tony's other wrist joined the first.

"Warm enough?" Lana asked. "The water, that is."

"Almost." In one lean, lithe motion he stood to heat the poker in the flames, then plunged it into the melted snow. He repeated the process, replaced the poker, and gestured to the tub. "Countess, your bath awaits."

Purposefully she let her breasts brush against his arm as she stepped into the tub. When she sat, she had to bend her knees to fit, but just as Tony had indicated, the water was warm. The corrugated surface was rough under her buttocks, but with Tony rubbing a rag across her back and with his breath hot on her neck, she decided that porcelain was greatly overrated; she much preferred tin.

Splashing the soothing water over her legs and body, she rolled her head back, a satisfied smile stealing across her face.

"Let me know if I'm doing anything wrong," Tony said as he rubbed the rag lower down her spine.

"I will. Maybe a little brandy in a few minutes." She purred contentedly. "Not right now."

"We can only trust that Billy Bob gave us a kind suitable for the countess."

Lana's conscience struck her. Mention of the bartender brought remembrances of the Fat Lady, of Cooter, and of Dusty John. This seemed as good a moment as any for confession—a moment that might put a quick end to any criticisms he might make—and, sitting straighter in the tub, she told him about her evening journey to the saloon.

Tony stopped the langorous designs he was making on her back. "You waved the gun around?"

"It convinced the gentlemen to leave me alone."

His voice grew solemn. "And John told you what happened to Jess.''

''John told me.'' Lana forced her voice to be light. ''And I decided in my own countess like way that you weren't the only one with a sad story.'' She let her eyes meet his for one brief moment and saw understanding in their depths. ''And so here we are,'' she said, looking away from him and into the flames.

Tony brought the rag around her neck and down over first one breast, and then the other. ''So here we are.''

When the rag dipped past her waist and settled on her abdomen to rotate in widening circles, she covered his hand with hers. ''I'm ready to get out now,'' she said huskily.

''Is that an order?''

She nodded, and they both stood. Wrapping her damp body in a blanket, Tony lifted her into his arms and carried her to one of the narrow bunks.

''Do you think we will fit?'' she asked, casting a dubious glance at the mattress.

''Ah, the countess planned on both of us in the bed.''

She glanced sideways at his face. ''Some servant you are. You can't even read my mind.''

Lana had no trouble reading his. The passion was there to read in the glowing depths of his dark eyes.

He held her close against his chest. ''Consider this, Countess,'' he said, and she reveled in the roughness of his voice. ''We will not be lying side by side. If it is your wish, I can place myself on top of you. Or perhaps it is your desire to reverse our positions.''

''An interesting idea. We must compare the two. First—''

Her voice broke, and she found herself unable to keep up her pretense. Tightening her hold on him, she pressed her lips against his cheek and chin, then ran her tongue around the edges of his ear. The sweat from his work outdoors tasted salty on her tongue.

A low moan sounded in his throat, and she was swept with such a longing that she almost wept for joy. She bent her head and whispered against his neck, *''Yah vahs*

309

loobloo, Tony."

I love you.

When he placed her gently on the bunk and began to undress, she read on his face an expression of the same longing, the same needs that must surely be visible on hers. A sense of regret lingered in her heart for only a second. He had not understood her words.

Chapter Twenty-Seven

"I can't believe you bought these for me!"

Lana stared down at the dark blue men's trousers she had managed to work up over her woman's hips. The bottom of the trouser legs rested in folds over her bare feet. Her breasts were covered with a lacy undergarment, and in her opinion she looked ridiculous.

It was morning on the third day of their isolation, and she was standing beside the bunk she sometimes shared with Tony. Glancing to where he sat sprawled across one of the benches in the center of the small room, she shook her head.

Tony brought his lean body upright, stood, and made a slow circle around her, lingering at the rear. "I rather like them," he said.

She cast a sardonic look over her shoulder. "And I rather thought you might." She rolled her eyes as if to say *Men!*

"Just don't wear them for anybody else but me."

His words had a nice, proprietary air about them, but she refused to give him the satisfaction of agreeing to his order.

He reached for the red flannel shirt lying on the bunk. "Much as I prefer what you're wearing, you better put this on. I want to take you for a walk."

"A walk!" She looked at him in surprise, then let her eyes drift in the direction of the closed door.

The thought of going outside aroused mixed emotions

311

in her. She liked the isolation and coziness of the cabin. It was like a protected cocoon, one she had thus far declined to leave except for brief stints to help Tony bring in the wood and one nearly disastrous trek to the cave to feed the horses.

She had insisted on taking care of the chore; Tony's standing by the corner of the cabin to watch had been an irritation. She was used to weather like this, and she was certainly used to work. But she had been glad of his attention—and his rescue—when, thinking more about the observer behind her than her path, she plunged into a drift of snow and found herself engulfed by powdery crystals.

It was back to the safety of the cabin for her; after an hour or two—she had lost count—of being undressed and dried and being made love to, she had not thought any more about leaving. As much as she wanted Nicholas to find her once again, in her heart she hoped he would hold off for one more day.

But that was yesterday; today stirrings of restlessness were beginning to crowd her protected cocoon. Walking outside with Tony was just what she needed, and she slipped into the flannel shirt, knotting it at her waist instead of tucking the thick fabric into her already tight pants.

She turned to face him. "What do you think?" she asked, extending her arms to each side in a questioning gesture. The wrists of the shirt rested across her upraised palms.

"You already know what I think," he said warmly. Kneeling in front of her, he began to roll up the trouser hems.

"I can do that," she said.

"I know, Countess. I like taking care of you."

"I don't feel like a countess." In answer to his questioning glance, she said, "I feel like a woman."

Lana felt a glow of happiness wash over her at the sound of her own words. She really did feel like a woman—a complete woman—and she wanted to feel nothing more.

"Promise you won't call me by my title again?"

He finished with the hems, then stood. His eyes locked with hers as he said, "I promise." He brushed his lips across hers to seal the vow.

"We won't be outside long, will we?" she asked, the taste of him on her lips tantalizing her as it always did.

"Not long. There's something I want you to see."

He seemed so endearingly intent that she almost told him then and there she would follow him to the ends of the earth. But since he had not asked her to do so, she settled for a softly whispered, "All right."

Reaching for her heavy socks and boots, she sat on the bench to put them on. "You know," she said, eyeing her clothes, "Boris bought me the riding habits and you buy me an outfit like this. Does that tell you anything?"

"It tells me we think about you in different ways," he said, strapping on the holstered gun he was never without when he went outdoors.

She fingered the coarse woolen trousers. "I won't try to analyze what that means." She stood and wiggled her feet until they were settled comfortably into the boots. "Now about that walk."

Tony had a surprise for her—two pairs of Norwegian snowshoes he and Jess had sometimes used and which he had found in the cave. Each shoe consisted of a strip of light wood eight feet long, four inches wide, and more than an inch thick at the center. Tapering at the back and curved upward at the front, they were grooved on the bottom and had a heavy strap in the center for the foot.

"We could probably get along without them," Tony said, "but I thought you might enjoy trying them out."

"We have such things in Russia," she informed him as she strapped the snowshoes in place outside the front door, her breath frosting in the air. She reached for one of the two balancing poles he held in his hand. "My country is really quite advanced."

Throwing him a challenging smile, she pushed off from the cabin and made her graceful way up the incline beside the window. Tony hurried to keep up.

The hem of her sable coat brushed against the crusty,

313

pristine ground. She had no idea the depth of the snow over which she was sliding. For all her bravado, secretly she was glad that it had packed so firmly during the day and a half since it had fallen; otherwise she might have made a fool of herself.

"Keep going to the top if you can," Tony said behind her. "There's something I want you to see."

There was something in his voice that gave her pause, an edge she hadn't heard since Hangtown, and she suddenly remembered the premonition of trouble that had worried her on the dock. She told herself she was just looking for trouble, unable to accept a little peace and happiness in her life for a change. At the least sign of change, she looked for the worst.

Things had gone all right for three days; with a start she realized it was the longest period of time she and Tony had spent together without trouble in some guise intruding itself.

Scattered fir and pine and an occasional juniper bush dotted the fifty yards leading to the eastern crest behind the cabin. Lana's snowshoes made a grating sound over the white, icy surface as she poled herself slowly upward toward the clear blue morning sky.

She was breathing heavily by the time she came to a stop, Tony close beside her, at the far edge of the flat, wide crest of the hill. The land on which they stood was like the jagged back of a monster animal, rising and dipping both to the north and to the south, brown granite boulders like broken bones protruding through the snow.

Farther on in the clear eastern sky, the sun had just cleared the snow-covered Sierra peaks, but from the curved front tip of Lana's snowshoes the ground sloped sharply downward for twenty yards, then flattened out once again, this time only for a few feet before coming to an abrupt end. Beyond the drop-off lay one of the countless ravines that had through the centuries been cut into the mountains. She was reminded of the scene where she had faced the grizzly.

With a shudder, she realized that if someone were

shoved—or fell—straight down the incline with its slick, icy surface, it wouldn't take much momentum to move rapidly to the edge; there were few rocks or bushes or trees to break the slide. Unconsciously she stepped away from the dangerous slope.

Glancing at Tony, she followed his gaze to the north where the ridge rose sharply. "The ambush came from up there," he said, gesturing with his pole toward a cluster of rocks.

Lana understood the tension she had felt in him. He was reliving an uglier time. "It looks as though an army of Cossacks could hide behind them," she said.

"Just one man." Tony's voice was bitter. "That's all it took. Jess and I had just come outside to begin work. It was spring and the thaws had set in. The creek was already flowing—it enters the valley from farther on to the north—and we'd decided to try until summer to see if there was any more gold washing down. Neither of us was armed, fools that we were, but then nobody but us had been here in a year."

Tony kept his eyes pinned to the cluster of rocks. "The bastard got the drop on us. Would have killed us, too, if we hadn't managed to duck behind the cabin and head for the cave."

Lana glanced back down the hill they had just climbed and tried to picture what the gunman must have seen— two unarmed men fifty, sixty yards away standing on the flat land outside the cabin. Armed with a powerful rifle and accurate sight, whoever he was, he would have found them an easy target. Having been married to a skilled hunter, Lana knew that even moving rapidly, Tony and Jess could have been felled with one shot apiece.

"Wasn't running like that dangerous?" she asked.

"No more than raising our hands and waiting for him the way he ordered us to." Tony managed a rueful smile. "Neither Jess nor I could ever take orders very well. At least from a man."

Lana reached out and squeezed his hand. "From anybody."

"Some of those rifle shots came damned close. Then we had to cower in that cave while he went inside the cabin. He came out quick enough. He had to know already about that storage place beneath the bunk. That's where we kept the gold."

"You hadn't taken any of it to a bank for deposit?"

"I said you could call us fools. We wanted to keep our strike a secret until we had taken all there was to take. Someone might have tracked us back here and maybe tried to claim jump. Such things were done. We decided to handle things our way."

A faraway look settled in Tony's eyes.

"Jess figured out before I did how we'd been found. That last trip he had made into town was when it happened. He had a tendency to drink too much, and when he drank, he talked. And bragged. This time he said it was to a redheaded whore, but when he went looking for her, she had skipped town. Probably listened carefully about the valley and the gold, and knew who would be interested in such information. Plenty of men around who would pay well for it."

"And it was on that trip into town to look for her when . . ."

"That's right. When bullets started flying and the Parson was killed. And when Maxwell Shader interjected his righteous self. He wasn't getting very far at prospecting, at least not then, and setting himself up as judge and jury occupied his time."

Tony paused only a moment before hurrying on. "There wasn't any way to recognize the gunman again. Average height and build, hat low and face covered. A little short in the legs, maybe, but that describes half the men around here. His voice was muffled by the bandanna. No help there, either."

Lana let her eyes trail back to the cluster of rocks on the northern ridge. She could almost see the muzzle of a rifle resting in a notch between the boulders, the front sight lined up with Tony. She squeezed her eyes closed, then opened them again. The rifle was gone, a figment of her

316

imagination and of her fear.

"Come over this way," Tony said, gesturing to the eastern slope. "There's something else I wanted you to see."

Shifting the snowshoes, Lana glided after him at an angle down the incline, taking care to stay well away from the edge. They came to a halt beside a tall sugar pine, at the base of which was a tumble of rocks that seemed no part of the natural lay of the land.

Tony was staring at the rocks; the expression on his face told her what his silence failed to say.

"Jess is buried here," she said.

"He always liked this view of the mountains," Tony said. "I thought about putting a cross in the ground, but he hadn't been a religious man. And I decided he wouldn't want a tree to come down just for something that would eventually rot. The granite rocks would last."

He fell silent once again, and Lana respected that silence with her own.

At last Tony looked up and smiled ruefully at her. "I've heard people say they can talk with the dead. You suppose there's something wrong with a man who can't?"

She took his hand in hers. "When Mama was buried, I tried to talk to her about things a girl asks her mother. I think the answers I got really came from my own head, but I was young and thought she was speaking. With Papa, all I really did was tell him good-bye." Her voice softened. "Have you ever done that with Jess?"

He squeezed her hand. "I think I just did."

They stood in silence for a few minutes more, then turned and headed back over the hill and downward toward the valley.

When they halted close to the frozen creek bed, Tony said, "Did I ever tell you all the gold wasn't in the cabin? That the thief didn't get everything?"

"No," she said, "but I'm not surprised."

"Jess didn't know about it. I figured just in case something happened . . . I wasn't really thinking seriously about a holdup, of course, but there are rough men

317

in the Sierras. It was back up on that hill near where I buried him. I thought about leaving it in the grave. Felt guilty when I decided he wouldn't want me to."

"Surely you don't think you were wrong to take it with you?"

"It seemed to me that if I left it, then the thief really would have succeeded in taking it all from us. No, that decision didn't bother me."

He moved beside the creek for a distance and showed her where they had placed the sluices. "I did tear those down. In case anyone came along and tried to take up where we left off, they could at least, by God, do their own work. The cabin I couldn't destroy."

A hint of his old despair was in his voice, and Lana shivered.

"Getting cold?" he asked. "I think I've had about all of the outside world I want for a while."

Lana agreed with all her heart and followed him back to the shelter. Propping the snowshoes and poles beside the front door, they went inside to the warmth.

Somehow the cabin had changed in the short time they had been gone. Removing the sable coat, she tossed it onto the table, along with her gloves and hat, and tried to figure out what was different. In an indefinable way the isolation of the small building had been breeched; when they returned they had brought a little of the outside in with them and were no longer alone.

Tony placed his coat on the table beside the sable, and she went into his arms, her face pressed into the warmth of his shoulder, her back to the door.

"Hold me for a while," she said. "Tight."

His hands stroked the red flannel shirt that covered her back. "Of course, Count—" He caught himself. "Lana. Forgot I wasn't supposed to call you that."

She raised her head and, cupping his face in her hands, kissed him long and hard. At last their lips parted, and she stared into his eyes, trying to read the meaning in their dark depths.

"I've been doing some thinking," he said at last.

A smile tugged at her lips. "I could be in trouble."

"About us."

She grew solemn. "Sounds serious."

"It is."

Lana's heart pounded. She was afraid to say a word.

His hands spread across her back, then moved lower to rest against her waist. "Coming here was a good idea. It's given me time to realize a few things."

She trained her eyes on his mouth, watching the words form, letting them warm and encourage her.

"Lana—"

Whatever he was about to say was lost in the crash of the opening door and the rush of cold wind that cut into the room.

"What the hell—" Tony said sharply as he thrust Lana to his side, his left arm tight around her, and reached for his holstered gun.

Lana twisted around to stare at a fair-haired man standing in the open doorway. With the daylight at his back, his face was in shadows and at first she saw only a stranger.

"I watched you outside for a while," the man said. "I was afraid I would find something like this going on."

His voice she would have recognized anywhere.

"Nicholas!"

"Hello, Svetlana," Nicholas answered as he took a step inside the room. A dark coat similar to Tony's covered his body, and a hat rested on the back of his head. His hair was longer than Lana remembered it, and as the light from the fireplace fell across him, she was surprised at the grim lines of his face.

"I've been trying to get here for days," he added, "but the way on the far side of the tunnel was blocked. Knowing Tony as I do, I figured your honor might need defending. My guess is, I'm too late."

Lana stared openmouthed at her brother. After all her time and trouble and anxiety, to be met with his sarcasm was annoying if not downright offensive. She hid the annoyance behind a smile. He was her brother and she was

319

glad to see him. Slipping from Tony's arm, she walked toward him. "Nicholas," she said, her smile warming, "we've been waiting for you."

"And passing the time very pleasantly, I gather. We need to talk, sister. I will wait for you outside."

Just as quickly as he had appeared, he moved away from the cabin door and out of sight.

Stunned, Lana shot Tony a look of alarm. "I . . . I don't understand."

Tony's face was as grim as her brother's had been. "I imagine I do. Nick is a very stubborn and proud young man."

Still confused, she said, "Let me go alone and find out what is wrong."

A look of impatience settled on Tony's face. "I'll give you a few minutes. Then I'm coming out. Whatever he has to say to you, he can say to me, too."

Lana nodded in agreement. Unthinking, she grabbed up Tony's coat resting on top of hers and hurried out into the cold. A horse was tied to the post in front of the cabin, and she looked around to see Nicholas treading through the thick drifts toward the top of the hill behind the cabin.

Thrusting her arms into the oversized wrap, she took strength from the odor that lingered. It was as though she were still in his arms.

"Nicholas!" she called out. "Wait." Forswearing the use of the snowshoes, she plodded after him up the hill.

Chapter Twenty-Eight

By the time Lana reached her brother's side at the crest of the hill, she was out of breath and her annoyance had returned in full strength. "Why did you come all the way up here?" she asked.

"I did not want to be overheard . . . or interrupted," Nicholas said, glancing back toward the cabin.

It seemed a poor reason to her. The folded ends of her trousers were soaked and her feet nearly frozen from the snow that had worked its way inside her boots. Adding to her discomfort were her bare head and hands; in her haste to follow Nicholas, she had forgotten both hat and gloves. Her teeth were chattering from the frigid weather and, more, from the anxiety that had built inside her as she followed in her brother's wake.

But she could not go back to the cabin right now, no matter how much its warmth and the man inside beckoned her. Waiting up here on the frigid, wind-swept hill, his back to her, was the brother who had defended her through the years and given her his love; to see him once again, she had traveled across several continents and sailed over more water than most people would see in a lifetime. No foolish stubbornness on his part would keep her from this moment of joy.

Even if she had to argue like the very devil for him to share it. When he turned to face her, she proceeded to tell him exactly how she felt.

"So where did all that talk about defending my honor come from?" she asked at last, taking time for a deep breath. Angry, she no longer felt the cold.

Nudging the narrow brim of his hat with a thumb until the crown rested on the back of his head, Nicholas looked at her in amazement. "Is it really my turn to speak, *sestra?*"

Lana swallowed, her anger gone as quickly as it had risen. *"Brat,"* she answered, using the Russian word for brother. "It is truly your turn to speak." She reached out and touched the sleeve of his coat. "It has been so long."

He covered her hand with his and massaged gently. "Far too long."

Nicholas was not much taller than she, and she studied the dear, familiar face now bristled and weathered since the days she remembered in Russia. Their earlier encounter on the trail had been too brief for her to realize how much he had changed. And yet he was as handsome as she remembered him, even-featured, a shock of fair hair falling carelessly across his forehead, and his blue eyes the color of the overhead sky.

"Why not tell me hello with an embrace and a kiss?" she asked.

The wind whistled over the top of the rise where they stood, and her long, loose hair blew wildly, catching in her lashes and against her lips.

Again Nicholas glanced toward the cabin, then scowled at her. "You come from a lover's embrace, Svetlana. Are you sure you need mine?" For all his harshness, he still held tightly to her hand.

"So! We are back to my honor, I suppose. You always were stubborn to the point of impossibility. But I will not let you deny me what I have journeyed so far to receive. Nicholas, tell me hello."

So saying, she threw her arms around him, the bulky coats that they each wore bringing an awkwardness to the embrace. Still, she had what she wanted, and she brushed her lips against his chin.

"What is this?" she asked. "Are you trying to grow a beard?" She realized with a start that her brother, always

322

so young in her mind—an eternal adolescent—was twenty-three years old. And looked much older. He had vaulted from youth to manhood in the months that he had been gone, she realized with regret.

"I do not think I will like your face covered with hair," she added.

Nicholas gazed at her for a moment, his scowl softening. At last he shook his head slowly. "You have changed, *sestra*. I left a timid countess who accepted what she thought she could not change. But this same countess travels halfway around the world to find me, and the first thing she does is put me in my place and then tells me that I must shave." A smile worked at his lips. "Have you reformed the count as well? I think he will not take so kindly to your orders."

Pulling away from him, Lana thrust her hands under the warm cuffs of Tony's coat. "The count is dead," she told him without emotion. "The doctor said it was his heart." She did not think it necessary to tell Nicholas more.

His eyes searched her face, as though he would read her thoughts. "I am not sorry to hear this news, unless perhaps the death has brought you pain."

"Would you think me cruel if I said there was no pain? Only regret for the wasted years of my marriage?"

"I would think you brave enough to speak the truth." He shook his head and grinned more broadly, a boyish gesture that took the extra years away from his face.

Lana's breath caught. His radiance seemed to light up the morning to an even brighter glow. Once again he was the younger brother that she had so longed to see. She thought sadly of the other truths she must tell him, the ones that would take the smile from his face, and she prayed for the strength to speak.

"Did Papa ever admit the absurdity of your marriage?" Nicholas continued. "Or perhaps the count died without Papa's ever realizing the truth about him. No, no, Svetlana, do not try to deny it. I knew the sort of man he was even before the wedding. He looked at me in a certain

323

way one night when there was no one but a gathering of men after a hunting party. I had never seen such a look on the face of a man. Only the village girls."

"I will not try to deny it." Svetlana blushed with shame and looked away. "How could I? You knew the truth before I did."

"There is no need for you to be embarrassed. And he made no attempt to do more. He seemed to realize the stupidity in approaching the younger brother of his intended bride. But I knew that if I ever wanted to encourage him . . ."

"Papa did not believe you."

"Papa believes only what he wants to believe. How did he ever let you leave? He has condemned me to hell, certain that California must be in its very bowels. And all because I spoke the truth. I hope only that the count's estate is as fine as Papa hoped. To me, it gave every sign of deterioration and neglect."

"Nicholas—"

But he would not be stopped. "I am certain that Papa did not send you to bring me home. He does not like to hear harsh truths."

"You do not understand."

"No, *sestra*, I do not understand. For Papa's pride, you were to live a lie. He is—"

"*Nyet!* You must say no more, Nicholas." Her eyes caught with his and welled with tears. "Papa, too, is dead."

He looked as though she had struck him in the face. "Papa?" Removing his hat, he slapped it absently against his thigh. "Papa? How could this be?"

"A sudden illness overcame him. He did not suffer long."

Taking great care not to go too near the slippery eastern slope, she took his hand and guided him to a large, flat boulder that sat downwind behind an ice-encrusted juniper bush farther south on the rise. Brushing the snow from the surface of the rock, she sat and pulled Nicholas down beside her. Tony's heavy wool coat was long enough to serve as a cushion for her to sit on, and she pulled the collar close around her neck and cheeks. Once again she had the sensation of being in his arms, and she drew courage.

In the relative warmth and calm, she told Nicholas about the last months of Alexander Kasatsky's life, making light of his loneliness over the departure of his son, playing up the strength he showed in the care of his lands and the bravery he exhibited when he knew the end was near.

She had not been with her father as much as she had wanted—he insisted he did not need her and there was so much work for her to do on her own estate—but she filled in with her imagination the details she could not know for sure. Now was not the time for the particulars of those waning days; Nicholas needed only the essence of the truth.

He sat quietly as she talked, asking occasional questions, putting in his own feelings when they seemed to fill his heart so much that he could not contain them. For a time Lana was transported back to that other country which she loved.

After a while, both Nicholas and Svetlana slipped back through the years and spoke of the childish tricks they had tried to play on Boris and of how he sometimes let them think they had succeeded in fooling him.

"How is he, by the way?" Nicholas asked. "I am surprised he let you come all this way by yourself."

Lana swallowed guiltily. "In truth, brother, he is not so many miles away from this very spot. In a Chinese mining camp laid up with a broken leg received when he saved me from an angry grizzly bear."

She sat back and let Nicholas digest that bit of news.

"Boris?" he asked.

"That is correct."

"Chinese mining camp?"

"You listen well."

Nicholas shook his head. "The only thing that does not surprise me, Svetlana, is that he saved you from the bear.

325

Such an animal would be no match for him if he thought his dear Svetlana was threatened."

"I almost cost him his life," she said, a catch in her voice.

"This is a dangerous country," Nicholas said. "Why did you come? There are two estates which must need your thorough care. You must have known that eventually I would return. I could not stay away. It is my home as much as it is yours."

Her home. Nicholas's words gave her pause, and she thought about the cabin at the side of the hill and the man waiting inside. For three days her home had been in that one room in that man's arms. Three days. For twenty-five years she had called Russia home. Could she so quickly change? When the American had said nothing about wanting her to remain with him?

She tried with only partial success to free her thoughts of Tony. This time belonged to Nicholas; he still did not know all the truth.

"I do not have two estates to care for," she said. "Only the poor remains that the count left me. Papa left the Kasatsky lands to you."

An incredulous look settled on Nicholas's face as he listened to the terms of their father's will.

"That is why I came for you," she explained. "You have the Blood of Burma, and I have possession of your land. But only until Rudolph has the right to claim it. And yes, I can see the question on your face. Our cousin is as unpleasant as he has ever been. He is in San Francisco right now hoping to make sure that you do not return for what he already considers his."

"Is there no one, Svetlana, waiting back in Russia? They all seem to be in America."

"I must ask, Nicholas, about the ruby. Is it still in your possession?"

"It is not on my person, if that is what you mean, but it is safe," he said. He would tell her no more except to say that a Celestial by the name of Sam Chin had helped him make certain the ruby would not be lost.

"Sam Chin?" Lana looked at him in amazement. "The one who runs the fan-tan parlor?"

"Should I ask how you know of him?" Nicholas slowly shook his head. "Perhaps I should not."

At that moment Nicholas reminded her more than a little of Tony.

"Besides," Nicholas continued, "I know what you are thinking. That I have gambled the Blood away."

He sounded defensive, and Lana could not hide her irritation. "It would be for the third time, would it not?"

"I see that Tony Diamond has been talking too much." Nicholas's voice was bitter. "You know about the game in which I lost it to him."

"I know. And about Lord Dundreary, too. As well as about his daugher Elizabeth."

Nicholas uttered an exclamation of disgust.

"She is not like the forward girls of the village," Lana continued.

He set his features in a mulish expression. "Elizabeth is my concern. I am a man of the world, Svetlana. No longer a child. No matter what you or Tony Diamond think. I will take care of her."

Lana saw her father in his face and, despite his stubborn words—or perhaps because of them—her heart warmed even more.

"And what about the gaming debts?"

"I am striving to clear them. That is why I am in the mountains. There is gold and there is gambling here. I can find it two ways. If only I had more time. I tried to tell you on the trail. It is why I left so hurriedly."

Nicholas's face turned harsh. "I think now, however, I made a mistake. If you had found me in San Francisco, perhaps Tony Diamond would not have found you. Tell me, Svetlana, is he your lover?"

Lana's answer caught in her throat.

"There is no need to speak. I see the truth in your eyes. Has he told you that he loves you?"

She looked away. "Not yet—"

"Bah! You condemn me for Elizabeth, and yet I hear no

words against Tony."

"Elizabeth is just a child."

"You have lived a harsh life, but in some ways you are just as innocent. Tony uses women as he uses other comforts."

"No—" Lana felt confused, unable to explain to Nicholas the way things really were, and yet deep in her heart she wondered if perhaps her brother was not seeing things more clearly than she. No, her whole being cried out. She could not accept such an unthinkable idea.

"I am the man of the family now, and I see what I must do. You will return to Russia with me. It is where we both belong."

"What if she chooses not to go?"

Startled, they both looked up in the direction of the deep male voice and saw Tony standing on the rise of the hill. Tall and lean, his dark features settled in a frown, he was wearing nothing warmer than a woolen shirt, his tight wool trousers tucked into calf-high boots. Lana's heart leaped at the sight of him. Her first instinct was to leave the protection of the juniper bush and rush to share the coat with him, but she held back.

Nicholas stood to face him, his jaw tight. "It is not a choice that my sister should make. I am old enough to care for both her and myself. I tried to tell you that before."

"Before you ran away?"

"Before I removed myself from San Francisco to a place where I thought I could settle my problems. Only," he said fiercely, "I found that people here still talked about you and the events of two years ago. I didn't know about Jess Tucker and—"

"Nicholas!" Lana stood and gripped the sleeve of her brother's coat. In the heat of argument, he could not be allowed to say such things that he must know would bring pain to Tony.

Turning from her, Nicholas paced through the snow away from the boulder, past Tony, and toward the northern ridge. Lana started to follow, then stopped when she came to Tony's side. Twenty yards away, close to where the crest began its downward slope, Nicholas came to a halt and whirled to stare coldly at them.

"Is this the way things are?" he asked, his eyes glittering angrily at Tony. "You would use her still?"

"Let's go talk about this inside, Nick."

"Let's talk about it now. After I rode away on the trail, I realized how much I wanted to see my sister. I got the insane idea that somehow she might need protecting from you. Too often have I seen you with the women of San Francisco. I did not want her to be treated as such a one."

Tony said, "You do not trust her to know her own mind?"

"For all her wisdom, my sister is an innocent woman. She does not know how to defend herself against a man like you."

"*Nyet*," Lana said, stung by his words. She felt herself pulled between the two men.

"I agree with you in only one thing," she said to Nicholas. "We must talk now. You must realize how wrong you are about Tony and me."

Nicholas waved away her plea. He was defending her as once he had tried to defend her against his father, and this time she saw, he was determined to be heeded.

The only thing she could do was move closer to Tony's side, to show Nicholas that he must not ask her to separate herself from the man she loved. She did not need defending; she needed to be understood.

Nicholas looked away in disgust. "The snows came and I could not return to the cabin where I knew the two of you must be. I have been circling this valley, trying to find a way in. The trip was not in vain, however. I came across a prospector who knew of Tony. He had some very interesting things to say. More than ever I wanted to find my way in and tell—"

A gunshot echoed across the mountains, drowning out the rest of his words. He arched his back, a look of stunned disbelief on his face, and he staggered in place.

"Nicholas!" Lana screamed. She rushed through the drifts of snow separating them; looking past him, she saw, in the notch of the boulders on the northern rise, the gun barrel she had imagined earlier in the day. But this time it was not a figment of her imagination or of her fear.

"Get down!" Tony yelled, crossing the distance in an instant and shoving both of them against the ground, his gun already in his hand and firing toward the north. The bullets ricocheted off the boulders and rang in the cold mountain air.

Lana clutched Nicholas to her, his moans pushing her close to panic. He struggled in her arms, then suddenly grew still, and she felt the two of them slide across the icy surface and down the slope on the far side of the hill, the slope which led to the drop-off into the seemingly bottomless ravine. The impossible was happening, and she was helpless to stop it. She cried out, her heart racing in terror, but she could no more stay the impetus of their careening than she could fend off the bullets from the ambusher's rifle.

Another bullet bit into the snow by them, but Lana paid it no mind, frantic as she was to stop the inexorable descent across the frozen, bruising ground toward what must surely be the abyss of death.

Tony's pistol answered the rifle shots. The sounds of gunfire, of Nicholas's moans, of her own pitiful cries of desperation mingled in the nightmare. She struggled, tried to catch her footing, kicked at the ground, at one point almost coming to a halt and rising to her knees, but she could not release her hold on her brother and his weight dragged her down again. She was dimly aware of the sticky warmth of his blood on her hands where she gripped his coat.

"Tony!" she screamed and heard his answering "Lana!" echoing around her, but she did not see him, only a rush of snow-covered ground and bushes and trees she could not reach. Still the gunfire sounded, but she did not know whether it was from Tony's pistol or the rifle higher on the ridge.

As if by divine intervention, she and Nicholas came to a halt not three feet from the edge, where the ground flattened. Sprawled against the snow, she clung to him, her eyes pinned to the edge of the drop-off. She was afraid to move, afraid to breathe. Not knowing if her brother were alive or dead, she could only cling to him and pray.

And then Tony was beside her, holding her, pulling her up, one arm on her and the other holding to the unmoving Nicholas, placing himself between them and the rifle.

"The bastard is still up there, and there's not much separating us and him but open air," Tony said, his words coming out in gasps. "This pistol isn't doing me much good. We've got to make our way to the south away from him. There are some bushes—"

Again came the rifle shots. Nicholas seemed to jerk in their arms. Lana thought only of holding onto him, of protecting him from the hellish bullets that kept them pinned in place. In her blurred and panicked mind, she told herself she must shift her body between him and the gunman.

Nicholas seemed to stir and she thought with elation that he was alive . . . as though his movement gave an end to the ambush. She raised her body, heard a deafening report, and felt a red-hot explosion in her shoulder.

For a moment time stood still, and they were all motionless on the icy slope, the three of them clinging together. The world seemed to spin around her. Another shot rang out. The last thing she saw before slipping from consciousness was the sight of her brother Nicholas falling from Tony's grasping hands and disappearing over the edge of the ravine.

Chapter Twenty-Nine

The next thing Lana became aware of was movement, a gentle rocking in a pair of strong arms as though she were being cradled and drawn slowly into wakefulness. But she was too weak to lift her head or to open her eyes. A soft moan escaped her throat.

"I've got you, Lana. We'll be there soon."

The words were raspy, more sensed than heard, but the voice was warmly familiar and wrapped around her as soothingly as did the arms, and she settled back into the comfort of oblivion.

She had no sense of time having passed when she again drifted into consciousness. The scent of a man and of a horse came to her, of a heart thudding against her bent head, of the rise and fall of a chest. She was wrapped in sable fur and was warm. She stirred. A dimly perceived pain stopped her from moving more. Something was wrong . . . something was terribly wrong . . .

"We're almost there."

Lana sighed. If she held very still, maybe the hurt would go away. But it didn't. Her mind struggled to understand the source of the fire that burned in her body. No, not fire. A knife slashing to get out.

She grew dizzy with the pain, but the dizziness was welcomed . . . blurred her thoughts . . . whatever was wrong could wait. Again she allowed the assuringly familiar voice to comfort her into blackness.

When she came to, the rocking had stopped. The arms were gone, and instead of the words of comfort, she heard only the low drone of voices whispering from very far away. No longer was she curled against a broad chest. She was lying down, alone, weighted by a thick blanket that seemed to lie upon her like a stone. She tried to open her eyes, but her lids were heavy and would not do as she wanted.

Suddenly, shots rang out in her head, and fire exploded behind the eyes squeezed closed . . . Twisting her head to rid her mind of the horror, she ignored the sharp pain that knifed through her. She was falling, falling, grasping for something to hold onto, and then when at last she gripped the solid strength of another body, she felt it ripped from her hands. A terrified face flashed across her mind, faded into the threatening dark, and she screamed out.

"Nicholas!"

She opened her eyes with a jolt. Her heart pounded in her throat, and she felt such a burning sensation wash over her that she thought she would retch. Her eyes darted around the strange room where she found herself, a whirling room that would not be still. She saw ceiling beams and rough walls and a man staring down at her, a man she had never before seen.

"Get Diamond," the man said. "She's coming around."

Was that the rustle of a skirt that she heard? Why was this stranger screaming? Why did she hurt?

"Nicholas," she said, knowing her voice was a whisper, unable to give it more strength. She had none to give.

"She's calling for her brother," the stranger said over his shoulder.

"Thanks, Doc." At last she heard the familiar voice that had soothed her in that earlier nightmare, and her heart and breathing slowed, the panic subsiding.

"She's lost a lot of blood. Don't upset her."

"Tell me how in the hell I can avoid that."

The voice wasn't soothing now; it sounded harsh and she felt herself cringing away from it. *Tony.* She tried to say his name, but it died on her lips.

Fingers brushed against her face. Familiar, soothing fingers. "You're in town, Lana. Doc's taking care of you."

Her eyelids fluttered. She swallowed and tried to speak. "What—" She could say no more.

"Hush. We can talk later."

Later was not good enough. She did not like this whirling feeling, this helplessness. She tried again, and this time managed a weak, "What happened?"

"You were injured. In the shoulder." The voice broke. "You'll be all right."

The pain . . . could it really be isolated in only one place? The lacerating waves seemed to begin on the left side of her body, yet at the same time she seemed to hurt all over. And there were those dreadful visions that slashed across her mind, of Nicholas—dear, dear Nicholas—close to her side and then slipping away, of gunshots rending the air, of a swirling nothingness more frightening than any clearly perceived object could have been.

And then she remembered. Nicholas had returned to her . . . they had quarreled . . . he had looked at her in disgust . . . and someone had tried to kill them. Again she was slipping down the endless, icy slope, and she felt the same panic as she groped for a boulder, a bush, anything to impede their fall. A dark face mirroring her panic suddenly appeared to her mind's eye. Tony was beside her, but he couldn't stop the bullets. Somehow he couldn't save Nicholas, and neither could she.

This time the fear that clutched at her heart was not of the unknown but of what she too clearly remembered. "Where is he?" she breathed.

"Later. We'll talk later."

Lana could not wait. "I remember holding onto him . . . and the shots . . . and then he was gone."

She stared up at Tony and knew that what she remembered was right.

"I couldn't catch him, Lana." Pain edged Tony's voice. "Everything happened so fast."

Helpless to do anything more, Lana looked away, her physical pain fading into a harsher agony of the soul.

Nicholas was lost to her, now and forever. She had gone halfway around the world to find her brother and had succeeded only in luring him to his death.

She felt the tears spill onto her cheeks, but she could not stop them, could not lift a hand to brush them away. Tony leaned close until his breath warmed her face, but she could not accept his comfort now. Her despair was private, and she turned her head away.

"You go on," a woman was saying. "I'll watch her for a while. She needs to sleep. Any change, I'll let you know."

Lana forced herself to be still, to keep her shallow breath regular. The lonely habits of the past years returned in a rush—the habits that had kept her sane through the darkest moments of her life. She must have time to sort through her own despair before she could share her thoughts with anyone, even Tony. After a moment, she heard the opening and closing of a door and knew that he had left.

Pacing along the poorly lighted hallway outside the Hangtown hotel room where Lana lay, Tony felt as though someone had ripped his heart from his chest. The torment from the past had come to him again, only this time it was worse. A thousand times worse. Nick was lying somewhere at the bottom of a Sierra ravine, given not even the few words from the Bible that Jess had heard read over his soul.

And on the other side of a thin wall lay the woman who meant the world to him. He trembled to think how close he had come to losing her. When he had seen the dark blood spreading on the tear in that coat, had watched her body twist from the force of the bullet, had seen pain and fright distort her features, he went mad.

Much of that madness was with him still. His beautiful, brave, willful countess harmed by a coward's bullet . . . He cursed the unknown assailant and himself as well for not protecting her.

"She's gonna be all right," said the man holding vigil

336

with him. "Doc swears she is. Got the bullet out and sewed her up neat. Says the bone wasn't hit. Just a little flesh."

If Dusty John thought he was consoling him, Tony could tell him different. The thought of a bullet piercing that tender skin, of one ounce of blood being lost because of that bastard gunman, filled him with a helpless rage.

He was the same man who had caught him and Jess unawares two years ago. Tony was sure of it. The odds against two such ambushers appearing in such an unlikely place were too high for him to think otherwise.

Why had the bastard quit when he had? After the death of Nicholas, Tony had managed to drag the unconscious Lana to a place of relative safety behind a boulder. Reloading his gun, he had let loose with a barrage of fire that kept the ambusher pinned down. But from that distance, the pistol was too inaccurate for Tony to do much more.

He had let up to reload, and realized that there were no rifle shots coming from the northern hill. Minutes had crept past, but still nothing. His searching fingers had discovered the warm stickiness on Lana's shoulder. He had known she was losing a great deal of blood. Taking a chance—it was all he could do—he had clutched her to him and had begun that endless trek back down toward the cabin, expecting any minute for a bullet to catch him in the back.

But all had been quiet, save for the wind whistling over the hill. His hands had been shaking too much for him to do more than apply a tight bandage to the wound and leave the bullet inside her while he brought her into town.

Doc had been sober, and Dusty John and Cooter had been determined to help.

Dusty John's voice gradually penetrated his dark memories. "You listening to me, Tony? Even Doc's taking a rest. Let's go to the Lady—"

"No, John. I'd rather wait here."

"Carmen's watching over her. Imagine she's seen more than one bullet wound. Besides, Cooter's waiting on the sidewalk. He can come running if there's any change."

Tony tried to take comfort from the words but could not. He knew now that Lana would live; Doc wasn't one to soften bad news with a lie. She was weak and would bear the scars of Tony's mistake the rest of her life, but no longer was her wound life-threatening.

He knew deep in his soul the twin sources of his despair. Nick Case had been a joyous young man, impetuous, maybe, and certainly not taken to walking on the safe side of life. Tony had interfered and tried to teach him a lesson or two. If he had stayed out of the poker game, Nick would have lost the ruby, all right, with no chance to win it back, but without Tony tracking him down, at least he would be alive.

And Lana. Just when he was about to commit himself to her and ask her to stay with him forever . . . just when he felt her needing him as much as he had come to need her . . . he had let her down.

And worse, she knew it, too. In that room when she had returned to consciousness, she had called out for her brother, not for him; when Tony had tried to comfort her, she had turned away.

The door to the sickroom opened and closed, and the prostitute known as Carmen joined the two men in the hall. She had been checking into the hotel when Tony arrived with Lana in his arms and Doc close on his heels. Remembering them from the steamboat and from Sacramento, she had offered to help.

"She's sleeping now," Carmen whispered, "but Lordy, I don't know how, not with the walking and talking going on out here. These walls are no thicker than sheets on a whorehouse bed." With a shake of her head, she returned once more to the room.

"Told you to get out," Dusty John whispered. "Cooter's keepin' watch down in the lobby, and Doc'll be back soon. Either one will let us know if we're needed. Which we won't be. What the countess needs is rest and quiet."

She needed that, all right, Tony admitted. But she needed peace of mind, too, and that would be harder to come by. He didn't think she would take it from him.

338

He glanced at the coat he had tossed impatiently onto the hallway floor during his pacing. It was ripped where the rifle bullet had hit; the fibers were stiff with Lana's blood. If for one moment he let himself forget the horror today, that coat would serve as a vivid reminder.

"You go on," he said. "I'm waiting here."

Dusty John studied him for a moment. "You ain't going crazy again, are you?"

Tony thought of the oak tree on the street corner not very far away. The sun was setting, and the branches would be stretching high and dark against the graying sky, but the tree held no terror for him now.

"I'm not going crazy again," he said.

"Good. Let's get that drink."

"But I'm not going to the Fat Lady, either. You drink one for me."

Dusty John was halfway down the stairs when Tony called him back. "You really want to do something that might help? I'm not too sure how much Lana will be wanting to talk to me, but there's somebody else that can maybe do her some good."

"Just tell me what you need."

"Thought you might feel that way. What I need is for you and Cooter to get out to that old mining camp called the Nugget Bar . . ."

Lana knew time was passing as she slipped in and out of sleep, but she knew little more. Except that she hurt. And that there was a heaviness in her heart that would not go away. She gave no lucid thought to the source of her troubles; they seemed so much a part of her that she supposed they would linger forever.

At last she came to a wakefulness that stayed. She looked across the narrow room and realized with a start that she had been here before. In another life she had lain in this same bed with a man and been happy.

Winter sunlight streamed through a window at her head and fell across the figure of a woman seated in a chair close to the bed. A blonde, Lana realized, full-figured and with unnaturally thick lashes and pink cheeks.

Lana swallowed. "Could I have some water?" she asked.

The woman's heavy lashes lifted, and when she smilingly said, "Sure thing, honey," Lana recognized her as the woman who had sailed to Sacramento.

She struggled for a name and asked tentatively, "Carmen?"

Carmen stood and poured from a pitcher on the bedside table. "Nothing wrong with your mind, that's for sure," she said.

Or with her memory, Lana thought with regret as the past came rushing in. She tried to steal herself against the hurt, but nothing could protect her from its onslaught.

"How long have I been here?"

"That man of yours brought you in day before yesterday, late. Now try to drink some of this."

Lana found she could do no more than lift her head, and even that took a great deal of effort. Her right hand lay limp on top of the blanket. Carmen held a cup to her lips, and Lana let the precious water trickle down her throat.

That man of yours. Where was he? She was filled with an overwhelming longing to see him, to hold his hand. She remembered vaguely that he had been in the room at some time. Surely he would return. Gone was the desire to handle her suffering alone. She needed him. She needed him now.

Lana let her head fall back on the pillow. Her left shoulder, bound and in a sling, throbbed mightily, and she was overcome with dizziness. Why on earth, she asked herself, did men ever play with guns when the bullets left such a terrible residue of pain?

"Got some broth here," Carmen said. "Doc told me to get some down you if I could. You'll be losing your strength instead of gaining it, if you don't eat something."

Lana let Carmen spoon some of the warm, salty liquid into her mouth before she once again fell asleep. When she awoke some time later, the procedure was repeated. Water, a little inane talk, a little more broth. But no mention of Tony.

"I thought you were going to some other town," Lana said after her third liquid meal.

"Coloma? No action there. A girl's got to see to business no matter where it takes her."

With a guilty start, Lana thought she must be keeping Carmen from plying her trade.

"I'll be all right alone," she said. "Surely I can feed myself now. I've never been helpless before."

Carmen laughed. "Don't fret yourself. I'm glad to do it. If it's worrying you, I'm being paid. Not that I wouldn't do this for free, but your man made the offer and I figured, what the hell. Do something I want to for a change and still make money. You can't beat a deal like that."

Lana managed a feeble smile. "Is Tony . . . somewhere around?"

"Pacing right outside that door. He's been real upset. Won't eat or sleep much. He's taking this mighty hard."

Of course he was, just the way he had Jess's death. Lana understood. He was blaming himself for what happened. But it hadn't been his fault. She was the one who had insisted on going to the cabin after Nicholas. She was the one who stood with him on that hill and argued with him. It was from her that Nicholas had turned in disgust.

If Tony would come to her right now, she would tell him how she felt. But the sight of her lying helpless must be for him too sharp a reminder of what had happened. As much as she loved him, it seemed they had no consolation for each other when most they needed it.

She squeezed her eyes closed, but she didn't try to forget. If she could not help Tony, the least she could do for her brother was remember each second of their last meeting, from the embrace she had demanded to the sweet reminiscences and talk of home, and on to their arguments about Tony and the final, tragic end.

Facing Nicholas for the first time in more than a year, she had been so filled with thoughts of Tony that she had not really believed what her brother had said.

She needed to trust him, he had insisted, to let him care

for himself and for her, to remove herself from Tony's presence, to return to her home in Russia.

Now she would have a lifetime to remember his words.

Lana had been confused on that wind-swept hill, pulled as she was between the two men, yet she had known from the beginning that America was not the place for her. It was too wild, too disturbing, too dangerous. It gave itself too much to the pleasures of the flesh. Like Tony himself, it was untamed.

She had immersed herself in those pleasures, but she should have known they could not last forever. Like a wild rose, the glorious bloom of passion could only live for a brief while.

She must not fight the passing of what she had known with Tony. She knew in her heart that he would let go more easily than she, no matter how much he might protest during the coming difficult days and weeks. She wanted to believe otherwise—desperately, unwisely—but she could not. She had learned to be a practical woman and deal with life as it presented itself. Until California, her dreams had been a long time forgotten; they would be so again.

Nicholas had been right. The pattern of her life was already set. Russia was home. Duty called her there. She must somehow return to her estate and accept once again the responsibilities awaiting her.

The Kasatsky lands, of course, were lost to her cousin, but she would make sure, by damn, that he did not let the estate fall into ruin the way the count had almost destroyed his. This silent vow was the one way she could begin to accept her loss.

And never would she wed again—not Rudolph, not anyone else, no matter how difficult her life became.

Resolve gave her the strength she needed to do what must now be done. "Tell Tony I would like to see him."

"Honey, I'd say that's a good idea."

Lana closed her eyes, hoping that Carmen was right. When she opened them again, it was to see Tony standing beside the bed and looking down at her. No one else was in the small room.

"Carmen said you wanted to see me." He knelt beside the bed and touched one finger to her cheek. "You feel nice and cool. Doc said there probably wouldn't be any fever." His finger trailed to the wisps of hair clinging to her face, and on to the dark locks spread across the pillow.

Lana looked away. How could she possibly tell him of her purpose while he was looking at her in such a way?

"How long will I be down like this?" she asked.

"Hard to say. A week, maybe even less. It depends on how much you sleep, how much you eat. The report I hear is you haven't been getting enough food."

"Then I will force myself to eat. I must regain my strength."

"Of course you must. Then I can take you back to San Francisco with me."

Lana made herself look at him once again. The force of his warm gaze robbed her of breath. For one unguarded moment she felt her resolve weaken.

And then the image of her brother flashed across her mind.

"*Nyet.*" The word was little more than a whisper, but her voice strengthened as she said, "I cannot return with you."

Tony grew very still. "What do you mean?"

"I must return to my home. For me, that can only be Russia."

Tony took her right hand in his. "Now is not a good time to make decisions."

"They have been made for me," she said tonelessly, still keeping her gaze locked with his. The darkness in his eyes frightened her, but she would not, could not give in to the impulse to do whatever he bid.

"Hasn't that country done enough to you? Brought you enough suffering?" he asked.

"No more than has America. At least in Russia I know I am needed."

"You are needed here."

His words coiled around her, and she was stunned by the

343

power he still had over her. With tears springing to her eyes, she looked away. "Do not speak from pity, Tony. I will not be pitied."

"In the cabin, before Nicholas arrived, I was trying to ask you to stay with me. To be my wife."

Lana would not let herself listen. She had expected him to protest her decision, but not with such an avowal. How much she had once longed to hear those words, but that time seemed to be have been in another life. His words came too late. With all that had happened, he would not know pity from love. And he had not said he loved her.

She pulled her hand free of his. He was as tempting to her as he had been that first time she had seen him on the San Francisco street and he had swept her up in his arms.

But with the joy and pleasure he had brought her had also come more pain than she had ever known. With Tony she had let down the guard she had built up through the years; somehow she must keep her vows and erect it once again.

"Please," she said, "leave me to rest. Perhaps it would be better if we did not see each other again."

"I can't accept that, Lana." For the first time since entering, he spoke harshly to her. "You're blaming us for what happened on that hill. I've had two years of carrying such a weight alone. You are the one who taught me acceptance of the past's unpleasant truths."

"Perhaps if we both had not been determined to find my brother when he wished to be left alone, he would still be alive. But that is no more than speculation. I do not blame you, Tony, and neither should you blame yourself. It is not guilt that makes me do what I must do. I have another life waiting for me faraway. I have always known in my heart that I must return."

Weariness washed over her; closing her eyes, she lifted a weak hand to fend off any argument he might make. "Please, Tony. No more."

She knew he waited for a long while before leaving; only when she heard the door at last open and close did she once again submit to the desolation that was too deep for tears.

Chapter Thirty

Boris appeared at the hotel the next morning, a wooden crutch braced under each arm. His complexion was pinched and sallow and his hair grayer than Lana remembered, but she had never seen a more endearing sight than his bent, thin figure standing in the doorway to her room.

Tony had arranged for his journey into Hangtown, Boris explained, and with no more than a quick flash of pain in his eyes, added that he had been informed of the tragedy by two gentlemen named Cooter and Dusty John.

Just then Carmen walked into the room behind him, a tea tray in her hands. "Here's just what you two need. I'll get on out and let you visit." She set the tray on the bedside table and exited, leaving Boris to settle awkwardly in a nearby chair, his still splinted leg extending in front of him a good distance across the room.

Boris managed to serve the tea, then turned his strong, sure gaze on Lana. "Perhaps it would be wise for the countess to tell me what she remembers. I know only that Master Nicholas is dead."

Lana caught her breath. She understood what he was doing—facing the tragedy with his typical forthrightness and courage. And she knew he would allow her to do no less. But knowing his purpose did not ease the difficulty of his request.

Propped up on pillows, her left arm still in a sling, Lana

345

stared at the cup of tea resting on her lap. She hesitated at first, then after a tentative, tearful start related the last time she had seen her brother. "He was a man, not a boy any longer," she said in conclusion, not dwelling on the manner in which his life was ended or of his harsh assessment of Tony. "He talked about our returning to Russia together."

"And is that what the countess wants?"

"It is what the countess wants," she replied tonelessly, unable to look at him. In this matter she could have none of his arguments, but, oh, how the sorrow of her decision rested heavily in her heart. Her eyes trailed to Boris's injured leg. "Surely America has done all the harm to us that she can. It is time, dear friend, that we returned home."

For once, he gave her no argument, even though she could sense he was not pleased with her words.

Lana used the few days to gather her strength, eating the food for which she had no hunger and spending longer and longer periods out of bed. The heaviness of heart did not lesssen, but she reminded herself that she had been trained to face difficult times. She tried to think only of the people awaiting her on her estate. They had bid her good-bye reluctantly; they would gladly welcome her home.

She was the Countess Svetlana Alexandrovna Dubretsky; as such, she must accept her responsibilities. Nicholas had been right. She needed to go home.

Carmen took her leave at the end of the week, saying that while she appreciated Lana's thanks, she didn't deserve them. "Told you your man was paying me. I'd hang on to him if I was you."

Tony wasn't her man, Lana wanted to say. Not now. Not ever.

He did not reappear, and she was told he had returned to the valley. She wanted to thank him for sending her Boris, an action that had not surprised her. Tony was Tony. He could exasperate her with his stubborn arrogance and then turn around and do something so incredibly brave or kind or thoughtful . . .

She could not let herself think that way. Perhaps it was best that he did not return.

But the thought of him alone in that cabin where they had known such brief happiness became too much for her and at last she broke her trust, telling Dusty John how to get there and asking that he make sure Tony was all right. She was too weak to make the journey herself. And she discovered a cowardice in herself. She simply could not go so soon to the place where Nicholas had lost his life.

A week after the good-bye to Tony, she and Boris made their arduous way back to San Francisco, first by a stage to Sacramento and then by steamer into the bay city. She didn't want to return to the Ace Hotel with its memories and with the unfortunate presence of Cousin Rudolph, but their belongings were still there, including the cache of money she planned to use for their return fare.

Also, it was the residence of Elizabeth Dundreary. Lana dreaded relating the sad news about Nicholas, but she had seen signs of strength in the young Englishwoman that would help ease the pain.

When she found that the girl and her father had taken an excursion to the ocean for several days, she was human enough to be glad that particular task could be postponed. She was even more grateful to learn that Rudolph had moved himself to less expensive quarters while he waited for her return.

Lana had one more item of business to take care of—the collection of the Blood of Burma.

For this second journey into Chinatown she would not have to sneak away from Boris, who was ensconced in a room on the street level where he wouldn't have to use so many stairs. Also he could make use of the small parlor behind the lobby desk when he grew restless in his room, an occurrence that happened often.

Two days after their return, she approached him in the parlor where he was reading. He had traded his rough mountain clothes for the familiar black suit, but the left pants leg had been slit to allow room for the splint. The crutches rested on the floor beside him.

"I have to go to Chinatown," she announced. "I assure you I am strong and rested enough."

She spoke the truth, or at least close enough to it that her conscience did not bother her. The pain in her left shoulder was tolerable now, and she had been practicing going without her sling. She had even managed to dress herself each morning without the assistance of the floor maid Maria, a feat she considered nothing less than phenomenal.

To herself, she admitted the dull ache in her heart was still with her and most likely would remain, but she couldn't let it slow her down.

Boris's eyes barely flickered as he looked up at her. "The countess has a reason, of course, for such an unusual journey."

"The ruby. Nicholas hid it there."

"And what does the countess plan to do with the jewel? There are, I believe, several claims outstanding against it."

Lana knew very well what she planned to do, but she did not want to get into that particular argument right now.

"That is a decision we can discuss later. First, I want to get it back."

"The countess, as always, is set in her ways."

"As always, I do what I must do."

For the journey she wore the black, hooded cloak she had left behind in the hotel. She told herself the choice was because the cloak was lighter in weight than the sable and did not hurt so much to wear. But she knew the truth. In her mind Tony and the sable had become inextricably bound.

Since the dueling pistol Lana was accustomed to had been left at the mountain cabin, she went armed with the one Boris had kept with him at the Nugget Bar. In the unlikely event she was forced into using it, she would have to remember that it didn't pull to the right.

In the daytime, Grant Street was just as brightly colored and ornamented as she remembered it, only more crowded and noisy. Hundreds of blue-coated Celestials, their queues bouncing against their backs, scurried along the sidewalks, their bamboo poles suspended across their shoulders.

And Stouts Alley was just as gloomy and forbidding, only after all she had been through, it held no fear for her. At the far, dark end of the alley, where little sunlight penetrated on this clear morning, she knocked boldy on the door of Sam Chin's fan-tan parlor.

She sensed movement over her shoulder, but when she looked hurriedly around the narrow alley, she could make out no other person in its dark depths, and she knocked once again.

The door opened to reveal the owner Chin, again wearing an elaborately embroidered coat; behind him were the scattered tables at which she could make out the Celestials hard at play.

"Madame," Chin said without a sign of surprise, "you have returned to our humble establishment."

Not waiting for an invitation, she stepped into the crowded room. "I have returned."

The chatter of the room abated; she looked around to see a hundred eyes trained on her. They were not friendly.

"Does the madame wish once again to part the Celestial from his coins?" Chin asked.

Lana got right to the point. "I am the sister of Nick Case. It was he I really sought on my previous visit. Mister Chin, we must talk." She paused a moment, then added, "About something Nicholas left in your trust."

For once she saw surprise registered on the face of the inscrutable Chinaman, but before he could respond, one of the fan-tan players, a bald, broad-bodied man she recognized from her previous visit, shook his beefy fist in the air and shouted out in his unintelligible language. Lana got the message all right. He was in a terrible rage.

As were the others, who took up his noisy cause.

"Why are they so angry?" she asked, as puzzled as she had been before. Could they really be such poor losers?

"They believe you have taken their money unfairly; they have been hoping for your return," Chin said, his voice rising over the increasing noise.

Lana resorted to her old defense. "Perhaps," she said haughtily, "if they knew I was a countess—"

"They would be in more of a rage."

Lana thought of her second protection—the dueling pistol. If necessary, she would extract it from her cloak and shoot another hole in the ceiling.

Across the smoke-filled room, still redolent with the opium scent Lana remembered from before, she spied Chin's fair-haired American wife standing in the portal leading to the back room, the strings of beads which served as a door thrust aside.

A look passed between the man and wife. "Come," Chin said as he took Lana unceremoniously by the wrist and pulled her back into the alley. "It is time that we leave."

Speechless, Lana could do no more than let him pull her through the semidarkness toward Grant Street. Suddenly a figure loomed in their path; with long arms outstretched, he blocked their way.

"Svetlana, where is it that you rush?"

"Rudolph!"

"Madame," Chin urged at her side, his hand still firmly on her wrist, "my wife is attempting to soothe the anger of the Celestials, but they have long awaited you. We have no time for a friendly discussion."

"With Cousin Rudolph, any discussion will not be friendly," Lana assured him quickly.

"Nonsense," Rudolph said. "I saw you leave the hotel and followed you here to offer my assistance." His narrow eyes fell on Chin's hand still gripping Lana, and he seemed to assess the size and strength of the smaller Chinese. "Is this man harming you in some way?"

Lana felt a sudden kinship with the Celestial gambler, one much stronger than any she had ever felt for her avaricious cousin. She knew full well why Rudolph had followed her. He wanted to know if she had found Nicholas and the ruby. Remembering that her cousin was now the rightful owner of the Kasatsky estate, she was filled with a fury all her own.

She turned to Chin. Nicholas had trusted him; she could

do no less. "I do not wish to talk to my cousin. He is not a good man."

Chin nodded once. "There is sorrow in your eyes that I did not see before. The young Nick is my friend. It is true that we must talk."

Noise spilling from the open door to the fan-tan parlor drew his attention; he released her and turned toward the horde of Celestials heading their way.

His shouts brought them to a stop; angry exchanges were made between Chin and the other Celestials, but at last the gamblers seemed to listen to his excited words.

His eyes shifted to Rudolph. "It would be wise for the cousin of Nicholas and of the madame to leave as quickly as possible."

Rudolph straightened to his full height, but he kept one eye on the angry men who were edging down the alley. "And why is that?" he asked. "I have done nothing wrong."

"It was necessary to reveal your identity. As well as the fact that you have taught the madame what she knows about games of chance. As well as how to win in unusual ways."

"I never—"

"Each moment you delay only adds to the danger. The Celestials have hesitated to do more than shout at the woman they believe deceived them. They will not be so reluctant with a man."

Rudolph's eyes darted from Chin to Lana to the stalking Celestials. Without warning the gamblers broke into a run, and with a low cry of fright, Rudolph turned on his heels and disappeared into the crowd moving along Grant Street.

Chin pulled Lana to the entrance of the alley out of the way, and she got a last view of Rudolph's black suit weaving in and out of the sea of blue coats, a line of angry, fist-waving men in his wake.

She leaned against the rough boards of the building which fronted on Grant. The sudden solitude of the alley, in contrast to the noise from the street, left her stunned.

"Mister Chin, I don't know what to think. Or to say."

"This is a rare condition, I believe. As I recall, the madame was seldom without words."

"Will they really harm him?"

"They will frighten him and demand he give them a chance to earn their money once again. But harm? Only if he tries to protest or continues seeking an escape."

"Rudolph is a poor gambler, but an inveterate one."

"Perhaps he can be cured of this evil habit."

Lana found herself smiling at Chin. "You can say this, the owner of a gambling den?"

"Who else better to understand the evils of chance?" For no more than an instant, Chin matched her smile. Then they both grew solemn. "How fares the young Nick?"

Lana knew of no way to soften the words. "He is dead."

Chin remained silent for a moment, his eyes lowered. He looked up to say, "It is with sorrow that I learn this. Did he not make the journey to the valley of safety he talked about?"

"He made the journey. But the valley was not safe." Lana blinked away her tears.

"And what of Tony Diamond? He, too, was a friend of Nick. And the valley was once his home."

Lana could not answer for a moment. At last she said softly, "He misses my brother as much as I." She was relieved when Chin did not ask more.

"I have no proof," she added, "that I am who I claim to be. I can only ask that you believe me."

Chin looked solemnly at her. "There is a sadness in your eyes that comes only from the heart. I believe you. And it is time," he added, "to speak of the jewel known as the Blood of Burma. It is for this you have come."

His words were a statement, not a question, and she kept silent.

"Come," he said. "Follow."

Turning from her, he led the way into the stream of Celestials in a direction away from where Rudolph had last been seen. A block down Grant, he turned onto an alley even more narrow than Stouts; it opened onto another street, and Lana struggled to keep pace with Chin as he moved rapidly through a series of steep streets and alleys, the smells of which she could not begin to identify. The morning light made rare penetrations into their dimness.

At last he paused before a narrow, three-story house much like the houses uphill and down from it, except that it featured a tall, encircling fence.

He stood before the gate, Lana panting beside him. The constant ache in her shoulder had sharpened, but she paid it no mind. Unlike Grant, the street was quiet. Above them hung a sign in Chinese characters, the only distinctive feature of the house other than the fence.

"The temple to the Queen of Heaven," Chin said. "For the devout subjects of the Flowery Kingdom."

A more unlikely temple Lana had never seen, accustomed as she was to the graceful onion domes of Russia with their Orthodox crosses rising above them against the St. Petersburg sky.

"It is called a joss house," Chin continued. "A corruption of the word *Deos* or God. Come. We will go inside."

Opening the gate, he stood aside, and Lana walked up the front stoop and through a creaking front door. With Chin once more in the lead, she followed him up two narrow, dingy flights of stairs. The scent of opium and other, unidentified odors wafted from the closed doors they passed.

The temple was on the top floor behind another closed door, which Chin opened. A Celestial hurried past him out of the room, leaving it to the newcomers. As Chin stepped aside, Lana entered into the dimly lighted place of wonder. She gave a quick thought to the dueling pistol hidden in her cloak and debated the propriety of carrying it into a place of worship, but there was no turning back now.

The smell of incense struck her first, as well as the pervading gloom of the curtained room. As she became accustomed to the close air and decreased light, she let her eyes slowly rove around. Against the walls were a total of ten platforms some three feet high, set back in arched alcoves. In the center of each platform sat the carved wooden image of what she supposed were the Chinese deities. Robed in fine garments, their faces half-covered by beards, they seemed not quite lifesize.

The alcoves themselves were draped with embroidered cloth and decorated with carvings and gilt. Glass lanterns hung above each deity, and at their feet in an urn of sand burned small incense sticks. On a table in front of each alcove was a pot of tea and bowls of rice and fruit.

Chin followed her gaze. "So that the gods will not go hungry," he explained, gesturing toward the repasts.

He stepped to a large brass gong mounted to the right of the entrance and struck it with a leather-bound mallet. The sound echoed in the small room.

"We arouse the sleeping gods," he explained. Guiding her around the room, he named them: the God of Somber Heavens, the God of Medicine, the God of War, the God of Wealth, and so on.

It was before the God of Wealth that he stopped. "The dispenser of riches," he explained. "It is to him that most knees are bent."

Lana was not surprised, thinking of the thousands of men roaming the rugged Sierra mountains in search of gold. Without realizing it, they too worshipped the God of Wealth. As entranced as she was by all that she saw, she was still puzzled. Since leaving the alley, Chin had made no mention of the Blood of Burma, but she could not believe he had forgotten their purpose.

He knelt before the shrine, and she thought he was lost in prayer. But when she knelt beside him, she saw his hand slipping forward toward an intricately carved panel that formed the right wall of the alcove. In the center of the panel was a grotesque dragon breathing fire, his head in profile, his lone eye sparkling red and hot as though he could see through the centuries and come down from the panel to protect his god if the need arose.

Chin plucked the eye from its place and rested it in

Lana's hand. "The Blood of Burma," he said.

Speechless, Lana stared at the jewel. Fifty carats of carmine beauty, it caught the fiery glow from the overhead lantern in its facets and seemed itself a source of light. Pigeon's blood, the color was called, and hence the ruby's name, for it had been found on the banks of the Irrawaddy River in Burma.

But the blood took on a harsher meaning for her, and tears welled in her eyes. To save the jewel, Nicholas had traveled inland in search of wealth. Her hand formed a fist around the jewel and she squeezed tight, purposefully letting her nails dig into her palms, welcoming the pain. For all the ruby's fiery glow and the religious shrine in which it had been hidden, she thought it had been delivered to her from hell.

Chin waited in silence beside her while she regained control. She had suffered much for this moment, but it was only a hollow triumph that she felt. Nicholas was gone, and Tony was lost to her. She had even forfeited the exterior shell of haughtiness that she had used to protect herself.

At last she looked up. "Thank you for being my brother's friend," she said. Standing, she hurried from the temple and down the winding stairs to the street. The brightness of the morning blinded her for a moment as she emerged onto the stoop, but when at last she was able to focus on her surroundings, she saw three men standing at the open gate.

Her first thought was that they were not Chinese—no blue coats or queues or slight, stooped shoulders. These men were burly and bearded; if she didn't recognize their scowling faces right away, she did recall the meanness they carried with them. It came across the small walk separating the gate from the front steps. These were the Sydney Ducks that had followed her and Tony and Boris along the mountain trail.

"Hello, there, dearie," said the one she remembered as the leader. She even recalled his name.

"Hello, Mick," she said. Her right hand slipped inside

the pocket of the cloak, and the ruby she had been clasping was replaced by the handle of her gun. "I assume you are still employed by Lord Dundreary."

Mick's eyes widened in surprise. Beside her, Chin said in a low voice, "Perhaps the madame would be wiser to return to the temple."

Lana shook her head. "These men hold no danger for me."

"The guv'ner wouldn't like to hear you say that, dearie," Mick growled. "We picked up your trail kind of unexpected like in Chinatown. We've got a job to do, and we got to do it."

"Is that supposed to frighten me? I've been through too much to be daunted by the likes of you. I would have to value my life more than I do to feel threatened."

"What in hell is she jawin' about?" one of the Ducks asked.

"Damned if I know," Mick responded and started up the short walk toward the stoop.

"Madame," Chin said insistently.

Lana's response was to pull the pistol from its place of hiding and point it in the direction of Mick's head. He came to an immediate halt a few feet away.

"Now, sir," she said with dignity and firmness, "beneath that disreputable coat you are wearing is a gun and who knows what other weapons. They truly do not frighten me. I cannot, of course, shoot all three of you, so I can only aim for one. Tell your men what they must do with me, because I promise that if you continue any closer I will pull the trigger. And I will not miss. You will not have another opportunity to give them the guidance they so obviously need."

From the puzzled looks on their faces, Lana suspected that none of the men realized what she was talking about. But they read the message in the pistol soon enough. And, she thought, they understood that she really was not afraid of them.

Mick hesitated, frowning. Making a decision seemed to come to him with difficulty.

"I would do whatever the countess suggests," said a familiar voice. Lana's heart leaped, and she looked beyond the Ducks and straight into Tony's dark eyes.

She caught her breath. Joy rushed through her. Against all logic and everything that she had been telling herself she must feel, she was overwhelmed with the pleasure of seeing him again . . . so overwhelmed that she almost pulled the hair trigger by mistake.

Tony simply stared at her, as enigmatic as one of the Celestials.

Swallowing, she forced her gaze back to the scowling Mick. "M'lord ain't gonna like this," he said. Both Tony and Lana remained silent.

At last, muttering under his breath, Mick turned and with the other Ducks close behind moved hurriedly down the street.

"Mr. Diamond," said Chin, "I am happy to see you once again. As always I am when the madame visits. She does not lead a quiet life."

Tony's lips twitched. "No, she does not lead a quiet life."

Lana could say nothing but stare at him. He had changed into another coat, this one following more closely the muscled shoulders and chest that she knew so well. He was hatless, and his black hair rested thick against the strong column of his neck. His jaw was tight, and his eyes were steady and unblinking.

Chin looked from one to the other. "It is time that I return to the temple and give thanks to the God of War that trouble has been averted." Lana barely heard him and was only dimly aware that he had retreated inside the house.

"You are looking well, Countess."

Lana shivered at his words. They seemed so cool, and he called her by her title when she had asked him never to do so again.

Suddenly she felt foolish standing on the stairs, a gun in her hand as though she were protecting the temple against infidels.

"You, too, are looking well," she said, glad that she sounded just as cool as he. "Were you following behind the Sydney Ducks?"

He shook his head. "Madame Chin told me where I might find the two of you. I had no idea they were anywhere around. Not that I helped you in any way. You seemed to be handling them all right on your own."

She knew what he really meant. He could see that she did not need him. Or so he thought. She wanted to rush into his arms and tell him how wrong he was—that she was empty without him and went through the days with no joy or hope. But her decision had been made. And he looked so distant standing there, almost . . . angry. She could think of no other word.

"You are right," she lied. "It was not necessary for you to seek me out." Her chin tilted defiantly. "I have taken care of myself."

"I think that perhaps I have been of some service," he said tightly. "Let me summon a carriage and take you back to the hotel. There's someone there I think you will want to see."

Chapter Thirty-One

"Nicholas!"

Lana could not resist calling out as she stood in the doorway of the Ace Hotel suite and stared at the prone figure of her brother stretched out in the bed. He was lying beneath a mound of covers, his eyes closed, his head resting against a white pillow. His complexion held little more color than the pillow slip.

On the ride from Chinatown, Tony had told her what to expect, but she had feared that when she arrived at the hotel all would not be as she hoped . . . that somehow her brother's return to life was all a cruel hoax. Tony would not be the perpetrator, of course. Grown used to bad news, she thought that perhaps he, too, had been deceived.

But Nicholas was alive and in San Francisco. The slight movement of the blankets told her that the breath of life eased through him. And his eyelids had fluttered when she called out his name.

A dark-suited man that Lana did not recognize was standing on the far side of the bed; by the footpost stood Elizabeth Dundreary and her father, returned that morning from their journey to view the rugged California coast.

As Lana hurried into the room, Elizabeth's wide blue eyes turned to her. "Countess," she whispered, "Nicky has been hurt."

"Oh, but Elizabeth," Lana exulted, "he is alive!" Hurrying past the girl, she knelt beside the bed and held

her brother's hand that lay on top of the covers. Beneath
her caressing fingers his skin felt cool and dry.

His beard had been shaved, and his dark lashes rested
against his smooth cheeks. His lips were soft, as pale as his
skin, and his fair hair was long and fine. He looked
no more than fifteen years old. She half expected him to
open his eyes and wink, to let her know his disappearance
at the ravine had been no more than one of his boyhood
tricks.

From behind her came the sound of a cough, and she
glanced over her shoulder to see Boris, splinted leg
outstretched, sitting in an easy chair on the far side of the
room. He, too, looked a little younger than when she had
seen him last.

"The countess departed too rapidly this morning," he
said. "Master Nicholas arrived soon after you left."

"Has he been awake to see you?" Lana asked.

Boris's face softened. "For only a brief time. The
physician brought by Mr. Diamond"—he indicated the
man Lana had not recognized—"has said the journey
naturally exhausted him. He will be sleeping much of the
day."

Too well Lana remembered the difficult stagecoach ride
she and Boris had undertaken on their return journey out
of the mountains.

Her gaze drifted to Tony. He stood between her and the
door, his dark eyes directed to her. She tried to read the
expression in their depths, willing to accept even the anger
she had seen in front of the temple; what she saw was
infinitely more painful—an indifference to the scene
playing out before him, as though any emotion other than
anger had been used up in the rescue and return of
Nicholas to San Francisco and he had nothing else for her.
In that moment he seemed very far away.

The light heart that Lana had brought into the room
turned heavy, and she looked away. Somehow she must
talk to Tony alone. She had a good enough pretext—if she
needed one. He had told her little about her brother's
rescue—she had been too excited to listen to details
anyway. And she wanted to give him her thanks. If in their

360

talk, she touched him . . . if she kissed him and he returned that kiss . . . Perhaps—she could not deny the hope—all would be well.

"Tony—"

"I'm sorry, Lana," he said, interrupting as though he could read her thoughts, "but I must leave for a while. There's something that I've got to do."

Stubbornly, Lana rose to face him. She would not let him go so easily. "May I talk to you before you go? In private, please."

He hesitated, then said, "I'll be in my room."

She waited for a few minutes after he had left, time spent reassuring herself with touches and a kiss on the brow that her brother really had returned from the dead, greeting Elizabeth with a hug and her stiff-necked father with a nod, and bidding Boris to let her know if there was a change in Nicholas's condition.

"Is he really all right?" she asked the physician as she prepared to leave.

"With enough rest, he will be. As I understand it, you are his closest kin. He's a lucky young man to have a friend like Mr. Diamond. Much more exposure to that mountain cold would have brought an end to him. You owe Diamond a great deal of thanks."

Again Boris coughed, only this time Lana ignored him. She knew how he felt about Tony. She could not agree more.

"As it is," the doctor continued, "he suffers from little more than bruises and some broken ribs. And a gunshot wound, of course. It's my understanding that was treated right away."

Relieved, Lana let herself out of the room. Nicholas had been placed in a suite on the third floor; waiting two stories above was Tony. Of course, she owed him her thanks, but more than that she owed him her love. The decision to leave America had not been made because of him, but because of how she viewed herself.

Since their first meeting, he had called her many wonderful things—smart, beautiful, mysterious, brave— but he had never called her his. The talk of marriage back in Hangtown had not really been a proposal, only a statement about what he had once been prepared to say. And she had rejected even that. She had no idea if there was still a chance for them. But she had to let him know how she felt.

Eagerly she hurried up the stairs, her thoughts in a jumble. So she had told Tony she would return to Russia. So she had told him that America had brought her too much suffering. She had been light-headed from the pain and loss of blood. She had been delirious with grief.

And how had Tony reacted? Burying his own grief in action, he had gone directly to the valley to rescue Nicholas's body and give it a proper burial. At least that had been his purpose, only Nicholas had miraculously been caught against a fir tree growing at an angle from the side of the ravine. Somehow Tony had clambered down the granite face and proven himself far smarter and braver than she.

On the ride from Chinatown to the hotel, he had given little description of how he had raised the unconscious body to the crest of the hill, but Lana could fill in where his details fell short. While she had lain in her warm bed surrounded by her sorrow, he had been on the cold mountainside risking his life. She had told him not to pity her, but wasn't that exactly what she had been doing herself?

The most she had done was send Dusty John to check on him. John had helped Tony care for Nicholas and then brought Doc from Hangtown out to the valley for more professional care.

Nicholas was wrong about Tony. Wrong, wrong, wrong. When he was strong enough, she would tell him so—if, in the unlikely event, he had not already realized the truth himself. And if he did not like what she was planning, he would just have to learn to live with it. After all, she was the older sister. Such a position ought to come with at least a privilege or two.

Her knock at Tony's door brought a firm response that she was to enter. Inside, she caught her breath. She had not been here since the day she had given herself to Tony. And that was exactly what she had done . . . given herself once and for all time.

Lana pulled her eyes away from the bed. Tony stood in the middle of the room strapping on his gun holster, and Lana remembered she still carried the dueling pistol in her cloak. As heavy as it was, she was surprised she had not thought of it earlier.

At least it was not loaded, a detail she had omitted in her threats against the Sydney Ducks.

Forgotten alongside it in her pocket was the Blood of Burma. The jewel was the reason she had traveled to California in the first place; at this moment it held no more significance for her than if it had been a piece of lint.

"You wanted to talk?" Tony said. His words held no hint that he still cared.

Lana turned coward. "I wanted to extend my thanks to you for saving Nicholas.

"Your thanks?"

She shifted nervously under his unblinking stare. "It was a brave thing that you did, especially when most of his last words had been said in anger against you."

Tony shrugged. "I knew he was upset to find you in my arms. And I knew I could convince him eventually that I wasn't the bastard he thought me. Everything I did was for his own good. Well," he said, his eyes narrowing, "not exactly. I didn't bed his sister for any reason that concerned him."

Lana winced, surprised at his harshness. "That's a crude thing to say."

"I'm a crude man. Or hadn't you noticed before? Remember, Countess, I picked up my ways on the streets. None of this aristocratic politeness for old Tony. Especially today. I haven't got the time."

"I see," Lana said, not really seeing at all. She understood only that Tony was anxious to leave her, and if he left her now, she did not know how she could confront him again. "I will try not to keep you too long," she added sharply, "but since you brought up the issue, you might tell me exactly why you did take me to bed."

"Because you're quite a woman. Beautiful, feisty, a real

challenge to any man."

On his lips, the words sounded insulting, and fear clutched at Lana's heart. She was losing him, if indeed she had not already, and she didn't know what she could do to bring him back.

"I said a few things back in Hangtown—"

"Not so fast, Lana," he said, interrupting her. "You said a great damned deal back in Hangtown. In another hotel room. I let you talk. Now we're in my room in my town and it's my turn to say what's on my mind."

He was angry, all right. She took it as a good sign. As long as he could work up any feelings, she had hope that he still cared. "I wish you would tell me what you've been thinking. I've never really known."

"No, I don't suppose you have. Do you have any idea how I felt back in Hangtown listening to you tell me I was no longer wanted? I couldn't tell you then, not with you flat on your back. At least I see you're looking better now. A little pale and thin, but better."

"You'll have to try harder, Tony. That's not up to your usual standard for compliments."

"Right now, I'm concentrating on the truth. I've never asked a woman to marry me before. Until you, I never met anyone who made me think about settling down."

"You make wanting me sound wrong."

Tony laughed sharply. "That's the way it has turned out. I don't think it occurred to you then that I was hurt by what happened to Nicholas, not as much as you, of course, but still I grieved for his loss. And what did I get? Good-bye, Tony. I'm going home."

He made the painful decision she had reached sound selfish, when she had been in agony deciding the right thing to do. She and Tony *did* come from two different worlds. Maybe—she allowed the thought to linger a moment—maybe leaving him was truly the sensible thing to do.

But oh, how she wanted to touch him. His face was lean and stern and dark and handsome and strong and forbidding. The words tumbled in her mind as she stared at him. Even faced with his scorn, she felt her body respond to him. Around him she became wanton, needing and wanting his kiss and his embrace.

"If you're trying to get back at me," she said, "you're succeeding. I came up here to thank you and . . ." She could not go on.

"And tell me that you have changed your mind and want to stay after all? That Russia isn't quite the wonderful place you were thinking it was?"

Anger sparked in her. "Do not assume what is on my mind, or make light of it, Tony. Not after all we have been to each other."

"I'm not. You want to show your gratitude, and I can appreciate that. But it's not enough for me. I want a woman who will stay by me when trouble hits. Someone who doesn't care what kind of bastard I am, or what anyone else thinks."

"I don't care what kind of bastard you are," she said, trying to smile, desperate to ease the tension between them.

He shook his head in resignation. "The problem here could be you come with just too much excess baggage. Too many memories and responsibilities calling you away. You've handled more trouble in a few years than most men or women face in a lifetime. It could be you handle it too well."

"Another compliment? I would rather not have any more if you don't mind."

He shook his head in disgust, his fingers raking through his uncombed hair. "We've come a long way down, haven't we, Countess? I hadn't really planned to say all this when you got here. The trouble is, when I saw you handling Mick and the other two thugs this morning, all I could think of was that you really didn't need me."

Oh, but I do. The words screamed in her mind. But she could see nothing in the depths of Tony's eyes, could hear nothing in his voice to give evidence that her avowals would be welcome any longer.

"So you will not hear me out," she said flatly. "I told you I didn't care what kind of bastard you are, but I find I do. You're arrogant, and you're hard on the people who disappoint you."

He flinched, and Lana knew she had scored a direct hit. Good. His insults had been striking her straight on.

He hesitated before responding, then said, "I'll hear you out, Countess. Only do me a favor and wait."

Stung, Lana could only stare at him. He seemed to be making some kind of concession to her, as though she were the only one in the wrong.

"I meant what I said about gratitude," he added. "I don't want it. And right now somebody else needs my attention. Nicholas found out a few things while he was roaming about the Sierra campsites. I've got a little delayed justice to take care of today."

"But—" Lana stopped. She could not force him to listen to her, could not make him love her as much as she loved him.

"Of course," she said, calling on her pride. She glanced at the pearl-handled revolver strapped to his thigh. "Be careful how you use that gun. I found out the hard way that bullets hurt like hell."

Hurriedly she let herself out and went to her room down the hall. Behind the closed door, she felt the tears begin. She had seen no signs of love in his eyes—only anger and hurt and at last a determination to get away.

But she would not cry. She could not. She had been planning to return to Russia; nothing had really changed.

Except that now she did not want to leave. As happy as she was that Nicholas would be making the journey with her, she could only think of the man she would leave behind. Returning to her estate, she would be without hope or joy; her heart would be left half a world away.

She slipped the ruby from her pocket and stared down at it. She knew exactly what she must do; indeed, she had already decided that the ruby was no longer hers. She would give it to Tony, its rightful owner; whenever he looked at its cold, hard beauty, perhaps he would think of her.

Chapter Thirty-Two

Lana spent an hour in the afternoon beside Nicholas's bed. They talked briefly, sweetly, and then he fell asleep; when Elizabeth came to relieve her, she sought the solitude of her room. She paced, tried to sleep, paced again, but she came to no decision about what to say to Tony when he returned. She loved him. That much was clear. After that, she could think of nothing else, and at last she fell asleep.

A knock at the door awakened her from the restless nap, and she bolted upright on her bed, heart pounding. Was Nicholas all right? Had something happened to Tony? Hurrying across the room, she flung open the door.

She did not recognize the woman facing her, the hood from her cloak effectively concealing her features.

"Hello, Countess," the woman said. "You probably don't remember me. I'm Isabel Wright."

Surprised, Lana hesitated, then said at last, "Of course, Mrs. Wright. The widow who was at Maxwell Shader's gathering."

"May I come in?" Isabel said. "I've got a few things I want to tell you."

Puzzled, Lana stepped aside. "Shall I send for some tea? There's usually a guard somewhere in the hall. He will take a message downstairs."

"Whiskey would be more welcome," Isabel said, her back to Lana. "But no thanks. I don't plan to stay long. I'm taking my stash of gold and getting the hell out of this town as soon as I can."

She dropped the hood back to reveal dark auburn hair twisted carelessly into a bun against her neck. When she turned, Lana gasped. The left side of her face was swollen and bruised, and her left eye was almost completely closed.

"Compliments of Max Shader," Isabel said with a shrug. She winced. "Shouldn't move too quickly. There's more bruises that don't readily show."

"Please," Lana said, "sit down. And let me get you that whiskey."

"Just listen. That's all I want you to do. Shader is a son-of-a-bitch, and I sure as hell don't want him to get away. Neither should you. He's the one that shot your brother."

Lana gasped.

"Thought he killed him. Wanted to kill Tony Diamond, too, but Tony keeps getting away from him." Isabel managed a small, painful smile. "Makes him madder'n hell."

"How do you know all this?"

"Max likes someone to brag to, and to beat up when things don't go right. When he returned to town a few days ago, he was ready to fight. A whore is as good a target as anyone for a no-good wimp of a man like him. Don't look surprised, Countess. I was working the mining camps when Tony's partner came into town bragging about all his gold. Never figured Max would set him up the way he did. Just a simple robbery, was all he said. That wasn't the last of his lies."

"Why do you come to me now?"

"Max found out that Tony was in San Francisco again, and that he brought your brother. One of his spies down on the dock saw them land today. For all his big talk, Max is afraid of Tony. Always has been. He's convinced Tony knows about him. He panicked, took a few swipes at me, and lit out. At least he's trying to. But he hasn't left town yet."

"Shouldn't you be telling this to the authorities? Or to Tony?"

"They're men," she said simply, as though that explanation would tell all.

Lana nodded. There was a time she felt much the same way. Before California and Tony.

"Don't suppose you know much about the Barbary Coast," Isabel said.

"I've been to the Gut Bucket Saloon."

Isabel looked at her in surprise. "And lived to tell about it, I see. That's a rough place for the likes of you. Seems to me I've come to the right person. You'll take care of things all right."

"Please," Lana said, "won't you at least let me get you some ice for your face?"

"Don't go soft on me. I want you mad as hell. You can summon whoever you want to for help. Just get Max Shader and hang him high."

Lana remembered her brother lying two floors below. "That sounds like a reasonable request. Is he somewhere in the Barbary Coast?"

"Shanghai Kelly's. He plans to catch a boat for Australia. Heard about the gold strike there. Figures he can take what money he's got stashed away from his creditors and clear out before Tony finds him. Kelly's specialty is setting men out to sea, only they don't usually want to go. What's worrying me is that Max could be leaving anytime now."

"Where can Kelly be found?"

"His place is over on Pacific Street. Most likely you'll find him doping some unsuspecting fool's drink with opium. Whoever goes there, warn 'em not to accept so much as a glass of water."

Isabel pulled the hood back over her head and moved toward the door.

"Where are you going?" Lana asked.

"Told you. Away. Can't say more than that. I took Max for some of his gold, but I figure I earned it. This pretending to be a widow was his idea. If I do say so myself, I pulled it off all right."

"I was firmly convinced you were what you said."

Isabel nodded. "Thanks for that at least. And tell Tony

Diamond that if I was ever to consider hooking up again with a man, it would have to be somebody like him. You're a lucky woman, Countess. Take good care of him."

Lana stared at the closing door. Everyone was advising her about Tony, as though she did not realize how lucky she was. Or how lucky she had been. Tony had as much as told her good-bye.

She began to pace. It was not very difficult to figure out that Tony had gone to find Shader. Nicholas had told him something, and he was determined to track the gunman down. But he wouldn't have any idea that Shader was at this Shanghai Kelly's. Please, she prayed, please, Tony, return soon.

But he did not, and an hour later Lana was close to panic. The afternoon was almost gone; at most there was only an hour of daylight left. Shader could slip away in the dark, and they would never find him.

There was only one thing to do. Thrusting a note under Tony's door, she set out on her own. In the cloak pocket she carried a few of the coins from her cache and the dueling pistol. This time it was loaded.

The carriage driver she hired did not want to go anywhere near Pacific Street, but she convinced him with some of the coins that he would not have to stay, only deposit her where she asked and leave. He thought for a moment and at last agreed.

Pacific was as rutted as she remembered it, only there had been few autumn rains and the ruts were at least dry. The crowds on the street, most of them men, were also as she remembered—rough-looking and scurrying as though they really had someplace to go.

Shanghai Kelly's was a three-story house built on stilts out over the water. The driver, knowledgeable about the area, said Kelly or one of his men could lower their victims through a trap door into a boat bobbing on the water and take them on a one-way ride to a ship waiting in the harbor.

With her hand in her pocket wrapped tightly around her gun, Lana hurried inside. Downstairs, Kelly's was not much different from the Gut Bucket—smoky, noisy, and filled mostly with men, although a few scantily clad women were draped across the arms of their potential customers. She half expected Big Jake to rise from one of the chairs and come after her.

A quick glance did not reveal Maxwell Shader, but she hardly expected him to display himself so publicly. Not if he thought Tony was on his trail.

In the same manner as Isabel, she held the hood of her cloak low and made her way toward a door at the back of the crowded room. Keeping close to the wall, she had to pass near only one table. A hand reached out to grab her, and without missing a step, she slapped it away. She did not have time for interruptions.

The door opened onto a central corridor. Other doors lined the walls; she did not try to think about what was going on behind them. The stairway leading to the second floor was at the far end of the hall, which was dingy and dirty and smelled of stale whiskey and sweat. In comparison, Shanghai Kelly's made the joss house look indeed like a temple.

A short, toothless woman in a faded, ill-fitting dress greeted her as she hesitated and tried to decide what to do. Her dark button eyes looked jerkily at Lana. "What can I do for you, dearie?"

Lana dropped back her hood. "I'm looking for Maxwell Shader. I'll pay well to find him."

She could see the calculation going on in the woman's mind. "What makes you think he's here?"

"I know he is," Lana said. "He beats up women," she added, as though that would give a bond to her and her interrogator.

The woman cackled. "Don't make him no different from anyone else around here."

So much for strategy, Lana thought. "I must find him before he gets away," she pleaded.

Down the darkened hallway behind the woman, a door opened. "Thought I was getting a drink," a man called out.

Lana recognized him right away, even though his hair was no longer slicked back and he was in shirtsleeves. He's getting fat, she thought inconsequentially as she stepped toward him. "Hello, Mr. Shader."

Even in the dimness, Lana could make out the sudden fear that flashed across his face. "Where's Diamond?" he asked.

"I've come alone." She wanted to gain his confidence, get closer to him with the gun, then tell him Tony was on the way.

Shader hesitated, then said, "Let her come on, Miss Piggott. It's all right. I know the lady."

Miss Piggott frowned, and Lana figured it was because with Shader showing himself so soon, she had lost her chance to collect a few coins. Maybe she would have another chance for bribery when Tony arrived.

"Countess," Shader said as he gestured her into the dim, bare room where he was hiding. The furnishings consisted of a wooden chair and table, and the only window opened out to sea, giving no opportunity for her to signal to someone on the street. On the table rested a flickering lantern; beside it was a gun and holster and a man's coat. On the floor in the corner sat a small valise.

Realizing she would have to keep him away from the gun if at all possible, Lana swept past him. It was time for dignity, she thought as she whirled to face him. He stood a half-dozen feet away from her, and as she studied him she decided he had no other weapon on his person.

"I have come about my brother. It is my understanding that you were the one who wounded him."

"Isabel." Shader spit out the name in disgust.

Lana ignored him. "Shooting Nicholas was not a smart thing to do, Mr. Shader," she said, her fingers curling around the handle to her gun.

"What makes you think—" He stopped and shrugged. "I don't know, Countess. It got you here, didn't it?"

Lana shuddered. "Little good it will do you," she said, pulling out the pistol and pointing it at his chest. It was the second time today she had threatened a man with a

372

gun; to her surprise she wasn't the least afraid. Shader had almost succeeded in killing Nicholas, had wounded her, and had threatened Tony. For the latter if for nothing else, she would not hesitate to pull the trigger if he gave her half a chance. She gestured for him to move away from the table and was almost sorry when he did so. He had taken away her excuse to fire.

"Don't be so quick to make up your mind about me," Shader said. "I know how to treat a woman. Better than Tony." He licked his lips. "I'll bet he's all politeness. May I do this, he says. Let me do that." He edged a little closer to her. "With me it will be different. I'll tell you what to do, and you'll love it."

Lana stared at him in amazement. Of all the things he might have done, this was one she hadn't expected. Was he trying to arouse her? He seemed to believe what he was saying, and for the first time she wondered if he were quite sane.

Her eyes dropped for a moment, and she saw a definite bulge in the crotch of his trousers. While he was only repulsing her, he was arousing himself with his own words.

His lunge came so suddenly and fearlessly that he caught her by surprise. The edge of his hand came down hard on her wrist, and the single-shot pistol discharged harmlessly into the floor. Knocking the gun away, he gripped her shoulders and pulled her hard against him.

His face leered close. "Well, well, Countess. Looks like I'll get to show you what I mean. We won't be leaving for some time yet, and then it's a far distance to Australia. You'll have lots of chances to practice what I like."

Lana struggled to free herself, twisting and pounding against his chest, thinking if only she could get to the gun on the table, she would be in control again. For all his flabbiness, Shader was a strong man and his grip was tight. He let loose with one hand only long enough to slap her across the face. Her head jerked backward, and she grew still. Fighting would not free her. She would have to outsmart him.

But Shader proved wilier than she had supposed. When she suggested he give her a chance to cooperate, he laughed. "I'll get your cooperation all right, but I want fight in you, too. Gives me a chance to rough you up a little. I've been thinking about this moment for some time now, Countess. I'll show you how a real man makes love."

He shoved her backwards in the chair. Immediately she threw herself sideways toward the table, but he shoved her back again. She landed hard, tried to rise again, but when her second attempt resulted in another slap, she sat quietly and tried to channel her racing thoughts. In dismay she watched as Shader pushed the gun farther away from her chair.

Her face hurt, her shoulder hurt, and she could barely reason out the situation. Gradually her breathing slowed. Maxwell Shader was a brute and a coward and a would-be killer, but he also fancied himself a lover. Men forgo themselves in the throes of passion. At least one man did. She would not begin to compare Shader with Tony, but in this respect they might be alike.

She swallowed bile at the thought of what she must do. Catching her breath, she looked up at Shader, who was standing with legs apart close in front of her. The bulge in his trousers seemed larger than ever, and she doubted it was only the angle from which she viewed it. He liked hurting a woman. It made him hard.

She looked up at him. "I guess you win, Max."

He grinned. "I don't trust you any more than I ever have, Countess. You'll have to prove yourself." He knelt down and reached under her skirt. She held her breath, but all he did was tear off a section of petticoat. "Now put your hands behind your back."

Lana did as he said. When he was behind her, she lunged from the chair, but he was ready for such a move and jerked her back down. A cry of pain escaped her, but Shader only laughed. Using the strip of white linen, he bound her wrists tightly, then moved around to tear another strip and bind her ankles to the legs of the chair.

With her knees spread apart, she felt vulnerable, even

though her hem brushed against the tops of her shoes. Her cloak had fallen from her shoulders, and Shader began to unbutton her high-necked gown. Each time his fingers touched her body, she jerked in revulsion. Each time she did so, his smile broadened.

When her dress was unfastened to the waist, he pulled the silk aside. She hadn't bothered to put on a camisole, since the movement required was too painful for her tender shoulder, and Shader stared down at her bare breasts.

She closed her eyes, waiting for him to fondle her, and decided to throw up on his hands. With the nausea building in her stomach, she felt certain she could do just that.

But he didn't touch her. She opened her eyes; to her surprise, he was simply staring at her and rubbing at the rise in his trousers. Nothing surprised Lana anymore concerning men and sex. She could only hope he liked nothing more than looking at a woman's body.

But Shader wasn't through. He unfastened his trousers and began to pull them open. He wore no underclothes, and she could see the thick hair on his abdomen. Repulsed, she again squeezed her eyes shut.

"You don't have to watch," he said with a chuckle. "I'll guide your pretty little lips."

And then Lana knew exactly what he was getting at. "Oh,' she cried out, more in disgust than fright, "how dare you!" And then she yelled, "Tony! Tony!"

The door slammed opened and crashed against the wall. Shader whirled, and Lana opened her eyes to see Tony standing in the doorway.

"Thought I heard you calling me," he said.

Shader jerked backwards, but the click of Tony's gun brought him to a halt. "I'm not armed," he said, raising his hands quickly.

Tony glanced at his open trousers. "That much is obvious, Max." He stepped into the room and closed the door behind him. "I almost wish you were. It would give me an excuse to shoot you, although I already have reason enough."

Lana shivered. Tony's voice was cold and hard an[d]
edged with hate. She knew beyond any doubt tha[t]
Maxwell Shader was a doomed man.

Tony gave a quick look at Lana, saw her bared breasts[,]
then turned his cold glare once again toward Shader. "Ar[e]
you all right, Lana?"

"I'm all right," she managed. "Mr. Shader likes to talk [a]
great deal."

Tony gestured with the gun. "Get behind the chair an[d]
untie her hands."

Max did what he was told, and Tony motioned for him
to back away.

When Lana's arms fell free, pain shot through he[r]
shoulder and she blinked to hold back the sudden tears[.]
She rubbed her wrists, then hastily refastened her gown[.]

Tony's eyes never left Max's face. "He likes to scheme[,]
too, as well as talk. You weren't content with getting th[e]
gold two years ago, were you, Max?"

"I don't know what you're talking about," Shade[r]
responded sullenly, still standing behind Lana's chair[.]
Unable to see him, she could imagine the petulant look o[n]
his face.

"And I suppose you never heard of a prospector name[d]
Ernie. Nick Case met him while he was looking for a wa[y]
into the valley that wasn't blocked. They had a ver[y]
interesting talk one night over a bottle of whiskey. Seem[s]
Ernie and a friend of his were paid to get Jess drinking
when he rode into town looking for the whore wh[o]
betrayed him. You'd been around town for a while. Yo[u]
knew what drink did to Jess."

"Jess Tucker got what he deserved."

"Like hell he did. Ernie remembered very clearly that i[t]
was his partner's bullet that caught the Parson. Not *my*
partner, Max. *His.* Only of course they were paid to take
care of Jess, and when time came to testify about the
shooting, they spoke right up and blamed him."

"You would have great difficulty proving all this."

"Not so great. I found Ernie's former partner today[,]

376

while I was looking for you. The two of you might even share a jail cell."

Tony's voice tightened. "You shouldn't have come gunning for Nick. You could have gotten clean away."

Lana turned her head slightly. From the corner of her eye, she saw Shader move a fraction of a second before Tony did. "Watch out!" she yelled just as Shader threw himself toward his gun.

The explosion of Tony's revolver reverberated in the small room. Lana screamed. The echoes of the gun and of her cry slowly died, leaving only the sound of her gasping breaths and the acrid smell of sulphur hanging in the air.

She glanced at the floor behind her. Shader lay unmoving, eyes staring upward, dark stains spreading across the front of his shirt. From his partially opened mouth came a slow trickle of blood.

"He's dead," she whispered, directing her gaze back to Tony.

"Yeah. I'm almost sorry," he said, but she could hear little regret in his voice. "The thought just occurred to me that I could have turned him over to his vigilantes and let them do the dirty work for me."

He smiled tightly at her. "Sorry I took so long, but I've been searching all over town for him. As soon as I returned to the hotel, I saw your message. The charmer out in the hall just didn't want to tell me exactly where he was."

"Miss Piggott," Lana said. She couldn't move her eyes away from Tony's face.

"Are you really all right?"

She nodded, then glanced toward the closed door. "Why hasn't that gunshot brought somebody by now? My gun went off earlier, but no one came then, either."

"In Shanghai Kelly's nobody pays much attention to a single shot. They figure what's done is done, and besides it's none of their concern."

Tony stared at her for a moment, then without warning dropped to his knees in front of her and cradled her face between his hands. "Woman," he said huskily, "you scared the hell out of me."

Lana's heart caught in her throat. The expression she had been looking for earlier was there on his face for her to read.

He kissed her eyes, her cheeks, her lips. The kiss deepened, a kiss that told her more than any words could have of his fear and his relief that she was alive. His hands moved to stroke her back, and when he touched the wound where Shader's bullet had exited, she involuntarily winced.

"Oh, God, Lana," he said, resting his forehead against hers as he drew in deep, ragged breaths. "I'm sorry. I didn't want to hurt you."

"You didn't hurt me, Tony. I didn't want you to stop."

He kissed her lightly, then sat back on his heels. As she stared at his beloved face, memorizing every bristle of hair, every line, she felt unbidden tears well in her eyes.

The pad of his thumb caught one tear, and he looked worriedly at her. "Why?"

She laughed shakily. "I like it when you call me woman. Not countess. Oh, thank heavens not countess."

"Is that a reason to cry?"

"For me it is."

"Did I ever tell you you're unpredictable? The tears fall now that you're safe; when I rushed in and found you half-naked and bound, you looked more angry than anything else. And by the way, it was a good thing you called out like that. I was about to head up the stairs."

"Calling for you seemed the natural thing to do," she said, a smile edging onto her lips.

"I see." His fingers began working at the knots that bound her ankles. He glanced up at her, a comforting glitter in his eyes. "I assume, then," he added, "that you have decided you need me after all."

Chapter Thirty-Three

A thick fog was rolling down the street in front of the Ace Hotel by the time Tony was able to return for the night.

"You have a message," the desk clerk said.

Tony read the note as he hurried across the lobby and, with a grin spreading across his face, immediately bounded up the stairs.

Lana was waiting for him in her fifth-floor room; he couldn't get to her fast enough. Three hours had passed since he left her there and devoted his attention to the legalities resulting from Maxwell Shader's death—three hours of bureaucratic questions and statements, officious police, wary denizens of Shanghai Kelly's watching from a distance, and assurances from Tony that the countess would give a complete statement tomorrow concerning the demise of Mr. Shader.

California was getting too civilized, Tony decided as he neared the fifth floor. Perhaps he wouldn't tell Lana that particular opinion, however. She might not agree, and he didn't want any arguments for a while. There were too many things he wanted to say and do, and her complete cooperation was essential.

He had been through a long list of emotions where she was concerned. Simple lust had come first. In his mind he could still see her standing at the edge of an impassable street, undaunted by the Gut Bucket's crude surroundings and, worse, the crude men and women hurrying past. That lust had never left him, but he had come to like her, too. Love had been the last, the strongest. When she turned away from him in Hangtown, he had thought the love died, leaving only anger and, at last, indifference.

Hell, he had even enjoyed putting her on the spot earlier today when she insisted on talking to him in his room. He fought dirty, as she had been quick to point out. A little of his self-pity had been showing there, not exactly a noble sentiment.

What a fool he was. When he found out she was at Shanghai Kelly's, he had gone out of his mind.

Impatient, Tony forced himself to stop by his room and change out of the clothes he had been wearing when he shot Max. Lana was tough, but there was no sense in reminding her of the events of the evening any more than necessary.

By the time he knocked at her door, he was ready to take her in his arms and forget all the fancy words he had been rehearsing. As usual where she was concerned, his body was working faster than his mind.

The sight of her did nothing to cool him down. She stood in the open doorway, her tall, willowy body clad in a red silk shirt and the trousers he had bought her in Hangtown. She was barefooted, and her loose hair fell in thick, black waves against her shoulders.

"Come in," Lana said, stepping aside. "I was afraid you might not have received my message, since it's so late."

"The questioning took longer than I expected," Tony said with a shrug.

The first thing he noticed in the room was the flickering flames in the fireplace, the second was the sable coat spread on the rug in front of the hearth. The pelt side was up, as it had been on the floor of his mountain cabin. He took a deep breath. He wanted Lana more than ever, but he wanted to talk to her even more, to tell her how much she meant to him.

"There's no snow banked outside the window, of course," she said. "Just the fog. Perhaps you could pretend we're trapped.''

"It's a minor matter. We're in for the night, right?''

"Right. I managed to find a bottle of that same brandy Billy Bob sold us. Or at least the clerk at the desk found it somewhere. Would you care for a drink?''

Tony took the glass from her hand and let his fingers brush against hers. Her eyes darted up to him, and he could have drowned in their dark depths.

"Here's to America,'' she said, lifting her glass.

"And Russia,'' Tony said on the second toast.

Lana turned and walked away from him. Tony watched the graceful, long-legged walk that set her hips to undulating from side to side. He definitely liked the fit of those trousers; he had made a good choice.

She stopped beside the sable and faced him. "There's going to be a wedding soon.''

Tony almost choked on the brandy. "Oh?''

"Elizabeth and Nicholas. Lord Dundreary finally agreed that the owner of a country estate outside St. Petersburg was good enough for his daughter. Especially when Elizabeth told him she was going with her darling Nicky whether Papa agreed or not.''

Tony took a step toward her. "Elizabeth sounds like a woman I could admire.''

"I am sure she is. All day she has been most insistent on caring for Nicholas, including bathing his body and changing his nightclothes. It is not, you understand, at all the thing for a proper young Englishwoman to do.''

Lana smiled. "Poor Nicholas. I can almost feel sorry for him. His bride looks innocent and sweet, but she is going to have him on leading strings.''

"What about his gambling?'' Tony asked, taking another step toward Lana. "Will Elizabeth approve?''

"He will be lucky if she lets a deck of cards in the house. I think even Lord Dundreary is shifting his sympathies toward his future son-in-law, a life without faro or roulette being in his view unthinkable. He apologized most humbly for the Sydney Ducks. Some more of Elizabeth's work, I'm sure. And he has promised to forget the gambling debt. After all, Nicholas will be a part of his family."

"Boris will be around to help the young couple, I suppose."

The smile on Lana's face died. "He's going back to care for Nicholas. He says there may be difficulties awaiting his younger charge as he takes over the estate."

By now Tony was standing close to her. He took the brandy glass from her hand and set it on a table along with his.

"More difficulties than arose with you? That's hard to believe."

"Nicholas was the wild one, remember? I was the offspring that saw to duty and responsibility, especially after I inherited the count's impoverished land."

Tony felt a sudden tightness in the pit of his stomach. If she thought for one minute she was going to return to that land, she had better do some recalculating.

Lana reached into the pocket of her trousers, then extended her hand. "Here. This is yours."

He glanced down at the Blood of Burma sparkling red and hard against the ivory softness of her hand. "Paying off your debts?" he asked, his eyes glittering into hers.

He gave her no chance to answer. Taking the ruby from her, he tossed it onto the table beside the glasses and pulled her gently against him. Damn but it was difficult to remember how easily he could hurt her injured shoulder.

"There's only one thing I want, woman, and it's not that jewel." His lips slanted over hers, his hands stroking the cool, slippery silk covering her arms. Her body leaned into his.

The kiss deepened. There could be no compromises now. He needed her in the basic ways a man needed a woman. For sex, that was for certain. He couldn't be in the same room as she without getting aroused. But more, he was incomplete without her. She brought purpose into his life, made him see the way things were, made him a better man. He wanted his children growing in her. He wanted her spirit and strength passed on to those same children.

He broke the kiss and looked down at her. "I love you, Svetlana Alexandrovna. And by damn, there better be two weddings or you'll have to live with me in sin."

"*Yah vahs loobloo*," she answered warmly. "I love you, too." A smile played at her lips. "Americans have a curiously romantic way of proposing."

Her hips moved slightly against his body, and Tony came close to losing control. "And Russians like to live dangerously."

She laughed. "I like to live, Tony. And I can only do that with you. Of course I will marry you."

"This country will never be like Russia, you know."

"I'm only following in the family tradition. My mother chose Russia over England. I've already written instructions to a St. Petersburg lawyer deeding my poor land over to Nicholas and Elizabeth as a wedding gift. Except for some faro winnings and the ruby—whose ownership we will obviously have to negotiate—I am impoverished. If you hadn't wanted me, I suppose I could have sought work in one of the San Francisco gaming halls."

She slipped from his embrace and, kneeling on the black pelt of the sable coat, looked up at him in innocence. Thick curls of hair covered her shoulders, and light from the fire flickered across the luminescent silk shirt and settled in her eyes. "I do want to be a dutiful wife, of course," she said.

"Of course," he answered, keeping a straight face. Her obedience was probably something else they would have to negotiate. Time and time again.

"Then please, Tony," she said softly, "join me down here and tell me exactly what you want me to do."

ROMANCE FROM FERN MICHAELS

DEAR EMILY   (0-8217-4952-8, $5.99)

WISH LIST   (0-8217-5228-6, $6.99)

AND IN HARDCOVER:

VEGAS RICH   (1-57566-057-1, $25.00)